GEMMA F

D1054695

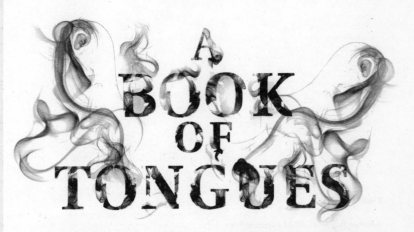

A BOOK OF TONGUES

VOLUME ONE OF THE HEXSLINGER SERIES

ChiZine Publications

FIRST EDITION

A Book of Tongues © 2010 by Gemma Files
Jacket artwork © 2010 by Erik Mohr
Cowboy Photo © iStockphoto.com/Nuno Silva
All Rights Reserved.

LIBRARY AND ARCHIVES CANADA CATALOGUING IN PUBLICATION

Files, Gemma, 1968-
              A book of tongues / Gemma Files.

(Hexslinger series ; v. 1)
ISBN 978-0-9812978-6-6

              I. Title. II. Series: Files, Gemma, 1968- . Hexslinger series.

PS8561.I5274B66 2010   C811'.6   C2010-900571-6

CHIZINE PUBLICATIONS
Toronto, Canada
www.chizinepub.com
info@chizinepub.com

Edited by Sandra Kasturi
Copyedited and proofread by Helen Marshall

For Callum, who can't read it yet
(and probably shouldn't, when he can).
But also for Steve, without whose support
nothing would be possible,
and Elva Mai Hoover and Gary Files,
without whom I would not exist.

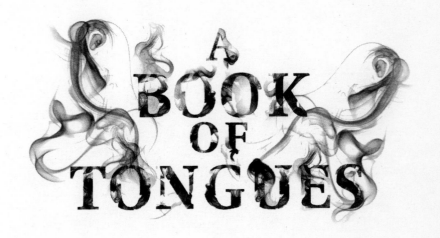

Here is a book of tongues.
Take it. (Dark leaves invade the air.)
Beware! I now know a language so beautiful and lethal
My mouth bleeds when I speak it.

—Gwendolyn MacEwen

I'll be true to my love
If my love will be true to me.

—"Two Sisters," Childe Ballad version

TABLE OF CONTENTS

BOOK ONE: CITY OF JADES

The Barbary Coast, March 6, 1867
Month One, Day Thirteen Dog
Festival: Tlacaxipehualiztli, or Skinning of Young Men

Today is ruled by Centeotl, the Lord of Maize, a version of Xipe Totec, Our Lord the Flayed One. Also known as Xilonen, "the Hairy One," he holds the position of fourth Lord of the Night.

The Aztec *trecena* (or thirteen-day month) Tecpatl, "Stone Knife," is ruled by Mictlantecuhtli, Lord of Mictlan. This *trecena* signifies an ordeal or trial that pushes one to the very threshold of endurance. It forebodes an abrupt change in the continuity of things.

By the Mayan Long Count calendar, the protector of day Itzcuintli ("Dog") is also Mictlantecuhtli, who rules that day's shadow soul. Itzcuintli is the guide for the dead, the spirit world's link with the living. It is a good day for being trustworthy, a bad day for trusting others.

These are good days to shed old skins; bad days to cling to what is already known.

PROLOGUE

The dream was always the same.

She appeared above him, blown by a black wind, her back-sloping forehead girded with a hissing serpent, her swirling hair stiffened with mud. Her round face was set with jade scales, irregular as leaves. The lids and orbits of her wide-spaced eyes were decorated, mosaic-style, with tiny chips of shell, mother-of-pearl and obsidian. Her breasts were bare, high-set, the nipples pale and small—a virgin's, or even a child's. Sometimes he thought this meant she must have died young. Other times, however, he looked deep into her painted gaze and knew that it meant she might very well never have actually *lived* at all.

Little king, she called him every time, ***little hanged man—you who are mine by right, as well as by choice***. And he saw a great darkness rise up around her, spreading wide: a hissing cloud of dragonflies whose wings dazzled, every colour in the world at once. Like a rainbow.

Water rose around his feet, burning cold, lapping at his ankles. The sky shone yellow and black. Knives fell like rain.

To either side, grey stone walls retreated into shadow, studded with what seemed at first glance to be rough, irregular stones—but a closer look revealed that the stones were grinning, all leering teeth and empty nose-holes. An endless rack of skulls from whose orifices flowers bloomed at random, luscious pinky-red as heart-meat.

Around her long neck a rope dangled, twisted from corn-silk and stuck all over with thorns. She held it up, looped around both thumbs—spread it wide, a cat's cradle, a pair of opening jaws.

Use this, she told him. *Use it, while you still can. Kill what you love, choose your ixiptla, make your necessary sacrifices. Pierce your tongue, run it through the hole, and pray words of blood.*

The time of earthquakes is at hand, little king.

The time of great floods, when the upper crust cracks, and the Sunken Ball-Court overflows.

The Gods return, at long last. What we have been promised, we will have. So feed us once more, and apologize, before it is too late.

He didn't know what she meant, by any of it—never had, and never expected to. But then again, maybe it wasn't even his dream to begin with.

Twenty days later, though, there he was again—right smack back in the same place, slogging through black-river water to his knees under the jaundice-yellow sky. Skulls to the left of him, flowers to the right, the very air itself an obsidian storm through which knives swirled by, drawing blood 'til it felt like all he had left for skin was a single walking wound. And as he struggled grimly forward, the only thing he could think was this—over, and over, and over—

Son of a bitch. Son of a bitch.

. . . that Goddamned son of a bitch, he went and left me behind.

CHAPTER ONE

For all it was just gone noon by the barkeep's (carefully hidden) watch, the Bird-in-Hand dance-groggery was nevertheless crammed full with people either drunk from the night before, or continually drunk for the last few days, and counting. One of these, a huge fool in miner's clothes, had spent the last ten minutes staring fixedly at Chess Pargeter, who stood sipping a shot of absinthe at the bar—a slim and neat-made man dressed in purple, head barely level with the miner's breastbone, whose narrow red brows shaded to gold over a pair of eyes the same green as the wormwood and sugar concoction he held.

"Queer," the miner said to the bar at large. "You can tell by the clothes."

"I really wouldn't, mister," replied another man—almost as tall, and armed with a double-barrelled eight-gauge—who'd passed a similar length of time with his chair tipped back against the wall, shapeless hat pulled down to shade his eyes in such a way that the company had hitherto mainly supposed him asleep.

The miner squinted at him. "Think I want your opinion, asswipe?"

With a sigh: "Think you *need* it, for sure. Entirely your own business whether you choose to believe me."

Chess took another sip, ignoring them both. His hair, twice as red as his brows, was close-cut enough to reveal he'd had one of his lobes pierced so that he could hang a lady's ear-bob from it: a modest gewgaw shaped like a Hospitaller cross, chased in gold wire and set with Navajo turquoise. It caught the light as he swallowed, making the miner snort.

"'I wouldn't,'" the miner repeated, low and sneering. Then called, in Chess's direction: "Hey, gingerbeer—didn't your Ma work the Bella Union, back when? I mean, *way* back."

"My Ma's none of your concern, tin-pan."

"So she *ain't* a whore?"

Chess shrugged. "Oh, she's that," he allowed. "Just don't see what it has to do with you."

The miner stared at him a moment, then blustered on. "Well . . . think I mighta paid for her, a time or two—she had that same red hair, and all." He pointed at the ear-bob: "Nice jewellery. Reverend Rook give it to ya?"

"This?" Chess shook his head, making the gem sparkle. "Nope. This, I bought for myself."

"How come? Everybody knows you're his bitch."

Chess narrowed his eyes at that, ever so slightly. "I'm his, all right, like he's *mine*. But I'm my own man still, and I pay my own way. How 'bout *you*, lard-ass?"

There was a general mutter, bringing the man by the door to his feet in one mighty heave. "Aw, here we go," he announced, both barrels up and trigger cocking.

The miner spat out maybe half a word—the phrase he had in mind might have eventually proved to be *damn faggot outlaw*, had it been allowed to come anywhere near full expression—before Chess shot him neatly through the head without even seeming to draw, let alone to turn.

Chess licked the last of the absinthe from his glass's rim, upturned it, and threw the barkeep money. "That's for my tab," he told him. "And more sawdust."

"We get that stuff for free, Mister Pargeter," the barkeep managed.

"Then use it to paint the wall again instead," Chess snapped back, and left. The tall man tipped his hat to the company at large, put up his gun, and followed.

"Some pretty rough work, 'specially on a Sunday," the tall man—

whose name was Edward Morrow—remarked, as they stepped out into the muddy street.

"Oh? How so?"

"Son-of-a-bitch never even had a chance, let alone a fair one—that's how so."

Chess snorted. "Hell, Morrow, I was just standing there, drinking my drink. *He* was the one convinced he had to say something about—it, or me. . . ."

"—you and Rook, more like—"

"Me and Rook, then, or what-the-Christ ever. Came at me asking for trouble, and he got what he asked for. I mean, I wasn't 'bout to start a damn fist-fight with him—you see the size of that idjit?"

"Looked 'bout *my* size, from where I was sittin'."

Chess shot Morrow a bare flicker of sly white grin. "Exactly."

A few steps on, they paused at the corner where Pacific Street met Moketown alley, under one of the many wash-lines of flapping coats and shifts—half-jokingly referred to by sailors on shore leave as "flags of Jerusalem"—which marked yet another of San Francisco's multitudinous Poor John clothing shops. Chess drew a watch of his own from the inner pocket of his purple brocade waistcoat, and flipped it open.

"Seventeen of twelve," he grumbled, peering down. "Man'll be late to his own funeral, you give him the option."

"People followin'," Morrow broke in, looking back over his shoulder.

Chess didn't raise his head. "From the melodeon? Yeah, I saw 'em—dead man's drinking buddies, annoyed he won't be picking up the next round. What do you suggest?"

"Head the other way, so's nobody else gets killed?"

Chess gave this idea about a second's consideration, before replying: "But here's where Rook said to meet, and I ain't shifting. So fuck that."

Luckily for them, the miner's "friends" had apparently barely taken time to arm themselves at all before giving chase, and only thought to do so with whatever came best to hand. Two men made straight for Chess, waving a broken bottle and a smashed-up chair; Chess cross-drew with a flourish and killed them both, then kept on firing, while Morrow made sure he just took the kneecap off a third, who fell back into the gutter, screaming. The whole exchange lasted perhaps a minute, at most—a popped blister of muzzle-flash and cordite smoke under heavy grey skies, spattering gaping passersby with equal parts terror and grue.

When it cleared, an only lightly wounded barfly could just be seen dragging the groaning cripple 'round a handy house-corner, his shattered ruin of a knee leaving a reddish trail through the mud. The rest were mainly corpses, though a couple were caught in mid-retreat with their hands held high, kowtowing awkwardly as Chess sighted at them down his left-hand gun barrel.

Morrow nodded back at them, not quite daring to touch Chess's sleeve. "C'mon now, Chess—that's enough for one day, ain't it?"

Utterly affectless: "Think so?"

"They were his *friends*, Chess, that's all . . . you know how it goes. Hell, you'd do the same for me, we all swapped places—"

"No I wouldn't," Chess said, letting his finger tighten. The penitent dropped face-down at the trigger's pre-click, shit-smeared and yelling for mercy.

"I can't leave you a minute, can I?"

The rasping basso voice behind them was audibly amused. Chess curled his lip and turned his back, reholstering, then stalked over to the big, broad-shouldered man in the black coat and stained white collar. "It's been *twenty*, Goddamnit," he complained.

"Yet I do see you managed to make your own fun, nonetheless." Though rumour told of Reverend Asher Rook once having been a melodious preacher, the crunch of hemp against larynx—from the Confederate Army's unsuccessful attempt to swing him rope-high—had left him with a rasp fit to strike matches on, so hellish dark and deep that whenever he spoke, you could almost smell the sulphur.

"Could've stayed in Arizona for that," Chess said, taking one last step, so he and Rook were safely nose-to-forehead—then dragged him down by the hair and kissed him hard, right there in the road for all to see. Morrow groaned at the sight, and not just from discomfort; even if the gunfire alone hadn't been enough to attract attention, the spectacle of two men treating each other the way neither would treat a woman whose favours he hadn't already purchased up front, certainly would.

Some might say Chess would never have dared be so open with his affections if the Rev wasn't so well-known—and well-feared— but Morrow doubted it. From what he'd heard, Chess had lived his life on the offence since long before Reverend Rook hove into sight. Still, now they *were* bound together, he was probably worse: every move a calculated insult, a slap to the collective face. A lit firecracker shoved up the whole honest world's backside.

A voice from the greyer parts of Morrow's mind, long kept carefully hid, came intruding: *"Asher Elijah Rook, Sergeant and unofficial chaplain for his unit, took up for desertion under fire and murder of a superior officer in the final weeks of the War. Some question as to the legitimacy of the charges, but the execution proceeded nevertheless. While other prisoners from the stockade waited, Rook fought with his captors and began to curse, quoting St. John the Revelator. . . ."*

And I looked, and, behold, a great cloud, and a fire infolding itself, and a brightness was about it, and out of the midst thereof as the colour of amber, out of the midst of the fire.

Also out of the midst thereof came the likeness of four living creatures . . . and every one had four faces, and every one had four wings . . . As for the likeness of the living creatures, their appearance was like burning coals of fire . . . and out of the fire went forth lightning. . . .

And when they went, I heard the noise of their wings, like the noise of great waters, as the voice of the Almighty, the voice of speech, as the noise of an host: when they stood, they let down their wings.

"I believe that's in Ezekiel, *sir, not* Revelation.*"*

"Yes, to be certain. *The more important point being that one way or another, a cyclone near thirty feet across whipped up almost immediately, and blew away most of the camp. Rook and his fellow escapees simply walked away, made their way to the Arizona desert and began to commit the crimes that have lent him notoriety throughout the West: robbing trains and stagecoaches, levelling entire towns, all aided and abetted by Rook's knowledge of Bible verse. In this manner, we see how graphic physical insult can cause talent for hexation to express, long after the normal parameters of adolescence have been surpassed.*

"Our next dispatches reveal him to have taken up openly with this wild boy, Pargeter—similarly freed by Rook's handiwork, after being convicted as an unrepentant murderer and sodomite. By all accounts an accomplished killer but no sort of soldier, Pargeter's records show him to be uniformly uncontrollable, contemptuous, loveless. Yet he bridles himself for Rook, suffering restraint and direction, and love—of a sort— does seem to be the key . . . so much so that it becomes impossible to tell exactly who the corruptive element in this mixture truly is. . . ."

But Rook and Chess were done at last, at least for now. They broke apart, Rook leaning to tell him softly, in one passion-flushed ear: "I will say this, though. You need to stop treating every place we go like Tophet in Hinnom just 'cause your timetable and mine ain't always congruent, Private Pargeter."

Chess blinked, then bit his tongue—literally—on whatever he would have never hesitated to say next, if Rook had been anyone else. "We still have that business of yours to do up in Tong territory," he said, finally, "so it strikes me we'd best get goin'. It ain't really a place you want to end up once the afternoon's gone, and it's getting hard to see what to shoot at."

"Lead on, then, darlin'—I'll willingly take your word. This *is* your home town, after all."

Chess hissed like an affronted cat, and pulled away from Rook before the Reverend could try to stroke him smooth again. Rook smirked, then noticed Morrow's expression.

"Problem, Ed?"

"Uh, well—ain't me sayin' so, Rev, but this's bound to bring down the law, what little they got here. Dead bodies chokin' up a central thoroughfare, and all . . ."

"I don't see any bodies," was all Rook replied. And Morrow saw his hand slip inside the front of his coat.

Oh, good Christ King Jesus.

But Rook was already thumbing through the small black Bible he kept pocketed there. Reaching something useful, he cracked the spine, lifted it to his lips, and *blew.* . . .

. . . and the grey sky rustled above them—*flattened itself out* somehow, a stretched oil-cloth—as a cold slaughterhouse reek drifted down. Chess turned to watch, a hand back on either gun-butt, eyes bright with excitement. His whole attitude and expression virtually crowing—*That's right, you fuckers, just go on ahead and get ready . . . 'cause* my *man here can do* any *damn thing, he takes a mind to.*

As the Rev began to speak, Morrow shivered, barely keeping his breakfast down. Because he could see the text lift bodily from those gilt-edged pages in one flat curl of unstrung ink, a floating necklace of black Gothic type borne upwards on a smoky rush of sulphur-tongued breath . . . feel the beat of syllables spread throughout his blood, each vowel and consonant its own dull explosion, larding even his thoughts with grit, so they stiffened and scratched his brain. Until the words spread like cataracts across his eyes, lidding them over with dim white horror.

"AND THE LOCUSTS WENT UP OVER ALL THE LAND OF EGYPT, AND RESTED IN ALL THE COASTS OF EGYPT," the Rev declaimed, and Chess laughed out loud at the sound, somewhere between delight and hysteria. "VERY GRIEVOUS WERE THEY; BEFORE THEM THERE WERE NO SUCH LOCUSTS AS THEY, NEITHER AFTER THEM SHALL BE SUCH . . . FOR THEY COVERED THE FACE OF THE WHOLE EARTH, SO THAT THE LAND WAS DARKENED; *Exodus,* 10:14 to 10:15."

The rustling peaked, became a chitinous clicking, and Morrow fought hard to stay still while the whole wheel-scarred road suddenly swarmed with insects—not locusts, but ants the size of bull-mice, their jaws yawning open. Neatly avoiding both Chess and Rook's boots, they broke in a denuding wave over the corpses, paring them boneward in a mere matter of moments. A wind followed, to scatter what few scraps of bone and flesh were left.

"As SMOKE IS DRIVEN AWAY, SO DRIVE THEM AWAY: AS WAX MELTETH BEFORE THE FIRE, SO LET THE WICKED PERISH AT THE PRESENCE OF GOD . . . THAT THY FOOT MAY BE DIPPED IN THE BLOOD OF THINE ENEMIES, AND THE TONGUE OF THY DOGS IN THE SAME."

Psalms 68, Morrow thought, as the rot boiled inexorably on, and the dead men reduced themselves to utter ruin and dust.

"That's just *wrong*," someone exclaimed from behind Morrow— man, woman or child he couldn't tell, but with a shaking voice, as though on the verge of tears. "Sin, a pure *sin*. It oughtn't to be allowed."

"*O God, thou art terrible out of thy holy places*," Rook murmured to himself, his voice abruptly human once more, as if in answer. And in his secretest heart, Morrow agreed.

But now the film was lifting—he could see the sky again. The ants resolved themselves to dust as well, sank 'til they and the mud grew indistinguishable.

Rook stood there a minute more, his face blanker than the page his thumb still marked. Morrow let out a long breath, echoed by one from Chess, whose excitement had ebbed along with the flensing tide. Gunslingers and hexslinger made an uneven triangle together, 'til Rook briskly cracked his neck from side to side, and stowed his Bad Book away once more.

"Well," he said. "Shall we, gentlemen?"

Morrow cut his eyes side to side, scanning what panting crowd remained: the various scum of San Francisco's roughest region, finally stunned to silence by the Word of God. Yet twisted rather than holy, songs of faith turned to faithless uses, and made there- fore to seem—though perhaps not tarnished themselves—somehow *tarnishing*.

"God damn, I hate this whole stinking city, and that's a fact," Chess Pargeter announced, meanwhile, strutting away like some pretty little Satan—the single brightest point of colour, from crisp red hair to gleaming boot-heels, in that entire dim sewer of a street. "Just the same's I hate *you*, Ash Rook, for makin' me come back here, in the first place."

Rook smiled at Morrow companionably. "Best not to keep my good right hand waiting, Edward," he suggested. "It's a long walk yet to Chinee-town, or so he tells me."

"Yes, sir."

Rook turned away, following Chess. Morrow shook himself free of his own dread, and did the same.

Thinking, as he did—for neither the first time nor the hundredth, and definitely not the last—*Oh Lord God of hosts, eternal friend and saviour: just what the hell am I doing here, again? With these two, or otherwise?*

But he already knew the answer.

CHAPTER TWO
The Previous November

The air inside the private train-car was oppressively thick, hot as new-cooked honey. Morrow felt his collar starting to rub a raw spot under the point of his jaw, and did his best to keep still while the old man in the frock-coat—Joachim Asbury, a Doctor of Sciences specializing in Magical Research, on loan from Columbia University to the Pinkerton Detective Agency—droned on, his otherwise fascinating lecture pulling out like so much taffy. He was silver-haired and mild-looking, his sober upper dress a stark contrast to the flash check trousers current Northern fashion seemed to demand.

"What we principally know of magicians—witches, wizards, shamans, et cetera—is threefold. Some are born with an inclination to such skill, yet only come to full expression of their talents later on, if at all; for females, generally at the onset of their menarche, while for males, generally during some great moment of gross physical insult. That once come to fruition, their powers seem virtually limitless, making it a foregone conclusion that if magicians were ever to act *en masse*, they would overrun the world within days.

"Yet the third most well-known fact is equally clear. Magicians do *not* work together, because they *cannot*."

Asbury's assistant changed the plate on his magic lantern, casting some gargantuan and disgusting insect's wavering light-skeleton on the train-car's wall. "Observe this specimen of the genus *Oestridae*, or common bot-fly—an endoparasite which deposits its eggs onto the skin of a host animal whose heat causes them to hatch, after

24

which its larvae burrow into the animal's skin and gestate, then drop onto the ground to complete their pupal stage. The bot-fly may also spread its eggs through the medium of an intercessor, by attaching them to a common housefly it has seized and restrained through superior power. In a way, this makes it somewhat representative of an *epi*parasite, a parasitical variant which feeds upon its fellow parasites.

"Appearances aside, gentlemen, magicians may be reckoned very much like these bot-flies—"

"In that they're all weird as hell and twice as scary," someone muttered, near Morrow's elbow.

"—since all fully expressed magicians cannot appear to help feeding parasitically upon each other's power, as a type of autonomic reflex. Which is why the best two examples of this oh-so-puzzling human genus can ever manage is a sort of brief accord for the duration of a shared task, during which they agree to consider each other not rivals or prey, but allies . . . until, task done, they move quickly on before they are forced to turn on one another, and hope devoutly to never meet again.

"Thus witches who bear witch-children to term (itself unlikely) must give their babies away at birth, or risk sucking them dry; thus there are no formal schools of magic, only apprenticeships, which all too often culminate in either death or murder. Thus two wizards cannot love, or live together if they do, for fear of their passion becoming mutually assured destruction.

"'Mages don't meddle,' as the old phrase goes. And for this, we who are not of that ilk must all, indisputably, thank God."

"Is the point of all this we're gonna be fighting hexes now, sir?" called out the same voice as before. Doctor Asbury opened his mouth to answer, but closed it again at Pinkerton's gesture.

"Let me take this one, will you?" As Asbury nodded: "Seems to me that what he's sayin' is—if we just play it right, we can trick 'em into fighting each other *for* us."

Asbury pursed his lips and made some ambiguous little movement of the head. "To some degree, yes, Mister Pinkerton. And yet—"

"Sorry, doc," another agent broke in, "but . . . what-all exactly could we even fight 'em *with*, if we had to? Silver bullets?"

"Och, I've found real bullets do just fine, long as you catch 'em off-guard," Pinkerton said, dismissively. Then added: "'Specially when aimed straight to the head."

A flood of laughter rippled through the assembly, levity washing away all but the soberest members' concerns. And sometime after that—when the train-car had long cleared itself once more, leaving Morrow alone with Asbury and Pinkerton—the true mission briefing began.

"We need you to find Reverend Rook, Ed," Pinkerton began, without preamble. "Chase down his gang, get yourself signed up, then move in close—close as possible, without recourse to the obvious."

"Can't think but Chess Pargeter might get a mite riled at me, I was to do *that*," Morrow said, flushing slightly.

"Oh, you know what I mean. Hell, chat *him* up too, while you're at it. No easier way to come next to Rook, considering where the little bastard usually spends most nights."

"And the—formal—goal of this particular sortie, sir?"

"Well, I'll let Asbury here fill you in on that. It's his baby, not mine." As Pinkerton stepped back, the doctor moved forward once more, reassuming his place at the lectern. He rummaged inside his pocket, withdrawing an utterly unfamiliar device. Once flipped open, closer study showed a resemblance to those magnetic compasses Morrow had handled during his service in the War—albeit with some notable differences. This apparatus seemed to have two needles, each spinning counter-clockwise, plus a slim, strangely curved tine of something blendedly green and red which fluttered in a completely different direction. The whole array involved no obvious clockworks, these indicators instead floating "freely" on a mercury-dollop housed in the shallow depression located at the object's centre.

Morrow could see no reason for the way the needles spun and flipped without pause, as if constantly re-orienting themselves to an invisible horizon—if *a* pole, then neither of the ones already mapped, those immutable icons of fixity. For whatever *this* object was made to measure obviously moved, consistently yet erratically, as though it was alive.

"I call it the Manifold . . . Asbury's Manifold, naturally," the doctor said, blushing slightly. "These needles I adopted from the Chinese science of acupuncture, which posits an invisible energy known as the *ch'i* that supposedly courses through every living creature. Medical difficulties are said to be caused by blockages in this energy-flow, necessitating the implantation of such needles underneath the skin at specific pressure-points throughout the human body. They know so much more than we do on so many different matters—yet never seek to share the information except under duress, these secretive Celestials."

Pinkerton broke back in, his tone almost as impatient as Morrow already felt: "With all respect, doctor, we've but a little time more before we pull into the next station."

"Of course, of course." Dr Asbury held the Manifold up for Morrow. "Do you take note of these markings around the rim, here?"

Morrow squinted. "I do, sir."

"Their purpose is to measure various gradients in the ebb and flow of this *ch'i*, which my researches have conclusively ascertained to be the driving connective force behind all hexation. Once its parameters are established, therefore, we may eventually use the Manifold to identify magicians whose talents are hidden not only from us, but also . . . from themselves."

"You mean the, uh . . . 'unexpressed,'" Morrow said.

Asbury nodded. "Consider what a stupid and terrible *waste* our dealings with the sorcerous amongst us have been, to this point," he said. "What a wanton slaughterhouse the past is, when gone over with anything resembling a Christian conscience. Have you ever seen a witch-burning, Mister Morrow?"

Morrow dry-swallowed. "Never had that inflicted on me, no," he replied, carefully. "Though I do recall an old harelipped woman took up in my home-town when I was but eight or so, for travellin' alone during a drought. They found cats living in her hotel room and a dried snakeskin in her bags, so they tied her to a cart and dragged her through town. My Pa said it was a miscarriage of justice against all of God's strictures, no matter what *Leviticus* might have to say on the subject—but that was 'fore she spat vitriol at him, and cursed him blind in one eye."

"And what happened then?"

Morrow sighed. "They buried her up to her neck in the sand," he said, reluctantly, "and told us kids to chuck rocks at her 'til she stopped moving." He paused. "Which . . . we did."

Asbury nodded again, without comment—as though he, too, could hear the irregular crunch of stone against bone ringing in Morrow's mental ears—that wet snap of cheekbone and teeth breaking, punctuated by the cruel laughter of children he still considered friends.

Said Pinkerton: "Only way, sometimes."

"If one knows no better," Asbury shot back. "But think, gentlemen—if we had gotten to that woman earlier in her life, before a few decades' worth of hatred and exclusion had warped her beyond salvage. If we had been able to treat her with kindness, with understanding."

"Break her to the bridle and *use* her, like any other animal. Turn a wolf into a dog."

Morrow noted that though Asbury seemed far less enamoured of this simile than Pinkerton, he made no overt protest.

Asbury continued: "Or consider the trail of destruction Reverend Rook himself left behind, when he first manifested—good men killed, law and order left in ruins, and why? Because he accounts himself abused, in large part owing simply to the circumstances of his . . . second 'birth,' one might call it. Using the Manifold, we could avoid all that horror by discovering witches and wizards *before* they come to their full power . . . our ideal being not to exterminate them, as in previous centuries, but to nurture—and, at length, *recruit*—them."

Pinkerton nudged Morrow, pointing to Asbury. "That's why we

call him 'witch-finder general,'" he confided.

"The point being, Mister Morrow," Asbury concluded, ignoring Pinkerton's joke, "that we are in desperate need of data. A reading from Rook would allow us to map out a spectrum with which to assess potentials."

Morrow frowned. "I wouldn't even know where to start."

"I'd teach you, of course—the process is simplicity itself. Observe." He held out the Manifold again, balanced in one palm, pointing it directly at Morrow. Morrow felt an instantaneous urge to bolt, for no very good reason, and fisted both hands at once to keep himself in check. But the needles simply spun on in their different orbits, clicking fiercely, and Asbury gave him a kindly little smile, probably prompted by Morrow's obvious trepidation.

"No visible reading whatsoever," Asbury told him, just to clarify. "We have two scales, one running clockwise, the other counter-; a power like Rook's would doubtless cause both needles to meet—and lock—somewhere along the red scale, in the upper numbers."

"So . . . what's that mean, then?"

Now it was Pinkerton's turn to smile again, clapping Morrow's shoulder once more for emphasis, like he was congratulating him on having knocked up his wife. "It proves you're no magician, Morrow—not even the beginnings of one. So we don't have to worry over you givin' us a false positive."

Thank God, was all Morrow could think.

"What do you say, son? You up to the task?"

Worth a promotion, Morrow knew, if he said "yes." Better pay. Some way of building a secure life for himself at the end of all this, 'stead of dying alone or starving on an uncertain pension after a bullet shattered something beyond repair. Wasn't like you could ever hope to live your whole life without dealing even once with hexslingers—not as a Pinkerton, and for damn sure not out here. Just wasn't . . . practical.

"Yes sir," Morrow said, at last, "I somewhat think I might be, at that."

Which was always what they liked best to hear, down at the front office—and easy enough to say, before he'd actually spent any sort of time in Reverend Rook's company.

Three months ago, and counting; an age, seemed like. Eighty days and nights, twice the length of time God took to drown the world, or Jesus to wrestle Satan in the desert. And in all that time spent standing idly by while Rook and Chess cut their bloody double swathe over an already-wounded landscape, he'd never yet been able to get close enough to take the reading which would kick him free from this whole nightmare for good.

Or remembered to do so, anyhow, whenever he *had* gotten that close.

So here he was, and here he stayed. *Would* stay, however long it took—until he finally got it right.

CHAPTER THREE
The Present

"They call this Whore City," Chess said, balancing back on his heels and surveying the area with a cold eye. "Though why folks make that distinction, given the rest of this crap-heap . . ."

"Weren't you born here?"

"That's how come I get to say so."

To the casual observer, 'Frisco's Chinee-town—or at least the part of it known as China Alley, a dingy passage extending from Jackson to Washington Street—was completely given over to a sprawling tangle of semi-respectable bagnios on the one hand, outright cribs on the other. It had begun to rain sometime during their trek down, reducing visibility considerably, with mist and mud conspiring to further dim the overhanging lurch of shadows. Outside the bagnios red paper lanterns had been posted, casting a hellish light.

Morrow thought they all looked tolerably enticing destinations, when compared to the cribs: cramped, one-storey raw-board shacks, at whose small barred windows girls leaned straight out into the alley, shamelessly bent on advertising their wares. Their top halves were covered with brief silk blouses, but the minute a man's eyes fell upon them, they opened their drawstrings wide and called out.

"China girl nice! You come inside, please?"

"Two bittee lookee, flo bittee feelee, six bittee doee!"

And most inexplicably: "Your father, he just go out!"

"A white woman would have to be pretty much on her last inch of trim, to end up like that," Morrow remarked. "'Course, this *is* where the smoke all comes from, I'll bet."

"There're plenty," Chess said, shortly. "And not all of 'em opium fiends, either."

For a split second, Morrow wondered how he knew—but he made sure not to let it show.

"Songbird's house should be along here somewhere," the Reverend broke in. "Selina Ah Toy's, they call it. Chess?"

"I ain't been down here in five damn years, as you well know, and my Chinee ain't worth squat 'cept for negotiating very *specific* points of sale."

The Rev fixed him with a sidelong warning look. Chess snorted, and grabbed hold of the next old pigtail who clattered by them.

"*Ai-yaaah!*" the man yelled out—then stared a bit closer. "You Ingarish Oo-nah's boy, *wei*?" he asked, at last.

Morrow noted how the tips of Chess's ears flushed bright red at being thus identified. But seeing how it was under the Rev's watchful eyes, he conjured some vile parody of a pleasant expression, replying, "Uh huh. Nee how, uncle—long time no see. Songbird ah?"

"Songbird? No can do!"

"*Can* do, uncle. Selina Ah Toy's, cash money ah. This fella jootping, same as her. You bring."

"Songbird no-go! *Chi-shien gweilo, ben tiansheng de yidui rou—*"

And here he went off into some further rattle-fast string of stuff, only stopping short when Chess stuck his gun to the old man's shiny blue silk-clad chest.

"Listen, granddad," he said, with surprising patience, "we ain't leavin' 'til the Reverend here and Songbird sit down together. So you go tell her that and see what it gets you, 'cause I can tell you right now exactly what it'll get you, if you don't."

The old man swallowed hard and drew himself up slightly, as if steeling himself to refuse once more (and be shot for it, a good Celestial soldier). But an imperious voice issued from just up the street, saying: "No need for that, gentlemen . . . I will gladly see the Reverend, if he cares to come inside."

Chess shrugged, and put up his gun. The old man ran off without a backward glance, calling out as he did: "*Chunren gweilo, waaah! Cao ni zuxian shi ba dai!"*

"That don't sound too nice," Morrow remarked.

"It is not," the voice—Songbird's, he surmised—replied. "He is a foolish old man, and I will deal with him later, harshly, for insulting my guests. But again, gentlemen, will you enter?"

Morrow thought he'd rather not, another thing he knew enough to keep to himself. Instead, he trailed Chess and the Reverend into what proved the most luxurious establishment they'd yet discovered: a snug red brick house, its dim-lit ground floor given over to gambling—fan-tan, mah-jongg, a creepily silent general click and shuffle of plain brass counters and polished elephant-horn dominoes. On a low stage, a four-piece orchestra sat playing some windy chaos which sounded to Morrow like they were still deep in the process of tuning their weirdly shaped instrumentation. Girls swayed back and forth on either side, doing a serpentine dance.

No sign of Songbird, though. Just a curtain made from jet beads swinging back and forth atop a flight of stairs, and the same voice calling down, impatiently: "Up here, Reverend Rook! Bring your men with you, if you must. I mean you no harm, and trust you mean me the same. You would never have come here at all were that not true, *wei?*"

"Yes ma'am," the Rev agreed, taking hold of Chess's arm.

But Chess dug himself in. "I ain't goin' nowhere near that bitch," he said. "You already got her parole, so you don't really need me. Just the stink of this hole alone's 'bout enough to make my head split open, anyways."

"Too much feminine perfume, and such?"

"Too much junk, more like. Take Morrow, you want some back-up."

Another rumbling laugh. "Your call, darlin'. Hell, though—I thought you were up for anything, Chess. When'd you get so damn nice?"

Chess nodded at the curtain. "You drug us down here to see some baby whore who does table-rappin' on the side; ain't my idea of a good time, is all. I'll stay in easy callin' distance."

Morrow, dubious: "Baby whore?"

"'Course," Chess snapped. "Chinee breed 'em that way—whores, witches, what-have-you. Same as them little mush-faced dogs, or them gold-colour fish with the floppy heads." He shook his head, nose wrinkling. "It's creepish, the whole damn thing."

"Sure you ain't just jealous?" the Rev suggested. "I'll be in fairly close quarters with her, after all." To which Chess's sharp face coloured and darkened, in equal measure.

"I'll stay close," he repeated. "Locked and loaded—all you gotta do is yell. Meet you back out front, soon as you're done your business."

Rook shrugged. "Probably the best place for you, you feel that strongly about it. Ed?"

"Sir."

So they left Chess behind, climbing to meet the only other magician Morrow'd ever run across so far, with nothing but a shotgun and Rook's Bible for cover. First witch-woman Morrow'd seen since Old Mother Harelip, too, for all she was barely old enough to . . . well, she'd have to at least be old enough to bleed, according to Asbury's strictures.

The curtain parted with a slither. Inside, one windowless room took up the whole of the house's second floor—spacious, yet cramped by a stifling forest of screens which had been arranged to turn one end of the room into a haphazard sort of pagoda. Where Songbird slept, Morrow reckoned, and maybe conducted other sorts of encounters.

"You are correct in this conclusion, Mister Morrow," the voice told him, with uncomfortable acuteness—and now issuing from somewhere roughly behind him, which troubled Morrow even more. "For while my maiden's flower is far too highly valued to be sold except at auction, there are no strictures levied against my allowing an occasional 'lookee' if some white man wishes to pay for the privilege, though I charge considerably more than fifty cents. I say *white* man, because most Celestials already know that the secret parts of their womenfolk differ in no way from those of any other female, be she yellow, white . . . or dead."

Morrow felt a small shoulder brush lightly against his elbow and all but fell back, the stock of his shotgun knocking one screen sharp enough that it rang against the sanctum's wall like a muffled bell. The Reverend, no doubt more used to these sorts of tricks, simply stepped aside, bowing as Songbird settled onto a throne set with a high silk cushion.

"Have to decline the kind offer, Honourable Lady," Rook said. "Though for all I probably couldn't afford it, I'm sure it makes a lovely view. What I'm more interested in, however, is your skill—"

"—as an interpreter of dreams? I know."

And here Songbird raised her face to what light there was, revealing herself as a truly spectral vision: twelve years old at most, a porcelain doll dressed all in red bridal silk whose features matched those of the painted courtesans decorating her walls almost exactly, aside from one peculiarity—a near-complete lack of colour in the face under her sheer red veil, pig-pale skin, crone-white hair and faded hazel eyes all bleached by some hideous trick of nature. Her hands she held folded in her lap, interlaced fingers covered with long, gilded filigree spikes which gave off a dry, squeaking tone as they rubbed together, a distant cymbal's clash.

"Albino," the Rev observed. "You must be almost blind, I'd think."

A tiny nod. "Almost. Luckily, I find it aids in my speculative endeavours. And now, since we have dispensed with formalities: your dream. It began when you first came to power?"

"Exactly at that same point, yes."

"When the gallows-trap opened? Or when your neck broke?"

The Rev took this in. Though still loomingly tall, he seemed suddenly smaller, less assured. "I don't think it ever actually *broke*," he said, at last.

Songbird smiled, thinly. "Such prevarication, for such a powerful man. Show me the kiss she gave you, your 'Rainbow Lady.'"

"Thought you said—"

"I can *feel* very well, Reverend." Voice dropping further: "Now—I have other business of my own to conduct tonight, as do you, no doubt. So open your shirt, and *bow down to me*."

Was there an extra thrum to the words she spoke? For Morrow, it was mere speculation—but from what he could see, Reverend Rook took them full in the face, a thrown glass of cold water. His huge hands were already rising to obey, unbidden, when he shook himself like a dog and hauled them back down again.

"Little girl," he said, "you'd best be able to give me what I want. Or I will tear this damn place of yours down around you, without ever even opening my Book."

Songbird yawned, covering her mouth with those huge gilt nail-sheaths. "We will see."

The Rev exhaled through his nose, then popped the requisite buttons, shrugging collar aside from the puckered rope-scar which still encircled his thick neck, bent himself until Songbird could reach up and place her naked palm against the furrowed flesh without having to rise. She stroked the burn, delicately, like she was planning to buy more of it by the ell.

Creepish, Morrow heard Chess's voice remark, from the back of his brain.

"Do you believe in ghosts, Reverend Rook?" she asked, at last.

"Sure," the Rev replied, straightening up again. "Why?"

"And do you believe in God?" As Rook stared: *Gods?*

This drew a frown. "Old heretic deities, the things they worshipped in Philistine times? Baal and Moloch, and such?" Songbird nodded once more. "I was taught those were devils, sent by Satan to fool with unbelievers. Like Solomon with his wives' idols, or Ahab and Jezebel."

Songbird shrugged. "Gods or ghosts, energy begets energy—prayer, worship, sacrifice, revenge. Like the *ch'i*, which you and I both carry inside us; a stream the whole universe drinks from, for good or ill. Nothing really dies."

"I do hope there's some point here beyond the merely philosophical you're eventually aimin' to make, for both our sakes."

"Certainly. This woman of yours—who watches over all hanged men, and claims you for her own—is both god *and* ghost. Doubly powerful, and thus doubly dangerous. She demands something from you . . . and until you render it to her, she will never let you go."

"Well, that ain't actually too helpful, since Goddamn if I know what that might be."

"You must ask her."

"She don't really speak my language."

"No—or you hers, I gather. Few probably live who do. This is why you must speak to her directly." Pinning Morrow with a red-tinged glance: "If you would be so good as to reach behind you, Mister Morrow . . . yes, there, exactly. Thank you."

The item in question proved to be a long slab of black stuff like congealed tar, four inches by six, inscribed all over one side of it with queer figuring. Peering closer, Morrow thought he could make out the remains of a prehistoric murder, some creature left in dismembered wreckage—but no, it was a woman, her cheeks picked out with spiral patterns, black breasts pendulous and stiff coif balanced by a massive pair of dagger-sharp earrings, fit to carve someone else the same way she herself had already been unstrung.

Rook shook his head. "That ain't her."

"Not completely," Songbird agreed. "And yet . . . I was given this in tribute, by a man from Tlaquepacque. He called it a 'smoking mirror.' Your Rainbow Lady will respond to it favourably, if given the right sort of impetus."

"Which would be?"

She beckoned him back down again, and whispered in his ear. Slowly, Morrow saw a cold understanding wash across Rook's face.

"Uh huh, all right. How much?"

"It depends. How much are you prepared to pay, Reverend?"

"Enough."

"And by . . . ?"

". . . the usual method."

Songbird breathed in, hungrily. "Aaah," she said. "I *had* hoped you would honour the traditions."

"I'm a man what keeps his bargains."

"Oh, not always, I think." Songbird's eyes flicked back to Morrow. "Perhaps you should send your friend away now," she suggested.

Rook nodded. "Go find Chess for me, Ed, would you? You may've noticed how he tends to make himself some trouble to get into, whenever he's riled."

"What about you?"

"I'll be back out in a minute."

Morrow nodded as well, but found himself lingering—so obviously, even Songbird couldn't fail to notice. She smiled, in a way that made Morrow's hair rise like quills.

"He will be quite safe with me, Mister Morrow. After all, I am only a young maiden . . . no fit threat at all to the Reverend. What he does here, he chooses to. Yes, Asher Rook?"

"Yes."

"Then . . . it is decided."

She grabbed hold of the back of Rook's head with both hands, so fierce and fast it made Morrow take yet another step back, rattling the screens' slick-painted forest. This sly little thing with her sugar-stick bones, digging her golden claws deep in the Reverend's hair, kissing him like she meant to suck out his very soul. Which she maybe might've, since he could see something pass between them, blurred and subtle, a sort of heat-shimmer that tugged at the corners where their two mouths met and puffed both their throats out like frogs'.

They prey on each other, Asbury had said.

Songbird gulped hard, and Morrow heard the Rev's usual rumble become a species of moan that scared him more than anything else he'd seen thus far. He knew that Chess would've tried to do something about it and screw the consequences, had he only been in range. Perhaps that was why the Rev had taken pains to make so damn sure he wasn't.

But that was Chess, and this was Ed, who didn't love Reverend Rook at all—not more than his life, at any rate.

So all Morrow did in response was grit his teeth hard, stop his ears and take to his heels, shotgun snapping up like a third arm, already cocked. And left 'em to it.

CHAPTER FOUR

That dream again. How many had he had already—a seemingly infinite roster of dreadful variations, each just as grotesque as the next? How many would he *have* to?

This time, he sat at his Rainbow Lady's left hand on a dais made from bones. Her dragonfly cloak spread out behind them both to form a living tapestry, each dim-brilliant wing aflash, their collective buzz a rising ghost-whine.

She laid her small hand upon his arm, murmuring: ***Even the dark world has its seasons, or tides. And this, Our Flayed Lord's young man-skinning month, is one of our shallowest points . . . when the waters recede far enough to show the mulch beneath. The endless death-muck swamp from which all life can—and will, and** must**—be reborn.***

Look down, little king . . .

Elevated far above the crowd, he saw the Sunken Ball-Court's fetid playing grounds teem with competitors—all splendid athletes, once upon a time. But now they were sadly denuded parodies, skins black with putrescence, slipping and sliding back and forth over drained-pale flesh rendered vaguely pink again with strain.

The skull-rack walls rang with groans of effort. Some played half-blind, their eyeballs long since spilled out upon their cheeks on glistening strings; others played by sound alone, sporting necklaces cobbled together from their defeated opponents' teeth, strung upon intestines.

Ixiptla, she called them. Even closer, her breath stirred his hair—but not rank, as he'd expected. Smelling instead of something fresh and green, a springtime scent, familiar enough to be doubly wrenching when re-encountered in *this* horrid place.

Ix-what? he asked, only to hear her rippling silver laugh, a many-layered chime of wind-blown glass.

Ixiptla, she repeated. ***Gods'-flesh. Sacred victims. How generously they spill their blood for us, even here! Playing out the old games, so they can serve themselves up to us like maize. For they have all been Him, in their time—all aspects of the Year-dancer, the Flute-player, best of all shared dishes. Xipe Totec, Our Lord the Flayed One, who breeds flowers from meat and flies from fruit, whose many deaths create and destroy the world.***

Crashing up against each other with a rotten gasp of impact while their rucked hides bulged, flapped open along the backbone, to display a sudden flash of naked spine: calculated as a whore's culottes, yet far more . . . intimate.

Ah, she breathed once more, she who had no real breath. ***Aaah, but the pulp of men is SWEET, little king. Red-ripe with pain, cradled in clicking yellow bone—and the heart itself, so precious when proffered thus, especially if given in love. Man's-heart set unwrapped in its cracked cage of ribs, a jade ball . . . earthquake anchor, skull-flower, jaguar cactus fruit. . . .***

I don't—he started to say, then choked it off. Seeing how each player's empty chest swung wide, then slammed shut again with the game's give and take, crunching. That they were nothing but raided lock-boxes given just enough life to blunder back and forth through the rising water, kicking up puddle-spray with their bare, bony feet.

A second hand hung from every wrist, cured-glove-limp, nails and all. Skeleton palms rose to spike the ball off whatever wall seemed nearest, sliming it with rot—after which the gamesters would yell out in triumph, catch it on the rebound, and start over again.

He shook his head, bile flushing his throat, and demanded— *What are you people? Goddamn demons?*

We are the Gods, she said. ***We were you; we love you. Why***

would we not? Your love keeps us alive.

I ain't no damn part at all of that *equation.*

And here she smiled, so sweetly, with her tiny green teeth—each of them filed to points, set with the same jade scales as her mask-face itself.

Replying, as she did: . . . *Not yet.*

And now . . . look up, through the moon's eye. See how I follow you, so closely, even here. See the door through which we two will meet at last, the hole through which I will climb back up into your world.

The moon in question was black, vaguely squarish—rectangulish? A tiny lozenge in the black-and-yellow sky. It struck him as somehow familiar.

Here: I will show you a great mystery, seldom seen. For though you witness me now in my glory, this was me, also, long ago: a girl just like the witch who tries to drain your power now, trembling on the cenote's lip, pierced tongue's overflow outlining her lips and chin in a bloody tattoo. She with the thorn-rope tightening around her neck, so that when she falls, she will not even feel her impact. The water will take her like a lover, suck her down and hold her fast, forever.

A massive sounding bell of rock, its sides jagged with lime, through which bats dove and screeched. The water, blue shading to black.

This well is full of bones, and all have them have "been" me, at one time or another. All of them, and none.

He looked up, looked down, looked back up; could not seem to stop himself. Saw the black moon swimming in the black-and-yellow sky. Watched as the rain of knives began to fall once more, slicing downwards.

Now wake, little king, before that witch-girl drains you beyond the point of being able to defend yourself. You are not wholly your own anymore, to give yourself away at will. Neither your own, nor hers, nor any living other's.

You are MINE.

Though most of Songbird's lower-floor Chinee-men didn't seem to know what the hell Morrow meant when he yelled Chess's name at them—even with the shotgun showing—he eventually blundered on one who spoke at least some sort of English.

"You go there!" this one yelled back, above the music's caterwauling, indicating a dim passageway that dipped twistily 'round and beneath the central stairs, before trailing into what looked for all the world like a genuine hole in the ground.

Why would Chess head down here? he wondered. *This place stinks worse'n the rest of it all put together.*

At his back, Celestials were already starting to gather, so Morrow squared his shoulders, and dropped down inside. His first thought was that this place was built far more for Chess's specifications than it'd ever be for his—but he bulled his way through nevertheless, the rock itself closing in on him mouth-wise, all teeth and no lip.

Eventually, he was spit out into a dead-end cave, its walls lined honeycomb-style with ragged little coffin-sized crevices—four apiece, moving upwards to the last length a man his height could reach while standing on tip-toe. The reek hit him face-on, a gag dipped in outhouse-water, as restless, shifting moans spilled down every-which-way from those same crevices' occupants.

All women, from what little Morrow allowed himself to recognize, and all of them sick to dying, too—maybe with the pox, the weeping syph, or spitting up blood with the dreaded lung-complaint: consumption, battening on them fast and eating them alive.

Suffice to say, it was the last sort of place Morrow'd ever thought to find Chess Pargeter, with his fancy store-bought clothes and his bath-a-night clean self. But here he stood, hands braced on gun-butts, looking down at a sharp-faced slip of a thing laid back in her shift, a smoking opium-pipe still clutched in one bird-thin hand, with her waist-long rusty hair piled beneath her for a pillow.

She opened her eyes just a slit, narrow and green as Chess's own, to say—hoarse and blurred by some Limey accent, but with no particular surprise—"Oh, so *there* you are, at long last. Where's that warlock fancy-man of yours, any'ow?"

"None of your beeswax," Chess replied. "*You* look like death warmed up, by the way."

The woman drew hard on the pipe, coughed rackingly and grinned, showing a reddened half-mouthful of teeth. "Don't I? Take a good long ken. This'll be you too, one o' these days."

"Not down here, it won't."

It was Chess's usual tone, all right—hot and cold at once, detached as though he was studying the world through the bottom of one of his just-emptied absinthe glasses. Still, Morrow heard a strange shiver run through it nonetheless: a crack, hairline for now. But spreading.

The woman laughed at that, rattle-harsh. "Ooh, *big* words. Fink I'm impressed, you cat-eyed bitch? Look at yerself. Could've 'ad a bloody soft life, you didn't run off an' act the fool, playin' at soldiers. An' look at us now."

"*Us*? No such thing, thank Christ Almighty. And don't rag me out like I'm knee-high no more, either—*this* bitch is feared 'cross six states. Might even go so far as to say I've killed more men than you've fucked, but I somehow doubt that's possible. So speak to me as if I got enough in my pocket to pay your fare, or—"

"Or what? Gonna shoot me? Least you can do—such a *big* man, you, wiv yer guns." And here she paused, her ghost-of-pretty face twisted, a bent tin mirror reflection. "Go on, *do* it!"

Chess considered her, until a look came into his eyes that Morrow couldn't easily put a name to. "Well . . ." he said, eventually.

"Well, what?"

"Say you was to tell me 'I'm sorry,' just the once . . . 'bout—oh, anything . . . then maybe I just might."

The woman took her own half-moment to think on this, before she shook her head.

"You'd like that, wouldn't ya? Go on wiv yourself, ya prancing molly. I ain't done nothin' in life worth apologizin' for, least of all to *you*."

For a split instant, the green flame Morrow knew all too well danced in Chess's stare—that sick-lit kill-flash which always came before lightning-fast trigger-cock and a body's downward thump. But it passed, and just as quickly.

"Yeah," he said, calm again. "That's what I thought. And that's why I wouldn't waste the damn bullet."

The woman sagged back, clutching her pipe in both hands. "Then what bloody good are you to me?" she asked. And drew on the pipe, its coal flaring up like she was sucking Hellfire—breathed it in 'til her eyes rolled back, each a mere green thread under a low-slung lid. All the vitriol drained from her, allowing Morrow a glimpse of what she might have looked like young, fresh, even happy, once upon a time. Or good enough at her calling to fake being so.

Conversation over, obviously. But Chess kept on standing there, hands a-twitch like a dreaming dog's, fingers reaching for the nearest trigger—or for something else entirely, perhaps. To tuck the sackcloth half-thrown across her up further, or at least re-right the opium pipe, so she didn't set herself on fire.

Morrow cleared his throat. "Hey, Chess—Rook sent me t' find you. Thought you said you was goin' to wait outside. . . ."

Chess turned, scowl immediately slapped back on. "Don't much matter, what I said or what I didn't—how fast you got here's your look-out, not mine." A second's pause. "So where the hell is *he*?"

"Uh, back up with Songbird, last I saw. Why?"

All at once Chess was up against him, close enough to lay hold of Morrow's throat with his teeth. "You *left* him back there, alone? Stupid fuckin' ox, you Goddamn skinned bear of a—"

"Jesus, Chess, he *told* me to! What the fuck was I supposed to—?"

"'Sides from come get *me*?" This last came called back over Chess's shoulder as he flashed ahead through the tunnel, close to full-out running as the narrow walls would allow. "Don't you know shit about hexes, Morrow, after all this time? They can't take just a *little*!"

Back through the half-dark, panting and heart hammering, barking shoulders and shins. Then up into Selina Ah Toy's proper again, blinking mole-ish, to find Chess already on point—both guns out and lips peeled back, ready to go down fighting, while customers and employees alike slid all sorts of crazy mediaeval weaponry out from beneath their coattails.

Above, Morrow could see Songbird stepping out onto her landing with the Rev's huge shadow looming behind, big as ever, though slightly sleepwalk-swaying.

"Ash Rook!" Chess yelled. "You all right?"

The Rev gave a grunt, neither enough to confirm or deny. But Songbird turned her head, back-tracing the cry and smiling in recognition at Chess's voice, with a hungry sort of interest.

"And here would be your lotus boy, Reverend—the redheaded man-killer himself. Did you enjoy your sojourn in the tunnels, Mister Pargeter?" Her voice dropped, a wintry whisper. "*See anything you like?*"

Chess levelled both barrels at her, without a second's hesitation. "Not too much," he said. "I'd spent any real money in this joint, in fact, I might feel inclined to put a ball right through your brain. So gimme back the Rev, quick-smart, and we'll call it even."

"Such discourtesy. I will excuse it on grounds of loyalty, however—or *love*, if you prefer."

There was a wealth of cool contempt packed into that one over-enunciated word. To which Chess gave a nasty little grin of his own, and replied, "My Ma always said *love's* the word they pull out whenever they don't want to pay you. But then again, yours too, probably."

A general hiss ran round the room. Songbird shook her head, sadly.

"Poor angry little boy," she said, softly. "And I might have been so hospitable."

"Uh huh, I'll bet. You want it in the eye, or should I just aim for anyplace convenient?"

But with this, the crowd surged forward again, and Morrow found himself abruptly kitty-corner up against Chess's side, wondering just how many blasts he could possibly get off—the full two? Only one? One and a half, however *that* might work?—before somebody grabbed his shotgun's stock and wrestled it away. Chess cursed as Morrow jostled his elbow, and let fly, like he was punctuating a sentence. At such close quarters, the same bullet reduced half of one pigtail's face to raw mash, wounding two others standing behind in the process.

"Now, listen all you motherfuckers—" Chess began, still keeping the other gun trained vaguely Songbird-wards, but broke off as the gal gave out a sudden teakettle-shrill shriek. She didn't sound angry, so much, as simply done with playing.

Her men cowered away, leaving Chess and Morrow to take the full brunt, as it eventually resolved itself into a string of imprecations: "*Mei, tamade hundan, liu koushui de biaozi he houzi de ben erzi!* To come inside *my* house and speak to me thus, as though you knew no better—"

Chess snarled. "Yeah? Well, koo nee day, po-foo! You bring your ass down *here* and say that, 'fore I come on up and—"

Aw, crap, Morrow thought, bracing himself. But at that very same instant, Songbird cried out in a very different way and slid sideways to avoid the Rev as he crashed through the banister, wood-splinters bursting to rain every which way, dropping to land heavy almost at Chess's feet.

Rook shook himself, groggy; hadn't quite recovered from whatever Songbird'd been doing to him, up top. Then reached 'round Chess's waist with one outsized hand, fisting it hard enough to keep them locked together, contact sparking between them in a way that made Chess stagger, guns drooping, like he wasn't quite sure what he was here for anymore. Rook rummaged in his coat with the other, tucking the "smoking mirror" he still clutched away, while Morrow used the distraction to empty his remaining shells: one in the nearest lamp, spraying lit oil, and the other into some gigantic Tong-boy who immediately came jumping back up with an axe even so, seemingly oblivious to the impact and looking to split a still-dazed Chess in two.

The shot's report seemed to snap Chess awake again, prompting him to gut-shoot his potential murderer, then catch Morrow's eye on the go-'round as they both went to reload. Morrow found Chess's glance uncharacteristically full of surprise and respect, admixed.

"Nice shot," Chess said, before going back to his usual business, as Rook finally got his Bible flipped open. Above, meanwhile, Songbird screamed out some new phrase, prompting Morrow to look up just in time to see—her *whole bottom jaw* unhinge, snake-wide, and a stream of live bats pour out of it like fluttery black vomit, filling the air around all three of them with shrieks and teeth. Chess pivoted with one of 'em already clinging fast to the side of his head, and emptied both guns in a matter of seconds. The results, though spectacular—delicate wings shred-torn, furry bodies popped apart like clay pigeons full of blood—were so sadly inefficient overall, he was soon reduced to trying to pistol-whip the damn things to death.

"Jesus fuck-damn *fuck*!" Chess yelled, in disgusted rage. "Fuck *all* y'all, you filthy fuckin' things! Rook, if you're gonna *do* somethin', best time'd be 'bout *right the fuck NOW*—"

Rook nodded. "THEN THE LORD SAID TO JOSHUA, SEE, I HAVE DELIVERED JERICHO INTO YOUR HANDS. . . . WHEN YOU HEAR THEM SOUND A LONG BLAST ON THE TRUMPETS, HAVE ALL THE PEOPLE GIVE A LOUD SHOUT. . . ."

"Chapter Six, two to twenty-seven," Morrow told himself, as the house began to shake and the Rev preached on. The text spiraled out of Rook's mouth flat and quick, a smoky snake-tongue of close-packed silver typeface, to dart inside the walls through any available route: old cracks, cracks newly opening in skeleton fans, every mislaid plank and empty nail-bed.

". . . AND WHEN . . . THE WALL COLLAPSED . . . THEY TOOK THE CITY. THEY DEVOTED THE CITY TO THE LORD AND DESTROYED WITH THE SWORD EVERY LIVING THING IN IT—MEN AND WOMEN, YOUNG AND OLD. . . ."

The cracks in Selina Ah Toy's foundations were wide enough now to both let in daylight and let out the bats, who almost immediately tried to get back in, blinded by the dull glare of 'Frisco's watery exterior. "AND AT THAT TIME JOSHUA PRONOUNCED THIS SOLEMN OATH," the Rev continued declaiming, implacably. "CURSED BEFORE THE

LORD IS THE MAN WHO UNDERTAKES TO REBUILD THIS CITY, JERICHO: AT THE COST OF HIS FIRSTBORN SON WILL HE LAY ITS FOUNDATIONS; AT THE COST OF HIS YOUNGEST WILL HE SET UP ITS GATES."

Quite some judgement, Morrow thought. But Songbird merely spat, unimpressed, maybe hoping it'd hit Chess on the way down. Hissing at Rook, in turn: "This cannot be forgotten, *gweilo ch'in ta.* Do you hear me?"

The Rev nodded, equally sanguine. "Goodbye, Songbird," was all he said, in return.

One final spasm, a crunching twist that ripped skin and muscle from the rack of the world, saw all three somehow thrown bodily straight from Songbird's bagnio to the muddy river-bank on 'Frisco's outskirts where they'd left the rest of their gang: a dry gold-panning operation with at least one shack left intact, just right for purposes of shelter and disguise combined.

The sudden rending—and mending—of their arcane passage was enough to make old Kees Hosteen spill the coffee he was boiling up, yelling out, as he did, "Christ on a coffin-nailed cross, boys! The Rev's come back!"

Above, the open sky growled. Chess hugged the Rev to him, wet to both knees and virtually holding him up—most of him, anyhow. *Frilly little catamite's a sight stronger than he looks,* Morrow found himself thinking—then kicked himself in the mental ass, hard, for being so surprised.

"You are a *damn* fool," Chess told Rook. "I *told* you them Chinee witches ain't worth the trouble of truckin' with, no matter the odds. But did you listen?"

Rook heaved a long sigh, bracing both hands on the small of his back and cracking his own spine 'til he groaned like he'd been beat all over. Finally managing to allow: "I did not."

"Nope. And considerin' we barely got out of there alive, I hope it was Goddamn well worth it."

"Well, since you ask . . . it was. Which means, I suppose, that I probably need to thank you for all your help on this particular campaign, in whatever way you might find most congenial. Always assuming that sounds like adequate payment in kind, to you."

A long, cool glance exchanged between 'em followed, with heat banked none too secretly underneath.

"We'll see," Chess said, at last. And turned away.

Half a night and a day of hard riding later, they holed up in a shanty barroom-whorehouse combo called the Two Sisters Saloon, where Chess insisted on laying out for a bottle all of Morrow's own, and stuck around 'til he'd drunk at least half of it. It was probably the longest he'd been in close quarters with Chess since joining up without the Rev there to mediate between them, and Morrow was vaguely shocked to realize he wasn't actually struggling to stay on his guard anymore. Mister (ex-)Private Pargeter could be fairly good company, when he wasn't determined to pick fights that ended in murder.

"Two Sisters," he said, thickly. "That who started this place up?"

Chess laughed, a genially smashed cat-sneeze cackle. "Hardly. It's the song, you know, with the . . . river, and the mill, and whatnot . . . you know that song?" Morrow shook his head. "Well, then maybe it *was* just my Ma, after all—some Limey jig she used to sing, whenever she got low. Goes like . . .

"*There lived an old lord by the Northern Sea,*
Bow we down—
There lived an old lord by the Northern Sea,
Bow and balance to me;
There lived an old lord by the Northern Sea
And he had daughters, one two three . . .
I'll be true to my love,
If my love will be true to me."

Morrow squinted, feeling the room lurch around him. "So he had *three* daughters."

"Yeah, and one of 'em steals the other's finance, so the other one throws her in the river to drown. Then she floats downstream and snags in the mill, and the miller drags her out—"

"So she's rescued."

Another laugh. "'Til he cuts the rings off her fingers, and throws her right back in."

"An' the third?"

"She don't even come into it, Morrow; three's a better rhyme than two, is all." Chess shot him a quick glance, and even mellow as he was, Morrow felt a quick stab of superstitious dread, unable to deny that even in the bar's smoky semi-shadow, the pistoleer's eyes really did throw back light like a cat's. "You're an odd sorta bastard when you're drunk, ain't ya?"

Morrow swallowed. "Yeah. When I ain't drunk, too—or so I've been told."

And then, because the Two Sisters was so warm and dark, maybe, packed full to the gills with outlaws and really almost too noisy to talk at all, Morrow found himself asking, without thinking twice, "What the hell *was* that place, anyhow? Back at Songbird's?"

But to this, Chess didn't answer immediately. Instead, he continued to study on his own empty glass a while, once more deep entranced by what he saw there: that cool, sticky green world where nothing mattered, 'cause everything was already well-drained hollow.

"Down in the hole?" he said, at length. "They call it the hospital— not that it's for gettin' better, you understand. 'Cause that's just where they put the whores who really *are* on their last inch of trim."

"'Bout how long you think they all got, then?"

"Oh, not too long. Undertakers'll be by tomorrow. If they ain't dead by then, they better try harder."

"So—that woman you were talkin' with . . ." Another gulp, as the room continued on its merry, wobbly way. ". . . who was *she*?"

And here Chess's eyes flicked over yet again, all the more disturbing for their unpredictable *lack* of anger.

"Well, hell, Morrow," he said, lightly, "I'd've thought you'd've already guessed. *That* there was the famous English Oona . . . Pargeter."

CHAPTER FIVE

That night, Morrow lay awake without wanting to, trying not to listen to Chess and the Rev fuck. Which was damn hard, since they were so damn *loud* at it—Chess mostly, Morrow reckoned, though the Rev sure did his share. The racket dripped down through the ceiling, incautious and unashamed as all get out; creak and thump of bedsprings and other accoutrements, plus Chess himself riding Rook like he was some sort of trick horse with a whoop and a holler, singing out his usual refrain at the top of his lungs: "Oh yeah, hit that, God *damn!* *Hit* that thing, uh, Good God Jesus! Christ Almighty, go on ahead and *hit* it!"

While Morrow didn't really want to know *what*-all was getting hit, necessarily, the sheer crazy spectacle of it still amazed him somewhat. God knew, he'd never heard a man and a woman get quite so rowdy with each other, not unless incipient physical damage was involved.

"There's things you need not to ask, concernin' Chess and the Reverend." Kees Hosteen had taken Morrow aside and told him, back when Morrow first joined up.

To which Morrow had blurted back, "Those two screwin' each other, or what?"

Hosteen gave him a long look. "Not *each other*, as such," he said, finally. "But Chess takes it from the Rev whenever the Rev cares to give it, and if you feel you gotta make hay on that bein' against nature, or some such—"

"Chess'll shoot me for it."

"Right where you stand, boy. I've seen it done, and more'n just the once."

51

"Reverend feel the same way?"

"Who knows what the Reverend feels? Them hexacious ones ain't for us to understand. But Chess don't seem to care either way—so watch yourself, or watch the damn wall."

Pinkerton Agency records didn't say much about Rook, or his proclivities, back before the hanging. *Had he always liked men?* Morrow wondered. Maybe the Rev just considered himself so damned it didn't much matter *who* he found himself at play with. Or did they consider themselves some version of married, with or without the Rev's former deity's permission? That seemed to jibe, though for all Chess might be the one on the receiving end, Morrow somehow doubted Rook thought he was the wife in their arrangement.

So Reverend Rook was a sinner and maybe a hypocrite, according to the tenets of his own Good-turned-bad Book. Chess, though . . . Chess Pargeter was by nature an outlaw born and bred, just like his Ma, and couldn't've ever been anything else, not even if he'd never robbed his first stage, or killed outside of the War. The big decision Chess had probably made before leaving San Francisco hadn't been to not be a *whore*, per se, 'cause from what Hosteen let slip, he'd certainly taken payment for favours since—it'd just been to not ever let himself be what Chess considered a victim.

"He's a mean little man, that's for sure," Hosteen had said, half-admiringly. "You know where Chess come from, right?"

Morrow nodded.

"Well, listen. I once went to a cat-house, up on Black Mountain— them gals was so tough they didn't even have pimps. They set their own rates; enforced 'em, too. I saw one cut a notch in a trick's ear 'cause he shorted her the minimum—said she'd've done it on his tallywhacker, but she wanted to give him a chance to pay her back. And the next week, there he was again! Chess strikes me that way.

"Very first time he come into camp, lookin'—and actin'—like he does, the men got to talkin'. Damn if he didn't even blink, though— just gave out how sure, he'd suck your cock for ya, long as you washed it first. But he always wanted something in return."

"Money?"

"Naw, trade, usually. Dry boots, bullets . . . you see that knife of his? I give him that. Wouldn't let you fuck him, though, no matter what. *You can do that with your wife*, he used to say. Then this one big bastard tries it, and Chess fights back so hard he gives him two black eyes. 'Course, he *was* big, and he had friends. After, he says: *Guess you're mine now, bitch.* But Chess didn't cry about it none, just said: *I ain't no-damn-body's, motherfucker.*

"And after our next engagement, what do you know? All three of 'em ended up in the doc's tent, and all three of 'em died 'of their injuries.' Which is real interestin', considering how the only thing that big fucker had was a cracked head, all one of his friends'd lost was a finger, and the last one'd just been shot in the ass-cheek. But there they were the next mornin', blue and stiff . . . with their throats cut, ear to ear."

"Is that what landed Chess in the stockade?"

"You'd think so, wouldn't you? But we was deep in Injun country at the time, so they let it go, 'cause it gave 'em an explanation—plus, the Lieut still had Bluebellies left needed killin', and Chess was the best we had at that particular game." Hosteen paused. "Then Rook joined up."

"And?"

"Oh, Chess wanted *him* right from the start, but the Rev wouldn't have none of it, 'cause he said what he really wanted was to save Chess's soul instead. So he used to spend a good part of each night preachin', while Chess just sat there noddin' and cleanin' his guns—bidin' his time. What surprised me was exactly how long Chess went along with it all, considerin'."

"The Rev seems to have given up on that idea somewhat, since," Morrow said.

To which Hosteen just laughed, and nodded. "I reckon how gettin' hung will probably do that to a fellow," he said. "'Specially when it's for somethin' you didn't even do."

Which probably bore looking into at some point, but not by Morrow, and especially not tonight. Because tonight would be when Ed Morrow finally either got that damn Manifold reading for Professor Asbury, or took off, either way. After the mess at Songbird's, he'd had just about enough spooky shit to last him the rest of this life, or any other.

God knew, it wasn't like he hadn't tried, before this. Those few times he had found himself observed at this practice (never by Rook or Chess, thank Christ, so far as he could ascertain), he'd claimed the Manifold was simply a tricksy sort of pocket-watch he'd picked up along the way. *Got it off a dead Pink,* he'd told Hosteen, and felt his heart drop over the way that otherwise so-congenial old man grinned wide at the very idea. Fact was, if any of Rook's bunch were to find out where his true allegiances were, they'd shoot him first in the back, then in the skull once he was down, like a broke-leg horse.

But every attempt had ended the exact same way, in confusion and doubt. Oh, the needles spun all right, into—and immediately back out of—the coveted red zone. What they *didn't* do was stay there long enough to register either way, let alone produce any numbers for Asbury's equation . . . as though something was interfering with the magical heat Rook threw off, or the man's precious *"ch'i"* was being blocked by something at least as powerful as *it* was.

Still, Morrow didn't know enough about the Manifold to guess at what that might be; if the thing was broke, he not only couldn't fix it, but he wouldn't even be able to tell. Which made this the best possible time for one more try, since at least he knew Chess and the Rev were both as distracted as they'd ever be.

Straining to move quietly as possible, Morrow levered himself up off the bed, feeling his ginger way across the floor, ears peeled for creaks. His shotgun he left leaned up against the door-frame; if anyone did happen to spot him in the already-chancy-sounding act of "looking for a pot to piss in," he surely didn't want to have to explain why he was doing it *armed*. As he shut the door carefully behind him, he could feel how the Manifold's indigestible lump, hidden deep in his waistcoat pocket, seemed to *wake up* at the mere possibility of getting back near Rook, clicking fast against his ribs like an extra, malfunctioning, heart.

He mounted the stairs, hoping the romantic din Chess and his boss were making would cover any mistake on his part. 'Cause they were deep in congress yet, for maybe the third time in a row, a faint blur of motion glimpsed reflected in the cheval-glass which hung overtop the bed they currently shared. And the closer Morrow drew, the harder he found to tear his gaze from that very same rude spectacle.

His first thought was, *So, Chess is red all over.* Second: *Do people really do that?* But there they were, right in front of him, so the first conclusion he'd have to venture was yes, "people" did—and when they did, they enjoyed it. Quite a whole damn lot.

Rook was half-sat up with Chess balanced in his lap, jouncing him up and down, their mutual effort almost bruising in its enthusiasm. Chess kept pace admirably, sweat-shiny, hands busy in his own lap the whole way. And when it seemed Rook finally couldn't take the strain anymore, he tumbled them both over and twisted around so he came out on top, which appeared to suit Chess even better.

"Oh *yes*," Chess half-snarled, half-squealed. "Pin me down, by God—go on, work your damn way with me—"

"My Christ, but you're an undomesticated son-of-a-bitch," Rook huffed.

"Sorry."

"No, you ain't."

"True 'nough. But I'd sure try to be, if I thought that's what you—uh!—*wanted.* . . ."

"Shut up, Chess," the Rev just growled—came in hard and fast, possibly hitting that unnamed *thing* a few times in quick succession, 'til Chess clutched and arched beneath him. The results sprayed up between them, splashing sheets and skin; Rook groaned, firing deep. Chess sprawled back, panting and glistening like he'd been shot through the heart.

Saying, a mere breathless moment later: "Let's do it again."

"Let's not, for now," Reverend Rook replied, "seein' how it ain't yet light out, and I'm thirty-eight years old." He closed his eyes on Chess's disappointment, stretching. "Go get yourself cleaned up, give me a minute or two to collect my faculties. After that, I'll fuck you 'til you can't ride, if you're still so all-fired up for it."

"That wouldn't be too smart."

"You make me a lot of things, Chess. I've never noticed smart to be one of 'em."

Me either, Morrow thought, as he watched Chess sigh, rise and pad away—the splash of a wash-basin, light flap of soaked cloth. Then saw the Rev jump a bit to feel that same cloth applied deep between his own thighs, with surprising skill and delicacy—gentle, almost reverent.

"That good?"

"Yeah, darlin'. That's damn good."

The intimacy of it all made Morrow blush, in turn, at the unlikely thought of ever taking his own turn under those pretty killer's hands. To distract himself, he eked a little further toward the door, sidelong, as Chess climbed back in to fit himself up against Rook's side.

"Yeah, well . . . you ever want to receive that sort of service again, Reverend, then you better get it through your head how San Francisco ain't *no* fit locale to do business, in future. Christ on a cross, I'll burn that damn place down myself, if I have to. An earthquake needs to swallow that shit-pit whole."

Rook laughed. "Poor angry little boy," he mocked, in fair approximation of Songbird's voice. "Aw, don't sulk, Chess—it don't become you. Let's talk 'bout something else."

"Like?"

The Rev's rumble dipped. "Hear your Ma's in 'hospital'; means she's on her way out, from what I gather. That a prospect bothers you much?"

Chess drew a long breath, and seemed to give the idea some fair amount of thought, before answering: "I don't rightly know. Best she go quick and quiet, I guess, considering."

"I could make sure of it. If you wanted me to."

That same cat-sneeze laugh. "'Course you could. Hell, I know *that*. . . ."

The Rev propped himself up on one arm, staring down at

him—cupped Chess's face in one huge hand, and said, with perfect seriousness: "But do you *want* me to, Chess? End her now, easy and pleasant, or let her go rough and slow, for all she done to you—all she *let* be done, 'fore you finally broke yourself free of that place? You just have to say the word, is all. Just say . . ."

You ain't no God, Ash Rook, Morrow thought, abruptly gone weirdly cold around the pounding heart, *not vengeful or benign . . . no matter how Chess Pargeter might set you up as a false idol; and do you worship on bended knee. 'Cause often as you might read that Bible of yours, it ain't exactly like you wrote the damn thing, is it?*

Morrow watched Chess stare back up at Rook, his green eyes gone somehow wistful. Saw the pistoleer's gold-shaded brows knit a moment, snarled in what almost seemed like genuine distress— then smooth out once more, signifying he'd come to a conclusion.

"Okay," was all he said.

Which was more than enough for Rook to work his magic with, or so his cold but gentle smile appeared to indicate. That, and the Bible on his nightstand.

"So be it," he told Chess, like it'd been Chess's idea, all along. And flipped the book's black-bound cover open.

Back in the lime-walled depths of Selina Ah Toy's, that pit of whoresome darkness, English Oona Pargeter stirred in fitful, over-drugged sleep—turned in on herself, shivering, and assumed the same position her son once had while he still floated inside her womb. Listening as Asher Rook's voice seeped through one wall and out the next, near fifty miles away, the close-packed silver Scripture typeface spiralling quick and deep as smoke inside her, some unanswered prayer made flesh.

Genesis, 15:16 to 15:18—

BUT IN THE FOURTH GENERATION THEY SHALL COME HITHER AGAIN: FOR THE INIQUITY OF THE AMORITES IS NOT YET FULL.

AND IT CAME TO PASS, THAT, WHEN THE SUN WENT DOWN, AND IT WAS DARK, BEHOLD A SMOKING FURNACE, AND A BURNING LAMP THAT PASSED BETWEEN THOSE PIECES . . .

Above her, the gals sharing her hospital rack began to twist and moan, sniffing the air like dogs who dreamt of meat. Because that familiarly enticing smell rising up toward them was nothing less than opium boiling off, issuing from Oona's pores as she cooked from the inside; eyes gone soft and gleeful under their heavy lids, glazing over, unaware even in death how much they resembled Chess's own.

Oh God, Morrow thought, that primal fear suddenly set back down bone-deep in every part of him. *How can I know this? Any of this?*

The Manifold burned and chattered against his sweaty palm while he leaned against the wall, bracing himself against the wave of nausea that swarmed from fever-froze head on down, roiling stomach on up. As though the Manifold had seized onto Rook's spell and conducted it *into* Morrow as a counter-natural lightning-charge, imprinting it onto him the way a daguerreotype's acid-etching made a plate. This ill beat in his blood, telegraph messages hammering silently, from one world to the next . . .

"So," Chess said, finally. "That'd be it, then."

"It would."

Chess nodded, and kept his eyes firmly locked ceiling-wards— not on anything in particular about it, so much, as just trained in that general direction, but it obviously helped him talk. "She'd've killed *me* if she could, a hundred times over; tried hard enough, 'fore I even came out of her. That was back when she still thought she could be some big man's kept girl, 'stead of a penny whore. But there I was anyhow at the end of it, redheaded and screaming, like Judas himself."

"Uh huh," Rook said, stroking lightly down Chess's red-and-gold-sheened belly, like he was gentling a horse.

"Kept me on her tit 'til I was three, 'cause she heard it'd keep her from gettin' knocked up again. Had me goin' through tricks' clothes by the time I was four. Oh, she'd pet me some when she was drunk enough, or gay enough on smoke, but otherwise—I wasn't even there. 'Til the day she figured out what I was, and what that could maybe get her, she let only the right sort of people know."

"Well, she's dead now, if that helps," the Rev said, still stroking.

But Chess reared back up, gaze abruptly furious as ever once more, and fixed Rook with it, so sharply Morrow could almost feel the big man's surprise. "Just don't *you* never leave me behind," he told him. "'Cause if you do . . . I won't be held responsible, for what comes after."

A weirdly ineffectual threat, one might think. Yet even from where he stood, Morrow could see the effect it had on the Rev.

"How could you even say such a thing? Look what-all I just done for you, Chess Pargeter." He hugged Chess to him in a way designed to make anyone's head swim, and growled, into his open mouth, "I'll damn my own soul for you, gladly, and that's a fact. Now—what'll *you* do for *me*?"

"Anything. Like you already know, you king-size bastard. . . ."

"Oh, yes. I surely do."

Now's another good time, Morrow thought, and hauled the Manifold out into the light—to find it still spinning with a horrid rattlesnake chatter, teeth shook in a box. To find *himself* simultaneously caught up and shook alongside: transfixed, unable even to cry out in agony. As though one long javelin made from glass barbs and Jericho thorns had entered through his mouth and bisected his tongue, plunging straight through his trunk and out between his shaking feet to pin him to the floor where he stood.

Don't anybody ever think to creep up on 'em when they're . . . engaged? he heard his own voice ask Hosteen.

Saw the old man shake his head, cheerfully: *One fool did, sure— planned on turnin' 'em in to the Pinks, and gettin' hold of that reward they was offering. But he run 'cross some mojo the Rev laid down all around the room him and Chess were stayin' in, instead, and it stuck that fucker right to the spot. We found him still there come mornin', after a whole damn night of hurtin' too bad to scream. Probably didn't even feel it, when Chess blew his brains out.*

That'll be me, Morrow thought, helpless. *Oh Jesus, what an idiot. I am so damn screwed.*

He met his own eyes in the cheval-glass, searching for something to take his mind off his current situation . . . 'cause when it stung this awful, any port in a storm would do, in terms of distraction. And there Rook lay on his belly, down between Chess's wide-spread legs, working away throat-first to the very red-gold roots of Chess's cock, so his spine jack-knifed with pleasure, while reaching up to cover Chess's face with one huge hand, at the same time—spreading it over him, like a blindfold. Morrow could see him kissing Rook's palm as Rook did it, licking at those long fingers and moaning gutturally, his eyes squeezed tight-closed.

Sighing out: "Oh Ash, oh God, oh *Jesus*—oh, God fucking *damn*, that's *good*—"

Rook gave a rumble of laughter, right into Chess's privatest spots. "Sssh," he managed, mouth too full for anything else.

Bad enough, but not the worst. Because even as Morrow trembled in the grip of Rook's spell, rigid with pain, he understood—with sick certainty—that his own drained-white face had *always* been visible in the mirror, from some angles. For example, the one Rook was looking up at Morrow from, *right damn now*—

Yes, it's true, a voice—*not* his own—said, inside of Morrow's head. *I see you, Ed; know why you're here*, and *what for. But, that said . . . watch this.*

Well, it wasn't like Morrow could do anything else.

Dimly, Morrow began to perceive a weird light forming around Chess's ecstatic, prisoned face, some ectoplasmic substance flowing off of him in a fluid, rotten caul up along Rook's arm, illuminating veins and muscles as it sunk beneath the skin, vampiristically absorbed.

What the Hell? Morrow wondered. Thinking, at the same time: *Bot-flies*, and knowing how "Hell" might be the exact correct word, given.

I said to watch *this, Edward*, Rook's mind-voice repeated—as, simultaneously, the Rook right in front of Morrow cupped his other hand beneath Chess's ass, two fingers teasing him open again so they could drive up high inside, feeling for that magic button.

Chess's flat stomach knotted, heels kicking, and a fresh blush blazed up toward his throat; he gave a hoarse half-yell, flailing, while Rook sucked even harder, draining him dry.

The phosphorescence hooding Chess's head flickered once and went out, a doused lucifer.

Rook grinned at Morrow, licking his lips. Then rose up, naked and dripping as some well-fucked ogre, palming Chess's lids delicately shut as he went, like he was blessing some corpse he'd just defiled. Didn't even bother to put on a pair of pants before he crossed back over to where Morrow stood, wavering in the magic circle's barbed-wire net, and pulled him bodily in through the Bridal Suite's door, kicking it closed behind them.

"So you're a Pink," the Rev said. "So what? That wasn't exactly hard to figure, even without my skills. Most men who'll go out of their way to join up with me got to have somethin' really, truly wrong with 'em, so the fact that you're a good man, let alone good at your job too? Dead giveaway, I'm afraid."

Though mortified by his own weakness, Morrow couldn't quite stop himself from making noise at that—a shameful sort of squeak—as the Rev looked back over at Chess, now fast asleep and snoring. "Oh yeah, that's right—Chess does hate Pinkertons, that's for damn sure. But that's how I knew I could trust you, Ed, if things came down to it—'cause since I could always give Chess good reason to kill you, I figured you'd probably do whatever it took for me not to."

Then: "But pardon me. I'm afraid I clean forgot you were still in . . . difficulty."

Rook made a sign in Morrow's direction, and the pain took flight all at once—such a relief, he all but collapsed into the Rev's plough-horse arms. Instead, he stumbled backward, almost flopping down on the bed with Chess before he realized his mistake.

"Naw, don't want to do that," the Rev pointed out, mildly. "Try over on that chair, instead."

Morrow did, straining not to sprawl every which-way. His joints burned like he'd been wrung out, heart tripping clog-step, bowels full of cholera-water.

"... thank you," he said, at last.

"Not so fast," Rook said, rummaging in the pile of clothes flung together by the bed's side. Then re-emerged, with Chess's knife at the ready.

"Aw look, hey, now—"

"Calm the fuck down, Ed, it ain't what you think. Hold still."

Spent as he was, Morrow sat there dumbfaced while Rook sawed a chunk of his hair away, sheep-shearing-quick, then touched the raw spot lightly, a soothing balm spreading briskly out wherever his fingers lighted. The tuft itself he tucked away in a small leather pouch he kept on his gun-belt.

"All right," he said. "*Now* we're done."

"The shit was *that*?" Morrow demanded, hoarsely.

The Rev shrugged. "Insurance, mainly. Know what a mojo is?" Morrow shook his head. "Well, the dolly-bag I'm gonna make from this hair says you're gonna do what I want, whenever and however I want it—or I'll throw it right in the fire, see what happens when it starts to burn. And you *really* don't want that, believe you me."

"I believe you," Morrow replied, his voice gone almost completely juiceless.

Rook nodded. "Here's the deal, then. I have to go somewhere, try out this mirror of Songbird's. Gotta talk to my Rainbow Lady, and I need to do it alone; she's gonna tell me things I don't want Chess tryin' to talk me out of. I need him kept away."

"All right. But he won't listen to me—not like he does to you."

Another grim grin. "Oh, I don't need him listenin' *that* hard. Just tell him I told you he has to take the rest of the gang to Splitfoot Joe's, lay low, and wait. That's where I'll meet back up with everybody."

"He won't believe—"

Brooking no opposition: "*Convince* him, then."

Rook turned his back, arrogant in his utter lack of wariness. And if Morrow hadn't been so damn drained, that alone might have been enough to *make* him try something anyways, just on principle.

But instead, he simply looked back down at his hands, still

trembling in his lap, and asked: "Okay, well—what were you doin' back there—with Chess? I mean . . . I know what *some* of it was, obviously. But—"

"Show me that 'timepiece' of yours, will you, Ed?"

Reluctantly, Morrow passed the Manifold over, as Rook stood waiting with one hand out. Rook took it, studying it from all directions.

"Very pretty," he said, finally, and passed it back. "Might come in useful, eventually."

"You gonna answer my question, or what?"

The Rev turned once more, finally rummaging for his small-clothes, and tucked himself safely away. "Oh, I think you'll figure it out, soon enough. If you just keep your eyes open."

Next morning, Chess came clattering down while Morrow was checking his ammunition, immaculate from head to toe, like he hadn't spent half the night taking it from behind—his bright hair combed and gleaming extra-sharp with fresh pomade, purple coat brushed out 'til it shone, and in about as foul a mood as Morrow'd ever seen him.

"How long that sumbitch been gone?" he demanded.

"Since 'fore dawn," Morrow said, counting shells. Then, like he'd just thought of it: "Yeah, he said you was to go to Splitfoot Joe's, and then he'd meet you there after."

"After what?"

"Fuck if *I* know, Chess. He don't make such as me privy to his thoughts."

"Well, why the hell wouldn't he tell me that his own damn self?"

"Uh . . . 'cause you was asleep, I guess."

"Oh, that Goddamn man!" Chess grabbed the bottle Morrow already had going, and flopped down in the chair opposite him to take a long drink. "Bible-beltin' son-of-a-*bitch* got business somewheres he thinks he don't need *me* for; thinks he can stick his dick in my ass to keep me quiet, then run the hell off on me."

Morrow squirmed, uncomfortably. "Aw, Chess, c'mon. I don't

need to know—"

"Well shit, Morrow, what was it you thought we was doin' up there? Playin' Goddamn canasta?"

"Hardly. Ain't stupid, you know."

"I *do* know, so don't act it. Oh, that damn man!"

"He's a hex. They ain't like other people."

Chess gave a bitter little laugh, then chased it with an even longer swig. "Oh no, they sure ain't, and neither is he—'cept from the waist down. 'Cause that part of him's pretty much like every other motherfucker I ever met."

Morrow didn't know what-all to say to that, so he just kept quiet. They sat together an interminable minute, locked back into a strange parody of companionability—Chess looking off, eyes narrowed, with Morrow too het up to do much more than keep his own breath steady. 'Til both of them were finally interrupted by a noise—all too familiar to Morrow—which grew ever more insistent.

Eventually Chess snapped out, "Just what the hell *is* that?"

"My . . . timepiece, I think," Morrow said, at last.

"You need to do somethin' about it, then, real damn fast. Thing's 'bout to give me a headache. Jesus *Christ!*"

Reluctantly, Morrow drew out the Manifold, popped its lid— and gaped, as both spinning needles instantly resolved, a set trap snapping: red on red, upper part of the scale, same as Asbury'd always claimed they would. Pointing, for all the Goddamn world . . . straight at Chess.

Morrow heard Rook's velvet rasp pick at his brain's folds: *Thing'll come in handy, eventually—you'll figure out why. Soon enough.*

That's *why I could never get a clear reading,* Morrow thought, helpless to not complete the equation, even when it'd already been made so mocking-clear. *'Cause Chess is always standing there, right beside Rook. And Chess . . . vicious little Chess Goddamn Pargeter, who used to suck cock for bullets, and'll shoot you just for standin' still if he don't like the look on your face while you're doin' it . . . Chess is a hex, too.*

The *start* of one, anyhow, seeing how true "grievous bodily harm" hadn't had its way with him. But more than enough for Rook to siphon a bit of it off whenever he'd been preyed on, and needed to do some preyin' of his own, in return.

All I need to trust about you, *Ed,* Rook's ghost-voice told him, *is that you at least know to do what I tell you. So . . . do you? We good?*

"Yes sir," Morrow muttered, out loud—then rose in one heave and walked away fast, while he could still be fairly sure Chess thought he was talking to *him*.

BOOK TWO: SKULL-FLOWER

California, Arizona, New Mexico—Beginning April 9, 1865
Month Three, Day Seven Reed
Festival: Xochimanaloya, or Presentation of Flowers

Today's Lord of Night (Number Six) is Chalchiuhtlicue, "She of the Jade Serpent-Skirt" or "She whose Night-robe of Jewel-stars Whirls Above." Chalchiuhtlicue was the ruler over the Fourth Sun, the world immediately previous to our own. That world was destroyed by flooding.

The Aztec *trecena* Mazatl ("Deer") is ruled by Tepeyollotl—Heart of the Mountain, the Jaguar of Night, lord of darkened caves. Tepeyollotl is Tezcatlipoaca disguised in a jaguar hide, whose voice is the echo in the wilderness and whose word is the darkness itself.

By the Mayan Long Count calendar, the protector of day Acatl ("Reed") is also Tezcatlipoaca, who provides the days' shadow soul. Acatl is the sceptre of authority which is, paradoxically, hollow.

Today is a day when the arrows of fate fall from the sky like lightning bolts. A good day to seek justice, a bad day to act against others.

CHAPTER SIX

Two Years Earlier

Once, the Rainbow Lady had told Asher Rook, in dreams, a human ball-player was enticed by owls to pit his skills against the lords of death, and made a descent into what was then called Xibalba. He swam the river of blood, yet did not become drunk with it. He reached the crossroads, the Place of All Winds, where he took not the red road, nor the white, nor the yellow, but the black. He entered the bone canoe, piloted by spiders and bats. He sank downwards, through cold water, to the whole world's bottom.

Xibalba, as it was called then. Mictlan, as it became. Mictlan-Xibalba, as it is now, and will be, forever more.

When he arrived, however, he was met only with mockery and betrayal. The Sunken Ball-Court's kings set him impossible tasks, then cheated the rules to make sure he would fail, and sent him to be executed, decreeing that his severed head should be set in a tree by the wayside, as a warning to other travellers.

Promptly, the tree flowered all over, producing a hundred succulent calabash melons that attracted the attention of Blood Maiden, the Blood Gatherer's beautiful daughter. She reached up to pick one, only to discover she held the ball-player's skull instead. The skull spat in her hand, and told her: *Though my face is gone, it will soon return, in the face of my son.* And she found herself pregnant.

Because this is how things begin, always, little king: in darkness, in chaos. In blood.

The world we know, a child conceived in death, a saviour made from bones. The flower from the skull.

This is what I want you to understand, as you already should. You died in my way, after all—a valid sacrifice, whether ordained or not. And ignorance is no excuse.

Think of it, now, she had ordered him, the black rainbow snapping around her like storm-clouds across a nervish, lowering sky. *When the rope tightened around your neck. That moment of flowering, when your skull cracked open, the seed inside you began to bloom. . . .*

Her words in his ears, ringing. Followed closely, as dream gave way to memory, by God Almighty's:

. . . and they four had one likeness: and their appearance . . . was as it were a wheel in the middle of a wheel. . . .

As for their rings, they were so high that they were dreadful. And their rings were full of eyes . . . and when the living creatures were lifted up from the earth, the wheels were lifted up. . . .

The verses were so familiar through long study—and equally long hours spent quoting them out loud, to prove one point or another— that he could no longer recall if he'd screamed them, moaned them, whispered them, in his hour of ultimate need. Only that they'd been on his lips when the rope finally snapped taut and the trap beneath him opened, plummeting him feet-first into night—

The drop wasn't long enough: inexperience on his killers' part, or maybe a sublimated urge to punish him further. So he slammed up hard against gravity itself, every inch of him instantly bruised, drowning in air. His heart stuttered, his own body's weight a millstone, spirits violently pressing upwards 'til they forced their way to his head. Where he saw a glaring light which seemed to vomit from his eyes with a flash so bright, so *deep*, it scarred the entire universe—

—and then, exactly as sudden, he'd lost all sense of pain. A glacial calm descended.

Rook looked up, saw planks and dust, the gallows' underside. A square of blue sky through the trap. His former brothers on the field of war looking down, some faces frowning, some blank. Some even, in a bitter way, amused.

Bastards, he thought. *You know not the day, nor the hour. . . .*

Then over further, to where Chess Pargeter still fought with his captors, next in line for the noose. Which somehow rubbed Rook rawer than the sight of his own death approaching—the idea of Chess pissing himself at the end of some rope, all that energy gone, without a final chance to redeem itself.

Chess, who was burning up with fever ever since he took that ball in the shoulder—probably turning gangrenous, not that that'd matter, in a minute or so. Chess, who snarled, and spat: "You motherless bitches! The Rev's worth a hundred of you, you slugs! He's worth ten thousand!"

"Goddamn queerboy camp-follower sure got a mouth on him, dirty as one of Hooker's gals," the soldier with Chess's right arm pinned back told his partner, who had Chess in a headlock. To which the other soldier just grinned, and tightened up his grip.

"He didn't even do it, either!" Chess screamed, twisting and kicking. "*I* was the one killed the Lieut, you morons! Good Christ, no wonder we lost the Goddamn war!"

Turned out there really was a bone in the throat, just as Chess had always claimed. Rook felt it go, and felt all the darkness inside him snap shut again, percolating, a stoppered steam-kettle. Heard his thunderous preach-voice shrink and grind, as everything went red.

And thought—prayed, though he no longer quite knew who to— *Oh, give me strength. Strength enough. Give me . . .*

But nothing answered save himself, or maybe the wind. And then, at last—

—her.

Save him, little king. As you know you can.

Kicking, turning. No voice now to scream.

And the blue sky, shrinking. The clouds, rushing in. Fat grey drops of rain falling, to slick his fevered face. As she spoke on, that impossible voice, only underlined by the thin, gnawing whine issuing from his own throat, endless and terrible and raw.

Saying, gently: **Save him, save them. Punish your enemies, reward your friends. Do as your God does. Become as your God is.**

Save yourself.

No breath left to speak with, not even to beg. Yet the words flew up anyhow, spilled from his mouth and swam in front of his eyes like sparks from cinder, molten-silver hot, and burned whatever they touched, until the whole world howled out in unison—

THEREFORE SAITH THE LORD GOD. BEHOLD, I, EVEN I, AM AGAINST THEE, AND WILL EXECUTE JUDGMENTS IN THE MIDST OF THEE IN THE SIGHT OF THE NATIONS.

AND I WILL DO IN THEE THAT WHICH I HAVE NOT DONE, AND WHEREUNTO I WILL NOT DO ANY MORE THE LIKE, BECAUSE OF ALL THINE ABOMINATIONS.

THEREFORE THE FATHERS SHALL EAT THE SONS IN THE MIDST OF THEE, AND THE SONS SHALL EAT THEIR FATHERS. AND I WILL EXECUTE JUDGMENTS IN THEE, AND THE WHOLE REMNANT OF THEE WILL I SCATTER INTO ALL THE WINDS.

The funnel, that moving finger, swept in on a slather of whipped dust, a froth of stones and swirling brick-bats. To either side, the sky remained clear—grey-blue with a messy touch of pink to it, frostbit flesh turned inside-out. But inside the twister was only rain and darkness, so cold it tore skin wherever it touched. And yet the wavering path of its eye swept over Rook's fellow prisoners entirely, while pivoting to tweeze the rest of Captain Coulson's company out of Heaven's reach. They scatter-shot in all directions, spread so far that the only sign that the camp had ever been inhabited was a single torn grey sleeve full of shattered bone and red muck poking up through the debris, its buttons still a-glint, intact.

Then the rope finally snapped, and Rook dropped to his hands and knees as the scaffold broke apart around him, watching through blood-dimmed eyes as the pieces flew up and away, into the whirling sky. Blood and spirits forced themselves into their former channels, a flash flood through a needle's eye, nerves pin-pricking so intolerably he spent a breathless moment cursing himself, paralyzed with pain—wishing himself hanged again, a thousand times over, for the unforgivable crime of cutting himself down too soon.

The twister spent itself in an outward rush and dissipated, slung clouds and rain across the horizon, leaving only wet dusk behind.

All around, nothing still stood except the things *he'd* allowed to survive. The rest was laid waste, sure as Gideon left Jezreel. Like Chorazin and Bethsaida, whose smoke goes up forever.

Which made him . . . one of *them*.

Exodus, 22:18. Fit only to be weeded out, burned and buried, their graves sown with salt. Just like that poor boy with the one goat's eye, trembling in fear with his sidelong pupil opening squarish, as he stared headfirst down into the flames.

Back in Missouri, in Rook's first parish, "good" people had tied a sick child to a ladder and cooked him over a flaming stack of hay, for the grand crime of being born a witch's get—while Rook had done nothing but watch and pray, because they were his, and he theirs. Which was why he'd left under cover of night soon after, fled as far as the stage-ticket bought with his flock's money would take him, then got roaring drunk enough to join up. Fleeing from what he'd seen, and done, by not arguing other parts of the Good Book, for fear of suffering similar excision and execution. *Matthew*, 7:3 to 7:5, for example. 1 *Corinthians* 13.

Born different, that boy—and through nobody's fault, not even his own. Same as Chess, always flaunting his slick little occasion-for-sin self around, with what he refused to pretend not to be writ large on every inch of him. Or Rook, too, with his doubts and deficiencies, the Bible leaping in his breast-pocket every time he heard something he felt he couldn't speak out against for himself, without using Jesus', Moses' or Ezekiel's words as back-up. Rook, washed white as snow with God's word, then damned black as night with the discovery of his own power.

"Whah . . . happen . . . ?" Rook rasped at last, shaking his head to flick wet hair from his eyes, down on his hands and knees in the wet black muck. Then looked up to meet Hosteen's horrified eyes—for between them lay Chess, his crumpled face pallid, wounded arm crooked behind him in a very unnatural fashion.

You could save him, that voice in Rook's head suggested.

At almost the same time, like he'd somehow heard her, Hosteen grabbed Chess up and dropped him almost in Rook's lap, intent plain, if impossible: *Here, you fix this!* Rook looked down, one palm cupping each side of Chess's slack skull—and God damn, but his hands were either far bigger than he'd ever thought, or Chess's face was far smaller. Or maybe it was just that he'd so rarely seen Chess Pargeter this still or silent, before.

I don't know what comes next, he thought—and knew he *must* be lying, because . . . well, shit, take a look around.

Rook shut his own eyes, squinched them hard and cleared his mind, swiping an elbow 'cross a spectral blackboard. Then leaned down, kissed Chess for the first time, on his own hook—deep and probing and tender—and whispered a Bible verse into his mouth, as he did it: "*Psalms*, 51-7 to 51-10. Purge me with hyssop and I shall be clean. Wash me and I shall be whiter than snow. Let me hear joy and gladness. Let the bones you have crushed rejoice . . . ."

The rain fell, a booming drum. Rook sat surrounded by his own words, glittering letters turning in the air, a slow cascade of evil stars.

While the colour came seeping back into Chess's face by degrees, Rook moved his broken shoulder back into place, as gently as he could, and felt the bone pop together once more, whole as though never split. Felt the sinews blossom beneath his fingers.

Eventually, Chess opened his eyes anew, pupils tiny, as though contracted against a bright, wild light. He grinned back up at Rook, happily, teeth sharp as some snapping dog's in the storm's half-darkness.

"It *was* you," he said. "I knew it. Oh, I *knew* it. Goddamn! You killed them all, them sons of bitches, didn't you? But *good*."

A sliver of ice pierced Rook's chest, then, encircling his heart so quick he wondered whether it would ever melt away again. Or whether he ever wanted it to.

"Yes," he agreed, unable to deny it. "Yes. I did."

CHAPTER SEVEN

Nine months before the twister. That was when Rook had first heard the Lieutenant say—

"And this'd be Private Pargeter."

A grey day, that first camp even greyer, all their uniforms dirt-stiffened and indistinguishable. But Chess still stood out, hair and beard bright as a brand. He'd been butchering livestock yanked as tribute from a local farm, and his hands were bloody to the wrists.

Looked up mildly from cleaning his knife, to answer— "Lieutenant. Reverend."

"Pargeter's our very best man for close work, 'specially during nighttime incursions," the Lieutenant told Rook, an odd note in his voice blurring what seemed like praise with something else. "He rode after us when we passed through California, rarin' to volunteer. Fair scout, excellent killer."

Eyes like sweet poison, too, Rook thought, and blushed.

Chess caught him at it, and grinned. "You're thinkin' how I'm small-made, to merit that kind of reputation," he said.

"Oh, no, I . . . hadn't thought about it, really," Rook replied, reddening further. "I didn't mean to . . ."

"Accuracy hardly counts as insult," the Lieut said.

Chess nodded. "Oh, I ain't insulted. But then again, that's the glory of the army, ain't it? For folks like me."

"Meaning?"

Those green eyes narrowed, as one hand sought out his most convenient gun-butt, caressing it the way most men might a pretty girl's dropped handkerchief. "*Meaning*, Lincoln may aim to free the slaves, Rev, but it was Colonel Colt really made all men equal—my size, your size. And everything else, to boot."

That night, Rook gave a homily from *Jeremiah*, 7-26 to 7-34, as martial a passage as any he could think of. The Lieut sat there nodding, his transplanted Bushwhacker hair groomed like Custer's, while the other men mainly got about their business, not ignoring Rook, exactly, but not exactly cheering him on, either.

All but Chess, that was, who watched him with a quirked gold brow and an odd little smile playing about his mouth—those deft hands of his cleaning and reassembling his guns by rote, without any need of close attention, while his gaze travelled the length and breadth of Rook's long body . . . complimentary and predatory, at once.

The next two weeks brought three separate engagements, fast and hard as anything Megiddo's plains might eventually deal out. Almost every day, the Lieut received fresh intelligence by bird, inevitably coded—and since only he had the cipher, they were forced to take his word for each subsequent target. Their primary duty, he often told them, was self-sacrifice. To rush any given breach, paving the way for more potentially damage-inflicting crews like Captain Coulson's, who moved far more slowly, on account of the cannon they still dragged along behind them.

The cost was dear, both in men and morale. Rook buried three in shallow graves that fourteen-day span alone, and one sewn in a sack, far too crushed for any sort of memorializing. The Lieut told Rook to cheer them up, or at least on, and he did what little he could—thumbed the Bible for inspiration, looking out on a narrowing clutch of faces whose eyes slid from his, increasingly emptied of anything but fear and doubt.

And there in the background, Chess, always whistling at his work, untouched by any of the above. Chess, for whom war seemed a form of recreation—something he revelled in excelling at, with no hint of regret that such victory always came at someone else's loss.

They were fighting hard over some sand-bar, one day, with mortar-fire felling trees in the distance. Rook found himself trapped by the coattail behind an overturned stagecoach that Kees Hosteen had set flame to, in order to create a brake and cover their retreat. As the older man tugged at his sleeve, a pair of Northerners managed to spill overtop and came down thrashing, blind, out to do whatever damage they could. One spitted himself on Hosteen's buck knife, knocking him to the ground, where they scrabbled around in gruesome play—Hosteen carving out loops of gut, as the man tried hopelessly to stuff them back in.

Meanwhile, Rook wrestled with Bluebelly Number Two, the both of them too entangled to do each other much damage, yet unable to quite break free. As Rook laid the man up against the stage's undercarriage, he saw him glance up, and followed the eye-line to see a new gun barrel pointing downwards, right at his head, wielded by yet another suicidal Abolitionist.

"Die, you secesh fucker!" this one spat out, then slumped face-forward, his eye a red mess of ruin. Rook's dance partner eked a garbled name, but fell silent when Rook cross-punched him in the throat, freeing himself up to look back—and catch Chess Pargeter maybe forty paces behind, gun still a-smoke, smiling at the damage he'd done.

"Best keep alert, Rev," he called. "Odds are, there's more where that one come from." A thin, hungry grin: "Sure *hope* so, anyhow."

And turned away once more, with a rakish tip of his blood-spattered hat-brim and both guns up, already discharging fatally in two entirely new directions.

At his feet, Rook could hear Hosteen breathing ragged, almost like he was sobbing. "C'mon," he said, scooping him up, kicking the disembowelled soldier aside, "your boy's right, and so were you. Better fall on back."

Hosteen nodded, shoulders heaving. "Oh, Jesus," he said. "Why'n the hell did I ever come here—why'd I even join up? To kill *them*, or get *myself* killed?"

"Little of both, I expect," Rook replied, dragging him along.

Much later, when the fire and drunken joshing had both died down, Rook heard whispers, and opened his eyes to see Chess deep in negotiations with the old Hollander. They muttered together a while about the varying utility of knives and such, from what little Rook could make out, 'til Chess finally said: "Okay, fine, that's settled—now take them down, and be done with it. I ain't got all night."

Hosteen cleared his throat, and looked down. "That . . . ain't what I want, this time."

"Oh no?" Chess's voice hardened. "Well, best be careful, old man—sure hope you ain't forgot so soon about Chilicothe and his pals, for your own sake."

"Chew coal and shit-fire, Chess, don't take on—we all of us remember Chilicothe, the Lieut included. God *damn*, but you can be a mean little bastard!"

"Got *that* right." A pause. "What *do* you want, then?"

Hosteen bent to Chess's ear, voice dipping too low to follow. Chess listened, then snorted—half a hiss, half a snicker. "You're an ill old buzzard," was all he said.

Hosteen's face fell, comically swift. "Just 'cause *some* of us got human feelin's. . . ."

"Yeah, yeah. Cry me a river, grampaw. I want that knife first thing tomorrow, handed over in front of God and everybody, the Lieut included—like we bet for it at whist, all legal."

"It's yours."

Chess huffed, lips twisting. "Oh, men really are fools, like my Ma always says," he announced, to no one in particular. "Dogs, too. Do any damn thing they take a mind to, long as they think they'll get what leaves them feelin' happiest, after."

Here he pushed Hosteen backwards, without warning, 'til he had no option but to let Chess *sit down on him*—one hard shove, far too quick for Rook to quite take it in. And straddling Hosteen's lap just a shade primly, almost side-saddle, he admitted, with a further smirk, "And as for me . . . I'm certainly no exception."

Then he twined his fingers in Hosteen's shaggy grey hair, letting the man draw him close enough to kiss and met him open-mouthed, without restraint, tongue-first.

Oh, Rook thought, numbly. *So* that *was it.*

He didn't stay to watch much longer, merely turned away, as quietly as possible. It seemed more than a bit uncouth—almost impolite—to treat their revelry as a sideshow. Particularly since it struck him as not so much *revelry* as maybe . . . necessity, on Hosteen's part. Maybe even kindness, on Chess's.

It did startle Rook a bit, however—as a Christian—to realize that he hadn't previously thought Chess might have any real kindness in him.

Later, in his journal—just notes scribbled down in an *aide-memoire*, leather binding sewn 'round a tablet of block-paper—Rook wrote:

His fine looks and indubitable skill aside, Pvt. Pargeter lives most securely in a state of nature, which is, as we know, also a state of sin. Yet does the prospect of damnation really hold any terror for one so utterly unrepentant? He seems almost soulless, and happy to be so, like an animal; guiltless in his actions, and thus (perhaps) blameless of their consequences.

Much later still that same night, Rook woke suddenly, so stiff in the trousers it made him sore—thinking on Private Chess Pargeter's green eyes, his freckled shoulders, that smooth dip where his belly met his belt. And thought: *Ah, so my sin—my liking for the Other, in any form—has come upon me, even here. . . .*

He lay there quite some time with both eyes open, searching the sky for stars, and finding none.

"Oh, Pargeter's a harlot in trousers, to be sure," the Lieutenant said, dismissively. "The very worst sort of Sodom-apple. Rumour has it his dam's some 'Frisco lily-belle—and she certainly must know her business, too, for that son of hers has managed to sully more than half my men, distributing his favours without qualm. That a thing like that should seem so outright *made* for war, meanwhile. . . ."

He trailed off, shaking his head, before concluding: "Well, it's a conundrum I simply cannot fathom. But there's no sentiment in the creature, thank God, sparing us all the usual fluttery Grecian nonsense inherent in such attachments. So while we have need, we'll gladly pay the fee to use him . . . as is traditional, no doubt, in his family."

"No doubt," Rook said.

"Private," he spoke up, around noon-time, as Chess passed him by, toting a pair of looted shotguns, "might I speak with you a moment, perhaps, tonight?"

"Well, that depends. What on?"

"A matter of Scripture?"

Chess turned back at this. "Really," he said, and narrowed his eyes, then broke out into a wide smile.

"Well hell, Rev, why not? You may've grilled the Lieut on all my bad habits, but you never peached on old Hosteen—that's worth somethin'."

"So . . . you knew I was there, the whole time."

"You're a damn man-mountain, Reverend Rook. Whenever you walk, it's like a tree movin' 'round, no matter how quiet you may dream you're bein'."

"You don't seem too upset I asked the Lieut about you, though."

Chess stretched the smile into an outright laugh. "Oh, you've probably already figured out just how much of a damn I give what people think of *me*."

Predictably, however, there was no single part of that evening's personal sermon which went anywhere near the way Rook'd hoped it might, when he'd first issued Chess that fateful invitation. He came prepared, with all the relevant sections of his Bible pre-marked; preached mightily on Lot's visitors and the destruction of Gomorrah, on it being better to marry than burn, on trouser-wearing women and other such unnatural oddities. But Chess just sat there while he gesticulated—interested but unimpressed, with the same tiny smile playing about his lips that'd annoyed Rook since the day they'd met.

Rook paused, finally, and sighed. Then asked: "Is *any* of this getting through to you?"

Chess shrugged. "Not much. But feel free to keep on talkin', anyhow, 'cause I sure do admire how your lips move."

"What do you mean by—"

"Oh, Rev. Just what in the hell d'you *think* I mean?"

For a second, Rook almost convinced himself he didn't understand.

"I'm . . . flattered, Private Pargeter," he said, at length. "But even leaving the strictures of my calling aside, I'm really *not* that way inclined."

Chess shrugged again. "Oh no, course not. Man of God, and all— what was I thinkin'."

"I very much hope you're not mocking my faith, Private, because . . ." Rook trailed away. "Have you even *read* the Bible?"

"Enough to know it ain't got too much to do with me, or them that's like me. I'm a bad man, Rev—that ain't debatable. So I don't aim to debate it."

"*Leviticus*, then—how 'bout that. Ever heard of it?"

"That's the part of your Book says all queers should die, ain't it?"

"Essentially. Doesn't that bother you?"

"Seein' how I'm funny as Union script?" Chess snorted. "Look, Reverend. Anyone wants to string me up just for who I'm drawn to dance with, I invite them to go ahead and try. If I can see them comin' and they still manage it, then it was probably my time. 'Til then . . ." Another thin grin. "Well, you've seen me at my exercise. What's *your* opinion?"

"I think you're the best pistoleer I've ever come across, though I'm sure the Lieutenant'd say your soldiering leaves a bit to be desired. What I don't understand is why pursuing this line of . . . abomination means so much to you, 'specially at the risk of your immortal soul."

"Where I'm from, we're all born bound for the Hot Country. I ain't lookin' for no chariot to Glory, not even if you're offerin'."

"What about those others you're pullin' down, though? Can't you see you're draggin' any man you let take advantage of you straight into the fire along with you? Hosteen, for example. You *seem* to care—"

"I don't 'care' 'bout shit but me, myself and I, thank you kindly. As for the rest—I never put a damn gun to anybody's head to get them near me, and they sure weren't complainin', either." He turned back. "Oh, and speakin' of which: *God's* the one made me this way in the first place, Reverend. Maybe you should just take it up with him."

Rook sighed. "Hell doesn't have to be a foregone conclusion, Chess, that's my point. Salvation—that's God's promise, open to all who want it, no matter what they may have done beforehand. There's no sin so black it can't be washed away, if you only ask for it to be."

"Yeah? Thanks for that, anyhow."

"The option to be redeemed? That's God's, not mine."

"Naw, that you can keep—probably wouldn't take, anyhow. But thanks for callin' me by my given name, Reverend. Maybe you'll even let me return the favour, one of these days."

Flirting with him, still. The man was damn well incorrigible. Yet Rook found himself smiling back, all the same.

"Maybe," he heard himself say.

Things continued bad, shading fast toward worst. There were rumours everywhere—that recent action at Five Forks and Sayler's Creek had left the Confederacy crippled, that General Lee himself was on the verge of surrendering to that drunken farm-burner Ulysses S. Grant. That Lincoln had been either assassinated or elected king by popular acclaim.

That afternoon, the Lieut received one last message, read it, then broke the pigeon's neck, before crumpling the offensive cipher up and throwing it into the fire.

"It's official," he told Rook, a tic in his brow fluttering wildly. "The rats have infiltrated. All further communiqués must from now on be reckoned a mere tissue of Abolitionist lies."

"Yes sir," Rook said. "I'm very sure that you're right."

That night, he dozed off, then came to, to find himself restrained by a hard little set of limbs, as somebody hissed: "Sssh!" in his ear.

"Damn, Rev," Chess Pargeter said, shifting to pin him closer. "You want to get us both swung?"

Rook breathed out through his nose, slow, while simultaneously struggling to resist the urge to see exactly how far he could kick the smaller man, if he only gave it a good enough try.

"Get off of me, Private," he replied, finally.

The same snicker again. "That an order? Hell, Rev, you're three times my size, at least. What is it you're 'fraid of, exactly?"

"Of . . . hurting *you*, mainly."

"Uh huh? Well, that's nice, but don't worry yourself overmuch— it's been tried."

"You want to talk? Then let me up."

Chess shrugged. "Okay," he said, and moved back.

"So," Rook said, once he'd regained his dignity. "What was it you had in mind, Mister Pargeter? Besides the obvious."

"Oh, I wasn't even thinkin' of *that*," Chess lied. "All seriousness, though . . . you do know the Lieut's gone stark starin' crazy, right? How he's probably right now dreamin' on the best way t'get himself killed for the honour of the South, and take us all along with him?"

"I don't see what either of us can do about it, saving desertion . . . or worse."

"Like blowin' his brains out in his sleep? Yeah, I've thought 'bout cuttin' his throat, too—or maybe smotherin' him, since that wouldn't leave much of a trace. But I ain't got anything on me exactly suitable to the purpose, more's the pity."

"Private!"

"Aw, Rev, I was 'Chess' just a week back. Can't we try for that again?"

"Not if you're counselling murder, we can't—'cause I won't stand for that sort of cold-blooded mortal sin, not even as a joke."

Chess sighed. "Desertion it is, then." Continuing, as Rook's heart rose in his throat: "Listen—I've done most've these boys a service here and there, as you know, but they won't listen to *me*, 'specially not shit-scared of the Lieut the way they are. Not like they would to *you*."

"You want me to—incite a mutiny."

"I *want* you to tell them it's all right to leave while they still can, given the circumstances. You got that Book on your side; tell them God told you special. For all we're privy, the damn War's been over a sight longer than it took that bird to reach camp, and throwin' yourself in the cannon's mouth after Lee's already kissed Grant's ass ain't honourable, just stupid."

"So?" Rook shot back. "Best go on, then, if you're goin'—which I'm sure you aim to, considerin' that's how you feel. Go on, and good riddance."

Yet here he saw Chess was biting his lip, a flush beginning to pink *his* face, for once.

"You really *do* care," Rook realized, aloud. "Chess Pargeter actually *cares* what might happen to somebody, other than him—on occasion, anyhow."

"You need to maybe just shut up with that Do-As-You-Would-Be-Done-By charity-school crap, Rev," Chess said, between his teeth. "I really do mean it. 'Fore—"

"'Fore *what*, little man?"

Chess looked up at him. "Don't you dare laugh at me, Goddamnit, Asher Rook," he said, low—then hove in and kissed him, same's he'd kissed Hosteen.

Except this time it was Rook's mouth that pink tongue was hard at work in, all rough and hot and silky. Rook's lap taking Chess's full weight, the delectable print of Chess's ass cupping him through two pairs of pants at once, rendering him instantaneously hard. Before he quite knew what had happened, Rook had both hands dug deep in Chess's fiery curls, just letting Chess keep on kissing him with never a word of protest, 'til they were both left gasping.

"Oh my," Chess said at length, emerging, that devilish smile of his already back full force. "Oh *my*, Reverend. Sure you don't need

some of my more—specialized—help? 'Cause from where *I* sit—"
(and here he ground his hips just a bit for emphasis, half trick-rider,
half gaiety-hall girl) "—it pretty much feels like you could pound
nails with that thing."

"Never said I didn't *want* none of your stock in trade, you
contentious tease," Rook replied, hoarsely. "Just how I at least know
that wanting it—let alone doin' anything to *get* it—is *wrong*."

Chess smirked.

"Wrong, huh? Well, let's try it one more time, to be sure—maybe
I ain't brung out *all* my best tricks, just as yet."

Now it was Rook's turn to grind his teeth, 'til they fairly squeaked.

"I can't," was all he said.

Unconvinced, Chess went to kiss him again, but Rook grabbed
him by both his wrists and bent them behind his back—not in a
nasty way, not calculated to hurt, just to immobilize. Still, Chess
must've felt the emotion that drove it, 'cause he slumped forward,
suddenly boneless, to lay his passion-flushed brow against the
hollow of Rook's equally feverish throat.

"Maybe not," he replied, quietly, right into Rook's clavicle-skin,
like he was trying to reach the Rev's heart by sheer osmosis. "But
you do know there's nothin' good gonna come of lettin' the Lieut
have his way, and that's a damn fact. You *know* it, Ash."

"No. I don't." Adding, as he shifted to deposit Chess safely back
on the ground, with far more gentleness than many might have
thought the situation merited: "And I never yet said you could use
my Christian name, either. Did I?"

Chess turned his head away, and replied: "You did not."

"You're a dangerous man, Chess Pargeter."

Another snort. "Bad, too. Don't say I didn't warn you."

To which Rook simply shut his eyes and commenced to pray, not
quitting 'til he finally heard Chess move away. Then opened them
again, only to find himself once more alone.

The Lieut came out of the bushes, tucking himself away, just as
Hosteen was pouring Rook a tin mug of coffee. He had a wilder

look than usual in his eyes, and Rook perceived that both his pupils seemed blown, as pin-prick as any concussion case's. Hell, he even had his hat on backwards.

"All right, boys!" he announced. "Due time for a last hurrah, don't you think?"

"Sir?" Rook asked.

"I have received fresh intelligence, Reverend, and sent for reinforcements accordingly. We, along with Captain Coulson's troop, are to immediately assault the local township of Farnham Ridge. We must then burn it to the ground and kill all within, so that the pernicious seeds of kiting Abolitionism shall flourish no more unchecked. Hallelujah!"

Hosteen spoke up: "But—that's over the border, ain't it?"

"What matter, if it is?"

"Well . . . sir . . . that's what direction the bird come from, yesterday. So . . . I'm thinkin' it's probably all already been took by Union forces, and . . ."

A bit further back, Rook could spot more soldiers nodding. He didn't glimpse Chess amongst them, for which he was thankful.

Cut and run, he thought. *Practical as the very Fiend himself, is our little Mister Pargeter. Well, good. I should've too, and that's the truth. We all should.*

Too late now, though. As demonstrated.

"Plus, how'd you get new word so fast, anyhow," someone else called out, "considerin' you *killed* that damn pigeon? Let alone call in Coulson, on top—"

The Lieut drew and shot him while he was still speaking, cleaving his jaw like a split log—then waved the gun's barrel slightly to dispel the smoke, and told the rest of the company, "I will brook no opposition, gentlemen. We are come at last to the moment of Apocalypse, where each must make his choice. Stand together, or fall forever. Are you rabble? What say you?"

Rook caught Hosteen's eyes, widening further than their orbits seemed made for, and shook his head just slightly, wondering: *Will Bible-quoting even work here, or is the Lieut far too gone for even God's word to resonate? Think fast, damnit: false revelation, uh—dreams sent by Satan, not by the Almighty—Daniel versus the Babylonians, Joseph in Egypt?*

Before Rook could choose, however, one more shot rang out, cracking the Lieut's head apart like a blood-orange set up for target practice. He gave a little spasmic shiver, then fell without complaint.

Behind him stood Chess, who'd simply walked up in the Lieut's blind spot as he blathered on, clapped gun to skull, and pulled the trigger. He gave the corpse a single sharp kick and reholstered, asking it: "That do, for an answer? *Sir.*"

Rook felt something on his face, and found on closer inspection that it was the Lieut's blood, already a little tacky to the touch. By mere trick of proximity, more had sprayed on him than had ever touched Chess, who looked immaculate by comparison.

"I do wish you hadn't done that," Rook said.

Chess shrugged. "Somebody had to."

Then Hosteen stepped in, suggesting: "Better get goin'. We wanna be elsewheres when they find this fool's body. Which way, Reverend?"

Chess looked to Rook, lifting a brow. Rook swallowed hard, and pointed. "That-a-way, I guess," he said, at random.

Which did seem a good enough route, to be sure—in those few minutes before they met Captain Coulson's boys coming back over the very same ridge, to rendezvous with the Lieut before that fabled final charge.

"Who did this?" Coulson demanded, staring right at Chess, who bared his teeth, shifting both hands to his gun-butts. But there were twenty of them, all armed, to maybe twelve of the Lieut's ragged Irregulars, too ground down by fatigue and shock to offer much response beyond a general gasp. And Rook knew what he had to do.

"I did," he said, at last, stepping forward.

CHAPTER EIGHT

Even long after the twister'd moved on, Rook could remember with exquisite urgency how it'd felt when Chess first knelt down in front of him in its wake and brought him to absolute ruin. How he'd fetched himself so hard he'd seen genuine stars flare like Pit-bound souls in the redness behind his eyes, then hauled Chess up by both shoulders and told him, hoarsely, "I don't want you doin' that with anyone else again, not ever. Hear me, Private?"

"Or what?"

"Or—I'll find them. And I'll kill them."

Chess just grinned, like this threat was the best compliment anybody'd ever given him.

"Suits me," he said, and let Rook lift him further—kissed him with the taste of Rook's own seed sour on his breath, wound his legs around Rook's waist, and gave him his sin again.

The decision to become outlaws proved a surprisingly practical one, in the end. By limiting Chess's choice of partners, Rook found, he'd unwittingly created a situation of scarcity which began to wear on the gang's remaining members, as the camp and its horrors fell steadily behind.

"Find them whores," was Chess's sage advice—but whores meant money, of which they currently had none.

They'd already crossed into Arizona almost by instinct, making for the empty places, and spent a length of time wandering amongst the stones there, like Legion. Occasionally, they saw what they took for Apaches off in the distance, and Rook wondered if any of these could be numbered amongst those myriad spectral intelligences he now felt crowding in on him whenever he closed his eyes—as he had almost since that first morning he woke up sprawled next to Chess, sore with love-wounds, his head already a-ring with other people's voices.

Chess stirred and murmured, sleepily. Rook hugged him a bit closer, and knew himself reborn, in far more ways than the not-so-simple fact of having merely fucked another man could ever explain.

"Hey," he asked Chess, poking him lightly. "You think they heard us?"

"What, Hosteen and the rest?" Chess replied, muffled, into the broad expanse of Rook's chest. "I think dogs for a mile 'round could probably *hear* us, if I was doin' my job right. Why—prospect of bein' known as queer make you antsy, Reverend?"

"Not . . . as such, surprisingly."

"Well, ain't you sweet." With a smirk, Chess sat up, right into a particularly luxuriant stretch—stark naked, and not seeming to give much of a damn who might be watching. Rook saw scars on him, both old and fresh, which hadn't been quite so obvious in the hours before: a pink curlicue tracing one rib, the pale flowery knot of a plugged bullet hole punctuating one shoulder blade.

Chess turned back to catch Rook gaping at the fierce white slash that hooked from right-hand sideburn to just under his jaw—suddenly visible, even beneath the red—and said, airily: "Yeah, that's where my Ma stuck me with her yen hock, same night I told her I was signin' up. Stung like a bitch, the whole time I was growin' out my beard to cover it."

"My God!"

Chess shrugged. "Suited me fine; I'm prettier shaved, which gave her the grand idea she might rig me up as some she-he, sell me that-a-way to fools who crave somethin' extra up under the skirts. But I ain't fit to be no girl, much less a poor jest of one—while I may not be the sorta man most think they are, I'm a *man*, just the same. Made to ride and fight, take what I want or swing tryin', not die on my back or live on my knees. Knew *that* the minute I first touched a gun."

"Colonel Colt, et cetera."

"Exactly so." He cast Rook a sidelong glance. "Think you'd like me better if I *was* a gal, Ash Rook?"

The Rev looked him up and down, and answered, without a hint of equivocation, "I don't really see how I *could*, Chess Pargeter. Seein' how you already move me absolute best of any damn thing I've come across, thus far."

He got to his own feet then, towering over Chess, and smiled at the way his shadow seemed to knit them both together, long before he gathered him fiercely back in. They collided, mouths open, tongues working sweetly.

When he pulled away, at last, he was equally pleased to see how Chess's pale eyes seemed all but dazed with arousal. And then something entirely brand new came into his look, an angry sort of hope.

"I . . . wasn't raised to—care—for no one," Chess told him. "But if I did grow fond of any man, outside the usual transactions, well . . . you might be that one, Rev."

Rook nodded, carefully.

"I think I'd like that," he replied.

"You're damn right, you would," Chess agreed. And gripped Rook by both biceps at once, his fingers leaving bruises, kissing him so hard spit mingled with blood.

They raised the subject of outlawry that night, 'round the campfire, and watched it pass unanimously. "Always did think I'd probably end up robbin' folks, once the War was done," was old Hosteen's only comment.

"It's dangerous work, is what I hear," Rook pointed out.

"Sure," Chess said, "same as anything else. But we'll be right enough, I expect."

"How's that?"

That crooked, dazzling smile. "'Cause we got *you*."

True, Rook thought, as far as that went. The only problem being he didn't actually know, himself, just how far that was . . . not with any true degree of accuracy. Particularly not under pressure.

Magic had its price, was what Rook had always heard, and that price was mighty hard. On the one hand, whatever he preached did come true, indisputably—and since everything he preached came straight from the Book itself, the direct and truthful word of God, he believed he might be forgiven for having assumed it would be *good* work he did with it overall, rather than the reverse. Yet everything he preached went bad, in the end—swiftly, and often inventively.

In the Painted Desert, for example—waiting for information on which trains might be best worth robbing, with what food they'd brought along running out fast—he turned to the tale of Elijah, who was fed by ravens. Soon, a plague of black-feathered birds huge as his namesake descended, dashing themselves to death against the canyon walls. The gang, starved enough to overcome their disgust at this haphazard delivery system, handily ate them roasted, only vaguely plucked and splinter-crunchy with hollow broken bones.

So Rook turned to Moses and his manna instead, bringing unleavened bread falling from the air (straight into dirt, soft and sticky, not exactly nourishing). It was blander, but kept better.

"Maybe you should seek for other hexes," Chess suggested. "Chat them up, get them to tell you what they do, or don't, in similar situations. Couldn't hurt."

"Couldn't it?"

(Minds always touching his, feeling him out, harrying him: *Go here, do this, do that. Stay clear.* Most he couldn't put a name to, 'sides from a Chink gal called Songbird to the west whose thoughts coiled and spat in a venomous centipede nest. Rook hoped to never come near enough for her to see what he looked like, let alone lay hands on him directly.)

"Hell, I don't know—I ain't no hex. But I got *my* best advice from other gunslingers, same's I got my worst. Take it all, pick through it at your leisure . . . and *practise*."

That morning, before dawn, Rook woke first and left Chess wrapped in both their coats, careful not to wake him. Then sat down in the dust bare-assed, stretched out a hand, frowned at the largish, greyish rock set opposite, and ordered it—"Come here, to me. C'mon, now."

Nothing happened.

"*Here*, I conjure thee. I . . . *command*."

Still nothing. Rook felt ridiculous. Even his voice seemed flat, dry, without a shred of its now-normal rope-rough timbre. As though . . .

You are only talking for yourself, one of the voices told him—right in his ear, yet resonating considerably deeper: inside the hills around, the earth itself. Inside *him*.

A woman's voice, but not his Rainbow Lady, who hadn't spoken directly to him since his escape, for all he glimpsed her face in dreams. "And who *should* I talk for?" he asked her, out loud—more to see what would happen, than because he actually wanted an answer.

One man's voice is only that, she replied—*one small part of the whole. We must be larger than that, in order to keep our balance.*

Sounds like an Indian, he thought. And felt, rather than saw, her smile curve, with the same quality to it his grandmother's used to have, back when Rook was still Little Asher.

She is not to be trusted, your Lady of the Snares and Traps, she told him. *But then, you know that, in your heart. And as for you, grandson . . . perhaps you must continue to speak in your blackrobe Lord's voice, until you have the time—the inclination—to finally come find me, and learn better.*

Then she was gone, leaving Rook alone in the desert, looking at a rock. His mind slid, automatically, to whatever Biblical claptrap might serve best, given the situation:

THE LION'S WHELPS HAVE NOT TRODDEN IT, NOR THE FIERCE LION PASSED BY IT.

HE PUTTETH FORTH HIS HAND UPON THE ROCK. HE OVERTURNETH THE MOUNTAINS BY THE ROOTS.

HE CUTTETH OUT RIVERS AMONG THE ROCKS. AND HIS EYE SEETH EVERY PRECIOUS THING. . . .

Job, 28:8-10.

And the rock cried out, he thought, feeling the words come up through him, scar 'round his throat left raw again, in their wake. The rock, at the very same time—a seed-pod stuffed with granite dust, cleft with an invisible axe—split wide open.

Oh, sinner-man. Where you gonna run to?

Behind, Chess slept on, hearing nothing of any of it, 'til Rook woke him with a kiss.

A week after, they rode down to No Silver Here and waited for the train to come smoking down its track, laid skeletal atop the new-blasted ground. Intelligence suggested it would be guarded by Pinks, equipped with at least one Gatling and a brace of pepperboxes; this Hosteen confirmed, via telescope. So they separated into two columns, Chess drawing fire on the right, while Hosteen made sure Rook could pull close alongside and catch the engineer's eye, gesturing at him to haul on the brakes—thus giving a man they all called Big Al time to jump in through the back and clap a pistol to the man's temple, making sure he would.

As the train started to slow, the accompanying gear-jerk threw one Gatling-operator into the other, spinning the gun's muzzle in such a way that it laid two of Chess's posse down. Rook dug in his spurs, surged maybe thirty yards ahead, reined in and slid off, stepping directly into the dreadnought's path. As it bore down on him—the uppermost Pinkerton already back on his feet, grasping for the Gatling's crank—he opened his mouth and preached, from *Corinthians*:

Though I speak with the tongues of men and of angels, and have not charity, I am become as sounding brass, or a tinkling cymbal.

It was one of the sweetest verses known to man, quoted at every wedding he'd officiated. But when his lips shaped the words, something else *came out* through his mouth along with them—a lashing ghost-tongue spear of silver-gilt which rammed full-speed through the boiler without jumping the train off its tracks, just pinning it there like a massive iron bug, releasing its entire compliment of steam in a hissing cloud.

And *that* was the problem, in the end. It was a bit too dense for Rook to completely calculate what he was doing. So though he'd meant for whatever effect he produced to stop short, or just slap the Pink silly, it split the man's skull and neck alike, spraying everything around it with gouting red.

The gang met it with a half cheer, half yelp—alternately disgusted, and pretty damn impressed. 'Course, that all changed once Rook turned to yell fresh orders at Chess, not realizing the spell-spear was still trailing along with him. Before he knew what was happening, it'd sheared off Joe Skopp's left arm at the shoulder, and Joe fell, screaming.

Rook clapped both hands over his face immediately, unmindful of what damage he might do to himself (none, it turned out). Hosteen tried—and failed, miserably—to tourniquet Joe's stump.

Meanwhile, Chess sprang up into the breach, yelling: "C'mon, you bastards! There's lootin' to be done!"

The others streamed after him, automatically—all but Petrus Kavalier, Joe's best buddy, who stopped in mid-stride and looked back at Rook, eyes gone blank with shock. "You're the damn *Devil*, Rev," he said, wonderingly, like he'd just worked it out. Raising his gun, cocking it back—

Maybe I am, Rook thought, while THE LORD IS MY SHIELD AND THE POINT OF MY SALVATION knocked *hard* against his teeth from the wrong side 'round—so easy to simply let it out, and watch what happened next. But it was a moot point, because that was when Chess shot Kavalier through the heart over his own shoulder, without even turning—an impossible feat, for impossible times. Almost . . . magical.

You ever notice how Chess hardly ever reloads? Hosteen had asked Rook. *Or how he can fire in two separate directions at once, and still shoot straight? He fans the trigger, just for fun, and he actually* hits his target. *Ain't no motherfucker on this earth can do that.*

I don't know that much about firearms, Rook had found himself replying, which wasn't exactly untrue. Yet—

Chess's hair lifted slightly in the wind, a tight blood-halo, and Rook could tell from the way he stood that he was grinning.

The train was taken five minutes on, with most of the remaining Pinks kneeling in surrender, down on their knees so fast they must've bruised the caps. But by the time Rook had coughed enough times to be sure his killing words were well-dispersed, Chess had already head-shot three of them, and was taking aim at the fourth. Rook slapped his gun up, annoyed.

"The fuck you do that for?" Chess snarled.

"We need one of them left upright, at least. To tell what happened."

"So they'll be warned, next time? Where's the fun in—"

"Not all of us're quite so fond of murder as yourself, Chess. Or maybe you hadn't noticed." He indicated Hosteen, staring sick-white down at what was now Joe's corpse.

Chess just sniffed, disapprovingly. "Well, you don't have to coddle them, do ya?"

"Like it fine enough when I indulge *you*, don't you, darlin'?"

Back to the grin. "But that's different. Ain't it?"

Rook couldn't deny how something in him came ticking up to meet that wicked smile, even right now—like sticking his dick inside Chess had turned the key in a door that the whole world would've probably been better off keeping shut. And it would have been shamefully easy to believe it was Chess's fault, but Rook knew the truth: he was changing *himself* to fit *Chess.* To be the mountainous man Chess dreamt on, fit to finally crush his rebel heart into submission—a man truly worth kneeling before.

"Think Kavalier was right?" Rook asked him, that night. "*Am I the Devil?*"

Chess snorted. "I've been called that, for a hell of a lot less. What I think's that if there even is a Devil in the first place, we're *all* him—and as for God, him and me ain't ever met, 'less you count him puttin' me in your path."

He nipped hard at Rook's lip, the pain of it both increasing familiar and increasingly pleasant. But the Reverend wasn't quite done.

"With Joe, though, or the Gatling-operator—I never meant to do that. Jesus Lord God of Hosts, that was awful."

"Yeah, well, Joe knew what he was gettin' into. We all of us do, or should. As for the rest, meanwhile—hell, they was just Pinkertons, and I surely do hate all them fuckers. Stole my first gun from a Pink, I ever tell you that?"

"Not as I recall, no."

"Yeah, I lifted his roll while he was busy feelin' up my Ma, so he hauled me out into the back alley, beat me somethin' bad. Didn't know I had a razor in my boot, though—more fool him. 'Cause that's the first damn thing that junked-out lunatic ever taught me, the only one I ever found worth remembering: sell yourself high, and dearly."

They drifted off at last, soaked and sticky—replete, even in the face of Rook's own deepest doubts. And Rook dreamt that old Indian lady again, sitting so close near a fire he could almost glimpse her face, nested in shadow beneath the overhanging folds of her shawl.

You should come and see me, grandson, she told him, without moving her lips. *And soon. Before your Lady finishes the web she weaves, and sets her snares for you.*

And how would I know where to go?

She shrugged. *Easy enough, to let your feet move where your instincts point you. There is a mountain which we Diné call the yellow Abalone-shell. She is a good place to go, if one wishes to make one's vision quest . . . which you have not, as yet.*

Thought that was just for—your people.

The People, *we call ourselves, as all peoples do. But we are both of a very different tribe than those we were born into, you and I—and your Lady, too, once upon a time.*

Meaning you're a hex. Like I'm a hex.

We say it differently, of course, but . . . yes. And in my tradition, grandson, we do not wait for misfortune to push us headlong into power—nor shun and spurn the powerful, as your blackrobes counsel. What would be the point of that? But for the gods, we alone see the future, and make it come to pass. There must *be balance. If we break it, it breaks us. Should we not help each other to keep it, then, if we can?*

Rook hesitated. On the one hand, it did sound logical—hell, the idea of seeking out mentorship'd sounded logical even coming from Chess, and that was really saying something. Yet he also recalled hearing rumours to the contrary, especially as regards to magicians.

I . . . don't know, he said, at last. *What's happening to me?*

This I have told you already, grandson. Until you do come to me—or to someone—you will always be a danger . . . to yourself, as well as to others.

Got no reason to trust you—

No more than you have to trust anyone, even yourself. Yet there is *someone else involved, after all—one you would do no hurt, if it might be avoided. Am I wrong, grandson?*

She wasn't.

Well, then. Come, if you decide—when you decide. I will be waiting. And do it soon.

But they both knew he wouldn't.

CHAPTER NINE

Another few months flew by. In Solomonville, up near the New Mexico border, the gang's object was the land office, where a fat payroll lay prepared for banking. Chess brought the company fast and hard—both guns already cross-drawn, guiding the horse with his knees—while Rook strode in front, hovering a yard above the ground and leaving no prints behind with a cloud of dust boiling out beneath him, like he was wearing Ten League Boots.

A dreadful flame lifted from his head, leaking out of every orifice, and whenever Rook blinked or spoke it guttered and danced, lighting up their way through the sandstorm-lively murk. By its baleful glare, Rook saw "good" people—parishioners much the same as his own, probably, once upon a time—scurrying from him and his in mortal panic, fast as their little legs would take them.

Fuck them all, he caught himself thinking, a grim smile curling his lips.

"No unnecessary casualties!" he roared down at Chess, who already had the land office manager in his sights; Chess brought his horse up short, reholstering, so he had both hands free to aid with his dismount. The manager just stood there trembling, too scared to even squirm.

"What-all do you men *want*?" he finally got out, through chattering teeth.

Chess returned Rook's grin. "Fair question—ain't it, Rev? What *do* we want, exactly?"

"Money'll do, for now," Rook replied. "That suit you?" he asked the manager. Adding, as if just struck by the thought: "Might end up bein' blamed for all this, though, I suppose. For not puttin' up an adequate defence of yours bosses' funds."

The manager coughed—a sound one-quarter laugh, three-quarters retch. "Ask me how much I care, long's they don't turn up here lookin' like *you*."

Rook smiled, yet again. Couldn't help it, really. It was all just so *funny*. He could see his own teeth reflected in the man's eyes as he did it, horrid little flickering red stars.

"Good man," he said.

A<small>ND THE</small> LORD <small>SAID UNTO</small> M<small>OSES</small>, S<small>TRETCH OUT THINE HAND TOWARD HEAVEN, THAT THERE MAY BE DARKNESS OVER THE LAND OF</small> E<small>GYPT, EVEN DARKNESS WHICH MAY BE FELT.</small>

A<small>ND</small> M<small>OSES STRETCHED FORTH HIS HAND TOWARD HEAVEN.</small> A<small>ND THERE WAS A THICK DARKNESS IN ALL THE LAND OF</small> E<small>GYPT THREE DAYS:</small>

As it turned out, the book of *Exodus* proved wonderfully fruitful quotation-fodder for far more than just Solomonville's aftermath. Might've made it to an even ten, eventually, had Rook not decided that three plagues in a row were probably good enough.

News of their exploits ran ahead of them as they rode on into the dark, a dry and bitter wind. By the time they reached Total Wreck, a waiter-gal sidled by to show off their very first official "wanted" post-bill, slapping it down along with their drinks. Chess was—to put it mildly—unsatisfied with the crudely inept artistic renderings attached thereto, especially the one apparently meant to look like him.

Rook let out a raspy bark of laughter. "You're peacock-vain, is all, Chess Pargeter! Don't cherish the idea of anybody thinkin' you're a skinny little snip with wall-eyes and a beard like the Wanderin' Jew, the way this seems to prove."

Chess studied the thing one more time, then spat on it and crumpled it up.

"I ain't *so* vain," he maintained. "But I damn well know I look a sight better'n *that*."

Rook nodded. "And every soul in here knows it, including me." Voice dropping further: "Care for a demonstration?"

That night, Rook turned Chess's many lessons in mutual pleasure back on him, and drifted off with the ragged sound of Chess's breath coming and going straight into his open mouth, head like an echoing sea-cave. But when he opened his eyes once more, he found that the bed had somehow dropped away into darkness, and that the body in his arms was even smaller, far softer—a girl's. Lady Rainbow, dead far longer than Rook's former faith had existed, with her black hair spread out beneath them like a pair of wings carved from funeral jet.

This close up, Rook could see how each of her delicate ears was flared in fans of beaten gold, the rope of thorns heavy between her little breasts. Her gaze seemed both fixed and dead, sheened to a terrible lustre and unnaturally long-lashed at its lower orbits—'til those lashes fluttered, and he realized she had painted false eyes upon the lids of her real ones, for what reason he couldn't possibly stand to guess at.

If Rook really was twice Chess's size, then he must be four times hers, yet she held him child-helpless with just a feather-light touch on either wrist. And beneath him, the jungle vipers which made up her skirt crept apart, rustling, to disclose the sticky lips of her hairless sex, then twined fast once more around them both, pulling them together: cock into cunt, feel of it already slightly unfamiliar—a flesh trap, snapping shut.

Desire laid lit powder up Rook's spine, a spasm of pure betrayal. But when he tried to pull away, she simply laughed, and reached up to stroke the scar around his neck, twisting its painful residual energy 'round her fingers somehow, like haltering an invisible lariat.

This is mine, little king, she murmured, ***along with the rest —can you really have forgotten that, so soon? To give and to take . . . your death, your luck, your very life.***

I don't owe you a damn thing, you devil! Rook roared, soundlessly.

With a shrug, she drew what Rook all at once knew was a stingray spine from her hair, licked quickly along its crabbed grey length (splitting her tongue crossways, to show meat within), and then—without even a wince—ran it through her bottom lip, piercing herself so deeply her chin slicked red, and the spine rang sharp against her teeth. She dragged him in so hard his neck cried out and smeared their lips together, laughing as he bit at her instinctively, the dew of her dripping straight onto his taste-buds, with all the kick of wine steeped in garbage.

There, she told him. ***You have tasted me, in honour of our marriage-pledge. Now—return the favour.***

He shook his head. Then roared again as she slid the spine through his earlobe, freeing another hot spurt.

I have told you already, she said, as he clapped his palm to the wound, ***when I pulled you from the tree: you are Becoming, magician. You are the seed, the flower from the skull. So you will bend to me eventually, or go back down into darkness—under black waters, deep and deeper. Never to return.***

Rook snarled back at her: *You talk like I got no choice. Like I'm not still a child of God, free-willed from my mother's womb, same as I was born from Original Sin into tribulation.*

True, the Rainbow Lady agreed, ***I do not know much of this Fatherly One-God of yours, except as He may twin with my brother Feathered Serpent, the God-Who-Dies. Yet you do not have a choice—nor do you want one, in truth. You enjoy what you are Becoming far too much, for that.***

A lie, he could only hope. Because yes, he could feel it curl inside him now, waiting to explode outward with wild new growth, to spray its poison pollen over everything he touched.

Then the world tipped up, and Rook realized they were flipping over. Lithe muscles gripped him, inside and out, the juice of their exertions drenching them both further in sweet foulness. The skirt-snakes rose up hissing in every direction from their sudden shift in momentum, tongues like little flickering flames, and the Lady's dragonfly cloak rippled outwards, wrapping them as tightly as his sword fit her sheath.

Enraged, Rook fought her harder than he would have most men, but got nothing but laughter once more, for all his pains.

Enough talk, she said, at last. *Bow your head to the yoke, little husband. The king must give blood, always—give blood to get blood. Or the land dies.*

Rook scoffed. *This ain't* your *land, woman—mine either, come to think. This is the desert. It's been dead a long damn time.*

But it could be . . . something else.

And the red vine exploded, everywhere. Blooming and burning, flowers opening like firecrackers with a sound of fifty thousand dead hands clapping, a tumult-choir of stone bells and thighbone-carven flutes. The Rainbow Lady closed her true eyes once more at the sound of it.

Do what I tell you, little king, she warned him. *Or I will take it back—all of it. And not from you only, either. . . .*

Chess, he thought, helpless. *She means Chess.*

You . . . leave him the hell . . . alone, he managed, as the rest of it began to fade—knowing full well how useless it was to threaten her with anything.

She licked at his wounded ear, utterly predatory, weirdly loving. Whispering: *And what will you do, to make me?*

. . . whatever I have to, Rook thought, drowning in his own blood.

Instants (or years) later Rook woke, sun in his eyes and head buzzing, to find Chess watching him—already dressed, his eyes uncustomarily impossible to read.

"You're bleedin'," Chess said.

Startled, Rook slapped at his ear, and saw his palm come away thinly red-smeared, though the lobe itself seemed still intact.

"So I am," he agreed, at last.

"Must've been some dream you were havin'."

"I . . . don't rightly recall."

"Uh huh. So who is she, exactly?" Adding, as Rook looked at him: "Yeah, *I* heard you, yellin' her damn name in your sleep!"

Rook shook his head, as though to clear it, then looked over at

Chess again, and this time found him fairly bristling mad. Like he wanted to get into it right then and there, only held back by not knowing where to find this phantom woman whose face he so yearned to scratch.

"Are you *jealous*?" Rook asked.

Chess's eyes flared. "Why? You think I *can't* be?"

"Well, uh . . . no, 'course. Just seemed . . . somewhat unlikely."

"Think I don't care, right? Or shouldn't, maybe. 'Cause whores' boys grow up whores themselves, no matter what . . ." Here he broke off. In a savagely choked voice: "Well, fuck *you*, Reverend. Even a whore—"

Rook wasn't about to argue the point. Especially not since he felt the definite flicker of something rising up in him to meet Chess's rage—similarly hot, if far blacker. Half of him could taste Chess's true pain buried beneath the bluster, more fully than Chess himself was equipped to, and ached to salve it even while the other half savoured it, drank deep. Licked its lips, and wanted more.

Ah, but the blood of men is sweet, little king.

"Chess . . ." Rook began again, ". . . who is it you think I've had instance to get close with, in all this time, 'sides from you?" Chess didn't reply. "I was *dreamin'*, sweetheart."

"Don't you 'sweetheart' me, Ash Rook."

"What's all this about? C'mon, now. You can't possibly think yourself cheated on, not 'cause I had a damn nightmare—that woman's not anybody I *want* to spend time with. And I don't think you're a whore."

"Then *don't treat me like you do.*"

A whole new note quivering at the very lowermost range of Chess's voice now, plaintive with injured pride and barely masked need. It hit Rook in a dark stream pumped straight through the heart, and he rode its current without effort, fascinated by the ill strength of his own arousal.

Rook laid one huge hand on the younger man's jaw-hinge, and turned his face 'til their eyes locked fast. "Look at me," he ordered. "C'mere—sit a while. Be with me."

Chess shook his head. "I got things to see to—"

"What'd I *say*, Private? *Come here.*"

Rook wove the geas instinctively, fingers flexed like a mountebank's, shuffling Fate's card-rack. The gesture kicked up a fresh ripple of energy that drew Chess close enough so the Reverend could collar him by the shirt-neck and kiss him hard, suck down breath and soul-juice together, in a dizzying, drunken exchange which left Chess looking drained.

"God *damn*—" was just about all Chess could say, once he had most of his breath back. "You work a hex on me, right then?" he demanded.

"Was that what it felt like?"

"What it *felt*, was . . ." Chess stopped a moment. ". . . like I didn't like it, was how. You hear? Do any damn thing similar to me again, and I'll—"

Rook laughed out loud, needlessly cruel. Could've said, *You'll do what, little man?*—just to add insult to injury—but in all fairness, he didn't see the point.

So he crushed Chess's mouth back to his, instead, before Chess could even think to protest, flipped him prone and squirming with one hand shoved quick down the front of his fly, and worked him 'til Chess's eyes rolled back. Lowered him onto the bed and rumpled him all over, not letting go 'til he was good and done with him.

There, Rook thought. *That's an end on it, for now.*

In Calvary Cross, to cover their escape, Rook turned to *Exodus* once more, and sowed a rain of fire. It worked the trick, all right—then kept on falling for three more full days and nights, pinning them down into a humid, smoky and woefully over-extended billet with the staff and patrons of Ollemeyer's Saloon. Knowing that fear of Chess's guns and his own witchery were the only things keeping the company safe from night-slit throats, Rook put the two of them on rotating watch—six hours up, six hours asleep, with one ready at all times to spill blood, should any of their terrified co-residents make a move.

As early as the first changeover, Chess growled under his breath, as Rook got dressed: "Ten minutes, Ash. I could clear this place for good in ten. *You* could do it even faster, I bet."

Rook pulled on his boots. "Might, at that."

"Then why *don't* you?"

"'Cause I've no clear idea when that—" Rook nodded through a window at the dull red streaks lashing down outside "—will be lettin' up, and no great wish to share the roof with a score of corpses on the rot. Or to send one of our own out to die, trying to toss them out. 'Sides, you know well enough my work ain't the equal of yours for precision . . . not yet."

Chess snorted at that, and let him go with only a kiss, laying down to get what sleep he could. But as the hours wore on into days, Rook could see that unwillingly banked fire burning ever hotter in Chess's eyes, an inner mirror of the fire-rain falling relentlessly outside.

Yet it still startled him when Hosteen caught him alone in the saloon's rapidly emptying pantry, and told him what he hadn't been awake to see: Chess, whetting Hosteen's former buck-knife to a sharp edge right in front of Ollemeyer's wife and children. Forcing the house pianist to play the same tune over and over again, at gunpoint. And checking, every few minutes—sure as clockwork—up the stairs to Rook's room, as if his gaze alone could make the Rev wake faster.

"I thought you'd want to know," said Hosteen. "That you already *would* know."

"What is it you're sayin', Kees?"

"Look, he loves you. I know *that*. I just thought . . ."

"What?"

". . . nothin'."

But it wasn't fear that silenced Hosteen, not alone. It was resignation. Doubt.

You wonder, sometimes, thought Rook, *if I love him the same way he does me. And sometimes—so do I.*

Thankfully, the rain of fire ran out before Ollemeyer's pantry did, and never set the roof on fire. Even more thankfully, it ran out on Rook's watch, not Chess's. So it fell to Rook to get the rest of the gang up and moving, then haul Chess into the street—had him up on his horse, still groggy with sleep, and halfway out of the town long 'fore he was sensible enough to think about killing.

Nevertheless, it did worry him somewhat—not just that he was continuing to dictate gang policy around Chess's offhanded murderousness, but that Chess's bloodthirstiness seemed to be on the increase, generally. Like he never had recovered from Rook working a hex on him, that one time.

I always thought he was changing me, Rook thought, *from the very beginning. But what if I'm changing* him, *just like I set out to? Only—not for the better.*

They rode on to the Two Sisters, where Chess—still off-colour, still uncertain why—started in on a bottle of absinthe, while the rest of the gang made various sorts of hay. Rook sat in the corner and watched, nursing a whiskey shot of his own, while Chess cleaned his guns and hummed to himself tunelessly.

"So here's the latest," Hosteen told Rook, sitting down next to him, and brandished a fresh-printed newsbill in front of Rook's face, as he did so. "Turns out, we got us an honest-to-God posse bein' formed against us." As Rook took another sip, not even deigning to look. "Could read 'bout it yourself, right here, you cared to."

"Why don't you go ahead and summarize, instead? Seein' I know you're literate."

For a second there, Rook almost thought Hosteen was going to snap back at him, in reply—*Saved your life a few too many times, back when we was still at War, t'play your damn secretary, Reverend!* But the glance Rook turned his way seemed to freeze the older man in his tracks, making him clear his throat instead and commence, stiff but steady:

"*Various recent train and payroll robberies executed at No Silver Here, Solomonville and Calvary Cross are all to be laid at the feet of one Asher E. Rook, late of the Confederate Army, a convicted murderer and so-called* 'hexslinger.' The so-called 'Reverend' Rook . . ."

"I think we both know who I am, by this point, Kees."

Over Hosteen's shoulder, Rook could just glimpse Chess casting drink-narrowed eyes at three newish gang-conscripts playing a clueless game of whist to his left, all haplessly unaware of how close they were to risking injury for the grand crime of obstructing his door-ward sight-line. Even from here, Rook could almost *hear* the way Chess had begun to tick, an ill-wound watch with just a hint of lit fuse in the background. That sulphurous *hiss*.

I could stop this, he thought, whatever "this" turned out to be. *But . . . why should I?*

Hosteen ran a blackened finger down the newsbill's centre column, and continued: "Uh . . . *the posse against Rook's gang will be led by Sheriff Mesach Love, who retired from the Union Army upon announcement of Armistice. Once a gentleman of leisure, he has since invested in a small cattle ranch nearby the township of Bewelcome, New Mexico. The fees paid by Union Pacific for Rook's capture will go to raise a permanent church for this district, where Love himself is well-known as a Nazarene preacher of avid devotion. . . .*"

Rook ground out a short laugh. "Don't want the competition, might be," he suggested.

Hosteen half-shrugged, half-nodded. "'*Having heard ample testimony that this man-witch Rook quotes Scripture while practicing his vile sorcery,*' Love states, '*I take it as a holy charge to see him caught and punished for propagating such blasphemy. For how can any Christian stand to see God's Word perverted, especially by one who—if rumour holds true—is guilty not only of using Satan's power for gain, but of all the sins which saw Gomorrah blasted, along with her even-more-infamous sister city?*'"

Taking a quick shot of whiskey to distract himself, Rook found his eyes automatically drawn back to Chess, only to find him already looking his way—tracking one of the Sisters' resident whores, as she sashayed in Rook and Hosteen's direction. Toying with the ribbon which anchored a faded sateen flower just above her overspilling cleavage, the woman slung a leg up over Hosteen's startled lap, fixing Rook with a sleepy smile.

"Buy a gal a drink, Reverend?" she drawled.

"I'd've thought the house already stood you a few per shift, to be frank," Rook returned. "Ain't that what the surcharge is for?"

She made a practiced moue. "Oh, now; we both got our parts t'play in this affair, don't we? Go along to get along, that's what they say...."

Always assuming you're my kind of destination, in the first place, Rook thought. But—

"Move by, woman," Chess snapped, stepping up behind her in one quick stride, at the same time. "He ain't for you."

The whore barely turned a hair. "Oh no?" she asked, one brow arching. "Well, I know *you* for damn sure ain't interested in my wares, little pussy ... but I'll bet the Rev here can prob'ly speak for himself, one way or t'other. What'cha say, darlin'?"

Rook gave her a sad smile, and shook his head. Before he could finish shooing her away, however, Chess had already broken his empty bottle across the whore's head, knocking her to the ground in a shower of dirty glass.

Then leaned down and snarled, right in her ear: "'Cept he don't *have* to, 'cause *I* just did. So how's your hearin' *now*, bitch? Better? Or worse?"

The fiddle and squeezebox wheezing away at each other in the far corner fell silent, and some drunk cried out a name—Sadie, Rook thought it was. Another barfly lunged Chess's way, only to end up froze in place with a barrel to his jaw, while Chess used his other gun to cover the rest of the patrons; probably couldn't really shoot all of them, or at least not all at once. But he certainly looked game to try.

Hosteen threw Rook a begging glance: *C'mon, Rev!* While Rook just sat there, stony, a fresh-poured shot already in hand.

"Look, mister," the barfly told Chess, his voice shaky. "I ... don't know what sorta beef you'n her got with each other, but take a gander. She needs help."

"Why bother? She'll be dead in a year, either way—pox, or gut-rot. She fuck you for free the once, so now you think she's sweet on you? Or . . ." As Chess's thumb caressed the firing pin, his voice dropped into a purr. ". . . is it that *you*'re sweet on *her*?"

Sadie's prospective saviour blushed. "None of your affair!"

"Sure ain't. Then again, slow as she moves, I guess she's probably pretty easy for any dumbass to throw a leg across. . . ." Confidingly: "It's the *syphilis* does that, most times, so best make sure and check your pecker, once you get somewheres a bit more private—"

"Oh, you son-of-a-bitching little redhead faggot motherfucker!"

Rook sighed, and rose, before Chess could finish the fool off. "Stand down, Private Pargeter," he rumbled.

"What do you care?"

"I don't, except that my word not be taken lightly. So stand *down*."

"Make me."

"Think I can't?"

"Oh, I know damn well you *can*! You think that makes me apt to trust you anymore? Who knows *what*-all else you mighta made me do, when I wasn't lookin'?"

"*Nothing*. Not one single friggin' *thing, ever* . . . that you didn't already *want* to."

They were outright yelling at each other, now, right in front of the appalled eyes of everyone, Chess's kill-to-be very much included. And though Rook wasn't exactly sure how things had gotten quite this far out of hand in quite so short a time, he did know they weren't going any further.

"*Put up*," he growled, slapping Chess's piece away from the barfly's face so the man fell to his knees like his hamstrings'd been slashed, then scrabbled crabwise 'til his back hit the nearest wall and stuck there. Pissed beyond measure, Chess swung his other gun 'round, only to have Rook grab *that*, too.

"Let Goddamn go, Goddamnit!"

"Chess—" Rook said, warningly. Then: "C'mon, darlin'—you know you're outmatched, so don't be an idiot, for Christ's sake. Least . . . not where folks can see you."

Provoked beyond endurance, Chess dropped both guns outright and lunged straight for Rook like a rat-killing dog, all ten fingers hooked into claws. Without planning it out at all, Rook flung Chess's weapons down and caught him by the neck, lifting him neatly off the ground.

"That how your *Momma* taught you to fight, boy?" he demanded, voice almost too low to recognize himself.

Chess tore a laugh out through his rapidly bruising throat. "Yuh, wuh—works pretty well, don't it? 'Sides which . . . my *Ma* could've wiped the floor with any one'a these fuh . . . fuckers, and she don't even pack a gun."

Rook hauled him closer. "Don't make me do something we'll both regret, Chess."

"I'd like . . . tuh . . . see *that*. . . ."

A darkness seemed to fall between them, ecliptic. Barely noticing how fast the Sisters had already cleared out, Rook let Chess fall momentarily free—doubled up and hacking—before pinning his arms from behind and hauling him upstairs parcel-style, virtually tucked under one tree-limb arm. With that same *charge* flashing back and forth between them, energizing and exhausting, all the while: each touch a dry powder-burn, a branding iron's kiss.

And here was where he truly knew it, for the first time—how with every touch, he was sucking *something* out of Chess. Gulping it down, the way a gut-shot man will drink 'til he bleeds out and dies, regardless of the gaping hole where his belly should be. The darkness rising in him spurred a similar darkness in Chess, rendering him ten times as dangerous as usual to everything around him (himself very much included). And though Chess fought *it* tooth and nail, exhausting himself, he also fought to cleave *to* Rook just as hard, if not harder.

Rook had been the true trap. And now Chess was caught, fast as any fly in amber.

Reaching the second floor, Rook kicked in the first door he saw, popping it clear off its hinges. Then threw Chess down on the bed, face down, and let the unnatural take its course.

After, he felt bad—as bad as he'd felt so all-fire good, just a hot, gasping moment previous. The hurt and injustice of it crashed over him in a wave, sticking him chest-first to Chess's spine, and he buried his face in the nape of the smaller man's trembling neck, hugging him fit to bruise. Chess stiffened for a moment, mouthed at Rook's wrist like he wanted to bite, then curled back into him, with a little sighing sob.

"I ain't just *yours*, you know."

"I do."

"You're *mine*, you witch-rode ox."

"I am, Chess, yes. I—surely, surely am."

The things I'd do, to keep you safe, little man, Rook thought, tongue gone abruptly cold and sour in his own mouth. *What I'd do . . . you can't imagine.*

Thankfully.

CHAPTER TEN

"You got to take the fight to him," Chess said. "Don't wait for this bastard Love to come lookin'—they don't know what they're dealing with, which puts them to a disadvantage. And even if you don't know what *you're* dealin' with either, half the time, you still got good tricks to pull out, long as you can control the field of battle."

"So you think I should count coup on Love in Bewelcome itself, right where God and everybody can see." Rook looked at Chess, genuinely curious. "That what *you* would've done? Back in the War?"

Chess snorted. "Hell, no—I'd've snuck in under his lines, waited 'til he was asleep, then cut his damn throat. But I'm guessin' you probably want to make more of a splash than *that*—send a message. Am I right?"

"Maybe."

So it was decided—and five days after that night in the Two Sisters, Rook and Chess sat looking down on Bewelcome on horseback, from the same sharply sloping outcrop over which sunrise reached that threadbare-pleasant little settlement, most mornings. Had any Bewelcomeites chanced to glance their way, however, they would have seen nothing but what was rapidly becoming one of Rook's favourite illusions, a heat-haze which repelled the eye without inciting even the briefest comment, and bent the reflecting sky like water.

Located several miles past the very outermost edge of the Bisti Badlands, Sheriff Mesach Love's stronghold was the sort of place Rook's gang would normally ride through at top speed, not looking 'round while they did, then never think of again. Its folks were almost universally the sort who'd probably call themselves "poor but honest"—more poor *than* honest, by Rook's reckoning—and hadn't even put up much in the way of a Main Street, thus far. But maybe they were just waiting 'til Love got his church built.

"This place really is the asshole of the world," Chess observed, idly.

"You truly do *despise* simple people, don't you, Chess?" Rook asked. "Why is that, I wonder?"

Chess shrugged. "Just don't think too much on them, that's all."

"And I'm sure they'd be happy to keep it that way, too, they knew you like I do."

But all that would change, and soon enough, if things went according to the plan they'd roughed out back a mile or so, squatted in the shadow of a startling green cliff, surrounded by a wild moonscape of sandstone and shale.

"They'll beat on you, I reckon, once they catch you," Rook said, to which Chess gave that same shrug again, since they both knew he was only stating the obvious.

"Reckon so. But given they already eat a steady diet of Love's holy horse-crap down there, I'll bet I've had worse."

"Holy horse-crap?"

"Aw, Ash, you know—'for God so loved the world,' et cetera." Chess's glare turned vicious. "Like any God worth his salt wouldn't know what a bag of filth he'd shit out on top of every one of us, and make himself sick laughin' over it."

"Sheriff Love believes in a good God, no doubt." Chess didn't answer. "Okay, then how's this: I find I might still believe in the Lord myself, Chess, down deep. Hate to disappoint."

Did he, though? The Lord, yes. but a *good* God? A *forgiving* one?

God is always good, Brother Rook, the old preacher in his home town had once told him, so long ago. *And He always wants to forgive. It's just that we so seldom allow Him that opportunity.*

Rook felt a vague knot form in his chest, right where his heart should be. Didn't want to think too hard on that, though, so he looked over at Chess, instead, smiling at the thought of his pocket-sized Satan ever begging forgiveness—and the knot swelled up even higher, bruising his lungs, making his stomach clench.

"As for God," Chess said, "you choose t'believe in him, that's all well 'n' good, I s'pose. Does *he* believe in *you*, though? My personal bet would be—not like *I* do."

But to that, of course, there was nothing to say.

They laid in their heels, and galloped down in opposite directions.

It was Joseph in *Genesis* which gave Rook the words to lay a misdirective glamour over their camp, just as the sun finally sank beneath the horizon: "AND THE KEEPER OF THE PRISON COMMITTED TO JOSEPH'S HAND ALL THE PRISONERS THAT WERE IN THE PRISON. AND WHATSOEVER THEY DID THERE, HE WAS THE DOER OF IT," he murmured, back to the town, while Hosteen and the others watched uneasily, and red light fell bloody on the pages. "BECAUSE THE LORD WAS WITH HIM, AND THAT WHICH HE DID, THE LORD MADE IT TO PROSPER."

The verses thrummed in his mouth, as yet another heat-shimmer distortion washed over the camp, and all of them vanished at once.

Walking into town took an hour. By that time, the "streets" were lit with lantern overspill and pit-bound cook-fires here and there between the tents. There was a rising ruckus already to be heard, even from a distance—gunshots, hoof beats, shouts and blows: Chess, doing his job.

Truly amazing, the amount of trouble one small man can cause, Rook thought. *Especially if he really puts his mind to it.*

Watch the dust, he'd told the rest, *and keep your weapons handy. Remember, they won't be able to see you, not 'til I'm done . . . so make your own way and look out for yourself, 'cause any man's dumb enough to wander off, he's gonna find himself stranded in the desert. And we're not stoppin' to pick up any damn strays, afterwards.*

And now, he could hear somebody yelling, from 'round the next "corner"—an alleyway down the side of that half-raised frame where the church was eventually set to plant itself.

"Rook! We know you're out there, blasphemer. . . ."

"Best come collect your catamite, 'Reverend'! 'Course, he ain't too good-lookin', anymore; had to dirty him up a touch. Hope ya don't mind."

Yelled a third voice: "Oh, he's plenty good with a gun, I'll give you that. Get hold of him in close quarters, though, and the bitch fights like a damn bar-room gal!"

Close enough to make out features, now. There was a variety of scuffle and tug going on, somewhat obscure—'til all at once, Rook figured it out. They were hauling Chess out through the crowd's heart, running him down a vicious little gauntlet of slaps, punches and kicks as they did. One particular thick-set roughneck reached back into the thick of it to grab Chess by whatever ear came handiest and threw him bodily forward into the dust, where he landed doubled up, gasping out a curse.

"Just shut the fuck up, faggot," the man said, and kicked him in the side. "Might as well keep your mouth free for other things, while you still got most've your teeth."

Now, Rook thought, hands curling into claws.

But a calm voice from further to one side was already warning— "That will be quite enough of *that*, gentlemen."

The crowd swung 'round as one, Rook following, as a figure almost as tall as Rook's half-stooped to step out through a backlit tent flap. Straightening up, this resolved into what couldn't fail to be Sheriff Mesach Love himself: a far younger man than his reputation suggested—one-and-thirty at most, forming an almost-exact mid-point between Rook and Chess—and a touch gangly, his classic preacher's broad-brimmed hat jammed down over a mop of brown hair tied back in two uneven, little-girl pigtails.

"We've been waitin' on you quite the spell, Mister Rook," Love said, lifting haughty zealot's eyes to address what must look to everyone else as nothing more than empty air.

"Fine choice of words," Rook answered—and let himself blink back into being all at once, a blown-out candle flame blooming high in reverse. Chess's tormentors all took an unconscious step back at the sight, while Chess looked up and grinned, revealing the extent of the damage.

"Well, hell," he remarked, to the general company. "Now you're *really* gonna see some fun."

Rook stared. "What the Christ'd they *do* to you, Chess?"

"Nothin' I didn't expect. Now help me up."

He did, automatically—yet still found himself horrified, and downright furious. Chess's face was all bruises, nose mashed flat and eyes blacked like a 'coon's, the left one puffed 'til just a thin green slit peered out. And the more Rook saw, the more his rage began to whip sand up around them in a tightening funnel, without him even thinking to quote the Bible beforehand.

"Aw, shit-fire!" The same tree-trunk fucker as before yelled out, throwing his hands up to guard his eyes and roaring at how fast his knuckles got skinned bone-deep, for his trouble—only to freeze silent, when Love turned those prayer-burnt eyes his way.

"You hush up on that profanity, Meester," Love snapped. "There's womenfolk present."

"Sorry, Sheriff."

Rook took this opportunity to rein himself in, and huffed out a laugh. "Got them well-trained, I see. Which means I guess I must have *you* to thank for—all *this*." A nod here at Chess, now wavering slightly by his side, angrily wiping away blood.

Love shook his head. "Mister Pargeter's the one's at fault here. You sent him in scoutin', he killed five of my men."

"Oh, I don't doubt it."

He threw this last over to Chess, as a compliment. But Love simply nodded.

"Yes—that being his calling, or so I hear. And you . . ." Love gave Rook an appraising look, as though he aspired to rifle his soul's pages. "You once proceeded from the Wesleyan tradition, Reverend, like myself. Which means you know that though depravity is total and grace resistible, atonement *is* intended for all."

"For all that wants it, yes. Must admit, though, I hadn't thought you were chasin' me down to debate finer points of theology."

"You're the one came to *me*, Mister Rook," Love pointed out.

Like you knew I would, obviously, Rook realized. For oh, this *was* a clever young man stood in front of him indeed, with all his War-time honours no doubt well-merited. Yet Lucifer-arrogant all the same; this stand-off alone proved that, with the two of them squared off in the middle of the street like veritable duellos, so Love's cohort and congregationalists (the latter even now starting to peep their heads out shyly, prairie-dog style) could admire his fortitude in the face of impending wizardish mayhem.

"True enough," Rook allowed. "What's your sermon's subject, then, Sheriff Love? Assuming you think I merit one."

From the crowd's back ranks: "He don't!"

"Don't deserve nothin' but a short rope and a long drop, for all he's done!"

"Naw, do his kept boy *first*, for them Anniston twins, an' Meester's cousin. An' make Rook watch!"

Love ignored these hecklers, keeping his gaze on Rook. "On the proposition a man's best-known by the company he keeps, perhaps. And since yours is that of a she-he *thing* who flaunts his unnatural proclivities as a martial banner . . ."

Chess spat once more, bloodying the toe of Love's boot. "She-he? You give me back my guns, Bible-thumper, we'll see who wears the damn skirts—"

Rook didn't bother looking 'round. "Hush up now, Chess, the Sheriff's preachin'. Been a long time since I confabbed with a fellow Scripture student, and I mean to enjoy it."

"You're going down Satan's path," Love said. "That much is clear."

"Uh huh. By robbin' trains and boosting Railway payloads, or by letting Private Pargeter ride my dick?"

Far too blunt for comfort, given circumstances. Rook saw Love purple right to his ear-tips, then avoid looking over to where a statuesque blonde woman with a beauty mark set just off-centre on her high, smooth forehead was suddenly all caught up fussing over her swaddled baby, which already had a hint of Love's nose, along with the very beginnings of his wayward hair.

"I'll thank you to stay civil, if we're going to settle this dispute like gentlemen," Love said, at last, savagely quiet.

Rook just smiled. "So you put my behaviour down to influence," he said, "rather than free will; frankly, I don't know whether to be flattered, or insulted. Layin' my liaison with Chess aside, though— you told the papers what you objected to most was me quotin' God's word for the Devil's purposes. But we both know no Christian performing miracles through gospel does it by Satan's power. Jesus said, *'Do not stop him, for no one who does a mighty work in my name will be able soon afterward to speak evil of me. For the one who is not against us is for us.'*"

"*Mark* nine, thirty-eight to forty—which makes you a Continuationalist, Mister Rook? Tongues and prophecy will only cease when Jesus returns?" Leaning closer, at Rook's nod: "Yet *'Beware of false prophets, who come to you in sheep's clothing, but inwardly are as ravening wolves . . . A healthy tree cannot bear bad fruit, nor can a diseased tree bear good fruit.'* And *'Every tree that does not bear good fruit is to be cut down and thrown into the fire.'*"

"*Matthew* seven, fifteen to nineteen. A fine counter-argument, from the Cessationalist view—and son, that's equal-fine load of pride you're carryin' there, even without the Good Book to back it up. Hell, it's sorta like lookin' in a mirror, give or take the sodomy."

Again, cries rose up—and again, the wind Rook could barely recall summoning whipped up along with it, cutting Love, Rook and Chess out in a wedge from the rest of Bewelcome's herd, then circling tightly 'round them, on endless patrol. Love's woman ducked under Tree-trunk's arm, wrapping her baby closer, while those few congregationalists who tried pulling their pastor free of his dimly rotating cocoon got their fingers well-sanded, for their troubles.

"Where're the rest of your men, Mister Rook?" Love asked him, the noise alone enough to render their conversation extra-intimate.

"Not too far. One or two might already have beads on that wife of yours."

"Then this *should* probably be kept between you and me, wouldn't you say?"

"As 'gentlemen'?" Rook gave out a true belly-laugh, at the idea. "Sheriff, you don't have one touch of hexation in you, or I'd've smelled it by now. We tangle, I'll crush you like an egg."

"You're forgetting—these folk are in my charge, as minister for this town, which makes it up to me to defend them. 'Sides which . . . I have the Lord, on *my* side."

"Uh huh. Well, you're young still—but in matters of answered prayers, I think you'll find God most often has nothin' much of import to say back, savin' the occasional 'I told you so.'"

Love studied Rook, almost sympathetically.

"He does to me," was all he said.

Rook sighed. To Chess: "Step back, darlin'."

Chess looked mutinous, but did it.

"At least throw me your guns," he complained. "Ain't like *you* need 'em!"

Rook did.

He turned to face Mesach Love head on, both hands rising to assume an arcane, unlearned posture—entirely intuited, each individual finger snake-crooked to spit, or strike. Only to realize Love was already doing something similar, in reply—hands first tented to bless, then canted forelong so he could sight at Rook over his own linked thumbs, a two-fisted shooting stance with no bullets behind it but those faith alone might supply.

Rook felt a tweak of sympathy himself, at the sight: *I'm somewhat going to hate having to kill this up-stood fool, if he makes me . . .*

"Ready, 'Reverend'?"

"On your mark."

They squared their shoulders as one, two stags in rut, and laid straight on into it.

CHAPTER ELEVEN

The sand was a moving wall all around them now, and Rook felt the Word come up through him in a wave, not even consciously summoned. It spilled silver-black and wickedly sharp-edged from his open mouth, a flood of sickness fit only to burn and scald.

Then was brought unto him one possessed with a devil, blind, and dumb: and he healed him . . .

. . . But when the Pharisees heard it, they said, This fellow doth not cast out devils, but by Beelzebub the prince of the devils.

And Jesus . . . said unto them . . .

. . . if Satan cast out Satan, he is divided against himself. How shall then his kingdom stand?

(*Matthew* twelve, twenty-two to twenty-six.)

He'd pictured it hitting Love in a swarm, eating that holier-than-thou snarl off his face. But Love stood firm. Spitting back, from the very same chapter: "*O generation of vipers, how can ye, being evil, speak good things? For an evil man out of . . . evil . . . bringeth forth evil things.*"

Obviously, Rook thought.

Love raised his "gun" hands higher, declaiming: "Get out, Satan! Oh, I am strong in the Lord. I cast you out, you sneakin' Serpent! I am full in His power, filled up brim-full with His infinite and unforgivin' might—"

Rook regarded him with curiosity. "You're fulla something, that's for sure," he replied.

Chess, from behind him: "Can I shoot him *now*, Ash?"

To which Rook just shook his head, firmly—*Not while I'm still enjoying myself.*

Since this first engagement had proved such an obvious stalemate, however (his power just *jumping away* from Love, like hands off a lard-slick hog), he must need to up stakes a tad. So, with full awareness of the irony, Rook reached down deep into the anti-Sodomitical grab-bag he'd once used on Chess and began to quote it back at Love, wholesale.

"Nice little town you've built here, Sheriff—shame to see it fall on your sin alone, don't you think? For—Behold, THIS WAS THE INIQUITY OF THY SISTER SODOM, PRIDE, FULLNESS OF BREAD, AND ABUNDANCE OF IDLENESS WAS IN HER AND IN HER DAUGHTERS, NEITHER DID SHE STRENGTHEN THE HAND OF THE POOR AND NEEDY.

AND THEY WERE HAUGHTY, AND COMMITTED ABOMINATION BEFORE ME: THEREFORE I TOOK THEM AWAY AS I SAW GOOD."

Beyond the swirling barrier, Rook heard the creak and crack of timbers, the shudder of opening earth, as Love's church-to-be folded in on itself, a house of cards.

Further on, Love's wife was crying out thinly into the wind's heart, her terror all for *his* life, rather than her own: "Meeeeeesach! Where are you? Fear nothing—God will help you, husband, in this your hour of need! God will—"

Rook forced himself a pace or so forward, catching long, tall Mesach Love by both wrists and pulling him close. Saw those God-drunk eyes of his widen prettily, their pupils suddenly aflutter in the wind-tunnel's ever-changing grey light.

"Scared yet, Sheriff?" He asked.

Love bared his teeth. "Not of *you*, I ain't."

"'Cause you got the *Lord* on your side."

"Miracles go both ways, 'Reverend.' Long as I'm doing his work, I trust in His good will."

"'His work,' huh?" Rook threw a glance back at Chess's wrecked face, and felt his rage whip up higher than the wind itself. "Well, all right, then: Try *this* on for size."

The verse was from *Psalms*—139, to be specific. This close, it rained down on Love in molten silver-black, a cursed shower of wriggling worm-words blind-seeking for every entrance-point they could essay, to the very pores of Love's straining skin. A blood-beat soul choir run anticlockwise, screaming out.

SURELY THOU WILT SLAY THE WICKED, O GOD: DEPART FROM ME THEREFORE, YE BLOODY MEN.

FOR THEY SPEAK AGAINST THEE WICKEDLY, AND THINE ENEMIES TAKE THY NAME IN VAIN.

DO NOT I HATE THEM, O LORD, THAT HATE THEE? AND AM NOT I GRIEVED WITH THOSE THAT RISE UP AGAINST THEE?

I HATE THEM WITH PERFECT HATRED: I COUNT THEM MINE ENEMIES.

Love took it full to the face, but Rook had to give him credit; all it seemed to do was make him madder.

"How *dare* you?" He demanded, bitter-thick, through near-clogged lips. "How *dare* you take the Lord's Word in vain, when you stand already on the edge of damnation—"

"Oh, it ain't in *vain*, believe you me. Still, if this ain't proof enough of that, already . . ."

Rook clapped one hand against Love's forehead, knocking the preacher-hat groundward, and forced himself inside: a healing in reverse, opening that invisible third eye in Love's skull up like a glory hole with one violent thrust forward into darkness, sure to his back teeth he could fuck anything he found inside 'til it screamed. And fully expecting that what lay beyond would be nothing more (or less) than the contents of his *own* brain-pan—a hollow core of ignorance and doubt, wrapped in memorized words. Good intentions, masked in a bag of wind.

He'd never seen any angels, after all. Never heard any still, small voice . . . not 'til after he was hung. And even then—only *hers*.

Instead, Rook gasped out loud, staggered and went down hard, all a-tremble. Around them, the sand stuttered, thinning far enough in places to show the crowd outside what was happening, and Love's champions literally leapt to his defence—Tree-trunk at the fore and grabbing for Chess yet again, only to take a bullet straight in his growling mouth. Meanwhile, more shots rang out from a handful of very different positions, as Hosteen and the rest weighed in at last.

Love's woman hit the dirt, baby tucked against her with both arms. And Love—nose bleeding, but otherwise unscathed—yelled back at her over Rook's head, which had begun to flail back and forth as the contents of Love's soul coursed through him: "Sophy, take the boy and run, 'fore our Lord's vengeance busts its banks! He'll keep you too, girl! Run run *run*—"

Sophy, Rook knew, wishing he didn't. *Sophronia. And the boy, the boy is—Gabriel. Like the angel.*

Chess grabbed hold of Rook's shoulder and shoved, hard. "Ash! What the shit—"

"That's right," Love told Rook, drawing himself to full height, while the tunnel around them shook and spat. "Now you *see* the true power of God Almighty at work, at long last."

Was that more sympathy he heard, just a touch of it, in Love's clarion voice? Rook almost hoped so. He lay caught between two equal-matched forces, prey to Hell's undertow.

"Goddamnit, Ash, you Bible-drunk king prick—we're under *fire*, soldier! Get your big ass *up* and do your damn *duty*!"

The central mistake—the *hubris*, for which Rook was now paying—had been trying to take hold of Love's soul in the first place, seeing how that obviously belonged to one far more equipped to fight for it. Christ knew, if Rook'd just picked up a damn mountain and dropped it on him, faith alone could never've kept the son of a bitch uncrushed.

"That's right, Serpent," Love said, sadly. "On thy *belly* shalt thou go. Of the *dust* shalt thou eat—"

Not just another opportunist—the Lieut wouldn't've been fit to shine this one's shoes. He loves this shit-flat place, these stupid, quarrelling people. Wants to do right by them, no matter the cost. Sophy over there's his wife, or will be—and little Gabe's fruit of their sin, 'til they get that reward money, and raise the church he'll marry her in. Sinners or no, though, they're firm in their commitment, their hope in redemption not so much a lie as telling the truth in advance.

He knows it'll happen. *God* told him so.

Mesach Love's done bad things in his time, like all men, but he's certain in ways you never were, about anything. Except . . . Chess.

Chess, even now grabbing fast hold of Rook's hand and *pulling* at him like he was a skinful of water on the Devil's griddle, without knowing he was doing it at all. Sucking power from him in waves, his face re-ordering itself, nose straightening with a visible ripple, eyes re-emerging from their bruisy nests, as mean and bright as ever. Bound and determined to pound Sheriff Love into the dry ground, on both of their behalves.

And Love don't stand a tinker's dam of a chance against him, poor bastard—God or no.

Rook's head swam as he tried to form the words, but his dazed mouth wouldn't obey. Thinking, instead—*Oh, let me go, sweetheart, let me go. This fight's one I don't deserve to win.*

To which he somehow "heard" Chess reply, over their mutual nerve-strung telegraph-wire: *Yeah? Well, too bad, Rev. Fuck that bullshit, right in the Goddamn ass.*

Chess drew careful aim on Love, right between the eyes. "Eat this," he said.

While, at the same time, Rook reached desperately up—*stop Chess shit* stop—

His hand spanning Chess's, fingers and thumb overlapping, so Chess wore them like a huge flesh glove—Chess's index tightening sure and vicious on the trigger, Rook's slippy-sliding in cold sweat. About as restraining as a wedding ring.

It was like the doubled force of both of them came rocketing right out through the barrel, along with the bullet. Hitting Love not quite square-on, but with enough force to spin him 'round, one spurt of blood arching up to break apart on the sandstorm's churning maelstrom.

Only winged him, thank God . . . guess he'll thank Him himself, after.

Chess, rightly amazed by his point-blank miss, swore ably.

"You shut your mouth," Love ordered. To Rook: "And as for *you*,

you hypocrite antidinomian . . ." Here he stopped short, however.

Because *something* was already licking out from the wound in his shoulder, all white and icy-sparkling: salt, blanching him the way flame blackens paper. His long body froze, all bones and glass, eyes wild in a calcinate mask. Rook saw Love's flesh bloom pinkly through here and there, a breathed-on coal, before stiffening forever into an almost-featureless pillar. His saint's gaze forever lidded over, in a single terrible blink.

So *fast*, Jesus! Like judgement.

At the same time, the sand-wall blew away, allowing young Missus Love-to-be to catch sight of her man's fate. She screamed, while others fought to pull her to safety—the baby already having begun to wail too, mimicking his Mama's grief, if all unknowing of its cause.

Chess laughed out loud, to hear it. "*Yeah*," he snarled. "Go on ahead and *cry*, little boy—your Daddy ain't comin' home anytime soon, not now, not ever—"

Rook retched a sour lick of spit, genuinely sickened by Chess's cruelty, the anger that had spawned it, his own complicity in both. Then cringed back a half-stride when he saw bits of verse glinting in the spew-up, silver-black and stomach-mucky—verse he didn't even recall thinking up. Genesis again, Lot in Sodom. Abraham the Patriarch, begging: *Give me but one honest man, my Lord, and stay Your hand against the city*—

And Abraham gat up early in the morning to the place where he stood before the LORD:

And he looked toward Sodom and Gomorrah, and toward all the land of the plain, and beheld, and, lo, the smoke of the country went up as the smoke of a furnace . . .

The words came torn straight from Rook's head, unbidden. And in that same puking breath, he felt the tide turn—swigged deep, sucking all the power Chess'd taken from him back again, and more. The sheer jolt of it lit him up, then backwashed, and sent the same salt that had snared Love quick-dripping down the Sheriff's legs, curdling the earth beneath into a floodplain mire. Each of his congregationalists sunk to the ankle, the knee, the waist, salinified from their extremities up, so they crumbled and broke apart even as they struggled to flee.

"Don't look!" Rook could hear Hosteen screaming from somewhere behind, to the rest of the gang. "Cover your face! For Christ's sake, shut your God damn eyes!"

The salt skirted both him and Chess, though, avoiding them like *they* were the plague at hand. Like he'd suspected it might, so long as they only kept fast hold of each other.

And Sophy No-Last-Name curled in on her child, praying, 'til the rising wave of white choked her. 'Til only Mesach Love's name was left on her bitter lips.

Hours after, as the sun rose, Bewelcome gave it back from every angle, a bleak wilderness of mirrors. In the end, *everything* had turned to salt—no exceptions. Oh, there'd be wind-wear and erosion to come, 'til the town's edges lost their clarity, and travellers struggled to identify the place as made by human hands. For now, however, it was pristine, so clean it cut.

Rook looked over at Chess, so triumphant before at Love's expense—and saw him waver, reeling under the full weight of what'd just happened: the spectacle of Love's dead congregation, his woman fallen to her knees and bent double to hide her baby from the tide of rime. Same baby whose pudgy hand still protruded from the folds of her shawl, the two of them already blurred together, inseparable.

"Jesus, y'all *right*?" Hosteen asked Chess, genuinely worried. Chess spat and shuffled himself back upright, batting the older man away from him.

"Fine, idjit!" was all he said. But Rook, like Hosteen, knew better.

Because they could both see what Chess had brought up, shining there amongst the drifts—a spray of liquid jewellery, bright red on endless white.

I can't see him killed, Rook cast out into the ether, his mind reaching for that Indian woman's—Grandma, why not? *I won't.*

To which she sent back, faintly, from someplace far away—her Yellow Mountain?—*You do not* want *to. But you will have to see it, eventually, knowing what he is . . . what you are. Unless . . .*

Unless?

"You're *goin'*?" Chess demanded. "Where? Why? *Alone?*" He paused. "For how long?"

"Don't know, exactly. It's this mountain over in Injun territory, back by the border—"

"You're a Bible School-bred liar, Ash Rook. I come in here alone, get myself beat to shit for you, and you lie right to my face? I killed the Lieut for you!"

"You *were* plannin' on killin' him anyhow, I believe."

Chess threw up his hands. "Yeah, sure . . . but when I *did* it, I did it for *you!*"

Rook grit his teeth, and began again. "Chess, what happened here just ain't right, and you know it. I don't whip this thing, I might hurt—somebody—I don't *want* to."

"So you're gonna leave me behind!"

"I don't want you hurt, Chess. Is that so hard to understand?"

"Yeah, well—talk's cheap, Rev. Prove it!"

Rook paused, sighed, heavy as Balaam's laden ass—and clapped a hand over Chess's face, willing instantaneous sleep into him with one muffled burst, a soft mortar-round. Chess folded back into Hosteen's grip, without a hint of protest.

"I just did," Rook told him, knowing Chess couldn't hear. To Hosteen: "Look after him."

"I will," Hosteen replied. "I mean, much as he'll let me."

Not much point in further goodbyes, from Rook's point of view. So he just nodded—*I know you will, Kees*—and left, heading for open desert. Thinking, as he did: *Okay, then.*

Show me somethin'.

CHAPTER TWELVE

Two days later, as Grandma's Yellow Abalone Shell mountain rose to scar the sky, Rook suddenly realized that this was the longest he and Chess had been apart since the day he'd been hung. But the desert was a shockingly empty place once you faced it alone, and he'd been walking slow enough now, for long enough, to let it steal a good portion of the daily sound and fury of Chess's companionship away, though parts of him ached for lack of what he'd increasingly come to regard as their due reverence. In fact, without Chess here to do him worship, Rook's formerly swelled head was deflating like a popped pig's bladder.

Like coming down off a three-week drunk, your very piss still alcohol-laced enough to light up blue and high-flaming at the slightest touch of a dropped lucifer. Or maybe the morning after signing up, when he'd come to already in uniform.

Now, Rook stood in the peaks' shadow, knowing San Francisco lay somewhere on the other side: that terrible city which had spit his own true love out into an unsuspecting world—all teeth from the very start, yet still quite the prettiest thing Rook'd ever seen, let alone killed for.

You're doing this for *him,* he told himself. *So you can build something together—something ain't just bed and bullets, something no one can touch but you. Not even—*

(*She*, deep in the murk with her dragonfly-cloak flapping, where all shed blood sluices away down steep black chutes to keep the world's gears grinding.)

Dragging himself away from the cold touch of Lady Rainbow's

shadow, with some not-inconsiderable effort, Rook forced himself to look up at the mountain instead. He opened his mind wide, and waited.

Eventually, that *other* voice-in-his-head sent thrumming down the line from the centre of it all: "Grandma," as he lived and breathed.

Climb up and see me, grandson. Set your feet to the great rock's hide. You are well come, though perhaps not soon enough . . . well come, and welcome.

Rook looked up the mountain's face, and sighed. *Should've known,* he thought, shifting his travel-blistered feet. But far as he'd come already, there really was nothing left to do now but either refuse, or obey—stand fast, shout useless imprecations at the sky, fight, flee. Or climb.

He climbed.

Not until Rook had covered two-thirds or so of the upwards-rearing crests of stone, and lay panting on a ledge barely wide enough to hold him, did he wonder why he hadn't simply pulled one more miracle from the Book to loft him upwards, 'stead of busting his already-bloody finger-pads with hauling himself up—levitation, bilocation or chariots of fire, he hadn't lacked for choices. Yet somehow, the very notion'd never even entered his head.

Instinctive wariness, knowing himself to be entering the domain of another hexslinger? Or had Grandma's command to *climb* held occult force so subtle he'd simply been unable to sense it wrapping its geas around him?

Sudden sweat broke cold on Rook's forehead as he clung to the mountain with both raw hands, thinking: *There are reasons we stay away from each other . . . and maybe what she wants is you out here, all alone. To take what you have. How foolish must you be, how trusting—*

(little king)

(husband)

Grandson: CLIMB.

Finally, everything levelled off, and Rook lay—gasping, drenched, so mortal dusty he might as well've been hewn from the same stones cradling him—in the shallow slope of scree that lined the inside of the mountain's pinnacle. The sky above was reddish-purple, draining to black. His lungs felt stuffed with grit. Gulping air and smelling something he couldn't put a name to, immediately—

. . . heat, smoke. A fire. She laid a fire.

Well, that made sense. Had to see, after all—and eat.

Then came the juicy smell of cooking meat, making Rook's days-empty stomach spasm painfully. Hunger-driven, he rolled over, huge and clumsy—got his hands braced against the pebbled slope and levered himself up, with a groan of effort.

The woman who knelt over that delicious-smelling fire wore her hair in a waist-length pair of braids, thin and fine and strong as sunbleached corn-silk. By contrast, the rest of her was shockingly thick, sturdy to the point of squatness—nose flat and cheekbones broad, her wry-set mouth so wide it seemed virtually lipless. A slant pair of coal-in-paraffin eyes, small as currants, cut sideways over to Rook.

"Grandson," she said, voice at once a gravelly rasp and a smooth, pure tone. It took Rook a second to understand what he was hearing: "inside" *and* "outside" voice, blended together, to bypass their mutual lack of common language. Trusting his instincts, therefore, he closed his eyes and felt 'round for the currents of power, for once riding them rather than shaping them.

"Grandma," he replied.

The word itself was spoken in English, by necessity. The *meaning*, however, went back out to her just as hers had come to him—portmanteaued inside a visceral understanding which neither needed anything as crude as mere *language* to clarify.

"So. I see you have not forgotten *all* your manners."

"Well, I do hope not . . . ma'am."

And this drew an actual husky *laugh*, straight from the belly. Shaking her head, she got to her feet, brushing down her shawl and stamping ash off her shoes.

"Men," she remarked. "They always hope to charm. But then, even we of the *Hataalii* are still steered by what the First People put between our legs."

"I meant no insult—".

She shrugged. "Of course not. What else can be expected? You know nothing."

"Hey, now," he began, flushing—but she merely gestured, curtly, for him to sit . . . and he surprised himself, by obeying. Another laugh followed, equally gruff.

"That angers you, eh?" she asked. "To be ordered, like a child? That boy you've roped yourself to . . ."

"*He'd* just shoot you, you pissed him off bad enough."

"Oh, he might try—and fail. But why charm, when honesty is better? You barely know what *you* are, 'Reverend,' your head still stuffed with blackrobe chatter-nonsense, while your boy does not even know *that* much, let alone how easily I have stopped bullets before. I am elder to you both, and worth respecting for it."

Rook gritted his teeth. "I'd've thought the simple fact that I'm *here* was evidence enough of my respect."

"Yet you took your time in getting here, and many have suffered. I see no reason for compliments." She paused, stirring the fire. "And where is he now, your apprentice?"

"Hexes don't take apprentices, is what I heard."

"Yet here *you* are, nonetheless—come to learn from one you think knows more than you do, without even bringing me proper payment, and having left *him* behind. Did you not think *he* might benefit from a lesson or two as well, once his true nature is revealed?"

"Well, it ain't done that just yet, and I don't aim to enlighten him, either. He's hard enough to handle as it is."

"Mmmh. Selfish, secretive. Spoken like a true . . . hex."

Rook shrugged. "Takes one to know one," he suggested.

Again, Grandma glanced down at the fire. "The bird has minutes yet to cook," she said, "which leaves time for one question."

Rook had to smile. Carefully: "I'd consider it a kindness to be allowed to know my teacher's name."

She clapped her hands. "Ah, more manners! How I love the *bilagaana* way, so long as greed outweighs the fear which makes you burn down everything you do not recognize. But here is a thing you *should* know already, and do not: no smart *Hataalii* ever tells their name, to anyone. Most especially not to their own kind."

"You know *my* name."

Grandma nodded. "Exactly so. The more fool you, for telling me."

Sparks flew up, and the moon blinked like an eye. Then Rook and she sat opposite each other, cross-legged on the dirt, while each tore at the meat they held, firm and hot and full of juice. The swiftness of it all disturbed Rook a tad, as it was probably meant to.

Grandma gave a small belch and licked her fingers, neatly, 'til they shone clean, while Rook wiped his on the tail of his coat.

"So," she said, abruptly natural, as though their conversation had never been interrupted, "since you present yourself as my student, you will *earn* the knowledge of my name—until then, I shall stay Grand-mother. Now . . . let me ask *you* a question."

"Ma'am."

"I told you 'climb,' and you climbed. Did you forget how to fly?"

"Well . . ." Rook paused. "Seemed . . . I couldn't think of quite the right way to put it, if I wanted to." He saw endless flickering telegraph-transcriptions of Bible-verse fragments scoring its way through his brain's centre-slice, tendrils digging bright hooks into either lobe, and shivered. "Just couldn't—find the words."

"From that Book of yours? Though you yourself know you have done without them, before."

"True enough. But—" *That was when I had Chess with me.*

The sudden truth of it stopped him mid-breath. With blessed courtesy, she gave him a moment to ride it out before answering.

"You still think of yourself as what you *were*, grandson . . . tied to your *bilagaana* One-God, even when you know yourself to have already gone beyond His narrow way out into the wider world, where the threads of true Balance may be woven. So when His Book failed you, you climbed. You forgot your own powers, because you thought yourself unworthy of them. That is the first truth.

"The second truth? Your powers are not all you are. To believe you are nothing without them is to *be* nothing but your own magic.

And no *Hataalii* who makes himself so hollow can still retain his soul."

"All right, then—yes. It does seem . . . right, somehow."

"Even though I might be lying."

Rook stared at her, hard. "Why would you?" he asked, at last.

A shrug. "Why indeed?"

Those flat eyes, so unreadable in the reddish ebb and flow. Rook made himself meet them nonetheless, thinking: *Liked you better by far when you were just one more voice in my head, woman—when you had to tempt, not browbeat, in order to get whatever it was you wanted. But that's just what always happens, I guess, when the honeymoon's over.*

And with that, sure as iron to a magnet, his thoughts went skittering on back to Chess.

If he was here, this old lady'd be no match for us—it'd be Bewelcome all over again, and she and Mesach Love could lick each other's wounds in Hell. But, then again—maybe she ain't *lying. Maybe she does want to help. And what am I, in the end, if I need Chess to fight all my worst battles for me?*

With deliberate care, he took another small bite of the fowl, chewing it slowly before swallowing—then another, and another. Musing, as his vised stomach began to gradually unclench: *Been a long time, for her, I expect—out here, all on her own, no other hex to feed from. She must be starved for company indeed. And yeah, could be she really* does *mean me well, just has a funny way of showin' it . . . but even if she don't, well—I think I can take her.*

They finished their meal in silence, consuming the bird down to the bones, which the desert witch cast into the fire. Then squatted down to peer at them as they smouldered, and said, "Now, Preacher Rook—look closely, and listen. Let me show you how the world *really* works: how every world grows out of the one which came before, *into* the next—and just as all worlds are connected, everything must be paid for."

"Could you . . . be a touch more specific, maybe?"

Grandma snorted again, tossing back her braids, and rummaged inside the skin pouch she wore on her belt, cross-strapped right at the vague indentation where her waist should be. Withdrawing a smaller bag, she shook a few pale yellow grains out into her big, scarred palm.

"Cornmeal," she explained. "Now: one more time, listen. And *see.*"

With two fingers, she twisted a hole in the sand at her feet, shook the meal down and bent to breathe a low croon in after it, then sat back, smoothing it over. Above them, the sky hung heavy with stars . . . until, gradual but unmistakable, those same stars began to go out.

A cloud, Rook thought, and Grandma nodded, like she could hear him. Like she knew he'd already forgotten how she probably could.

"Come down, *nilch'i biyázhí,*" she called up, into the air. "Wind's children, hear me—spin your wool to my loom, gift me with threads to weave this working, keep my heart clean. Keep me from misstepping upon the Witchery Way."

Rook could all but feel their two species of magic pass by each other in the night—her own strong faith, versus his sorrowful lack of it—and when she smiled back over at him, he realized he'd never before been so aware that a person's teeth were also part of their skull. The sight made the hairs on the back of his neck prick up, a thin violet whining sound echoing through his head. And yes, bellyful of fresh-cooked meat aside, it also made him . . . *hungry.*

"Give me your hand," Grandma told him, her deep voice oddly shaky, and Rook felt his scalp tighten. Was that a note from the very same famished scale he heard, behind her words' bone-born "English" translation?

"Why—"

"*Give* it."

He hesitated—and saw it jerk forward of its own accord, her power a taut-snapped leash around his wrist. Heat flowed swoonishly outwards, dizziness mounting up fast as blood-loss. Scraping down deep to his very marrow, like she aimed to eat it with a spoon—and letting him know just how helpless he was to stop her from doing so, if she happened to choose to.

Two conclusions to be gleaned here, neither welcome. First off: she was *much* stronger than Rook had thought, or hoped.

And second—*is this how Chess must feel,* he thought, *when I do it to* him?

"This sort of spell cannot be done through natural means alone," Grandma told him. "It needs more than one *Hataalii's* power, whether or not the other aims to give it. Which shows us why it should probably not *be* done at all."

With a flourish, Grandma shook her fingers over the hole, and Rook saw two types of hexation rain down into it, glinting hotly: his and hers, admixed. The earth drank it gladly, puffed up the way dough does in hot oil and shot up one green sprout, blindly seeking for an absent sun.

"Things must be what they are," Grandma said, stroking the corn-stalk lightly. "From one grain I can make a kernel, and then— from that kernel—"

Sprout became stalk, grew to nodding-height with startling speed—leafed out, a dancing-girl's flapping skirts, spun all of a sudden with dry-rustling silken tassels. Ears whose ripe husks budded quick as grenades, golden-juicy fruit beneath aglow with an inner light that stunk so high of artifice it made Rook's mouth fill with sour water.

"Take one," she ordered. Rook did, gingerly. Even its weight felt *wrong.*

"Now eat."

Rook bit savagely into the ear of corn, chewed, and was halfway through his second bite when the taste struck him at last—dust and ash, warm-slimy with decay. And as he choked down the third, the whole cob disintegrated in his hands, stalk curling over upon itself, shrivelling to the ground. Rook breathed deep, feeling his own stolen power flood back into him.

"That was never meant to be," said Grandma. "Do you see, now? If I must steal from you to create a good thing, no matter how I try, I cannot make it stay. It cannot be other than it is—one grain of cornmeal in a new dress, sewn from dreams."

Bread falling from the air, tasteless, unnourishing: Rook remembered. *But the* bad *things you used your own—and Chess's—power to do, all of them . . .* those *things stand still. The train, bisected. Bewelcome, in all its salt-slick glory.*

Grandma reached down, prising up a rock to reveal the fossil which clung close beneath it, froze in mid-crawl, as though excreted straight from stone.

"Or this," she said. "*This* slimy thing . . . something from the Fourth World itself, perhaps. Suck from you—'til you sleep, or die, and I grow fat and drunk—and I might be able to make it creep, free to roam once more. But how far would it get, before it drowned in air it was never meant to breathe? Its time has passed. So I could feed you for years out here, grandson, just as I have kept myself fed—but never on corn, or sea-insects."

"Not much of a miracle, then, is it?"

"Only gods do miracles, Asher Rook. Your own Book says as much."

"And . . . we're not gods."

"Powerful, yes: *Hataalii*, born to Balance or un-Balance, to do right or walk the Witchery Way, perverting our own magic for profit. But we are *not* gods, and never could be."

"There's one I've spoke with, now and again," Rook replied, slowly, "who might tend to disagree with you."

And we both know who that *is, now, don't we?*

No need to even nod. 'Cause from somewhere far below, the threads of his dragonfly-cloaked Lady's influence came spinning up 'round both of them in a slack silk knot, just waiting for any excuse to tighten. And as she sat on the Sunken Ball-Court's sloshing sidelines, Rook knew she grinned to hear herself discussed—she, her, the One Now Woken.

You, Rook "heard" Grandma blurt out.

And heard the reply in turn, a barest liquid murmur—***Ah, yes: me.***

A surging snap lit Rook from within, at the very sound. Not fear, so much, as a terrible urge to run wild and aimless in any direction, run 'til his skin rucked up and his muscles unstrung themselves, leaving his slick red bones to rattle at last into a sticky heap, reconfigured by their own momentum.

Before he could, however, Grandma's hand moved again, and the unseen leash jerked him taut, puppet-stiff. When he made to protest, she sewed a quick seam across his lips with one needle-sharp nail, muffling them shut—a locked purse, his tongue curled too tight in on itself to even move.

"Stay *still*," Grandma told him. "The Lady of Traps and Snares has made threats, made you promises—of this I have no doubt. But even she, powerful as she has become, is no true god, grandson. She is *Anaye*, a monster. Enemy to all. Did she tell you *you* could be a god, perhaps, if you only did her bidding? Or was it . . . that *he* could?"

There was a note in her double-voice which rung through Rook like a bellyful of angry hornets, and made him just pissed off enough to wrench his sealed lips free—just pop them back open, uncaring of what might rip, and spit a mouthful of his own blood up, before answering: "Don't you . . . talk about . . . *him*."

He'd at least hoped to startle her, but had to settle for a bare smidgen of genuine respect, instead—before, with a flick of her fingers, she wound him tight on himself again.

And here the Rainbow Lady came whispering once more, from deep inside his ear's shell—***You are in a bad place now, little king. Do you wish my help?***

Grandma's head whipped 'round, bent low and seeking, as if she might be able to find the words' source somewhere in the dust at her feet, if only given enough time to study it. "Do not answer her!" she ordered Rook, peremptorily.

The Lady, ignoring her, continued: ***For I will give it. That is how close we already are, given the blood we have shared, our marriage pledge. You have only to say the words . . .***

Rook managed a groan, nothing more. Kicked out hard against Grandma's net, and got the blood cut off to all his limbs at once, in return.

"*Ohé*, grandson—you will only hurt yourself, if you continue to struggle," she warned him, without much sympathy. "I might have broken you of these bad habits gently, but my dreams tell me there is no time. If you do not learn your business quickly, she will hang you once more, and finish the job, this time—you, me, everyone else. Even that boy of yours."

"His *name* is Chess. And he ain't no *boy*."

"No. He is rage and fire, a fierce warrior, one whose blood would enrich any tribe, did he not prefer to lie down with his own sex. I have seen many such, in my time: two-spirited as Begochiddy himself. But love is love, and you *do* love him, after all."

Rook swallowed. "The hell'd you think I'd even come here for," he managed, finally, "if I damn well didn't?"

"Then why do you fight me, fool?"

Say it, husband.

"'Cause . . ." His head swam, lightening like the sky, as the dying fire sunk lower. ". . . she threatened to kill him . . . then promised to *save* him—"

"From what, *herself*? In her time, the gods ate ones like him every day—the beautiful, the gifted. They ate their hearts, and drank their precious blood, because they could. Because that was what *tasted best*."

Little king, say—

"That ain't even vaguely what she—"

"Oh, save me from all men, *bilagaana* or *Diné*—do you really believe no one but you knows how to *lie*? Wake up!"

Say it, say the words—

Rook opened his torn mouth wide, only to have it twist shut on him yet again, so fast it burned worse than a swallow of sparks.

"Your mouth stays *shut*, grandson," Grandma repeated. "Or—"

Or what, *old woman?*

Had he ever truly thought her gentle, kind? Damn, if the bitch wasn't right: between her and the Lady, he might well be the stupidest whoreson alive.

Grandma gave a sigh, similarly frustrated, and pressed both palms to her eyes, as though to soothe an aching brain. Then continued, after a moment—"When North and South went to War, Rook, you fought, yes? And that young man of yours, too—not because either of you cared one way or another who owned land, who kept slaves, but because you wanted to die and he wanted to live. Because he knew himself born for killing, and saw a chance to trade that skill for a long ride, far away. And neither of you cared who else might be hurt by it—not least because, unaware of your own true natures, you did not see what would happen when one of you was hurt badly enough to come to power.

"Meanwhile, for we *Diné*, your War was one more theft in a long string of thieveries. Treaties which signed away the land from under us, leaving our horses no place to graze. Two of our sacred mountains taken—as though that could happen! Your greycoats offered us alliance against the bluecoats, but threatened us with death if we did not accept. After, the government men sent Kit Carson to burn us out, calling us traitors. And then, the Long Walk . . . men, women and children driven to *Hwééldi* like cattle, three hundred miles in eighteen days, on foot."

She shook her head, her braids' double shadow lashing the ground. "Bad blood between us, always. Soon my people will march home once more, and there will be war again—a war we will lose. My dreams have shown me. Like the Steel Hats who drove your Lady and her kind under the ground, you will make it so we are forgotten even by ourselves.

"And I might have stopped it—I, and every other *Hataalii*. When the tribes sent warriors to ask us for help, we *might* have banded together, even at the usual cost. When they said, *These* bilagaana *do not think of us as people, given how they treat us, so why should we think of them as people?*, we might have answered, *You speak the truth. Let us go to war. Let us answer force for force, and make such a slaughter as the land has never seen.*

"But I am the true fool, here. I told them no: *Bilagaana* are only human beings, and to kill human beings by magic is the Witchery Way. *We* would become skinwalkers, *Anaye*, were we to do so. Yes, you 'whites' think no one as good as yourselves. You think you own everything, and care for nothing. Yet you are not evil spirits, or even dumb beasts—you love your children, at least, enough to cry for their pain. And even if you do not, you still piss and shit as we do, and know to go outside your own camps before doing so, for the most part. This is human enough, for me."

That's quite the little philosophical dilemma you got yourself entangled in, Rook thought. His ears burned, and his forehead was clammy—was that his own tongue leeching iron between clenched teeth, or a knife? How could he have possibly cut himself so deeply he could feel it in every pore, without having said a single word?

Why the hell're you even tryin' to sell me this cart-load of Indian horse-crap? he wondered, shame and hate struggling venomously inside him, two snakes in the same bag. *Just go on and kill me, same's I would you, if I thought I was capable of it. 'Cause I could face* that *a sight better than I can the prospect of being damn well* talked *to death.*

"Because I do not *want* to kill you," Grandma said, to herself, her voice full of a dull sorrow. "If only I could be sure you were fully a monster! If I killed you, it *would* upset her plans, I know that much—I do not think she could get another man to serve her quite as willingly, as quickly. And so long as you practise only for your own pleasure—or your lover's—you both come closer and closer to being something anyone can kill without guilt, without even having to cleanse themselves of the deed, afterward."

Chess's voice, now, answering for him—distinct as the Lady's, though licking hot against his opposite eardrum—*Yeah? All right, then. Bring it on, bitch. Let them damn well try.*

"Yes. And this, too, is a monster's answer."

As though resolved, Grandma got to her feet, flicking back her braids. Rook found himself jouncing upwards as well, knees popping painfully.

"Has your Lady told you the full extent of her plans?" she demanded. "I doubt it. Even an uneducated *bilagaana Hataalii* would not consent, if so. Remember what I showed you—there are things which must not be done, because their cost is too dear. To bring the dead back to life tears a hole in the world's fabric. It is a great crime, a sin against Balance. What your Lady wants is to remake the world, to poison everything. It will destroy her, and everyone else." She glared at him, suddenly furious. "Yet *you* think nothing of helping her, if it gets you what you want."

Rook took her contempt, which stung, but at least gave him enough strength to speak again. "Yeah? Well—screw you, you crazy squaw! All I ever *wanted* was her out of my head, away from me, from Chess . . . and I thought you were gonna help me with that, by the by!"

Rolling her eyes, at the very idea: "Oh yes, of course—because it makes such *sense* that another *Hataalii* would offer to solve your problems, free of charge. Or that I would ever wish to help any white man, let alone *two*."

Put like that, it *did* seem foolish—and though he overshot her by a foot at least, when she thrust her face alongside his, it was *he* who felt dwarfed. That marrow-deep *suck* turned on full, guttering him 'til he watched himself fade away by shades, like windowpane breath.

You can still stop this, husband, the silver-bell voice reminded him. *If . . . you want to.*

"So . . . this *was* a trap, right from the start. Right from that first time you spoke to me."

Grandma nodded, a touch sadly. "Always, yes."

"Was always my *power* you wanted, the whole time, like any other hex—"

"*Your* power? Tchah! You have nothing *I* need. But when I saw in my dreams that if you were not stopped everything would die, how could I refuse that call? This being the only time at which I *could* stop you from Becoming—"

"Becoming what?"

And here . . . he heard what she was thinking, two equally strange ideas laid overtop each other, contradictorily at odds. Grandma's double voice with Miss Rainbow whispering underneath, translating the unspoken:

A god's lover,

Husband to
two gods at once,
And your own lover's
Killer.

Fear spiked down through Rook at those last four words, a shooting metallic pain. He looked down at the ashy remains of the conjured cob, and it was almost a relief to realize how sick he still felt at the thought of Chess hurt, dying. Let alone—

"So." Grandma reached up, prodding his cheek, and brought it away wet. "If you do still care, this much . . . then there may yet be a way to save you both. A way to live in Balance, without one of you devouring the other—if you are willing to pay the price."

"What . . . price?"

"There is a binding," Grandma said, "that makes a circle of two willing *Hataalii*. It sets their power to feed each upon each other, a combat which becomes partnership, perfect Balance. Each takes power from the other, and is instantly restored by the power they have taken. They may then live together, so long as chance permits."

Rook blinked. "Doesn't sound so—"

"*Listen*, fool: they *may* live, I said. But not as *Hataalii*."

It took a long time for Rook to find the words. But even when he said them, they sounded meaningless—ridiculous.

"You mean give up the hexation. Both of us."

Grandmother didn't move, even to nod—so Rook leaned forward instead, barely aware that some range of motion was beginning to return. "But . . . not permanently, right? You *can* break it, when you need to. . . ."

I could live with that, his mind gibbered to itself; Chess need never know what he didn't already suspect. Keep the law's eyes off each other, mask themselves to stay safe then unsheathe the power only when absolutely necessary, a lock-boxed magic shotgun.

And now Grandmother *did* shake her head, of course. Dashing all his hopes with one simple word: "No. It can be broken, yes. Once broken . . . never remade. Because the power, once bound and balanced, cannot be divided again. It must go with one or the other.

And the one left empty . . ."

. . . dies. Anyhow.

"Did you really think there would be no price?" Grandmother asked, after long silence—more honestly curious than contemptuous, for once. "Even foolish as you are, have you really learned so little?"

No, thought Rook, numbly. *Knew there'd be one, 'cause there always is. Just—not* this.

Take away the magic, and Reverend Rook was just a fallen preacher turned outlaw, gone in one fell swoop from demigod to dirty joke. Everything Rook had been, he had thrown away for hexation's sake. If he gave *that* up, what was left?

But then again . . . *Chess* would be losing more than he knew, too: his miraculous marksmanship, lizard-swift recovery from wounds and such. Hell, even the slow-burning brightness that turned men's heads might drain away, leaving nothing behind but a too-pretty little man with a too-bad attitude, no longer fit for his formerly natural-born twin occupations of shooting and screwing. Could he ever forgive Rook, if he learned the Reverend had bargained away what made *him* special? Even if it saved his life?

If neither of us were hexes, could we even stand *each other?*

Grandma still held him down, a hundred ghost-hands 'round his throat, unwilling to give him even the slightest chance to refuse. Like she didn't trust him far as she could throw him—by magical means, or otherwise—to not want both his cake and eat it too.

Knew him pretty well, all told, considerin' how recently they'd met.

". . . no," he managed, at last, then coughed hard and spit, half-expecting to see a chunk of lung in the sputum. "I think—not."

Grandmother's brow, already hard-rucked, threw up fresh lines. "What?"

He could see it in her eyes, again—that brief flash of weary sympathy. *Oh, grandson, do not make me* make *you do right—*

Don't worry, lady. You won't get the opportunity.

"I accept," he said, out loud. And—not to *Grandma.*

Then saw her draw breath to protest, just barely—begin to,

anyhow. But the answer was already returned before the old woman could even complete the action, through channels so obscure he had to strain to even perceive them fully: a tintinnation, borne by dust and blood.

That silver no-voice, so sweet and dry and dreadful: **husband, husband, yes**

(you will not regret this)

No? Rook thought. Then: *Probably not, no. Knowin' me.*

And—back to Grandmother, still caught in that half-tick of timelessness, her brown face turning purple. Rook felt her influence fall away, probably only accelerating as her head grew lighter, her eyes stung and swum. It occurred to him that putting her out of her misery sooner rather than later would be a truly Christian mercy.

And the glow starting to leak from every pore, laid overtop her lines like a badly exposed plate, emulsion popped and bleeding black light . . . all *that* wouldn't have the slightest bit to do with him feeling oh-so-forgiving, would it? The magnetic pull of one hex for another, increased thousandfold by proximity to death.

A departure-born mutual arrival, rape and sex combined, with only one still left standing to savour the doubled load. . . .

Oh Jesus, it's not like that. Can't be. I just want—I don't—I don't hate her that much.

The Lady, then, in reply—triggering her Traps, flicking shut her Snares, with him a mere struggling fly at her web's sticky heart:

But she would have done the same to you, given half a chance. For all her talk of sacrifice and Balance, of Doing Right, she is our kin, her hungers the very same. Would you refuse a meal offered in starvation, on moral grounds?

Embrace what you are; take her defeat, my gift to you. Grow strong, to shelter him from your needs. Then find your way back to me, at last, and give me—in turn—due payment.

I'll do it before Chess has time to manifest, Rook thought, *to Become himself—'cause oh, but he'll burn and shine, shed light so hard it hurts to look, a bonfire of bones. Gotta pay her back before that, or there'll be great feasting indeed, on that day. . . .*

So: done deal. He took a step, grabbed his "Grandma" by one braid, brought his free hand up instinctively, and *plunged* it somehow through her chest, elbow-deep—not into gristle or grue, but right into the seed-sac of boiling energy she carried 'round her heart.

Saw her grimace and *almost* cry out, and "heard" someone else—many someone elses?—call back, in answer: a vague sympathetic notion, her solitary hurt multiplied and reflected, fragmentary, fleeting. And along with it, the realization that she herself was severing this contact, breaking it off mid-stream before he could think to back-trace it—crying out (a warning? an order?) in her own language, all trace of English kicked to the wayside.

Gone, now, with only they—*three*—left.

Rook sucked hard, piggish, already brim-full of everything which had made Grandma *her*, and slid hid hand down even further, with a wet, hot *crack*, to touch her heart's fluttering meat-lump through broken ribs. There was a last rising sigh, warming him to his own hollow core—the sound a coal makes when it cracks across, releasing a last rush of embers.

"You *are* . . . a monster," Grandma told him, painfully, blood leaking from her mouth. "*Bilagaana* with a Bible . . . your One-God tells you this whole world is yours, so you . . . think that means you can use it up, throw it away. That all things conspire to serve you."

And now *she* spat, hot and sizzling, to scar the ground. "Such *shit*. If I could help that boy of yours drain you dry before you get the chance to do the same to him . . . teach him to dance with your heart in his mouth, as one should, after slaying foulness . . . then I would. I *would*."

Rook didn't try to deny it. Just shrugged, and answered, "Well . . . that's kinda what I thought, all along."

One more wrench, and she was emptied—he saw her spirit pass him by obliquely, a star falling the wrong way.

Rook just stood there panting, and watched.

Damnation didn't feel so bad, on consideration; not bad as he'd feared, anyhow. Felt like, well—nothing, mostly.

Which was probably why it gave him not a moment's pause when all Grandmother's blood humped itself up and sprayed blowhole-high to form a geyserish pillar—the midtop of which bowed slightly, spread outwards in a cowl, to let a too-familiar face push through.

Rook gave the Lady a stiff little bow. "Ma'am," he said.

Little king, my affianced. It does me good to see you, face to face.

"Likewise."

We are allies now, after all. Such courtesy is the least I owe you.

"'Spect you're right," Rook agreed.

Go back to your lover, now, she instructed him. *Do not feed overmuch from him, if he can help it. Just keep yourselves alive and free, until you find a way to speak with me directly.*

Rook frowned. "But—how'm I supposed to—"

Oh, it will come to you. It comes even now, as we speak. Have faith, husband—as I have faith in you. The blood-face smiled, too full of sly glee to bother approximating anything recognizable as human, any longer. *You knew how to do that, once. . . .*

With that, the inevitable wind whipped up—pillar boiling back to dust with nauseating speed, a pale red cloud which blew away, leaving him alone, in silence.

Sighing, the Reverend turned back for Bewelcome, and Chess.

CHAPTER THIRTEEN

Things went quicker, after that—like every other foregone conclusion.

Rook returned to find Chess still waiting for him in Bewelcome's frozen ruins, even more parched and sunburnt than he otherwise might have been, due to the salt's coruscating glare. Hardly the best place for any redhead to linger, let alone one who'd apparently fallen asleep—or lightly comatose, perhaps, after what Rook later worked out had been near two weeks of dehydration—with his shirt spread out under him, to keep the ground from rubbing his back raw.

Two days, from Rook's point of view. One less fourteen, for everybody else. But that was magic for you, he thought, idly—ten pounds of trouble in a five-pound sack.

Rook drew a stream up from beneath the lumpy white crust, cracking it open 'til the fresh water bubbled free, and fed it to Chess a fingertip at a time, for fear he'd puke and die. Then hoisted his slack weight high, carried him over to the same hill they'd once stood on and kicked it open, creating a cave. Since the trip hadn't drained him overmuch, Rook was still so stuffed-full of stolen power he felt bloated as a tick—like he just *had* to use it, or pop.

Inside the cave, he nursed Chess through a day and night more of fever, flensing his lover's burnt skin away gently throughout, onion-careful. Beneath the worst of it a fine new layer of skin had already re-grown, bright pink, painfully smooth and sensitive to the touch.

Ignoring its delicacy, Rook folded Chess close and refused to let go, even when he cursed and kicked and bit—dripped the run-off from Grandma's legacy into Chess's mouth along with their kisses 'til the energy he was giving out began to return to him, as Chess's fierceness rekindled. Eventually, the blaze of him rose to such an intoxicating level that Rook had to rein in hard, pry free of Chess's grip and leave him sleeping, lest hex-hunger tempt him to push the little pistoleer back over the edge and suck him dry once more . . . permanently, this time.

When the sun set, the cave stayed warm—an oven-stone cut to just fit two, so long as they lay close. Chess's skin had firmed to the point of cooling, his sweat no longer smelling of anything but itself. So it came as no grand surprise that when—as though to celebrate his escape from death—Chess curled a bit further into Rook's chest, slid one hand down the front of Rook's flies, and commenced digging for treasure.

At the cusp, however, he suddenly opened his green eyes wide, staring at Rook as though he were a dream conjured to offputting life. Like he'd never thought to see him again outside of sleep, and wasn't too sure how he felt about finding himself proved wrong, even under such delirious circumstances. And the next morning, while Rook was pissing in the scrub, Chess came wavering out after him, barely able to stand—weak as a newborn colt, but with guns still a-droop from either hand, cocked and ready.

"You son of a bitch," he said. "You son of a *bitch*."

Rook tucked himself away, and turned to face the music. "Don't you slander my Mama just 'cause *yours* ain't worth a damn, Chess Pargeter," he replied.

"You left me behind, when I told you Goddamn not to. *One* fuckin' thing I told you, *one*. And . . . you went ahead and *left* me."

"But *I came back*."

To which, a breathless moment on, Chess gave only a hoarse cry for answer—and fell, headlong, into Rook's open arms.

They found Hosteen back at Splitfoot's, drinking himself incontinent, perhaps as a crude form of mourning them both. Rook and Chess came in with the hot breath of the desert still on them, and once they recognized exactly *who* was letting in the flies, the bulk of the barflies leapt back—not just 'cause they remembered all Chess had done the last time he was there, either.

Hosteen turned at the sound, gaping. "*I wanted t'stay!*" he yelled out, voice a whole octave higher than usual. "T'look after him, like you said! He wouldn't let me!"

Rook: "I know, Kees."

"*Shot* at me, point-blank, wouldn't let up! 'Til I ran, yeah . . . but that was 'cause I just *had* to, honest, Rev! He'd'a killed me for sure, else!"

Chess laughed. "Hell, I already *told* him all this, you old fool. Ain't nobody here holds a grudge."

Rook pulled a pair of chairs out from around the nearest table, settling himself down in a third. "So there: all's forgiven," he concluded. "Now sit, Kees, 'fore you go ass-over-teakettle. 'Cause if you're really all we got left for a gang, seems we got plannin' to do."

"Need to find us a nice, fat strike, first off," Chess said. "And if you want to pay me back for leavin' me all that time in the sun, I'm gonna need new clothes."

"Oh, we'll get them for you, all right—store-bought, tailor-made. You'll be fine."

"Sounds expensive."

Rook smiled again, wider—"Anything for *you*, darlin'."

After news of Bewelcome spread, other bad men either flocked to join up, tried to take Rook and his newly resplendent lieutenant on directly, or got the hell out of their way. Rook paid little attention, letting Hosteen handle such affairs. He had Chess, and Chess had him. Familiar now with the feel of power's thirst for power, from both sides of the circuit, Rook found himself able to control the flow from Chess to him more finely—slow it to a trickle, enough so that Chess seemed well-able to replenish himself, without ever noticing the loss. Grandma's education had been good for that much, at the very least.

1865 slid over into '66 in a haze of loot and murder, the seasons indistinct in the desert dust, and the Smoking Mirror drew ever closer. Vague rumours of pursuit, by army or locals, rarely came to anything much. Whenever the Railway wasted their money to hire Pinkertons, Chess killed them, with or without Rook's help. Claimed he had a nose for that sort of stink, and that usually proved true.

So yes, Rook found himself startled when Hosteen brought Ed Morrow by, 'round about Christmas of '66. He said he'd found the tall man moping at the back of yet another Border-bar, looking for dishonest work. One glance told Rook Morrow was a Pinkerton, almost down to the number on his badge—sent in Bewelcome's wake, more to gather information and assess the sort of threat could reduce an entire township to Dead Sea salt, than as any sort of inside man placed to save fellow agents from the Wrath of Pargeter. But the funny part was, Chess's sharp eyes skipped over Morrow, like he'd been wax-coated.

Another hex's influence? Intriguing, if so. But Rook knew it didn't matter, in the final go-'round. Things were much too far along already, for that.

"Glad to make your acquaintance, Ed," was all he'd said.

My oracles tell me you must seek this grim Lady who sends you her dreams at the Place of Dead Roads, Songbird had told him back in 'Frisco, once Morrow was off looking for Chess. Adding: *And do not rush to demand of me where that* is, *Reverend—that business is for you and she alone, to settle between you. But though she may not want exactly what you want, your wishes do* coincide; *she will certainly take you there, if you only allow her to lead.*

Granted, he hadn't felt too inclined to believe her, right then— with her still drawing energy from him in crackling bursts, the way a church's weathervane draws lightning. So he'd quoted on Jericho City and pulled Selina Ah Toy's down around her, easy as stamping on an anthill . . . but taken the Smoking Mirror with him nonetheless, all the same. 'Cause Christ knew, he'd damn well earned it.

And then, finally—leaving Chess safely asleep, with Morrow set to watch over him, or get shot as a damn Pink—Rook had left the Two Sisters without a backward glance, moving so quickly his boots barely skimmed the desert floor. Above, the moon shone on, dead as Judas. It was almost full.

You'll have to do something about that, little king.

"I *know*," he said, out loud. "Heard you the first time, woman."

I know you did . . . husband.

Funny how even with both hands in his head, Songbird still hadn't been able to figure how it was no mystery at all to Rook where this Place of Dead Roads might lie. 'Cause—where was the single deadest place he'd ever stood? Only the place he'd killed what little good was left in himself, with Chess's unknowing help.

And here it was now, glistening bright beneath a spray of stars, like granulated marble: Bewelcome. Where Rook touched down lightly, skidding a bit, 'til his heels snagged in salt, then flipped open his coat's front flap, and took out the Smoking Mirror's uneven black disc.

He held it up high, balanced in both hands—thumbs and forefingers gripping its outer edges, the rest curved for additional support, a shallow flesh funnel—before angling it to fit neatly overtop the moon itself, like a cold iron skillet-lid.

A moment later, darkness came scuttling along the desert's floor to engulf all in its path, from east-west to north-south, the way a photographer's black cloth reduces the world to nothing but an upside-down reflection trapped inside a box. And the moon's whole light was dowsed at once, in horrid sympathy.

We call that an eclipse, he told the Rainbow Lady, arms still extended, already beginning to ache. *When it happens naturally, that is.*

Even in this darkness, though, he could see her shake her head—that stiff coronal of hair slicing the air, axe-heavy, like she could make it bleed.

But—there is nothing natural about such things, little king, in any event. When tizitzimime eat the sun and moon, horror follows: fields fall fallow, water sickens, unborn children wither. Bats fly up out of an empty cave, spreading disease and death.

Rook snorted. *Sure they do,* he thought, mostly to himself. But when she laughed as though he'd made a particularly witty quip, he knew the truth at last: there wasn't one single thought left inside him, about anything, he could truly call his own.

It was . . . oddly freeing.

There, he told her. *Done. Now what?*

The words came back on the wind, night-scented, from infinite distances. Saying, only—**Watch. And wait.**

He did.

And finally, from the north-east . . . someone came walking, out of the dark.

It was a woman, full-grown and full-figured, well-made as a statue. Her fine features were stamped in a mould which might mark her anything from Navaho to Mex, skin copper-sheened, and from the unconscious swing of her hips and the sureness of her light-shod feet, Rook reckoned that—on any other given day—she would have stepped proudly even here, in the midst of this desperate solitude.

But there was something *wrong* with her overall, visible from a fair distance off—a wounded gait, with two hectic spots blazing at her cheekbones. Her skirt itself seemed stiff, stained darkly 'round where her belt should lie, while a kerchief had been thrust down her shirt-front to cushion her swollen, leaking breasts. Her dark hair was braided back haphazardly, the part frankly crooked. Both eyes sat in shadows so deep they seemed bruised.

Childbed fever, maybe. Or something more: cholera, smallpox. Dying anyhow, probably.

You just keep on tellin' yourself that, "Rev," he thought.

Though she was already looking straight at him, it seemed to take the woman a moment or so to realize he was actually there.

She cleared her throat, licked sticky lips and asked: ". . . who *are* you?"

But Rook just shook his head, by way of an answer; after the fiasco with Grandma, he wouldn't be makin' *that* mistake again. Assuring her instead, as gently as he could—"Doesn't matter. You come a long way?"

She half-shook her head, half-shivered, teeth chattering audibly. "Far enough. But I . . ."

And here a fresh uncertainty clouded her stare, drawing it back down to both outspread hands. They were muddy from palms to wrists, nails choked with dirt, like she'd been digging without a shovel.

". . . had a dream," she told him, finally. "A woman—she told me where to come."

I'll just bet she did, Rook thought, wishing he felt worse over this nameless sacrifice-to-be's obvious plight, her probable fate. Yet all he could summon, by this point, was a sort of random ethical weariness, too shallow to reach anything that counted.

You know what to do, husband, the Lady reminded him.

"I . . . don't know why I'm *here*, is all," said the woman. "You know?"

Rook bowed his head, and shot her his most trustworthy smile. "Yes, ma'am. I can well understand how frightening that must be, for you. But it's okay, because . . ."

. . . I do.

CHAPTER FOURTEEN

Up from Mictlan-Xibalba, a crack came extending by slow degrees, like the first small tear in a rolled snake's egg—splitting, re-splitting, fine and flexible as dead woman's hair. Meeting on its way with the same artesian wellspring Rook had teased forth once before, it washed the earth beneath their feet free of salt to form a mucky circle 'round himself and the woman, roughly twelve feet in diameter, like it'd been measured out with a pair of coffins for compasses.

Then the crack's furthest finger opened up a smallish hole right in the off-centre of this depression, through which—while they both watched, with similar fascination—a dark tendril poked and furled, coiling the way kudzu does, pumping with evil juice. A quarter-breath, and it had swelled cock-thick. A half-, and it bloomed big as a big man's wrist. Three breaths later, a young sapling.

Bark like unclean fur, leaves quill-sharp, pine-needles from a giant's Christmas wreath. The tree spread itself out above them, its low-slung limbs hung with vines so heavy they reminded Rook of nothing so much as serpents. But its fruit did shine: satin-silvery, casting light down on the woman's face as she stared upwards, mouth open, wondering—a thin rain of glitter, spores heavy with sleep, and dreams.

Open your mouth, little king; she teeters on the brink. We must be careful how we steer her, if the right outcome is to be obtained. Speak only the words I send you.

No help for it, then. At all.

"This tree—" Rook began.

155

"Beautiful," the woman agreed. "What do they call it?"

"*Yaxche*. Tree of Heaven. It's a . . . calabash, I think. But that ain't the point."

"No."

"Point is—you want to die. That's why you came here, right?"

She looked down again, as if shamed—at her weeping dress-front, the mess between her thighs turning her hem to rust. Whispered, mouth barely moving: "Yes."

"Well, then . . . there you go."

He pointed to the tree, which was already letting down a helpful extra length of vine—close-plaited, easy to tie, hard to break. A hangman's rope.

"That's a sin, though," she said; more of a question than a statement, going strictly by intonation. Like she was hoping he'd try and talk her out of it.

Wasn't as though that was a strict impossibility, either, it suddenly struck Rook. Sure, the woman'd come out to Bewelcome on her own, who knew how far. No food or water with her that he could see, which meant—if he was to give in to a foolish impulse of mercy—he'd have to waste most of the latest jolt he'd sucked from Chess on healing her alone. But then he'd be so weak, even if he did get her back to a place half-civilized, the citizens there'd simply shoot him where he stood once the first of them put a name to his notorious face. Scatter his brains, burn his body, atomize him beyond even Lady Rainbow's recall . . . if she didn't kill him herself, long before, for breaking faith with their subterranean compact.

You cannot save her, little king. As you know, in your bones.

No. And . . . yes.

We are complicit in this, husband, as in all things else. Is that not the meaning of marriage?

Not really, not for everybody. But then—*I ain't everybody.*

"What's your name?" he asked the woman, on further impulse.

"Adaluz," she replied, the terminal "zee" a faint "th" lisp—but didn't ask him his in return, as one might've thought only polite. Then again, it probably wasn't anything she particularly cared to know, right at this very instant.

"Mexican, huh?" No reply. "Well, leave that by. You cleave still to the Holy Roman Catholic faith, Adaluz?"

". . . I did . . ."

"Yeah, 'course. But that was before God killed your child, right? Or—let *you* kill it."

She took the implication straight to the jaw, slap-hard, with barely a flinch. Just kept her gaze locked fast to that half-born noose, its tail already curling in on itself, forming an unslippable knot for her convenience. Her mouth gave a twist, skewing a drawn purse-string way that rendered her entire pretty face a badly sewn mask.

Matthew, *2:18*, Rook couldn't stop himself from thinking. *In Rama was there a voice heard, lamentation, and weeping, and great mourning, Rachel weeping for her children, and would not be comforted, because they are not.*

"I can't *reach* it," was all sad Miss Ada said, at length, hopelessly. "It's . . . too high for me."

"Well, I can help you with that, ma'am. I mean—I'm surely tall enough to spot you a lift. Ain't I?"

A long, wet sniff. Then, with her tear-blurred voice even softer than her words' slight Spanish tinge could make it—"You're very kind, *señor.*"

"Oh, no such thing, darlin'. No such thing."

He went down on one knee in the salt, like he meant to propose, and cupped his hands in a makeshift stirrup. *Step up, now, honey, 'fore you change your mind. Best to strike while the iron's hot.*

She did.

And then . . . stood there a second more with one foot up, one foot down, like she couldn't decide whether she wanted on or off this dirt-bound ride, after all. Listened quiet, while Rook mouthed the "hey, rube!" spiel his Lady dictated, from her sodden, death-stink home. How there was nothin' to any fine degree wrong with stretching your own neck, if the circumstances warranted. How this tree was a gallows grown for Adaluz alone, to end her pain and see her set up on high for all to gawk at, a new constellation of loss fixed at the very apex of an empty black sky. No need to think it over, since in Rainbow's suicide paradise her child would be returned to her, whole and grown, to live by her side forever—

"You'll never want for anything again, either of you," he told her, throat dust-dry. "No hunger . . . no fear. Woman who dies of childbirth, God smiles on her, something fierce. Her baby too. You're a pair of soldiers who went down fightin', and there's not much more honourable than that."

"No," she said, eyes tight-shut, head shaking like palsy, like fever. Like the only way she could keep herself from stopping was to turn eyelids and brain inside-out, and slip into voluntary blindness like a hangman's all-too-welcome hood. "There isn't, is there?"

Rook shook his head right back at her, even knowing full well she couldn't see him do it. It was that, or scream.

Adaluz reached up, face abruptly slick with tears, La Llorona herself; the tree reached down to meet her halfway, wrapping itself helpfully tight 'neath her chops. And when Rook let his clasp part at last, she didn't even struggle—just hung there, slack yet straining, 'til her own weight broke that throat-bone Rook knew so well, long after midnight but longer still before dawn.

'Til her lips crept back, bruising blue, and her tongue ground bloody between two uneven rows of small white teeth. 'Til a weak little spurt of piss ran down her legs to splatter on the ground, washing the profane circle even wider.

Oh, this better *all be worth it, in the end,* Rook thought. *'Cause if it's not—by God,* all *gods, I deserve every damn thing I get.*

Rook watched her sway to and fro a span, continent-slow—her skin warm enough, yet, to mist just a bit, against the cold night air—before laying the Smoking Mirror carefully on the wet ground beneath her, so that her shadow crossed over it on the very next swing, crossed and then *locked* to it, impossibly fast. With only the key-in-lock *click* of an opening door as accompaniment, along with a rumble that might be thunder, if thunder normally came from down rather than up.

That Hell-deep crack, opening wider. Yawning to send a fresh new wad of darkness sprout forth, lolling, a wet black tongue.

Say my name now, husband, while her heart's precious blood stays hot. Say it, out loud.

"I don't *know* your name," Rook snarled. But his mouth opened yet one more time, and he heard the alien syllables spill out, burning his throat the way bile does, when you vomit—a mouthful of foulness. Bones boiled to burnt stock.

She *of the Rope*

She *of the Traps*

She *of the Snares*

Lady **Rainbow**

Suicide *Moon*

Psychopomp **Mother**

Eclipse's Bride

Ix

 Tab

   Ix*Chel*

     Yx*Tabay***Tlaz***TleOtl***CoYoTl****ax***Qhui***Chal***Ch***iuh***Tlicue**

All of them, and none of them—or just the first. Or—maybe not. Or—

The baroque chorale echo of it took Rook from inside, a tin hornet's nest shook hard and set ringing, hammering, buzzing, poisonous-sweet and *painful*, shit, *so fucking painful.* . . .

He fell to his knees, which was probably where she liked him best. Pawed and beat at his own head like it was a nut he was trying to crack, as the mirror winked open—a staring eye, a hole. As it stretched itself to let a veritable snake-bag of new tresses burst forth, geyser up the tree's trunk and swarm down the rope, cocooning Adaluz's corpse in black: a silk-drop seed-pod, heavy and full and *ripe.*

Only to tear itself open, thread by thread, and let her fall free once more, hitting the ground beneath in a feral crouch—with such *impact*, the eclipse itself shattered, leaving the moon unscathed and coldly shining once more above. Shining, the way her eyes—

and teeth—did, as she caught Rook by the chin and grinned, before crushing his mouth to hers. Like brightly polished bone.

"Oh, little king," she said, tearing at his buttons, pinning him wide with her hard-muscled legs and screwing herself right down on top of him, regardless of wounds or muck—not even pausing to wipe the filth from her loins as she hiked her vehicle's dress high, naked and unafraid. "I'm cold, cold so long . . . *so* long. Warm me, now. *Warm* me."

I'll do no such thing, Rook wanted to say—meant to, anyhow. *Call me "husband" all you want, don't make it so. Don't remember gettin' fitted for any ring with you, either, just 'cause we once had carnal knowledge of each other in a* dream—

Far too late for such equivocations, though.

She pressed him down with both palms on his chest, punch-hard, like she aimed to leave bruises with her fingers—rode him the way he'd seen Chess break horses which truly *were* three times his size, with a sneer at the very idea of being trampled. He was glued fast to her, every point of entry a brand-new orifice, ripped wide and gasping. Behind them, the tree was already folding itself back to the ground, dissolving into her unseen dragonfly-wing train—used once and then discarded, with not even a shred of regret. Her hair was in his mouth, waterfalling over his eyes in a septic blindfold—arousing and dreadful, a charnel aphrodisiac.

Her cheek pressed to his, a strange little pit starting to open at its very centre, twisting so sharp he could *feel* it form, without even having to watch: a black spiral raw as a new tattoo, the colour of decay. Her breath already in his lungs, incense-laden, hotter than a furnace. To try not to breathe it would be to suffocate.

Horror and desire, too mixed by far to separate. She yanked his own palm up to span her neck, collarbone to collarbone, arrogant against possible treachery; he could've strangled her one-handed, and she knew it. The same way she knew he never would.

"Call me Ixchel, *husband,*" she commanded. And ground his sensitized skin against where the rope's puffy burn bulged, flaking—where what had once been poor Adaluz's pulse fluttered and skirled, flushing the damage brightly. Saying, "See, here: *I* have let blood too, to show you my good faith. We match now, you and I."

Not your *blood to let,* Rook thought, eyes rolling back. But his scar was tightening in sympathy—a vascular choir singing, red and salt, washing him away, where no one but she could follow.

Oh, Chess is really gonna kill *me, once he finds out. Though that's only if he does, and she don't kill me first.*

Fuck it, though.

Reverend Rook growled at his own hypocrisy, hard enough to hurt, like every damn thing else about these supernatural shenanigans. Then flipped them both, to at least give himself the *impression* of being on top—and let her have her way.

Later, clothes re-ordered, they stepped out together beneath the salt-encrusted lintel of Love's church, back into the moon's harsh purview. It shone down on Bewelcome, illimitable and pure, the same way it once had on the dark-stained marble steps of Tenochtitlan, and both of them cast stunted black shadows beneath its too-bright light—though Rook's did stretch far longer than Ixchel's, to be sure. And seemed far less divided.

"Thought that was just s'posed to be a way for us to *talk*," he said.

She took a moment's pause, before answering—stretched luxuriantly, every joint cracking, and yawned wide, trying to taste everything at once. "*Aaaah*, the *air*," she murmured. Then: "We have held congress a long time, one way or another, you and I. So I ask—do you know what I want yet, little king?"

"I got some small notion. But I'd really rather hear *you* say it."

She—*Ixchel*—nodded Adaluz's head, black hair disordered and enticing. "What I want is what I had. What *you* want is for what you already have to last forever. You fear Hell, and rightly. I live there. So you have seen."

"Yes."

"You know I speak truth, then. As all gods must."

"Uh huh. If *that*'s even true—'cause not havin' met as many as you, I can't really tell. You ain't *my* God, lady. I don't know you from a hole in the ground."

A shrug. "Then I will enlighten you. It costs me nothing."

Stepping lightly into the circle again, she sat, cross-legged, and patted the wet dirt next to her. He lowered himself down across from her, by aching degrees, assumed a similar posture—like she was 'bout to spin some schoolyard tall tale, and with probably just as much weight to it. But then again, why *would* she lie?

Hell, why *wouldn't* she? *To get her way, fool. Same as everybody else.*

"Once there was a girl of the Mexica—that great empire which once lay to the south, where those lands you call Mexico are now. Her name I no longer recall. She was born without flaw, and raised to pay her family's debt to the gods until—one day—her mother took her to the temple. She was to be *cihuatlamacazque*, a god's wife. The girl lived her days in endless prayer, letting blood each morning into the sacred brazier, so that the perfume of it rose up to please her husband-to-be—He By Whom We Live, Enemy of Both Sides, who the Maya called God K. He who the Mexica called . . . Smoking Mirror.

"But one night the moon was eaten, and the people cried out in horror. Such a thing was too dreadful to let stand; the star-devils and small female gods might burn back onto the earth without the moon to prevent them, snatching up children and eating them. In their despair, however, a god—perhaps even the Enemy himself—whispered in the temple *cluazvacuilli's* ear that she should select the girl who shone brightest and persuade her to allow herself to be sacrificed. Then the moon would return. And this was done.

"That girl Became me, little king, and then I Became myself—again and again, I Became. She was not the first, though she brought me forth at last from the Maya gallery of gods to the Mexica one . . . re-embodied, alive once more to receive my due, to eat the precious blood spilled in *my* name from then on. To choose my *ixtiptla* for beauty and strength, accept their willing deaths and clothe myself in their bodies, over and over—as you see." She ran both careless hands down Adaluz's curves at once, proprietary, shivering slightly at the feel. "Neither the first . . . nor the last."

Rook nodded, for lack of anything better to offer. *Keep talkin'*, he thought.

"I do not know why Smoking Mirror did what he did for me, even now. Perhaps, since he loves to fight, all he wanted was a worthy opponent. Yet I cannot complain, for certainly I profited from it. Because I was one of the oldest of the gods, one of the smallest—because my cult was eaten away by time and forgetfulness—I endured even after the Steel Hats came with their One-God babble, when the greatest of the new began to fade away. They thought me no threat at all, until they were too weakened to offer me resistance. And then, after we had sunk back down into the Ball-Court once more to wait for renewal, there in the dark when all other gods forgot even their own names—"

"You hunted them down, and ate them. Took their juice, like Grandma tried to do with me. Didn't you."

"I did. And why are you so sure?"

"'Cause . . . that's what I'd've done."

She smiled. "See, then: we do understand each other."

Darkness above, yet far greyer, the moon starting to fade. Darkness below, all but infinite.

"My blood was shed by those who wanted gods," Ixchel told Rook, "and so I became one. I fed the engine, as it fed me. But as you are now, so once was I."

"The engine?"

She laid one hand over his eyes, death-cool enough to make him shudder. "This world, with all its pleasures, its wellspring of misery—light and heat expressed through blood, the only fuel strong enough to keep everything going. Look."

See:

A green, steaming jungle or an arid plain. Both. Maybe. Or neither. White cities rearing up huge as Egypt's pyramids, their sides gingerbread chalet-stepped, plastered with gleaming lime—all but their central staircases, each one the shining metaphorical fulcrums of this alien word, atop which sat kings so hung with jade and gold they could barely move, surrounded by priests in huge, nodding masks and feather-cloaks, dancing, drumming, speaking in tongues. And wooden-armoured warriors carrying swords fringed with black glass, dragging endless coffles of prisoners tied at the neck and wrists: grist for the mill, meat for the altar-stone.

The same four moves, over and over, done until no part of the whole seems *real* as the whole itself, the object of all this sanguine worship. The dance which does not—*cannot*—stop, or the whole universe dies with it.

Cut the victim free, press him (or her) down. Let them rave with prophecy, the gods' favour. Feed them *pulque*, that they may die drunk and happy, giving themselves over wholly.

With your stone knife, slice across the front of the chest starting between the second and third rib, cutting across the breastbone to the opposite side. After, break the bone transversely, with a sharp blow and a chisel. A gaping hole opens, exposing the lungs, which deflate like moonflowers at dawn.

While the heart continues to beat, reach into the chest and sever the arteries and veins. Grasp the organ, and lift it from its bloody cradle to the sky.

The blood is then deposited in a green bowl with a feathered rim, into which a hollow cane—also feathered—is placed. Through this reed, the gods suck their nourishment.

Again, and again, and yet again. Without cessation. Until those once-white stairs run red and slick and steaming, a gigantic gutter of constantly shed grue.

A machine, Rook thought, forced to consider it through her eyes, but still able to retain his modern perspective. *Men as parts, blood as oil. Cogs and wheels.*

To which she replied, equally silent: *Show me this . . . machine.* Then added, once he had—*Ah. Yes. Very like that, yes.*

So that was the world she wanted to bring about again, in a nutshell—the Mayan-Aztec Death Factory, a cotton gin of severed heads and heart-smoke, built on whitewashed bones. And he was going to help her do it, he supposed. Not so much in order to get what he wanted as . . . not lose what he had.

"Look you, little king—our reign was long. Four worlds came and went, cracked to pieces beneath us. We were well-fed indeed. A thousand thousand fellow magicians died unborn, their powers unrealized, to help keep us alive. But instead we grew fat, we quarrelled, we squabbled—like children, but with less reason. We could never bridle ourselves to work together, even at the very end . . . which is the only way your Steel Hats and desert-prophet howlers ever overcame us. We fell down to the Sunken Ball-Court, a dreamy morass, all blended together, and now we do not even recall who we once were, let alone how we might Become again. But the one great truth which watching four worlds come and go has taught me, is how that which *is* dead need not *be* dead forever, if the right sacrifices can only be made."

Here she drew a long breath, oddly ragged. Almost sad.

"Yet of a hundred gods, only I—as yet—remain awake, alive," she said, as though to herself. "Only I."

"Not even that Smoking Mirror of yours, huh?"

Remote: "Not even he."

Rook snorted, not overmuch inclined to sympathy. "So you *are* just a ghost, then," he said. "A jumped-up Goddamn ghost, nothin' more. You're *me*, savin' the meat."

"Oh, but I am far more than *that*, husband. Now that I have fed on my betters, if not my elders, I am six gods at once—two more than Smoking Mirror himself—and the very least of them is far beyond *your* comprehension. You have heard their names already, remember?

"*Ixtab*, Mother of all Hanged Men . . . she was the one who first made contact with you, who reeled you up and hooked you in. *Ixchel*, Suicide Moon, Lady Rainbow—she of the Ropes and Snares—bound you fast, spun her web around you, anchored you in time and space. *Yxtabay*, She of the Long Hair, drew you into the wilderness, to tie you tight in desire's meshes, with *Tlazteotl* Filth-eater ready at her left hand to redeem you of all the sins you've committed in love's name—to eat them up, then shit them back out. Then comes *Coyotlaxqhui*, the Broken Moon, who opened the door to bring me up into your world. And *Chalchiuhtlicue* herself, with her spinning serpent skirt, is the womb that birthed me into flesh once more, the way she births and re-births the whole world. The way she drowned the last sun in order to make way for this one, which will shiver itself apart in earthquake and calamity."

Rook looked at her askance. "The fuck you . . . look, shit. *Look*, now . . ." His words ran out. Then, weakly: ". . . I never asked for *any* of this."

Another laugh. "Did you not? Well, it does not matter. You were to hand—the perfect instrument. Your utility will yet exalt us both."

She laid her cool palm on him again, this time at temple, and let her silver voice's tone drop accordingly, slow and soothing, murmuring, plausibly, "You want to keep your own power, as is understandable. Yet you want to save your lover, too—from himself. From *you*. The old woman lied to you, little king, perhaps without knowing it. Nothing must be given up. These things are not incompatible, so long as one of the magicians involved is—something more."

"And how would *that* happen, exactly?"

"A man who beds with a goddess becomes a god, or dies. Or both."

"Oh, is that so? Well, I don't think I'm much cut out to be a god, really. Hell, I wasn't even barely fit to serve one, by the end."

"Perhaps. Things might differ, however, were the god you *served* one . . . you already loved."

And at last, all at once, he saw what it was she'd had—always, from the very beginning—in mind.

Not him at all, not ever.

Oh, you cheatin' bitch.

Rook schooled himself hard, and drawled: "Hate to tell you, Moon-lady, but—if you're lookin' in *Chess's* direction, you may not have exactly struck pay-dirt. 'Cause he just ain't much of a one for beddin' women, full stop."

"Oh, all men burn to return to their mother's womb, little king— even your wild boy. Desire has nothing to do with it. The universe's very spark will pull us together; I will mark him as my bridegroom and he will come, raving. Like you, he will be unable to help himself."

"I don't want him hurt," Rook repeated, stubborn. "Or—*to* hurt him."

"But if you *had* to, Reverend, to reap the greatest gain? For both of you?"

He didn't answer—couldn't.

"Aaaah," she breathed once more, hungry as ever. "And that is the god-seed buried in *you*, husband—the deep-laid root of the calabash, poking its way between the rocks and blossoming with succulent fruit. Hun Hunaphu's severed head, crying out amongst the bark and leaves to be born again, at any cost."

Rook closed his eyes. And thought, helpless: *The gods are chosen for their youth, their beauty. They live on blood and worship.*

Chess could do that. He'd be happy with people fearing him, as always, and even happier with people having to *love* him, or the sun goes out.

(In the machine, one cog is as good as another.)

She whispered: "The king is priest, too—always. Did I not mention? And as *his* high priest, you would lose nothing. Nothing but blood, in its season."

"I'd give him that anyways, gladly."

"As you say."

His heart beat on, a hammer on flint, drawing sparks.

"What'll I have to do?" Asher Rook asked, at last—eyes kept firmly closed, so he wouldn't have to see the pleasure in Dread Lady Ixchel-Adaluz's awful, answering smile.

That tripping giggle, ringing out—icy, abyssal bells.

"You won't enjoy it, little king," she told him, softly—like that was any sort of news.

Rook sighed. And said: "Tell me anyway."

BOOK THREE: JAGUAR CACTUS FRUIT

March 9, 1867
Month Two, Day Seven House
Moving from Arizona to Mexico City through Mictlan-Xibalba,
along passages sacred to Xiuhtecuhtli, First Lord of the Night

Xiuhtecuhtli, the Old God, is also Huehueteotl, the gatekeeper of Mictlan-Xibalba's tunnels. There he appears as an elderly man, bent over and carrying a brazier, or small stove, on his head.

But sometimes he is accompanied by another: either the Mayan god K'awil, "God K," who is drawn with a sacrificial knife in his forehead and one leg replaced by a snake, or perhaps Tezcatlipoca—the Smoking Mirror—whose right foot is replaced by an obsidian mirror.

Tezcatlipoca is associated with hurricanes, the north, rulership, divination, temptation, jaguars, sorcery, beauty, war. At times he is called Night Wind, Possessor of the Sky and Earth, and—most threateningly—We Are His Slaves.

Tezcatlipoca ruled the first world that ever existed, before it was destroyed by Quetzalcoatl. Quetzalcoatl created the second world, which Tezcatlipoca subsequently destroyed. Yet they worked together to create the fifth and present world, along with their "brothers"—Huitzilpochtli, god of war, and Xipe Totec, the god of maize. These four gods—Tezcatlipoca, Quetzalcoatl, Huitzilopochtli and Xipe Totec—are referred to respectively as the Black, the White, the Blue and the Red Tezcatlipoca.

In fact, some even believe that *all* other gods and goddesses are, ultimately, only aspects of Tezcatlipoca.

CHAPTER FIFTEEN

The morning the gang made Splitfoot Joe's—there to wait for Reverend Rook to join them, just how he'd instructed—Ed Morrow woke up aching, long before everybody else, and crept off into the bushes to do his business. The needle of pain he felt still dug deep in the meat behind one eye wasn't even one splinter as bad as when he'd got caught in the Rev's wards, a mere week previous, but it did have that same very particular stink about it, nonetheless: a spiritual marking, same as Cain's. A hex-bag hangover.

Thrust deep in his waistcoat pocket, the Manifold whirled and chittered, like it aimed to break his rib. Groaning, Morrow dragged the damn thing out and popped it open, then glowered down at the face reflected within its glass-set lid—not exactly unfamiliar, but not *his*, either.

"Rev," he rasped.

"Took you long enough to answer."

Morrow squinted hard through his hurt, which was rapidly spiking worse. "Well . . . sorry, I s'pose. Just not quite used t'this method of communication, as yet."

"Understandable. So—how're the boys? Chess gettin' cranky yet?"

"Like a cat on a Goddamn skillet."

Rook laughed. "Sounds 'bout what I expected. Well, he won't have much longer to fret—won't be but a half-day more 'til you reach Splitfoot's. And once you do, I'll be home before breakfast."

"Okay, that's—good. I guess."

A moment of silence passed, during which Morrow could only

wonder if there was something further—something specific—Rook had expected him to volunteer. Unbidden, his mind jumped back to their last layover, where he'd caught three separate instances of what he now knew must be magic welling up inside Chess, stagnant and explosive, before backing up and leaking out: one new-signed gang member's gun misfiring in practice, blowing off his thumb; eatery plates exploding when the cook dumped a scoop of stew into them; a store windowpane cracking right across as Chess's shadow passed by. In the town's single saloon, Chess had look stank-eye on some fool who'd just taken the trick in a card-game he was barely bothering to play—and when the idjit was dumb enough to grin back, a lamp flared up blue-hot behind him, throwing sparks that set his cards on fire.

The longer Rook wasn't around to siphon it off, that influence Morrow could sometime feel boiling off of Chess at times kept ramping up, fit to blow. And though Chess didn't seem to feel anything beyond ordinary orneriness, overall, something still made him want to keep Morrow close, like a lucky piece—to sit with, drink with, demand jokes from.

It raised Morrow's hackles . . . and Chess's, too, eventually.

"Just what the hell you lookin' so scared of, anyhow?" he snapped, when Morrow failed to meet his eyes directly. "I mean, God damn! Got on fine enough back at the Sisters, didn't we?"

Which was true enough, as far as that went. Trouble was, Morrow knew Chess for a hex now, and couldn't *un*-know it—couldn't stop wanting to treat him careful, no more than cheerfully juggle lit dynamite.

But from Rook's point of view, all of the above was probably just his problem. So Morrow sat tight, keeping whatever trepidations he might have strictly to himself.

"You still there, Ed?" The Reverend asked.

"Yessir."

"Thought I'd lost you, just for a minute."

Oh, how I wish you had, Morrow couldn't keep himself from thinking—then almost jumped upright when he saw Rook smirk, as he did. Then, before he could stop himself, another thought followed: *Christ Almighty! He can't really* hear *inside my head, 'stead of just talk* there . . . *can he? Even this far away?*

"Well . . . that'd be the key question to ponder on, Ed, 'specially in your current position," Rook replied. "Wouldn't it?"

And then, while Morrow stood yet agape, struggling to compose a suitable rejoinder—Rook was simply *gone*, leaving him staring at his own reflection.

The Manifold whirred down within seconds, gave a final death-beetle click, and slept once more.

Legendarily, Splitfoot Joe's had gained its infamously catchy moniker from the axe-split bottom edge of its sign, where (supposedly) the first "Joe" had once painted a bright red cleft foot with a grinning devil standing upon it—a symbol that served, in place of words few of his customers could read, to signify that the saloon was open for business. And since it also stood not five miles from the Mexico border in a conveniently hard-to-find valley, Splitfoot's—along with the town surrounding it—had since become an unofficial way station for cross-border traffic of questionable character, a place with a foot in two lands.

After Chess, Hosteen and the rest—what was left of Reverend Rook's gang, some eight to ten gentlemen of fortune—took up their residence that evening, the task of dickering over rates fell to Morrow, for reasons he found mysterious.

"Okay, we're square," he told Chess, when negotiations were concluded, and passed him the absinthe Joe had thrown in on top. "This here's your bottle, by the by."

Chess nodded, popping the cork. "He try anything?"

"Wanted ten cents on the dollar, but I jewed him down. Nothin' I couldn't handle."

"Yeah, old Joe's a tricksy fucker." Then, contemplating the room through twin scrims of glass and gently sloshing green liquid: "Might be *I* should go have words with him, later, 'fore we get to orderin' up our bill."

Morrow and Hosteen exchanged a glance. Chess had started drinking pretty much the minute they'd left the Two Sisters and hadn't let up yet—just seeking to muffle the lack of Rook, maybe. Which certainly argued for him having Honest-to-Christ feelings, just like anybody else.

Or not. But feelings, anyhow—fairy-coloured ones, hallucinatory and mean, drawn closer surface-wards with each fresh swig.

"Oh, we're well set up, Chess," Hosteen assured him, tapping his money belt. "The Rev gave us plenty of gelt. No need—"

"—for trouble?" Chess swivelled 'round, grinning nastily. "Aw, that's sweet of you to care, Kees." To Morrow: "And where'd *you* learn to pinch pennies so fine, anyhow? Half this band'a numbskulls can't count to twenty-one, 'less they're naked."

"Just careful, is all. Best to be, not knowin' exactly when the Rev's comin' back—"

"Rook'll be *back* soon 'nough," Chess said, a bit too quick for comfort, "whenever and however he damn well pleases. He told— *you*—he'd be back; that's good enough for me. In fact . . ."

"Chess Pargeter?"

This was a new voice entirely, drink-roughened and shaky, from directly behind Chess—some cowboy, barely old enough to shave. Morrow stared at the scarred tabletop, suddenly more exhausted than scared. Thinking: *Aw, great.*

Looked like the Bird-in-Hand all over again, at best. And at worst—

"Chess Pargeter," the cowboy repeated. "You're him, right? If so, we're gonna have words."

"Seems I'm lettin' you have them now," said Chess, not looking up.

"You recall a waiter-gal used to work here, name of Sadie?"

"No."

"You broke her head open last time you come through here, over that damn Reverend of yours." He had a sun-reddened face, with spots of colour burned high on broad cheekbones. "She never woke up. Died of a fever, a week after."

"Boy . . . I've killed a *lot* of people."

"She *meant* somethin' t'me!"

"I can see that. Question is, what? You even think about that part yourself?" The cowboy laid hand to gun, flushing further. "'Sides which—you waited what, a half-year? Somebody killed the Rev, I wouldn't wait two minutes."

"Well . . . I had to train."

At that, Chess nodded. "Good thought, on your part. So—"

The kid caught his eye-flick, and barely had time to touch holster. Chess cross-drew at the same instant, so quick he'd already shot the kid twice before the boy even had time to realize what had happened. Then didn't bother to watch as the kid collapsed, skull cracking heavily on the saloon floor.

Morrow stared at Chess, who raised an eyebrow back at him. "What? You thought we was gonna have us an honest-to-shit shootout, in the middle of the damn street? Please."

Like some kinda fair fight, *or somethin'?* Morrow thought, his stomach clutching queasily. *Guess not.*

It must've shown on his face, though, because Chess snorted out a sour half-laugh—as though even he felt some inexplicable wrongness in what he'd just done, and was annoyed by it.

"Sit yourself back down, Ed," he ordered. "Joe'll get this—" he nodded toward the body "—took away, and I got most've a bottle yet to drink. I don't aim to do it alone."

Morrow had a giddy moment's thought of slapping Chess right across the chops and walking out, bullet in the back or no. But Chess—who might just as easily be well aware of that fact as blithely ignorant—just met his eyes straight on, unflinching.

"You heard 'im," he said. "Boy didn't know half what he oughta; be crueller to prolong the misery. 'Sides—he'd waited long enough."

Up on the wall, a greasy pastoral Joe'd hung to block a draft first fell sidelong, then detached altogether, hitting the floor with a clatter. The noise seemed to spur Joe's slim consort of musicians-in-residence to draw out a wheezy squeeze-box, and set to mangling a tune that sounded for all the world like Chess's Ma's favourite: *For*

I'll be true to my love, if . . .

Blood on the sawdust, coming up in clots, and a few flies, already gathering: perhaps this *was* the price of "being true," sometimes, sadly enough. Especially when you didn't take care to pick and choose who best to do it *to*—

But that was a lesson Chess himself might have to learn, someday.

"All right," Morrow said, finally. And took his seat once more.

CHAPTER SIXTEEN

One bottle became two, and Hosteen switched to rotgut early on, "to stay crafty"—but since Morrow'd been kept busy matching Chess at absinthe slug for slug, might be he'd already lost his ability to reckon such matters. Now they were upstairs, in Chess's quarters, playing a hand of cards while Chess supposedly kept score. Whenever Morrow looked over, however, he found him messing with his armaments instead—stripping one gun after the other, tallying up shot, stropping Hosteen's former blade to a keen gleam.

"Anyhow," Hosteen told Morrow suddenly, re-ordering his hand, "here's the latest from San Fran, 'fore I forget to tell ya 'bout it *again*—word is, after whatever the Rev got done doin', half that bitch Songbird's whole knock-shop fell down, leavin' her out on the street. Then, next thing she knows, the Pinkertons're there, too. Mister Head Agent Allan himself at the helm, b'lieve it or not, 'long with some fancy Northern professor he got hooked to his outfit."

"What for, exactly?"

"Well, as t' that . . . you recall back in th' War, when the Bluebellies tried t' put hexes t' work, fightin' on behalf of the Union? Reckoned if they looked 'mongst the Irish brigades, say, an' took up all those who turned after a sizeable battle—always *was* one or two, per major engagement—they could cobble a devastatin' force t'gether, 'specially if they added in every fled nigger with sim'lar inclinations in on top. But *Mages don't meddle*, so they got t' squabblin' midst themselves, killed each other an' sucked the corpses dry, long 'fore they ever drew anywhere near *us*. . . ."

Asbury's lecture in action, Morrow thought.

"Still, guess Pinkerton's fixed t' get back at it again, 'cause Miss Songbird cut her a deal, turned State's, for the cost o' repairs. That an' a license t' come after the Rev, no doubt, with just as many Pinks as they'll lend 'er." Hosteen threw down. "Annnd . . . Ace, king, queen, jack, ten. I take the trick."

Morrow frowned. "Thought we was playin' whist."

"*Whist?*" Hosteen rose, almost up-ending his own chair in the process. "Well, that's me done for. Gotta go fall down."

"We'll miss you."

"Yeah. Jus' bet you will."

He turned for the door, studying Chess, who barely seemed to notice—then sighed, and moved on. But—

"'Night, Kees," Chess finally called out, gaily, just as the door clicked shut behind the old man's back. And snickered, right down into his purple shirt-sleeve.

"You *have* to—?" Morrow snapped, then stopped. Not quite fast enough, though.

Chess sat forward, chin propped on one palm, as the other fell to stroke his favourite plaything's shiny pearl inlay.

"Don't much enjoy me playin' with old Mister H, do ya, Ed?" He asked. "And why is that, I wonder."

"'Cause he's my *friend*? Yours too, I always thought."

Chess shrugged, eyes narrowing. "Sure. But then again—you *think* quite a whole damn lot, 'bout a full spread of very different subjects. Don't think I ain't noticed."

Morrow held himself still as possible under that scrutiny, while in his pocket, the Manifold gave a shiver. *Just sit tight and shut the fuck up,* Morrow told it, and braced to wait it out, as though he could somehow *will* Chess's unconscious hexation back into him; bad enough Chess might be fixing to shoot him, without adding spells in, on top of the mix.

"'Bout that boy's woman," Chess said, suddenly. "Fact is . . . I just didn't calculate her dyin'. Hell, I had bottles broke on *my* head, lots of times, and I ain't dead."

"But you're a man, Chess. You're tough."

Chess snorted. "Ever seen the inside of a birthin' room? Stick a pin in the map almost anywhere, you'll find ten women tougher'n me—and you, for that matter." A pause. "Not many meaner, though. I believe I'm right in *that* estimation, anyroads."

"Yeah, you do got that goin' for you," Morrow agreed, taking another swig.

For Morrow, it all came back to that one word, sprinkled throughout every Agency report he'd read before first embarking on this misguided venture: **unrepentant** *sodomite and murderer.* The primary description anyone who'd ever heard of Chess Pargeter always slapped on him, and strictly on the sodomy part of it, Morrow felt he could safely give a resounding *yes.* But as to the other . . .

"Still and all," Chess continued, "you might have a point there, this one time. 'Cause thinking back, I find how I do feel kinda . . . *bad* about riddin' the world of Sadie's little friend."

"Well . . . you kinda should. That boy didn't have a chance—and seems to me you liked it that way. Like back in 'Frisco, with that miner; you lead them on, then lay them down, then you giggle about it after. Way you conduct yourself, it's—"

"Uncharitable?" Chess suggested.

"—*easy.* All a damn sight too easy entirely, considerin' how afterwards they're dead, and you're alive."

Morrow waited, but Chess didn't reply—simply sat back, and though his hand still hovered near his gun, it seemed less a threat than a habit.

"That whole thing . . ." he said, at length. "It was nothin' more than a damn *tiff,* 'tween Ash Rook 'n' me. Just this dance we were havin' with each other, spilled over into fisticuffs—and that boy, his bitch, they just got in the way, is all. And I . . ."

He trailed off, shook his head. And here Morrow saw something cross Chess Pargeter's face, shame-full and sidelong—a thing so alien, so out of context, he barely recognized it himself.

Regret.

"I don't want to think about this anymore," Chess said, finally. "So . . . you're gonna help me out with that, ain't ya, Ed? Yeah, that's right. 'Cause *you're* gonna get me so I *can't*."

Morrow couldn't begin to guess how—and even if he had, this wouldn't've been the first idea he came up with: Chess leaning forward all of a sudden, using both Morrow's biceps to haul him down hard. Chess friggin' Pargeter, at maybe half Morrow's height, dragging him eye-level, the better to stick his tongue deep between the bigger man's teeth.

Morrow reared back almost immediately—pants tight, stomach cold. "What—what the hell was *that*?" he demanded.

Chess smirked. "What'd it *seem* like?"

Somethin' might get me killed, Rook ever found out, was Morrow's first idea. But instead, he said, carefully, "Look, Chess—just how drunk *are* you?"

"Depends. How drunk are *you*?"

"Not drunk enough." But that didn't sound right either. "Look, I, uh . . . I like girls."

Chess shrugged. "Sure. Half the men I've messed with'd say the same. But you know better 'bout *me*: ladies ain't my meat, and I ain't theirs. I do like *you*, though, Ed—always have."

". . . oh?"

"Yup. You do what you say, and mean what you do. Don't run your mouth. And you're clean in your habits, too—I admire that in a man."

So I hear, Morrow remembered.

But now Chess was all up in his face again, nuzzling hotly 'round the pulse-point of Morrow's jaw and rubbing their bearded cheeks together like he was either grooming Morrow, or grooming himself *on* Morrow. Probably looked ridiculous, but the effect was soon enough to render simply breathing a difficult task indeed.

Morrow groaned, forcing out: "But, the Rev—"

"He cared enough to help me out, he'd be here already; he ain't. 'Sides which . . . this is his fault, too. So screw 'im."

"Now, that don't make a—"

"Just shut the hell up, Ed." Chess kissed him again, delving deeper. "Now . . . man up and skin off, 'cause I don't got all night."

Morrow bristled. "Oh, now I *really* want to," he threw back, oddly insulted by the implication that them getting to it had become an utterly foregone conclusion.

'Course, if a hex *made* you, it wasn't nothin' to feel shame over, was it? And Chess'd probably kill him one way or the other, if he refused.

While he waffled, however, Chess was already slipping one of his hands right down the front of Morrow's trousers, deftly plucking his buttons apart. And here came the thing itself, free at last: poker-stiff, drooling. It filled Chess's palm, fingers playing just as smooth and nimble on it as Morrow'd always thought they might, 'til he hefted it, and laughed out loud at the strength of Morrow's reaction.

"*Ah*, Christ shit Jesus—"

"Yeah, that's right. Quite uncommon instrument you're packin', Ed. Very—manly." Chess hauled a bit harder, then stopped to admire the result. "Oh, and I do like *this*, too—a big man, all raw and needy and beggin', and all because of me. Not to mention a nice, thick piece like you got right here, stuck in just as far as it'll go, justabout any damn place that's handy."

Morrow gasped, glancing down—saw himself magnified a size more than expected, purple-weeping, and looked away again, before he ended up with scarred eyeballs. Shaking his head, and demanding, "But what the hell do *you* get out of it, exactly?"

"*My way*, Ed. It's like killin', almost—*almost* as good. 'Cept nobody has to die. Anyhow—you *could* do something for *me*, in return, you were willin'."

"Like *what*?"

"Like you might could *fuck* me, fool. What'd you think I meant?"

"But—don't that hurt?"

"Oh, you poor innocent. 'Course it does." Chess was all but straddling Morrow now, yet swung in just a tad further, voice dropping, to explain: "That's what makes it *good*."

"Chess, I ain't that *way*."

"You ain't complainin', though, are ya?" As Morrow hesitated: "*C'mon*, for Christ's sake! It's the exact same act, no matter *what* the accoutrements—"

"Bullshit! How would you even know?"

Chess paused, actually seeming to consider this. And answered, at last—"Well . . . you got me there, Ed. Many the times as I seen it done, I guess . . . I still probably wouldn't."

They contemplated each other for a tick, chests heaving. Chess's eyes fell, unexpectedly, releasing Morrow—and even more unexpectedly, Morrow registered it as a loss, rather than a victory.

"Listen," Chess said. "I ain't no outrager. So hell, Ed—if you genuinely don't want to, I sure ain't gonna stick a knife to your throat. I mean, I *could* make you, and you might like it better than you think; blow-job's the best method of persuasion I know, savin' a gun. But . . . it wouldn't be worth the damn *effort*, that way. Would it?"

Chess's thumb stroked idly at Morrow's cock-head, drawing a hot bead, swirling it 'round. And, at once—it didn't seem so bad. After all.

That's the magic talkin', Ed.

Probably. But then again—who cared?

"Wouldn't, I guess," Morrow replied, fast enough not to think it over. And crushed Chess back to him.

They retired to the bed, shedding clothes and weapons as they did—a bit cramped for Morrow's liking, 'specially when two were involved, but it wasn't as though Chess wasn't providing a hell of a distraction . . . biting at Morrow's nipples on the down-slide, licking his navel, rolling his whole face (the beard scratching awfully, yet intriguingly) in the cradle of Morrow's pelvis like he was savouring the taste. Even pushing his thighs apart peremptorily—so *strong*, for one who still got mistook for a boy on occasion, if only from a distance—so he could lap at Morrow's too-full balls before opening wide and taking him to the root, grunting with effort, the thrum of it almost enough to fetch Morrow right there.

Seconds later, Morrow opened his eyes to find Chess arrayed on top of him, huffing in fresh pleasure while he fingered himself open, well-primed with what Morrow took—by its smell—to be some of his own brilliantine. Fair made Morrow blush, to see how Chess's own cock perked up at the sensation: red and shiny, crying out for further exploration. How would it be to grab hold in turn, do to Chess as he'd been done by? Jack him slow, then faster—keep on 'til Chess was the one rendered inarticulate, 'til he made him squirm, and arch, and pop—

Here Chess shifted downwards into Morrow's lap, however, breaking that train of thought all to hell—coming down in the saddle with a long groan, letting gravity do much of the work. Morrow let out a holler as he drove up into the very heat of him, lodged narrowly, stuck fast. Chess sat there froze a moment, all mussed up and panting, and said:

"Just, uuuuh, gimme one sec. Gotta find the angle, or it won't work like it oughta—"

"You *want* to, though, right? Say you want to, Chess—"

"Morrow, God damn! Do I any way seem to you right now like I *don't*?"

As though to prove the point, Chess forced himself down still further, 'til something inside him apparently *gave way* with a force that made Morrow shudder. And let loose with a whoop as he did it, triumphant and unashamed, the way an Injun trick-rider jumps a fence.

So tight and *nasty*, almost dry enough to scratch, for all the hair-oil Chess might've used—impossible to forget this was the *literal* back passage he was trying to breach, a secret place where nothing flesh was ever meant to fit, no matter its constitution. Yet more impossible still to fault the act further for that simple truth, given the sheer intensity of pleasure it obviously held, for both of them.

Because: Morrow could see Chess's eyes rolling back already, both their hips going twenty to the bar. Felt himself collide intermittently with a smallish, hardish lump inside, and saw how it made Chess gasp, whenever he did—that famous "thing," he could only conclude. As in *God, oh* God, *HIT that!*

I could rid the West of Chess Pargeter right now, Morrow thought, *with one quick snap. Tear his ear-bob out right now, when he ain't thinking—make him ugly—take away that lure of his, so he has to comport himself the same sad way all the rest of us do. Crush his hands, break the trigger-fingers at their roots, like chicken-bones. . . .*

But this was just sophistry, empty rhetoric, as the mere fact of what Morrow was doing even *while* he thought it proved beyond a shadow of a doubt. What with him still hammering hard into Chess like it was his first fuck, or his last—or both.

He almost laughed at the craziness of it all, right out loud. But let a cry of his own bust out instead, similarly squeal-pitched, as ruin broke through him all at once—clutched Chess to him, nipping automatically into the younger man's nearest sweaty shoulder, and felt his body go off in a chain of tiny explosions, a firecracker-string stuffed with spunk.

The cross-shaped earring flashed and jounced, sparking painfully at the very corner of Morrow's sights, as Chess juddered hard through his own climax, spitting hot trails up Morrow's stomach— throe-drunk, riding the wave. Energy crackling everywhere, out of his very pores.

If I was Rook, I'd want some of that, Morrow thought. *If I was Rook . . .*

But he wasn't.

No time to feel bad, though, just hold on and enjoy the ride, pumping every last drop of his own heart's-blood out through the head of his cock.

"—aaaaAAAAAh, fuck *me!*" Morrow heard himself yell to the empty air, so loud his voice gave out mid-way. Chess answered it in kind, then collapsed, pulling them both over in a graceless heap. They lay there a while, twinned and panting, as though neck-to-neck in yet another race to see who'd be able to catch their breath first.

"Guess you're . . . mine, now," Morrow managed, finally. His own voice so hoarse he barely recognized it.

Which was *also* a mistake, the single dumbest thing he could've said, goin' by prior report alone.

Chess simply snorted again, however, before rolling safely back on top.

"Not too damn likely," he replied. "I'm the Rev's, if I'm anybody's. But considerin' how *I'm* the one just busted *your* cherry, as regards t' queer frolics . . . way *I* see it, if anything—now *you* belong to *me*."

And *that* wasn't anything to worry about, now, was it? As a prospect.

Crap, Morrow thought, knowing damn well he was doing nothing but repeating himself, as ever. *Of all the bone-head moves to go and damn well pull, Goddamnit. . . .*

But here the words faded to white, 'cause Chess was kissing him again—grinding into him groin-first, his pretty little piece polishing itself industriously on the sweat-slick fur of Morrow's belly. And Morrow felt himself spring immediately back to full attention; more hexation-overspill, probably, not that he was complaining. Felt his slick head butt up hard once more against Chess's ass, like the dumb beast just couldn't *wait* to cram itself back up into a space so tight, it was just as well that part of the body didn't have no bones.

Cry 'bout it in the morning, if I have to, Morrow decided, knowing he wouldn't. And pulled Chess back down once more, to where he could get at him.

CHAPTER SEVENTEEN

Stay with me, Chess'd ordered Morrow, after their fun was through. So Morrow had, though he mostly ended up just watching him sleep, all sprawled out, absinthe-dazed and snoring aniseed.

Even his damn scars are pretty, Morrow caught himself thinking, wondering just how God expected to get away with letting anything be so fair and yet so unrelenting foul at once.

But here Chess yawned wide and stretched, breaking Morrow's reverie. He opened one lazy eye, winced at how the morning light pained him, and demanded—"Where in the hell's that damn bottle?"

"They only had the one of them left, Chess, remember? And you drunk it already."

Chess pulled a face, which seemed to hurt him in an entirely different way.

"I feel justabout the same, if that helps," Morrow offered.

"Oh, *do* ya? That's a comfort. . . ."

He levered himself standing, and stood there rude and proud as ever, though moving just a tad slower than he usually did, 'specially in and around the nether regions. Continuing, as he did: ". . . but if you really *don't* got any liquor handy, then what I want's a bath . . . so call me one, and get the hell out. 'Less you're thinkin' of comin' in with me."

And with this last part, he shot Morrow yet one more of those lash-veiled glances, causing him the now-requisite hot stab of equal parts shock and shame. *I ain't* like *that,* Morrow would've been able to tell himself, up to only last night—but here it was at least an hour past dawn, and that once-fine certainty had gone the literal way of

186

all flesh.

Now Chess was legging it over to the wash-stand, wincing slightly with each step. Casting back, over his shoulder—"Just so we understand each other, by the by, I ain't sayin' this didn't happen— just that the Rev don't need to know unless it's from me, and me alone. You take my meanin', Mister Morrow?"

"Oh, no damn fear, *Mister* Pargeter—you think *I'm* gonna tell him? I got at least as much to lose here as—"

"No. No, you don't."

They paused a moment, Morrow studying Chess closely—not the full spread of him, so much, as the far more telling details.

"Hell, you feel *bad*, 'bout what we did—you 'n' me, last night. Don't ya?"

"Don't be an idjit. I done a lot worse, with a *lot* of others. You think you're special?" Chess shook his head, reaching for his trousers. "Second after Rook gets back, I won't even recall that horse's-ass *face* you make when you're in your sin—that's the damn truth."

Morrow kept on staring, then shook his head in turn, grinning slightly. "If that don't beat all," he declared.

"If *what* don't, Goddamnit?"

Feel bad for killin' a man . . . feel bad for doin'—that—with another one. Hell, it's kinda like you ain't the Chess Pargeter I heard tell of at all. Like you're a whole 'nother man, entirely.

But: "How you really *must* love him, after all, strange as that might seem," was what Morrow said out loud, instead. "That you even *can*."

Chess ground his teeth at that, audibly, so loud it almost made Morrow take an actual step backwards—but let out his held breath a moment on, his anger set aside for the nonce: cooled, if never truly banked. "Yeah, I guess I do, at that," he allowed.

Didn't sound much of a happy insight, though.

"Okay, then. But love ain't so bad, Chess. Is it?"

"My Ma always said love was a trick and a trap; took her oath on it, more times than I can count. Not that she ever kept her oath."

"Well..." Morrow began, uncomfortably. "Might be . . . she wasn't really the best authority on the subject."

Wasn't sure what to expect, by way of response—anything from a sob to a punch seemed just as likely. But Chess simply looked at him once more, eyes suddenly considerably less forlorn—sniffed like he'd heard better jests from gut-shot men slow-dyin' but didn't necessarily want to say so. And answered, "Oh yeah, that's right, I forgot. You *met* her."

Scrubbed and dressed once more, Morrow walked out, and ran straight into Hosteen, who gave him a look the likes of which he'd never previously seen. Because he knew, of course—hell, the whole of Splitfoot's probably knew, come to that, since Chess wasn't exactly *quiet*.

"Hey, Kees," Morrow said, flushing hard.

Hosteen sighed. "So . . . you and Chess, huh? Boy, I thought you was smart."

"Says the same man who give him his knife!"

"That was *before* the Rev. 'Sides which—Hell, I s'pose it don't really matter much, in the end; just keep it to your damn self, is all. Considerin'."

"Considerin' what?"

"Scouts say they saw Rook comin'—that cloud he walks around in sometimes, anyhow, tall enough to block out the sun. Should be here by nightfall, if he ain't here sooner."

From behind them both, a fresh squeak of the door announced Chess's presence. The smell of hair-oil made Morrow blush afresh, but Chess didn't even acknowledge it—just gave the both of them both a cool nod, and said: "'Bout time that son-of-a-bitch showed up."

Hosteen nodded back. "They said he mighta had somebody else with him," he said. "A woman."

There was a general pause, during which Chess stared fixedly at Hosteen, while Morrow tried his level best to look pretty much anywhere else.

"She just better be a fuckin' hex, is all I'm sayin'," Chess announced, eventually, to no one. And stalked off past them, hips swinging, to take the staircase down.

Outside, a storm came in hard and fast—more dust than rain, bright orange-red, lighting up the whole sky from horizon to horizon. What denizens of Splitfoot Joe's hadn't already made themselves scarce, got busy either securing shutters or mudding up the various lintel-chinks, and since the chimney had to be blocked off first of all—no point in leaving it open, when all it drew was sand—the fire went out, leaving them to sit idle in semi-darkness, listening to the wind.

"Screw this," Hosteen said, and started fiddling with a lamp. Morrow felt his way closer.

"Need some help with that?"

"Had you a lucifer handy, I wouldn't turn it down."

Morrow took hold of the lamp's glass bell and kept it upright, while Hosteen struck a match. The lucifer went blue, then yellow, as he guided it in—but it wouldn't catch, nohow.

"Might be the wick's too short," Morrow suggested. "Or too soaked to light—"

"Might *be* you should keep your opinions to yourself, 'less I go ask you for 'em."

All of a sudden, the wick flared, light swelled to fill the room, and Morrow turned with a sigh of relief—that choked to a glottal sound of shock and fright as Rook's grin gleamed down on him, from above the sofa on the far wall. The Rev seemed to materialize around that grin, coalescing out of the gloom: slumped at his leisure, one long arm slug over the sofa's back.

And next to him sat someone entirely different, though—as advertised—visibly female. She was a dim blur, hair hung in a cowl, her haughty face the colour of good blonde tobacco. Had the same stone-black eyes as Songbird, too, albeit cut larger and far more lustrous: flat and glassine, much like the famous Smoking Mirror itself with that gal adorning it—broke apart in sections, forever caught falling downwards, froze in the instant before impact. Her hung-dagger earrings. Her flat nose, sloping forehead, swooped-up frieze of braids.

Her, by God.

Oh *yeah*, Morrow thought. *She's a hex, all right.*

The company cried out, almost as one. Rook's hand tightened on hers to hear it, in proprietary fashion; he was still smiling, though she looked like she might well not know how. And outside, the wind—that endless scraping trumpet, ubiquitous, deranged—went suddenly silent as an open grave.

"Shut the hell *up*, you buncha wailin' jennys!" Chess hollered out, reaching for his guns.

"Boys," Rook said, at the exact same time. To Chess: "Miss me, darlin'?"

But Chess's eyes were stuck on Little Miss Nobody, firm as though they'd been glued there. "This her? The one you been dreamin' on?" No answer. "She a hex?"

Rook's smile deepened. "Oh, she's more'n that." Raising his voice, "Ain't that right, Lady Ixchel?"

He pronounced the name so easily—*Eesh*-zhel, fluid and guttural as a snake spitting blood—that for an instant it sounded as if some other voice entirely had spoken through Rook's mouth.

Inside his waistcoat pocket, Morrow's hand clenched white-knuckled on the Manifold as it jerked Rook's Lady's way, holding its needle still and its gears frozen. Its workings bit into his callused fingertips, vibrating with the fierceness of their signal: ten times, a hundred times the strength of Rook.

Couldn't he tell what she *was*? That she was outside any of them—outside their whole world?

The woman raised her head slowly, as if her black gaze took effort to lift. "So pleasant to meet you at last, Mister Pargeter," she said to Chess, her tone absurdly gentle. "The Reverend thinks of you, oh, *so* often."

Rook placed a hand on her knee. "Don't scare him, Lady. Please."

And at that, she finally smiled, a slow and awful snake's-jaw stretch. "I doubt I could," she returned softly. "Husband."

The room went dead.

Chess's shoulders actually shook. "*What'd* you just call him?" he whispered.

"Never you mind." Rook stood, clapped his hands. "Boys, gather 'round—your patience is about to be rewarded. Got a few announcements."

He twitched his fingers toward one wall, then the other, and all the lamps sprang into flame, sending the gloom fleeing. Morrow had a queasy feeling they would have lit even without wicks, or oil.

"You boys already heard about Songbird, I take it." the Reverend said. "Well, since the Pinkertons turned her, seems they've been on quite the tear. Any hex don't sign up, they either clap them in jail or throw them to the 'Frisco Madam . . . grist for their mill, and hers. By reports, must be damn near a hundred of them arrayed 'tween here and the Border."

"A *hundred*?" Morrow blurted. "Pinks'd be lucky to pull an even fifty off of—"

Too late, he stopped, realizing there was no way he should know that—not plain Ed Morrow, outlaw. But the rest were too busy goggling at Rook and each other to notice, while Lady Ixchel barely seemed aware he had spoken at all.

"Well, be that as it may . . . it's Songbird I'm more worried over. Morrow here's seen her at her work—ain't you, Ed? Chess, too. She's no one to trifle with."

Hosteen lifted an awkward hand. "But Rev, you—you can *beat* her, right?"

"Fast enough to keep a hundred—sorry, Ed—*fifty* Pinks from drillin' the rest of you full of lead, in the meantime? Hex cancels hex, Kees. You know that."

"What're you saying, Rook?" One of the new signups, this one, a burly mean-eyed fellow named Wade. "You've brought a fight on us you'll be no good in? Maybe—"

Chess turned—but Rook had already flipped a hand up, the air between them whip-cracking. Wade catapulted away, struck the saloon's wall hard enough to shatter four-inch planking, then hit the ground, a render's discards.

"Sorry, darlin'," Rook told Chess. To the others: "Anyone else care to weigh in?" He waited, then nodded. "All right—best go get snookered. Come mornin', we're off for Mexico."

"And how is it you figure on gettin' from here to Mexico, exactly, without Songbird and that army of Pinks findin' out, and blockin' our way?" Chess asked.

Rook went to answer, but it was his odd companion who got there first.

"We will go by the low way, through the Place of Dead Roads," she told Chess. "As to the mechanism of entry, meanwhile . . . the whole earth is a corpse, little warrior—the corpse of my mother, whose mouth opens into the Land of the Dead. And she is *covered* with mouths."

"That's handy, ain't it?" said Rook.

Chess just blinked. "So . . . in other words . . ."

"That's right. In *other* words . . . we're goin' by way of Hell, itself."

Hosteen's eyebrows soared, but he kept whatever disbelief he might have to himself.

Chess, though—secure in what had always, hitherto, been his cocoon of privilege—snapped: "Say what?"

"He means the land which was once called Mictlan, or Xibalba," Ixchel told him, gently. "Now known as Mictlan-Xibalba, since all things run together down in the darkness, where even the gods forget their own names. The Sunken Ball-Court."

"Hell."

"Not *your* Hell, little warrior. But . . . yes."

"I'm not sure I trust you, woman," Chess said, bluntly, showing that same disregard for danger which had served him so well—'til now. "And seein' how every other hex the Rev's met so far has tried to drain his juice and kill him dead, I sure as *hell* don't know why *he* does."

Ixchel tilted her head at Chess, as if examining a bright-carapaced insect. Rook gave an exasperated headshake, and opened his mouth—then surprised Morrow by closing it again, suddenly thoughtful. For if Chess was the only one with the nerve to protest, none of the other men in the room looked particularly happy, either.

"Private Pargeter's reservations," he said. "Am I right in guessing they're shared at large, fellows?"

"Aw, Rev, c'mon—" Hosteen flushed. "You know we'd follow you into, um . . . wherever takes your fancy."

"I know, Kees, I know." He clasped his hands behind his back and took them all in with a level look. "But here's the thing . . ."

Oh good, Morrow thought. *It's damnation* and *a lecture, tonight.*

". . . since all of you know how hexes can't work together long, seein' me here with the Lady, you must think: what viper have we taken to our bosom?" He glanced at his "wife," who had not taken her black eyes off Chess even the once, in all this intervening time. "But Lady Ixchel here, she's *more* than just your ordinary hex—more than me, Songbird, or any other sorcerer you may have heard tell of. Where she comes from, them that use magic are powerful beyond the dreams of any minor mage or witch. They don't gobble each other up, 'cause they don't *have* to. They got other ways to get what *they* need—"

—by takin' it from us *somehow, no doubt—*

"—and that alone's what proves she's got the goods to show me how to bind any other hex—*every* other hex—I meet to our cause." He brought his hands together and knotted them in one another, as if strangling a ghost. "Or just suck the life outta any won't join up anyhow, whichever comes first."

As Rook's voice took on an unnatural resonance, the steel-spike pain flared in Morrow's skull once more. He saw the other men's eyes glaze over too, and knew hexation was at work.

"We'll live like emperors, boys, doing whatever we want, whenever we want. No more running and hiding, just sweet cream and an endless river of gold, once I gain my apotheosis—become a god, or damn near like unto one."

"*The* God ain't bound t'like *that* much, I'd think," Hosteen muttered. "I mean . . . ain't makin' yourself *a* god somewhat 'gainst Bible-lore, at least a little, for a preacher?"

Morrow felt the hairs on his neck ruff just a tad, and braced himself for yet more offhand killing. But Rook just smirked.

"Almost certainly so," he replied. "But I hate to tell you, Kees . . . me and the Good Lord ain't been on speakin' terms for quite some time now." He shot a hot glance at Chess, and added: "Obvious reasons."

Usually, Chess would have returned the look in kind—but not today. Not with Lady Ixchel looking on.

"Me a god, Chess," Rook said. "You too, maybe. How's that sound?"

Chess reddened. "Sounds like . . . well, no sorta fun at all, t'me," he finished, and fell sullen-silent, as if even he could hear the whine in his own voice. A balky child quibbling over wrapping, when the present itself was rare beyond belief.

That *did* make the whole room laugh, right out loud. Even Hosteen smiled, and Rook himself guffawed with deep hilarity. But there was an odd, almost unconscious affection in it as well.

"Joe," Rook called out, over the laughter, "uncap every bottle you got." He reached inside his coat, pulled out a purse heavy with strange metal, and flung it at the barkeep, who caught it one-handed. "Should be enough in there to cover it all, with gold left over. Gentlemen—tonight, the drinks're on me. 'Cause tomorrow, we spit in the Devil's eye, and take the world for our own!"

A general maddened hurrah erupted, with Morrow, Hosteen, and Chess the only ones who didn't immediately rush the bar; Chess stood still where he was, glowering at the Rev while trying to ignore Lady Ixchel completely—which didn't bode well, for anybody. So Morrow risked both a hand on Chess's shoulder and a nudge forward, praying Joe might have just one more bottle of absinthe he hadn't admitted to still in store.

"Look kinda green, Chess," he said. "Let me stand you one."

Chess didn't fight, but didn't shift his eyes, either. "Tryin' to get me gay? Hope you're not lookin' for some sort of repeat performance, Morrow."

"Hardly. Naw, I reckon you're still the Rev's just like he's still all yours, tonight and always."

"Just like," Chess repeated, with even less affect.

"You got any cause to doubt it?"

"*No.*"

"Well . . . act like you mean it, then." Glancing back at Lady Ixchel, Morrow added: "I mean—you can't be worried over *her* account, can ya? Long as you and the Rev been—together?" He shook his head. "Throw it off, son. It's a chigger-bite in a windstorm."

"You ain't my damn daddy," Chess snapped, automatically. Then, after a moment: "She smells like *him*, you get in close."

Morrow shrugged. "She *is* like him."

"That ain't what I mean, and you know it."

Any other time, this last would've come out as a sucker-punch, or even accompanying one. Instead, Chess leaned back against the bar with his arms crossed—trying for insouciance, yet almost hugging himself. His purple-clad shoulders rose high and he bent his head first right, then left, his tense neck cracking audibly.

"Been a while since he's had him one, I guess," he said, as if to himself. "That's all—somethin' familiar. Though . . . it *is* true how he ain't queer down to the bone, like me. Not really. And me . . ." Chess paused. ". . . me, I ain't no hex, Goddamnit."

Morrow had to bite his tongue. "Well—"

"Well what?"

"You never know, right? Do ya. I mean . . . *I* could be a hex, I just got hurt bad enough. That's the rumour, anyhow."

"Sure it is. Want me to gut-shoot you right now, so we can find out?"

That did succeed in drawing a laugh, after all—from both of them at once, equally sharp, yet genuine. Morrow felt an instant's strange stab of kinship with the little monster standing next to him, 'specially since there were two others within easy reaching distance who really did have him beat for scariness.

But here came one of them sidling up, a raw flicker of dark on dark, to lean past Morrow and loom over Chess with a small smile curving her lips, as she murmured: "Ah, but no . . . there is no power waiting dormant in your bed-warmer, little warrior. He is a man, nothing more or less—as good as any other, I suppose, for doing those things that men do." The smile deepened, letting out a sliver of teeth. "Though you may feel free to enlighten me, if I misjudge."

Morrow, unable to figure out *what* best to say in return, just stood there, a wax-hall dummy.

But Chess blushed deep, eyes fair throwing out sparks, and snarled back, "Ain't too sure how they do things where you come from, 'Lady'—but for my money, Ed and I were havin' ourselves a *private* palaver, and I don't recall you bein' invited."

Ixchel's own laugh rippled out, an ascending glissando of music—light and cold, yet weirdly innocent. "Aaaaah," she said, her teeth fully out now. "You *are* such an angry little man, Mister Pargeter. For so little cause, and with *such* small result."

"There's a host of dead men would disagree with you on that one—"

"But then," she continued on, without even seeming to hear, "he *did* warn me of this when we discussed you, earlier. . . ."

"Who did—Ash?" Chess blushed further. "Ash wouldn't—"

"And why would he not? Being, as he is, my very own. . . ."

Not the guns, then, but Hosteen's knife. Chess had it out and brandished before Morrow could blink, so close its shine lit Lady Ixchel's dolorous eyes from the outside-in. Saying: "Keep on callin' him 'husband,' you gimcrack bitch, and I'm gonna stick *this* right in your—"

"Oh, shhhh."

No pause in the surrounding rollickry, but as of that exact split-second Chess was stuck—eyes locked with hers, strung tight and humming. Unable even to close his own lips as she leaned near enough to steal the breath from them, crooning: "Here, child. *Here. Yes. This* is better." She gave him a protracted huff, sniffing him deep. "Aaaah, yes. It is as the Reverend implied. *So* strong, so singular . . . and so untouched, even now. So . . . inviolate."

Morrow looked for Rook, and found him closer than he'd thought—a step or so behind Lady Ixchel, near enough to look down over her shoulder—yet hardly close enough for comfort.

Chess's lids were fluttering now, ever-so-slightly, and . . . damn, if Morrow hadn't seen that look before, back at the Two Sisters, watching the air between Rook and Chess grow slimy-liquid and run like blown glass, while Rook sucked a portion of Chess's very life from him in the service of a Little Death.

And yet Chess managed to bite out, while the lover he'd thus far trusted to protect him simply stood there and watched—"*You* . . . don't . . . know *me* worth shit on a shingle, 'f *that*'s what you think . . . 'Lady.'"

A spasm ran through him, heel to head, as he struggled to free himself—and almost succeeded, before Lady Ixchel laughed again, and made a casual motion with her left hand's little finger, insultingly tiny. Which tied him up tight once more, jaws locked and straining. She leaned farther forward, to sleek her lips up the cords of his tense throat, spilling out a rope of foreign words whose syllables crackled and crawled, sluggish, bruising the eardrum.

On Chess, their effect was both immediate and horrid: it brought him up against her in a single hapless heave, pressing himself to her curves, inhaling her smell—wrapping himself in her torrential hair, which almost seemed to rise and embrace *him*, in its turn. Set his pupils skittering, frantic for escape, even as it hooked him *deep* between the legs, pushing his trouser-fronts tight.

Oh God, what? *What the ever-friggin' hell*—

The day Chess Pargeter looks t' engage himself with any woman's situation'll be a cold one in the Hot Place for sure, Hosteen had told Morrow, once—and though Morrow found he couldn't remember why, the remark had stuck with him ever since. Which was just one of many reasons why this, right here, was unnatural . . . *awful*.

Like he'd said last night, Chess wasn't made that way—and the Lady damn well seemed to know it. To *revel* in it.

Morrow looked back to Rook again, heart slamming, but registered no appreciable difference in attitude. In fact, the Rev seemed similarly statue-bound, one hand held mid-rise, on its way toward Ixchel's shoulder. The long span of it twitched, as though galvanized—or like he, too, were deriving a sick spiritual nourishment from Chess's plight. Were somehow piggybacking on the Lady's extraction, siphoning away its topmost layer for his own enjoyment while Chess hung in agony between them, made a meal of . . . predator turned prey, at the mercy of two hungry hexes.

Goddamn vampires, the pair of them, Morrow thought, as the Manifold spun and kicked with vile activity. *Yet not a soul around seems to see it, savin' me, Hosteen, Chess. Chess, who can't do nothin' to save himself. And us—who won't.*

Lady Ixchel stroked Chess Pargeter's cheek with one hand, deftly plucking his knife away with the other—turned it so the blade was toward him and briefly menaced one green eye with it, as though to see if he'd give out any betraying blink. But when he refused to, she only grinned the wider, reversed it once more and slid it straight down the front of her bodice. A single perfect brown breast sprang forth, grazed along its inner orbit, deep enough that one small blood-drop ran quick and sure to gild the sharp, red nipple.

Chess stared at it, hypnotized. And when Ixchel flicked that littlest fingertip of hers yet again—he went down on both knees, heavy enough to skin them. Mashed his face into her cleavage and opened wide, sucked at that poisonous orb like he was a baby once more, so unfamiliar with his own nature that he might think to take small comfort there. And groaned aloud as he did so, utterly overcome: his deadly pistoleer's hands aflutter 'round his stretched-to-busting trouserfront buttons, like he yearned to pop them all at once and bring himself off in a stroke or two, spill his seed in the saloon-floor's trash.

"Oh yes," Ixchel told him, stroking his head softly—while all around her his stolen power boiled off in waves, contemptuously wasted. "I know *you*, warrior. *Ixiptla.* Little god-to-be. I have known you a thousand times—you and all men who were *born* to die for me, in shame, and pain, and ecstasy. Your heart's-blood is fire. I could drink it a million years, and never weary."

"Lady . . ." Rook said, finally.

To which she responded by hugging Chess closer, whispering, into his ear, "But because my little king loves you, I will not; your blood is his, and his alone, to shed."

A few steps over, Morrow glimpsed Hosteen keeping his own gaze steady-trained anywhere else, unable to bear to watch. And Christ, how he envied the man for not having to see Chess and the Lady tandem-step in a funeral march, heading for the stair, while Rook followed after, his hand still on Chess's arm. *Pushing.*

"I'd move on now, Ed, if I was you," he said, all but throwing back a damn man-of-the-world *wink.* "I mean . . . you had *your* fun, already. Didn't you? But tonight's for us, and we really don't need no witnesses."

Chess moved sleepwalker-slow past Morrow's elbow, his stunned stare flicking just the once to lock with his, then fall as though cut free. And Morrow . . .

Morrow did nothing to stop him—stop it. Because there was nothing he *could* do.

At all.

CHAPTER EIGHTEEN

Come half of midnight, Morrow went looking for Hosteen and found him outside in the scrub, smoking and staring up at Chess's window, like he was expecting Shakespeare's Juliet to lean out at any second.

"You care for him, don't you, Kees?" Morrow said.

Hosteen shrugged, like he'd never made any real attempt to deny it. "Used to think it was because he was nice t'me, back in the War—but I paid him for it, so . . . hell, I *don't* know. Just do, that's all. . . ."

"Pretty sure *I* know the reason, if you're interested." Then, as Hosteen looked at him: "It's 'cause he's a hex."

"And he believed you," Allan Pinkerton said, four weeks later—in that cramped Tampico hotel he'd engaged for Morrow's debriefing, with Songbird and Doctor Asbury in attendance. The faint Scots burr still audible in Pinkerton's voice sounded doubly incongruous in the white-plastered, Spanish-style dining room, bright with rich sunlight falling through slitted windows. "Just like that."

Morrow sighed. "Hardly. But . . . yeah, he came 'round to the idea eventually, given time and talk enough. I made him a pretty good argument, obviously."

"Obviously?" Asbury repeated, with that same air of constant vague puzzlement Morrow had long forgotten attended most of his pronouncements.

"Got y'all here, didn't he?"

He knocked out another shot of the tequila Pinkerton had given him, to the skittery accompaniment of one of Miss Songbird's dry little laughs. "So he did, Mister Morrow," she agreed, smiling at

Morrow's bosses, her mouth safe-shrouded behind those filigree claws of hers. "Much to our . . . mutual satisfaction."

Four weeks after Rook had led them into Hell, and Morrow had clawed his way back up somehow, into the Agency's loving arms. And Chess—

Morrow decided not to think about Chess; not right now, at least. So he slammed the shot and continued with his report.

"Said it yourself, Kees. How is it Chess can shoot somebody standin' thirty feet behind him, 'fore they even have a chance to squeeze one off? How is it two men as dog-on-cat different as Chess and the Rev ever tripped over each other in the first place, let alone got stuck at the dick?"

"Hexation?" Morrow nodded, quickly. Hosteen just snorted. "Naw," he said. "You're thinking crazy, Ed. Rook's more'n man-witch enough for both of them, without tryin' to bring Chess in on it."

"What if I had proof?"

"Christ, what *if*? What'm *I* supposed t' do about it, exactly?"

A fair question. With, much as Morrow might hate to admit it, only one real answer.

"Kees . . ." He stopped. Then continued, reluctantly: ". . . there's somethin' I need to tell you—"

"Aw, shit." The older man put a hand over his eyes. "This never goes nowhere good."

"—I'm a Pink."

Hosteen stared. "Why . . . in the *hell* . . . would you tell me a thing like that?"

"Oh, *I* don't know. Have to be pretty damn desperate, wouldn't I?"

They glared at each other a spell, 'til Hosteen sighed deep, and Morrow let out his own held breath at almost the same exact time, in grateful sympathy.

"Look," he began, "Rook's got a mojo-bag held over my head, that's the long and the short of it. Chess and me, last night— wouldn't surprise me if he had a hand in it, though I'm damned if

I know why. But as it is, I have to stay the course, for fear of bein' blasted. So if anyone's left could do anything for Chess, Kees, it'd be you . . . assuming you were willin'."

"You offered him a pardon."

Morrow shook his head. "No, sir. For Kees it's all about loyalty to the old cohort, and he's known Chess a damn sight longer than he's known the Rev. I did tell him your plans, though, Doc—how you were fixin' to build a hexacious reserve. Gave him the idea that Chess might be worth more to the Agency alive than dead, for once."

"That's all well and good," Pinkerton said, and sat back to mop his shining brow. "But as to Pargeter—just what *is* he now, anyways?"

"'Sides from not to be trifled with, or only at your own peril?" All Morrow had to offer was another shake, for that—plus a further swig, while Asbury and Pinkerton swapped significant glances.

Songbird rapped her gilded knuckles impatiently on the table-top. "My choice would be your genuine opinion on the matter, Mister Morrow. If you please."

Morrow threw a glance upwards, speculating on exactly how high you'd have to go before the roof above became the floor of Chess's impromptu prison—that room where he lay asleep, ensorcelled deep in a trance of Songbird's own making. Maintaining the same fierce slumber he'd endured ever since they'd both . . . resurfaced from their scramble through the depths, with Morrow clawing his way up mindlessly with one arm dug death-grip tight 'round the raw neck of what he could have sworn was Chess Pargeter's gutted corpse.

How he'd ever found Chess down there, in the first place—laid a hand on his collar in the dark, once it'd all gone predictably to shit—that, even now, Morrow didn't quite know himself. Only that during what he'd thought was three days ago and the month or so Pinkerton assured him had actually elapsed, enough "grievous physical insult" had occurred to make Chess exactly what Rook and his dragonfly-cloaked Lady had planned for: a sacrifice to dead forces, a new-expressed mage not yet aware of his own power, a son-of-a-bitching reborn "god-to-be."

Songbird had to feel it, surely. Wasn't the tasty pull of Chess's power what had led her, Asbury and Pinkerton to Mexico City, where they'd dug Chess—and Morrow—up out of the earthquake's rucked hide? But then again, perhaps it was just *too* big, too . . . alien, for her to fully realize. Which was why she still had to ask.

And that, if handled correctly—could be an advantage, for Chess. Morrow, too.

"Fuck if *I* know what he is," Morrow lied, therefore, right to the former witch-queen of San Francisco's pig-pale face, with far more sass than was probably warranted, or safe. And went to pour himself another, regardless of Pinkerton's disapproval.

"Good enough, Mister Morrow," Asbury said. "You *are* no expert in hexology, sad to say, as we are all of us aware. But if, barring such sidebars, you might continue with your recitative nevertheless."

Morrow nodded. "Why not?" he asked, of no one in particular.

"Think they'd want Chess for that hex-army of theirs, if only we could get him took into custody?"

"Think Chess'd stand still for it, if we did?" Morrow shot back, without thinking. Hosteen's face fell at the idea, a whole dropped wedding-cake of dolefulness.

"Maybe not . . ."

"But . . . maybe so, too," Morrow suggested. "'Cause much as Chess may not mind dyin', he still takes awful good care to keep himself alive."

"Yeah. Maybe . . ."

They looked at each other, then, and knew it: a compact had been sealed.

"So here's what you do," Morrow told him—risking another glance upwards only to find the window gone dark, and shuddering to think what-all might be in progress behind it. "Go west nor'west, fast as you can. We got an outpost, maybe a day's ride to get to, but they'll bring you back a deal quicker, 'cause they got Songbird to work it for them—hell, she can probably slingshot Pinkerton's private train right into the middle of Joe's, she takes a damn mind to." Hosteen stared. "C'mon, Kees! Can't make fry-cakes without you break—"

"—eggs, yeah, yeah, I get it. But . . . Ed, you at least got credit with those fuckers, you pull out your badge. They ain't got no fit reason under Heaven's sky to believe *me*, on anything."

Maybe not, Morrow thought. *But they're gonna* want *to.*

"They will," he said. "Long as you show them this."

He reached inside his vest, where the Manifold clicked and chittered, to grasp it firm, pull it out, giving it no time for nonsense. And dropped it in Hosteen's outstretched hand.

"I was *very* happy to receive my little device once more, by the by," Asbury assured him. "The readings you'd taken, their impressive range of resonances . . . well, they were more than I'd hoped for. It was they which formed the spectrum allowing me to confirm your diagnosis of Mister Pargeter's—condition—last night, once he was . . . secured."

"Glad to be of service, Doc," Morrow replied. *And t' finally get the damn thing off my chest . . . literally,* he thought.

"Strange, however, that Reverend Rook would not have immediately gleaned your intentions in this matter," Songbird remarked. "Or this *goddess* of yours, either . . . powerful as you make her seem, in your report."

"Did seem to me how Rook was probably just a bit distracted, right at that very moment. And the Lady? Well—she probably didn't much care *what* we did, either way. From what I've seen, we're dirt under her feet."

Pinkerton: "Mmm. Well, then, by all means . . . continue."

"Mornin' came. Rook got us all together. Told us what was gonna happen. Chess . . ." Morrow paused, the image still fresh in his mind. "He just stood there, with that woman, that thing—Lady Ixchel—holdin' his hand. Didn't say a damn word. Like he was—"

"In a sort of trance?"

"Hypnosis," Asbury said to himself, quietly. "Or perhaps as in the *Codex Magliabecchi*, when the deity-impersonator is 'made drunken' and 'painted white' in anticipation of transformation . . . though that may only be a metaphorical intoxicatory state, to be sure."

"All right, Doctor," Pinkerton said. "I'd suggest we can address that issue in fine detail some other time, assumin' it even comes up."

"They didn't ask about Hosteen," Morrow went on, "and I sure as Christ didn't volunteer. Then, after the Rev'd said his piece, *she* just all of a sudden up and grabbed big Cow-Puncher Pete Van Damme by the head and bent him back over her knee. Pulled a knife out of her hair, cut his throat. And where his blood fell on the floor, it . . . opened up a hole. . . ."

"A hole," Songbird repeated. "Which . . . you went through."

"That's right."

"Into Hell."

"Yup."

Asbury gave himself a shake. "Gods and monsters," he said, musingly. "You have glimpsed wonders we can only dream of, Mister Morrow."

"Yeah, well—you'd seen even the half of what I saw down there, you'd be happy to keep it that way," Morrow replied.

In the end, the voyage itself had seemed . . . impossibly easy. A plunge, taken. Like stepping off a cliff.

That yellow sky, leering down. The rain of knives, falling. No wonder Rook'd wanted the rest of his gang to come along, haplessly unsuited as they were to hexacious labours—they made for perfect cannon-fodder.

The Rev kept them moving steadily forward, with Chess on one arm and Morrow clinging tight to the other, a protective envelope of lightning a-snap in all directions. And the Lady Ixchel glided on effortless behind all three—behind, beside, around. Ixchel, bent near-double in the darkness to murmur in Chess's ear—Ixchel, darker by far than anything around her, no matter how deep they went.

Wrapped in her buzzing dress of devil's darning needles, with her copper limbs unstrung at the joints and set drifting in Mictlan-

Xibalba's current like kelp—her flesh shiny as burnt bones, hair a net of hooks, voice like broken bells chiming: **. . . but there is nothing like death in war, a flowery death, so precious . . . I know you can see it far off, my husband's husband, as you always have. Far off, and not so far. I know how you yearn for it!**

The words thrumming *through* everything at once, every*one*, reverberate eternally on a shimmering thread of prayer, both answered and not. The yearning witchery of each dead and living supplicant, each made and unmade name all crying out, together—

To die for a god

To die *as* a god

To die, in Pain, in Glory, wrapped in Hot Heart's Blood, is

beautifulbeautifulbeautifulbeautifulbeautiful

Morrow heard Rook's voice rise above the din, so heartbreakingly *human* amidst all this spectral awfulness.

"Where *is* this place you're takin' us, woman? I didn't get swung by my neck and lose my damn *soul* just to get eaten by someone else's demons in a hell I don't even believe in—"

Be silent, husband. I will not be spoken to thus, not in my own place. There is nothing here that poses any danger.

"Says you!"

Yes. The only ones of any consequence awake down here are you, I and he, little king. All others lie asleep, dead and dreaming. These are their nightmares, nothing more. And besides—we are here.

"Cow-Puncher Pete," Pinkerton mused. "So that's who was on that floor. Was a five grand reward on for him, I recall—spares us that expense, any road." He gave Morrow a steady look. "They let us through, you know. First time we've ever been welcomed to Splitfoot's vale without gunplay; Joe himself wouldn't go inside his own tavern. And the body we found looked dried ten years in the sun."

He drummed his fingers pensively upon the table. "I've seen hexation. But . . . Hell?" He took off his bowler hat and turned it over in his hands, as if wondering how it'd gotten there.

"There are ten thousand different *Chinese* hells, Mister Pinkerton," Songbird put in. "And *our* explorers have drawn maps—detailed ones, or so my tutors claim. Fifty of them in the Emperor's library alone."

Pinkerton nodded. "*Hell* I know, same as every other man," he said at last. "'Gods,' well—no such except the Almighty, in my book."

"There *are* more books than *the* Book," Asbury pointed out, mildly, in return.

You're right about that, Morrow thought.

But he had no dog in either fight—and Asbury was already off again in any event, theorizing out loud.

"As for the idea of 'gods,' Mister Pinkerton, consider them as magicians writ large, truly cosmic predators. The bloodshed perpetrated by Maya and Aztecs in veneration of their pantheons is, indeed, legendary. In fact, some credit the entire fall of the Mayan Empire to their religious excesses: killing whole generations of beautiful youths and maidens, destroying forests to build pyres, polluting rivers with entrail, ash and gore. . . ."

"And *that*'s what-all this woman of Rook's aims to bring about again—that right, Morrow?"

"Far's I know? Yes."

Enthralled with his visions, Asbury just kept on going. "'Gods,' then, would be the sum of Expressed magicians plus worship, as a system of human sacrifice channels both the power inherent *in* such sacrifices—chosen without doubt from amongst the Unexpressed—and the power of human faith, of sheer zealotry and credulousness, into the 'deities' in question. A fascinating equation indeed."

Pinkerton smacked the table, sharply. "*Doctor* Asbury," he said. "Seems to me Mr. Morrow has not finished his account, some of which I gather may still be of interest to you—and *all* of which has earned him, at the least, courteous attention."

To Morrow: "Now then. Where did this Lady Ixchel take you, precisely?"

Morrow took a deep breath. "She called it the Moon Room."

The arch itself was perfect and smooth as any cathedral's, the rock in which it was set raw, rough and dripping with lichen. Above the arch, at its apex, sat a gouged half-circle curve, an inlaid sickle of flint splotchily patterned with dark stains: a moon shape, fit only for shed blood, mirrored in the yellow-black sky above by an almost-full real moon—skull-bright, a burst lantern.

This is the Moon's House, said Lady Ixchel. **A door between worlds and ages, poised to open. Be honoured, my kings . . . and you too, o blood-guards, my husband's retinue. For this is where the old age will come anew.**

They entered.

Inside, the moon seemed to loom closer still, making a pitiless roof that blocked the rest of the sky entirely. Under it sat that same black disk from Songbird's, re-grown to full size: ten feet in radius, from its ragged-punched central hole on out, its circumference a smaller, bleaker, reverse-coloured parody of the painfully white orb above.

Their boots clopped dull and dead upon the round black stone, as if swamp-thick air swallowed the noise, though to the lungs the cavern's air felt breath-hitchingly thin and dry—the painful draw of a mountaintop. The men ranged themselves around the stone's circumference without even being told to, an instinctive movement—the circle of the tribe in wordless wonder, agape at the blackness of the infinite night sky.

At the centre of the circle Lady Ixchel stood, hands uplifted and her hair stirring about her in a great black cloud, as if she floated in invisible water. To the right and left of her stood Rook and Chess, facing each other like bride and bridegroom. Between them, the hole in the centre of the stone yawned, so empty it went beyond black into something that seared with anti-light, anti-*life*—as sight-sore to look at directly as the sun.

Against that emptiness, the power in all three figures blazed, actinic and flashing. Morrow had to shade his eyes and fight not to double up, retching, to try and cough out the acrid stench of magic.

Rook lifted one hand, stroked Chess's jawline as if memorizing its feel. Then smiled, and murmured: "Skin off, darlin'."

Without a second's hesitation Chess flung away his hat, shrugged off his vest, blank face empty. His hands moved entirely of their own accord. But it wasn't until the gunbelt hit the stone with a clatter—until Chess's guns themselves went spinning away—that Morrow finally found the strength to protest. "You son of a bitch," he choked out. "Just what the hell you fixin' to do to him? He *loves* you."

Rook didn't look around, as Chess finished stripping down. His eyes seemed to shine in the murk—a tear, or just the gleam of power-lust? "Guess he really must, at that," he said, wonderingly. "The Lady tells me this wouldn't work, otherwise."

The air was so thick with magic now that Morrow almost felt he could *see* the cord of Rook's geas: a shimmering tension like a glass rod glimpsed in flowing water, running taut from Morrow's head to a point inside Rook's coat, the pocket where the mojo-bag rested. He sucked in the deepest breath he could and grabbed for the line of power—felt it quiver against his palm, a ghost-wire of air and static.

"No," Morrow ground out—and pulled on the geas, hauling himself a step forward, into the circle. It hurt like yanking his own brain out through his eye sockets. But Rook winced too, and put one hand to his head as if pained by a too-bright light.

Slowly, Chess's staring eyes blinked.

Lady Ixchel did not move, her rapturous gaze holding fast upon the gigantic overhanging moon. But a wavefront of fury struck the circle in a sandstorm, hot and stinging; the men cried out, dropped to their knees. Given that Morrow was already half-mad with pain, however, it didn't make much never-mind to him: he hunkered down and pulled himself another step forward. Two more, and Chess would be within arm's reach. . . .

Rook sighed, and brought his hand to the nexus of the mojo-bag, stroking his coat. Every nerve in Morrow's body went dead in an instant. He crumpled—slack, but for just that moment so blissful with numb release he didn't care at all, tears smearing over the cold black stone, as he gasped out sobbing breaths.

"Now that . . . is truly something special," Rook said. "Never once occurred to me you could pull on a binding from either end. Never thought anyone wasn't already a hex'd be fool enough to try."

"Ash . . ." Chess turned his head slowly, drunken. "Ash, I can't . . . can't move, Ash. Whuthah . . . fuck . . ."

"Shhh." Rook cupped Chess's face in his hands, and cold-kissed his forehead. "'S'all gonna be all right, darlin'. I wouldn't do nothin' to cause you real harm. I love you." Holding Chess's eyes with his own: "You believe that, right?"

". . . shouldn't I?" Chess's glance cut sideways, to the dark woman-thing nearby, and blazed with fury. "Oh, 'course I should. 'Cause you been *so damn nice* to me, lately—you, and her. . . ."

Rook smiled. "Hex can't stay true to hex, Chess. You saw me with Songbird—I paid her price, fair as fair does, and she tried to kill me anyhow. Just 'cause she knew damn well just exactly how nice it'd feel, if she did."

"The fuck's that . . . got to do with . . . you and me? I ain't no—"

"You *are*, darlin'. Always have been. Not awake like me, not yet—but you been wakin' slow and sure these past years, and once you came to full flower, wouldn't be nothing left for us but to feed. On each other. 'Til one of us was dead." Rook's voice roughened with sorrow. "'Cause that's what hexes *do*."

"You been . . . feedin' . . . on me?"

"Since always, darlin'. I'd have left you a long time back, it weren't so—and even now, I still want to *eat* you. *So damn bad.*"

"No." Chess's eyes went wide, all fear and desperation and rage. "I won't hear this. You're better'n me, always have been—you're a *good* man."

"Flattering, darlin'—but in this case, I'm afraid, you're much mistaken. Because—on this whole wide earth, there's nothin' worse than a bad man who knows the Bible."

"You . . . think . . . I'm scared?"

At that, the gleam in Rook's eyes showed itself after all: tears, runnelling down. "Never, Chess Pargeter. That's what I like about you the most. You ain't afraid to kill, or to die; you ain't even afraid of pain."

And here the Rev kissed him savagely, drawing power deep, so intense Morrow could see it swirl like inky water between them. "But don't try to fight me, sweetheart," he said, panting, when he broke off. "You ain't strong enough for that, not yet."

"Fuck off!" Chess writhed in his invisible bonds, unable to see his own aura surging black. "*You're* a damn hex, you cheating motherfucker. I ain't! I—"

Rook, covering Chess's mouth with his fingertips: "But . . . *you will be.*"

A blink, and the Lady was abruptly between them—pressing Chess down hard with both hands, all but *grinding* herself against him. Though Chess fought her, it did no damn good whatsoever, that Morrow could see.

She murmured, "My brother will ride you well, little warrior, once your flowers are brought to bloom. Husband of my husband, little light, little meat-thing."

Chess spat. "Screw *you*, you hex-Mex hellbitch!"

Lady Ixchel simply crooned back at him, tutting slightly, stroking his fever-flushed cheek—and Chess melted under her touch, losing energy like she'd popped a spigot on his soul. Beside her, Rook had finally withdrawn the Bible from his inner pocket and stood flipping through it, searching (no doubt) for some relevant passage to soothe Chess with . . . but that was when the whole of it burst into flames in his hand, each page going up like flash-paper and vanishing, with not even ash—his namesake—left behind.

"You will need that no longer," she told him. "We will write a new book together—a book in stone, and blood, and gold. A Book of Tongues."

The phrase ran through Rook, Chess, even Morrow, in a silver skewer. They shivered and nodded, as one.

"Now . . . kill what you love."

"Why?" Rook managed.

That is YOUR sacrifice.

Open your heart to me, darlin'. 'Cause there's no more time, at all.

But it was Rook who opened *Chess* up, skin-first, blood spraying—and Chess who screamed at the feel of it, high and harsh and sounding far more in rage than pain, though Christ knew it *had* to hurt. His flesh went flying—and as Chess spilled his blood on the stone it began to shine, its image humping up by parts so each section peeled and tore itself free and *added itself* to Ixchel somehow, making her huge, terrible, inhuman. Rook plunged his axe-blade hand under his lover's breast-bone, plucked out his beating heart like a dripping carnal jewel—

Jaguar Cactus Fruit, from which all of us will grow anew. . . .

—and gave it over to Lady Ixchel, who chawed it down, ate it whole, smashing it against her mouth 'til her lips ran with his blood. Then kissed Rook right in front of Chess's betrayed eyes—a kiss like clashing swords, like split skulls. A kiss with teeth.

"My little kings," she said, beatific, fond as any other mother. "My . . . husbands."

Screw all this for a game of Goddamn soldiers, Morrow thought, drawing his gun. And before Rook could maybe think to stop him—but would he even want to, seein' what she'd made him do?—Morrow'd already fired directly into the back of that dark and bloody goddess's head, blowing a gaping hole right where skull met spine.

But: The rest of her head spun 'round, a Satanic whipping-top, to roar full in his face, her mouth so wide, inside it a tangle of other tiny people screaming, rows on rows all *red*, and—

the earth quaked

the Moon Room walls rocked

the air went foul and full and stiff

darkness everywhere, all but where something blue sizzled, some awful coal-pot set atop a monster's skull and

an irregular chopping noise infecting it all, a sluggish wooden heart beating, getting

closerclosercloser

—but then it was four weeks later, and Morrow was already clawing his way back up, alone but for Chess Pargeter's broken body clutched one-armed to him—reaching out in the dark by blindest drive alone and catching hold of *somebody else's hand*, tiny and cold, its brass-hard nails curved and sharp as a harpy's—screaming out loud as he was dragged inexorably upwards, out into the light.

Where a hearty Scots voice greeted him, burred and blessedly familiar: "Damnable good to see you again, Agent—even under these sad circumstances."

Cries, screams, shrieks and Spanish oaths formed a howling, incomprehensible music around them, as mobs of panicked men, women and children rushed everywhere. Dust clouded the sky in a choking, shadowy veil. Amid broken brick, splintered wood and fractured stone, Pinkerton knelt over the disgusting ruin of what had once been Asher Rook's lieutenant. Songbird, who'd plucked him from the hole, had taken up position on Pinkerton's left hand, and was shielding her albino complexion with an incongruously dainty parasol of red-lacquered paper. And here came Asbury, toddling along in the rear, examining some sort of trail snaking—crack-like—up through the dirt.

Morrow glanced back at Chess, and immediately wished he hadn't: the man lay there flayed and gutted, only recognizable because his jaunty earring was held on by a few threads still, tenaciously attached to that slack flap which had once been his earlobe.

"Well, *he's* good and dead," Pinkerton remarked, while Asbury looked disappointed.

But Songbird, whose pale eyes saw more than either of them, simply shook her head. "Perhaps . . . not."

She put her hand almost *in* Chess's grievous central wound, hovering right above his open rib-cage, only to have it close with a sticky Venus Flytrap snap, trying for the fingers themselves. Startled, she tried to yank back, but seemed unable to move—was caught, squirming, that same meat-to-fluid *slide* of hex-on-hex drawing hard at her, the way a five-year drunk inhales his night's first jolt.

And all the while mould grew over Chess, flourishing with each wave of her stolen juice—a cocoon of green, a husk that turned gold, then brown. Then peeled away, in its turn to reveal a fresh new Chess, naked, re-skinned once again. Perfect as ever.

Perhaps more so, even . . . seeing how they all of them—even Pinkerton, even Songbird—gave out a collective hungry gasp at the sight of him, like it'd reached down into their privates and *twisted*.

"Aw, shit," was all Morrow found he had left to say, on the subject, before slumping backwards into similar unconsciousness.

The sunlight had angled and deepened only to afternoon, but Morrow felt he could sleep for days. "And everything after that . . . you know." He massaged at his forehead, fighting not to yawn.

Pinkerton stroked his beard. "You deserve a medal, Agent Morrow," he said gravely. "And were there any way to cast you one this minute, I'd do so." One side of his mouth lifted. "Though I'd dearly love to see the faces of the men, when we tell them how 'twas earned."

Morrow stared at the tabletop. "Thank you, sir," he replied, in a mutter so low he could only hope Pinkerton would put its distinct lack of enthusiasm down to a state of impolite but understandable exhaustion. After all, he hadn't found out until waking—in one of a convoy of stagecoaches thundering back to the Pinks' unofficial headquarters in Tampico port—that the pile of rubble they'd dug him from had actually been a too-damn-large part of Mexico City itself. The quake he'd kicked off down in that dreadful world below had wreaked sympathetic damage on a monumentally destructive scale.

This sort of thing starts wars, Morrow thought. *If anyone ever reckons just what exactly happened. . . .*

Once out of the debriefing, however, the air smelled suddenly clearer. He'd forgotten just how bad the incense-and-gunpowder stink produced by Songbird's opening ritual, when she'd stripped Rook's mojo-bag geas from him, must have clung. Still, a bath might be in order, before he bedded down.

Upstairs, he came on Hosteen conferring with a Mexican sawbones in front of Chess's chamber door—authority writ large in every limb of him, like he'd negotiated on the Agency's behalf his entire life. "Pinkerton says he needs Mister Pargeter fit to travel, Doc."

"*Señor*, he may not live out the night. That man is down in Mictlan again, I think. By tomorrow, he'll either be better or dead."

Hosteen clicked his tongue impatiently, and turned away—past Morrow, who he seemed intent on ignoring outright. But Morrow wasn't having any.

"Good to see you made it here all right, Kees," he said.

"Uh huh," Hosteen flung back, over his shoulder. "Too bad *Chess* didn't."

Morrow shut the door of his room, leaned back against it and let himself hang there, boneless. Felt how every part of him ached with roughly the same intensity, an all-over throb.

Sleep, he thought. *Sleep*. Until—

He heard it rise, slowly, softly—that shuttery click-clack again, wooden-soft, hollow as a rotted log. Blue sparks appearing at the very edges of his vision, sizzling.

Aw, hell *no, damn it. Just—NO.*

Morrow half-ran to the wash-basin, splashed his face and shook his head, as though he could throw the last three-days-that-were-thirty off just by willing it. Kept his eyes shut throughout, black shading to red, 'til the sound receded and there was nothing but his own pulse to hammer at the world's edges, his own breath to hiss in his ears like the sea.

But when he opened them once more, it was no dice: Rook's face hung inside the mirror, staring right into his own. Like they were contemplating each other through a damn window.

Ed.

"Reverend."

I see you got that spell of mine took off you, in the interim—she's a good one 'bout her business, that Miss Songbird. Ain't she?

"Sure is, yeah," Morrow agreed.

And you've told your tale by now, I'm certain—must've gotten quite the reaction from your boss. But you didn't tell them the absolute whole of it, though, did you?

"No, Reverend. I did not."

And now it was Rook's turn to smile, finally, awful as ever. Awfuller.

Good man, he "said."

Hardly, Morrow thought. And bowed his painful head against the cool tin surface, eyes shutting once more, to await further instructions.

CHAPTER NINETEEN

In the room next door, meanwhile, Chess Pargeter's body lay in bed, while his lost soul loped nameless against the Sunken Ball-Court's sluggish currents headlong, black water breaking in stagnant waves to his knees—stinking of old death, no part left of him that didn't hurt. Off in the distance, he saw a blue and smoking light sizzling beneath that constant rain of knives which fell, blade-first, all around him: a torch, maybe? Lantern? Something to anchor him in the endless darkness's midst, anyhow. Something maybe worth the following.

Skinless, he stumbled on, thanking the God he didn't believe in there were no mirrors handy. Because even without one, he knew himself horrific: nose's bone gleaming cuttlefish-white from a red mess of face, exposed eyes clicking dryer with every useless blink. And the pain, Jesus, *pain* everywhere, so much it faded to nothing whenever he tried to concentrate on reckoning it exactly. Like flies buzzing on exposed nerve.

At least he had his guns yet, as the belt's further torment proved, tenderizing the laid-open meat of his waist with every step. He didn't even want to think about what must hang, nude and knocking, beneath it.

At his chest's centre a gaping hole sat open, mouthing the awful wind.

The tunnels narrowed as he went, closing 'til all he could see was skulls, flowers, skulls. Eventually, he turned a sharp corner, and fetched up against a skeleton twenty feet high, leaning quizzical over the wall of bony brainpans, which set up a great wailing.

Ixchel, this said, inexplicably. ***You . . . are hers.***

No, I damn well ain't, the dreamer snapped back, fast enough—though he couldn't quite recall, himself, why he was so insulted by the implication.

At that very moment, though, another figure leapt up out of nowhere, squatted atop the wall, leering down at him. Wrapped in a mantle of feathers worked with skulls and crossed bones, this new phantom had a small disk set where its foot should be—pitch-black, yet still shiny enough to reflect the dreamer's current haggard lack of face, in horrid detail: all nude eyes, his scalp askew 'round his shoulders with the rest of his head-hide split wide in two rotten peels, turned inside-out.

Ah, this figure said, undressing him further with its awful gaze. ***So you are not sweet Sister Ixchel's ixiptla, after all. Who does that make you, then, little king? Little sweetmeat?***

And oh, he *should* be able to answer that one, he thought, cursing himself for straining after what was once so uncommon clear. But there was only the pain, worse than ever, everywhere at once. A white-hot eraser. A salt-lick scrape.

Then a chorus of voices entered his head, in fragment.

Reverend Rook . . . everyone knows you're his bitch.

You Engarish Oo-nah's boy, wei?

So there you are, at long last. Such a big man, wiv your guns. . . .

With the most important voice of all saved for last, rumbling low as thought up through hot flesh, gentle and terrible all at once: *What wouldn't I do, for you? Damn my own soul, gladly.*

And . . . that was it, right there. That was enough.

"Name's Chess Pargeter, you skinny motherfucker," he managed, at last, through lipless teeth. "I mean, seein' how you're prob'ly the Devil himself . . . you really ought t've heard of me."

And before the spooky bastard could tell him any different, he gave him both barrels, right in his damn fleshless skull.

Then he woke, but didn't. Saw himself on the hotel-room bed, gyved at wrist and ankle—hung above his own empty body and watched it glow, a flesh candle.

The smell of the place—burnt wood cut with garbage, plus a chamber-pot whiff of sex's unmistakable long-stood stink—reminded Chess fiercely of the last time he'd been fever-caught, when small. *Inflammation of the appendices*, the whorehouse's live-in barber-cum-abortionist'd called it—a churn of pain, pushing out the side of Chess's stomach in a sore, swollen curve.

How he'd kicked and raved! They'd had to hold him down, English Oona getting him briskly lit on smoke and cradling his head as the "doctor" cut into him without benefit of alcohol, let alone ether. Now and then, she'd turn Chess's head so he could puke in a blue porcelain basin with a chipped rim. It came in endless racking waves of pain and nausea, nausea and pain, eventually blotting him out entirely.

And much later, resurfacing to the agony of his wound—black stitches through seeping red skin, rucked like a bad seam—he'd been soothed back to sleep by the regular creak and heave of her fucking the Doc a bare hand's-breadth away, for payment.

But this was now—the agonies of Mictlan-Xibalba were gone at last. His body lay right there in front of him, intact as ever . . . aside from one little missing part, of course. For fine as it might look from the outside, it lay doubly empty—pithed, a shucked husk.

You took my heart, you son-of-a-bitch, he thought, "to" Rook—whose very absence, he found, hurt him almost as much. *Reached down inside and took it, and then . . . you gave it away to that evil whore from Hell, right in front of me. Let* her *take the damn thing, and* eat *it.*

Yet that wasn't entirely so, either: he'd *given* his heart away, gladly. Like the fool Oona always called him.

Yet here a voice intruded, neither thought nor conjuration, so much, as . . . simply *there*. And said: *Aw, quit foolin' yerself, you great pansy. You never even 'ad no 'eart worth the losin', to begin with.*

Yet forget that, pelirrojo, conquistador. Forget it all, and listen.

And gradually—Chess became aware of voices filtering through the chamber-walls, muttering and indefinite. Without making any sort of decision to do so, he sent his consciousness drifting thata-way, random and thoughtless as any eavesdropping bird. After a moment, the wall itself grew porous, seeping away in foggy sections, revealing—not another room, but the memory of another room, another place.

Outside Splitfoot's, the moon hung heavy, bright as the devil's coin. Under it stood Ed Morrow, looking north—'til Reverend Rook flickered into being beside him, and offered him an already-lit cigar, which Morrow waved away. And as Rook pulled deep, blew out, the smoke rose up languid into the night sky, catching light from the window Chess knew he himself had lain behind that same night, trapped in that bitch Ixchel's toils, having his rebellious body put through its paces.

You should've saved me that, you bastard, he thought, *with all the crap you'd spewed hitherto concerning love, and loyalty. Would've, for sure, you'd ever really cared for me at all.*

"Well, listen to you—big man wiv 'is guns, whinin' away at lost love like a baby whore. Ain't too proud *now*, are ya?"

She was sitting on the bed, behind him. Or—above him? Beside him. *Inside* him.

That same smell as ever, pussy-wash and opium-cookings, acrid on the tongue. Her hair fell rust-red around him, and as she grinned down, he could see the holes where her teeth had once held gold.

"You . . . you're damn well dead."

"'Cause your fancy-man says I am? Well, 'e'd know, of course."

"You wanna get the fuck away from me, old woman. . . ."

"'Ow old you think I *was*? 'Ad *you* when I was only fourteen, and damn if that didn't knock all the other kids I might've borne right out of me. So thanks for that, *son*, if for bloody nothin' else."

"That what you're here for? To thank me?"

"Oh, lovey . . ." She made a moue possibly intended as endearing, which might've even looked so, if it hadn't pulled her face skullishly gaunt. "Ain't you never thought maybe I went somewheres *better*— that I might finally be 'appy enough t'say all the things I never 'ad no inclination to, back there? 'Ow I might pray it ain't far too late to tell my son just 'ow much I always *loved* 'im?"

Chess stared—then finally burst out laughing. Insulting, and frankly meant to be—yet Oona's face didn't change. Over and over Chess tried to recover himself, then looked on that awful smile, and was helplessly swept up once more. It was only the sight of his own body on the bed below—so passive and still—that finally cooled the hysteria again.

Voice still shaky: "Oh thank Christ, you ain't her at all. Can't be."

"Can't I?" Smile still unchanging, more and more maskish by the moment. "Didn't I never make a joke, then?"

"Not when it was on yourself. So if you ain't her, then . . . just who the fuck *are* you?"

Oona reached out, put a too-long finger on his chin; Chess tried to twist away, but couldn't. The contact, he realized too late—along with a pressure that forced his regard back downwards again, into that time-echo slice of past where Rook and Morrow still held their secret confab—were both things of spirit rather than flesh, impossible to fight off, except through magic.

And I ain't no hex.

"Names later, little one. I fink you might not want to miss this."

So: Rook and Morrow looking up at the window, behind which Ixchel had Chess at her mercy.

"Why would you *do* that to him?" Morrow asked, wearing that same half-puzzled frown always made Chess want to punch it whenever he saw it, because Ed was far too smart to play dumb as often as he did. "Let her—"

"'Cause she needs it." Rook replied.

"And you need her. To make yourself a damn god, too."

"You really are a sight smarter than you look, Ed—but yeah. And no. I need her . . . to make *Chess* a god."

The hell?

"Oh, he ain't much enamoured of the idea right now," Rook continued, like he hadn't heard Chess—and why would Chess expect him to? "But that'll change. He'll be a god, I'll be his priest-king; hers too. It'll be choice."

"And her." Morrow jerked his head at the window above. "What does *she* get out of it?"

"Oh, the usual . . . blood, and lots of it. That's what her kind like best. How'd it go, by the by? You and him, I mean." As Morrow blushed: "Yeah, I knew. But don't think I'm jealous, Ed; you gave him what he needed, in the moment. And now—you won't be so quick to want shed of us after all, either, will ya?"

"What do you *want*, Reverend?"

"I'm playin' it by ear, somewhat. Goin' where the currents take me. All hexes can, or could, but most don't listen. So—you send Kees for the Pinkertons yet?"

Morrow reared back, and Chess could see in his eyes it was true. White-hot fury: Morrow, a Pink? He'd fucked a damn *Pink*?

You son of a bitch, Chess raved to himself. *Minute I wake, I'm gonna—*

"Aw, shit! Okay, I give the hell up." Morrow threw out his hands. "Why d'you let me do *anything*, exactly? Why ain't I dead a hundred times over, by now?"

"'Cause I need you upright, Ed." Rook came close, put a comradely hand on Morrow's shoulder. "Better yet . . . 'cause Chess does. I need you *for* him—to want to serve him, protect him, bad as I do."

"Why can't you do it?"

"All you need to know is I *can't*, Ed. Not right now." Rook looked away, eyes shadowed. "I lay down with dogs, and now I gotta deal with the fleas . . . you understand me?"

"Not even a little damn bit."

Rook sighed. "Well, it don't matter too much, really. We all of us only do what needs doing, or what we're made to do." He glanced at Morrow. "You as much as anyone, Ed, for what that's worth."

Morrow frowned. "What—what d'you mean?"

"I mean, that what he needed last night . . . well, that was what I needed too. To make this whole thing work. So—" Rook tapped the coat-pocket which held the mojo-bag "—I might've helped things along, with you and him. Just a bit."

"You *made* us do that? Both of us?"

"Ahhhh, I said I *helped*, is all." Rook waggled a reproving finger at Morrow, whose hands had bunched into fists. "Didn't need that much pushin', truth be told, for either of you. So what's *really* gonna drive you mad, Edward Morrow, is wonderin' just how much of that night was me . . . and how much was you."

For a moment it seemed Morrow might just let fly at Rook, spells be damned—but Rook just tipped his hat and walked away, whistling. Morrow watched him go.

Then he walked over to the wall of Splitfoot Joe's and punched it so hard the skin on his knuckles burst.

"Oona" shook her head, sadly. "So men are born fools and stay fools, steered 'round by their pricks 'til the day they die. Too bad the only way knowin' that might 'elp you would be if you *wasn't* one." She gave him a considering look. "Poor little bastard. If you 'ad been a girl, least I'd've been able to teach you 'ow love's nothin' but a mug's game. As it is, you'll go on doin' whatever the little 'ead tells you to, 'til you learn better."

Chess frowned, having heard all this before—too many times to count, or register.

"What's that noise?" he asked, instead.

The real Oona, embarked on a philosophical tear, would've slapped him for interrupting; this one just grinned. And replied, "A fair question. What's it sound like?"

Several phrases popped into Chess's head at once, all equally unlikely. In rough order—*slammin' door . . . a wood bell tolling . . . something . . . rotten.*

Back and forth, in and out, a decomposing heart's mushy beat. It had started low-down, but now it mounted steady, so the walls fair rung with it. *Don't rightly know*, he thought—had halfway opened his mouth to say—but stopped. Because his eyes had gone lower, drifted to "Oona's" skinny chest, and *seen.*

And now she was looking down too. "Ah, *that*," she said, unsurprised. "Want a better look, do ya?"

She shrugged her skinny shoulders, let the fabric fall away. Revealing—a torso like an awful wax-rendering, anatomically denuded: bloodless neck, skin to her cleavage, and from thence on down nothing but a set of flapping ribcage-sides all wet red and whitish yellow, gristle-strung haphazardly together only at the bisected breastbone, the glistening spinal column. Guts coiled inside, and above that the heart, hung like a fruit—bright, hot, fluttering with life. *Smoking* with it.

He felt the sight of it in his own empty chest, like a fist. Felt his own *response* to it setting brain and gut afire, and found himself not cringing away in disgust, but reaching forward, fascinated, almost desperate. Wanting to feel that sheer pulsing *force* under his fingers, unbarred by fat and skin.

"Reach in, little brother, if you wish." By pitch and timbre it was still Oona's voice, but the Limey drawl was fading, washing away into an accent like ink stirred into blood. "Reach in, and perhaps I will give you a *new* heart, to fill the hole."

Her smile was half invitation, half mockery—and it was the mockery that broke his daze, reminding Chess far too sharply of what no longer lay beneath his own scars. So he flushed, scowling, stopping his hand in mid-air . . . while, inches from his fingertips, cradled under dripping bones, the heart beat a little faster—as if amused, or excited.

The bony arches of the ribcage reminded Chess for a moment of the whorled-dome walnut halves old Chang used to run games for the waiting pikers, back at the whorehouse. The salient point of suchlike endeavours, whispered slyly to him one night while setting it up, having been: *Trick, boy-ah, is not put ball under one shell, make gweilo pick other shell. Trick is—*

"—make sure there's no ball in the game, at all," Chess murmured, almost under his breath. "That every shell's empty, no matter what they pick—so you can make 'em always lay something out, but get nothin' back in return."

Then added, voice rising again: "As you'd goddamn well know already, you actually *were* my Ma—'cause she's the exact bitch first gave me any version of that same advice, her own damn self. So you can keep your 'new' heart; old one'll do me *just fine*, once I find out where to go get it."

"Oona" stared at him, that sugary smile well-gone now, for good.

The movement of her upper body was so small that Chess almost didn't see it in time. It was the noise alone warned him, a dampish whicker, as the open ribs suddenly spread wide—then lashed back together, almost chipping each other with the force of it, to mesh sharp as a shut clam-shell.

"*Jesus!*" he shouted, whipping his hand back with only a cunthair's width to spare, feeling what had once seemed normal bone slice the air coldly over his skin. Because it was all black and matte and glassy now, like tar-smoked quartz, and made a horrible glutinous sound as its razor-edges sheared the heart in half, mid-beat.

Wide-eyed, Chess recoiled, cradling his hand to his chest.

Stone grated on stone as the obsidian rib-blades slid over and through each other, like interlocking fingers. *This is the church, this is the steeple,* Chess heard faintly sing-songing, in his mind. *Open the doors—*

A wavering pane of flat smooth blackness assembled itself before him, his own face dimly visible in its glassine dark. For a beat of the heart neither now had, he recognized himself.

Then—change.

Crimson feathers, gold, ivory-hued bone and strips of reddish-dark leather adorned him. A long black wig streamed glossy hair from his head, and a pale, oddly tailored coat clung tight around shoulders, wrists and waist. He seemed to have four hands, and his face—*his* face, still—looked slack and empty.

Yet even as Chess realized that the person in that mirror was wearing *his own flayed skin as a cloak* (his staring eyes rimmed not in red paint but the naked flesh left behind after their violent striptease), the image changed again. Now the headdress was a bright and virulent turquoise, and a monstrous head reared over it, while the figure clutched a serpent made of fire and considered him with a face similar to Chess's own, but older—a man past thirty, his wars all behind him, and settled into ruling . . . what?

Some place I ain't never seen, and ain't too like to.

A further ripple of light and colour brought change, once more. Now the man was white-haired, white-feathered, a pectoral like a conch shell cut in half dangling on his chest and books and scrolls tucked beneath one arm. Yet the face, the face . . . was still *Chess's*, old as he had never thought ever to be. Venerable, respectable, even. Respec*ted*.

And behind all the faces, he heard cries and chants in a language unrecognizable, the frenzied howls of thousands in ecstatic adoration. Felt the huge, tremendous pulse of the earth's long slow turnings, the piling up of seasons upon seasons into centuries. The taste of blood at the base of his tongue, salty-sweet as Rook's seed, but richer, hotter, smoother.

Blur yet again, and now the face in that reflection was nothing near Chess at all, barely human: black-skinned, monstrously tall, knives of night-coloured stone sheathed everywhere. A buzzing corona of blue flame lifting from its slumped head. And one foot, one foot . . . was gone. In its place, an oblong plaque of stone, ornately carved. Like that thing—hell, it *was* the thing! Same one Rook had torn down Selina Ah Toy's to get hold of. . . .

Smoking Mirror.

And with that, it was no mirror at all anymore. "Oona's" head was gone, her slender white arms now long and coal-coloured, the monstrous face he'd seen reflecting his now rearing tall above him. The thing sat on his bed, huge and inhuman and steaming, and still all Chess felt was that leap in his heart, that excitement, that alien, utterly natural-seeming joy.

This is me. I'm with my own, at last. I have come home.

He fought it down, though, tooth and goddamn nail. 'Cause if there was one thing Chess Pargeter had learned never to trust, it was happiness.

"You're *her* kind," he said, "that bitch of Rook's, Ixchel, or whatever. Ain't ya."

The enormous face tilted, pensive. "Might could be," it replied, tone—and jargon—now mimicking his.

"Thought she said all y'all were—"

"Asleep? Well, that was her error. She woke me. With *you*." Chess blinked. "She tried to make you into me, little brother. One of me, anyhow. But you ain't made to cooperate, for which I love you dearly—so now you're only half me, and *I* am awake once more, wholly. Which, given I woke *her* in similar fashion, once, will be interesting, yes. Perhaps even satisfying, eventually."

Which made sweet fuck-all sense to Chess. "How many of you are there? You got a name?"

"Oh, many." The thing chuckled like the largest railroad engine in all the world grinding forward into motion, indicating its reflective stone foot. "Some call me, on account of this—".

"Smoking Mirror." Chess scowled, suddenly faint, and struggled for his next idea. "Yeah, uh . . . I remember the Rev showin' me that . . . thought that was just the thing, though—the *plaque*, what-friggin'-have-you."

"That was *a* Smoking Mirror, carved in my sister's image, by worshippers so far removed from our glory days as to confuse us for each other. *The* Smoking Mirror—"

"—is you."

"Yes, little brother. And now . . ." Shockingly, the thing laid its hand on Chess's shoulder, fatherly gentle. ". . . you, too."

Chess's head swum and throbbed like that bisected heart. His mouth was wickedly dry, tongue all buds, barely cogent. "Getcher meat-hooks offa me," he said, or tried to—muzzily at best.

Such ridiculous creatures we are, in the end, the Smoking Mirror continued, as though Chess hadn't even spoke—and was *it* even speaking, as such? Not out loud, at any rate.

Oh Christ shit fire, my head, my head.

So powerful. So unrestrained. Yet so dependent on the very things we all too often kill with kindness, to survive. We blunder from Sun to Sun, seeking after humanity, nurturing it, destroying it. All the while refusing to accept that without it, we—the blood engine's crew, centrepiece of an entire universe—are nothing.

"Goddamn 'f I know what'cha gettin' at, ya skull-face sumbissh—"

Look down, little brother.

Chess did. There was a crack spreading fast across the floor beneath his bed, hairline to gaping—flourishing open even as he watched, humping the floorboards up, the same way roots break open cobblestones. And beneath, beneath—

—sure ain't the ground-floor, no sirree—

—was nothing but blood, and black, and cold water welling up, looking to breach the crack neat as a flooding river's banks. A wind of knives, rising.

A living man should enter neither Mictlan nor Xibalba, Smoking Mirror observed, ***and those who try, pay prices beyond imagining, as my sister well knows. Perhaps she thought your lover's retinue would suffice for exchange, allowing you, and he—along with that mutual toy of yours—to escape unscathed . . . and perhaps she would have been right, in less hungry times. But as it stands now . . .***

Chess stared, spat—saw it drop away into the endless gap, back down to where the skull-racks sang and the ball-players danced. Then, wrestling with his own slack mouth, demanded: "You . . . sayin' *I* did that, somehow?"

A shrug, and the voice in Chess's head became Oona's once more. *Just sayin' 'ow your warlock didn't even 'ave the guts to ask outright, so 'e gambled on it bein' easier to beg forgiveness after than ask permission before. Put you in a trance, tried to make you into one of me—an' damn, if 'im and 'er didn't succeed, but not the way they wanted. 'Cause when you're enspelled, you can't say yes or no, as such—can't submit fully, gladly, as a good* ixiptla *should. If you 'ad, things'd be . . .*

The clear implication: better. Less—apocalyptic, maybe.

Went on ahead and ended the whole world, him and you, with your Godlessness: that's what you did. Sure 'ope you're happy now. . . .

Chess spat again, a barely disguised snarl. Snapping, in reply: "Uh huh. And if my aunt had nuts, she'd be my uncle, and if things weren't the same, they'd be different. So fuckin' what?"

At that, cold wind from below met—abruptly—with an equally cold front of wind from above, a rush of "godly" disapproval: ***Don't***

mock, *meat-thing*. Chess flashed his teeth outright, this time, and bore it. Perverse as it might be, he'd match his own hotness 'gainst the coldest shit *on* this earth any damn day, let alone from *under* it.

But merely thinking this blasphemy alone seemed enough to work the turn. That blue flame leaking from Smoking Mirror's head-set coal-pot straightened in a quiff, rearing proudly once more. The monster itself loomed closer, holding Chess's defiant eyes with its own. Crooning, wordlessly: ***Oh, but I do like you VERY much, little brother. You have true mischief in you, fit to breed and burn. Let loose, you will seed this Flat Earth well with chaos and horror, carving roads for all the things even now escaping from the Ball-Court's gravity to follow.***

"Screw you, you spooky motherfucker! I already shot you the once, even if it *was* in a dream—"

Yes, I remember. And that . . . only makes me like you more.

Fast as it'd whipped up, the heat was draining out of Chess again, maybe through that same gaping, skin-shielded hole in his chest—he coughed and clutched himself, bent in over his own absence.

Naked, if not ashamed, he felt his numb-tongued incoherence return, and fought hard to demand, 'fore he was no longer capable of distinct speech. "Uhhmmmean . . . why the fuh sh'd I lissen t' yuh 't all, 'bout anythin'. . . ."

'Cause I'm you, little brother. No-voice sliding back to Oona's naff scolding tone, now, fast as sooty London winter: *Fink I can't be 'er too, just 'cause she's dead? All the dead are mine, no matter 'oo, an' all of them find their way down 'ere to me, eventually. They come an' go, like tides, but we endure, all my four faces—red, white, blue, black. All the same.*

"*Fuh* yuh! Sure's heh *ain't*, 'n' I . . . ne'er wih be!"

A shrug, so large it seemed to ripple the roof. ***No? Take a look, then—see for yourself.***

Though Chess tried hard to keep his gaze from going back to that meat-set blackness, both eyes returned nevertheless, as of their own will—spellbound, death-magnetized. Without fanfare, he beheld himself enthroned, splendid yet ghoulish—all turned inside-out and hung with corn-silk, a garland of ripe ears in 'round his blood-sticky head, and the green of his eyes converted to new growth—the spirules of budding stalks pushing out his sockets, bisecting both palms in imitation of Christ's passion, offered helpless to the world at large.

My body and blood, here, take, eat. All flesh shall be grass.

But that last, that *ain't me either, bein' how I'm a God-starved whoreson queer raised in knocking-shops who'd rather spit on the Good Book than have it read at him. I don't know any of that crap. That's . . . Ash Rook, you faithless fuckin' fucker, HELP ME . . .*

And Smoking Mirror, smiling down: **Pelirrojo, conquistador**. *Red hair, red face, my own red self, little brother, o brother mine. . . .*

"Born t' live fast and die young," it said, meanwhile—out loud—at the exact same time. "Born to raise 'ell. That's what your man an' my sister wanted, all right—a Flayed Lord fit to sow a fresh new crop of gods, all the way 'cross this empty West of yours. 'Course, the people as already live there might 'ave somethin' t' say on the matter . . . but then again, that's 'alf the fun."

"What are you?" Chess repeated yet one more time, hoarse and hollow.

"I'm your *Enemy*, son—yours, an' every other's. Chess Pargeter, English Oona's boy, Asher Rook's lover. Trickster. Killer. Destroyer of worlds."

Its voice dropped, intimately, effortlessly reassuming that other, interior tone—*But the real thing to keep in mind, when you're calm enough to do so, is this . . . I am your enemy's Enemy, as well.*

"The" Smoking Mirror gave Chess a push, right over the miraculously unscarred area where his stolen heart should reside: a mere flick, the easiest of keep-aways. And Chess felt himself drawn down, down, back down into his body again, the soft box of his flesh locked shut on him, a movable, woundable, wounding coffin—'til finally he woke up again, mid-leap, while rocketing out of bed: a spent shell, momentum-burnt, dead to the touch.

Still *screaming.*

Next door, in his hotel-room, Morrow heard Chess come to and whipped 'round, staring at the wall. From the mirror, Reverend Rook followed his actions, though only with his eyes.

Showtime, son. So . . . you do know what it is you gotta do now, right?

Chess's scream went on, arcing high, every new second of it a further lost opportunity—but Morrow hung back nonetheless, letting all his breath out in a huff, long enough that Rook's amusement started to slide to annoyance.

Right, Ed?

"I'm thinkin'."

Well, think fast, damnit. Songbird ain't but a few steps behind.

"No doubt." Morrow straightened up, full height, shoulders squared—then added, as he turned to stare deep into Rook's phantom face: "Oh, and speaking of which . . . *you* do know since she already broke your spell, that means you can't *make* me do shit, anymore."

Rook shook his head, sadly. *Aw, Ed, c'mon. It's Chess who's laid the spell on you now, much as he don't even know it . . . and deeper by far than anything I could've whipped up, seein' he's finally let loose all the explosive power of a lifetime's stored-up hexation at once—with not an ounce of skill to temper it, in the expression.*

The scream had long since lapsed to an air-hungry half-sobbing, less bereft than infuriated. Morrow could hear Chess blundering around, circle-caught and hammering at the invisible walls Songbird's wizard-trap had set up 'round him, cursing freely in a dry, exhausted whisper. In consequence, both rooms seemed quieter now, even somehow smaller—cramped with intentions, both good and bad.

"Lie down with hexes, that's what you get, huh?"

Dogs and fleas, Agent.

"So I'm fucked either way, is all."

Maybe so, yes.

Which was no sort of surprise at all, of course. And all Morrow could do, in the end, was take it, with a sigh.

"Best not to keep him waiting, I guess," Morrow told his suddenly empty quarters, as the mirror irised securely shut once more. And opened up the door.

CHAPTER TWENTY

Cramps racked Chess and pitched him back onto the bed, doubling him over. He managed to roll far enough to get his head over the edge and retched up onto the floor. No stranger, that particular feeling . . . almost comforting, for sheer normality. Until he cracked his eyes open again and saw what lay steaming on the floorboards: a wide, scarlet puddle of blood, with insects all a-wriggle in it, wings buzzing. Blood fell away to reveal rainbow glitter and huge crystal eyes.

Dragonflies.

They took to the air, filling it with a skin-crawling buzz. Several seemed to have been vomited up mid-bugfuck, careening awkwardly 'round in pairs, their black segmented tails still fused. Mouth open, Chess followed their flight and then froze, eyes locked on the corners of the bed's headboard, where two dark reddish rings of powdering metal hung broken from bright new chains. Like a score of years had passed in a night, making wrought iron shackles into useless rust, easily shattered with the flick of a wrist.

Two at the head, for his arms. Two at the foot, equally decayed, for his new-freed ankles. A folded set of duds on the nightstand, drab but serviceable. And—his guns, laid out neat, polished and repaired. With his belt and holsters coiled next to them.

How his hands itched to strap those back on, and draw! But there was no way *that* wasn't some sorta trap, same as the ring of Chink scrawl drawn 'cross the floor beneath—circling him with a net Chess couldn't seem to fight free of, no matter how hard he instinctually rammed and thrashed against it.

Heart trip-pounding, eyes wide and wild, ricocheting back and forth and back again: door, bed, floor, guns. Door, bed, floor, guns guns guns guns—

The door itself banged open, freeing Chess Pargeter to gladly obey his oldest and swiftest instincts—to snatch both sidearms up by their barrels, flipping them mid-way, and thread indexes through triggers like a damn magic trick. Thumb-cock the hammers, low and level, and train them both on whatever—*who*ever—was revealed.

Ed Morrow, as it turned out. *Agent* Ed Morrow, that was. And looking none the worse for his trip Down Under, either.

"Chess . . ." he began, then stopped short, the very sight of him apparently enough to drive a man's words out of his head entirely. ". . . I, uh—see you're awake."

"Uh huh. Figure that out all by yourself?"

"Um . . ."

Squinting hard at Morrow, Chess abruptly discovered that the additional buzzing he was "hearing" (above and beyond that of his sicked-up companions, who were already starting to die off, perhaps over-weighted down with a double payload of blood and impossibility) must be that of Morrow's actual *thoughts*, which almost immediately began to blunder through Chess's own skull. A goddamn offputting thing, not least since it made him inevitably wonder if Rook had always been able to read *his*, all along. . . .

The thoughts jumped forward, clarified and blew up hurting-large: himself staring back, looking *somehow older, even tougher than before—both less and MORE attractive in a strange way, even with a FIREARM POINTED STRAIGHT 'TWEEN MORROW'S EYES—*

—aw shit, God DAMN that stings!

"You . . ." Chess said, slow, and shook his head. Coughed again, wrackingly. "*You're* a goddamn *Pink*."

"Chess, it ain't like you think it—" But here Morrow seemed to register Chess's blood-slicked chin for the first time—along with the raucous, hovering debris of his recent supernatural up-sick—and stopped again, transfixed. "—just what the hell did you let Rook *do* to you, you damn crazyman?"

Chess scowled at him, drunk with pain and fatigue and fever. He couldn't keep both guns up any more, and let the left one drop to the bed, while the right one wavered. "Well—are you, or ain't you?" he demanded.

"That's neither here nor there. What did he *do*?"

Chess didn't glance down, though his other hand brushed automatically against the raw-to-touch skin where his scars *should* lie but didn't, stroking it.

"Cut out my heart, fool," he snapped back, annoyed by Morrow's incredulity. "Just like you saw."

"Literally?"

"You were damn well *there*, weren't you? Pinkerton man?"

Morrow sighed again. "Look . . . it ain't what it seems."

"Yes it is," Chess said, and pulled the trigger, which clicked hollowly against nothing. Enough of a surprise to make him pop out the barrel and gape at the empty chamber, thus allowing Morrow time to both roll his eyes *and* snatch the gun away with one sharp yank.

"I took the bullets out three damn days ago," he snapped, though he knew Chess wasn't listening (and Chess *knew* he knew, in a completely distinct way from how he'd've once meant that sentence—*Jesus*, this shit was *weird*). "Just left the guns so you wouldn't pitch a fit, if you woke up and found them gone. Now c'mon—you're sick. Get back in bed."

"Sure. Gonna try and hold me down?"

Morrow flushed, and Chess *knew*, precisely, to the last little drop—as if gauging the mix of a favourite drink—how much of that flush was memory, equal parts arousal and embarrassment, versus how much was exasperated anger . . . with something else lurking lower yet, gobsmacking in its urgency, its stark truth: fear. Of Chess—no surprise there. But also—*for* him.

Shuddering, Chess pressed the heels of his hands to his eyes. "I'm worse by far'n just *sick*, Morrow," he said. "*Sick* people don't heave up bugs, or puke cooked blood—and better still, when *people* ain't got a damn heart in their chest, sick or not, they usually go on and die.

Not to mention how there's no sickness I ever heard tell of lets you fuckin' well *hear what someone else is thinkin'*—"

But *that* was a mistake, 'cause the instant the words were out, Morrow paled, and Chess swayed under the cold blast of his fear before he threw it off with a jolt that rocked both of them: *No no no shit, get your head out of my head you sumbitch!*

Silence and numbness slammed down. Chess stared hard at Morrow, who stared back—then sighed. And replied, "Sounds like hexation, right enough . . . 'cause you're a hex, Chess. That's the sad truth of it."

Morrow crossed to the nightstand, flipped the plain denim clothes at him. They fell on top of the bed. "You don't wanna sleep, fine. Put those on, at least. We got business to discuss."

And I could stand not havin' to watch your tallywhacker jig free under there, while we do it.

Oh get out, get out, *get GODDAMN OUT!*

"I don't see how there's any sorta *business* left 'tween you and me, exactly—" Chess started.

But here Morrow whirled on him—faster than Chess had ever seen him move, 'cept maybe in the occasional gunfight.

"Inside this circle Songbird's done up here, you got no more mojo than I do, *Mister* Pargeter," Morrow snarled, his sideburns fair to bristling with the righteously angry effort of it. "There's enough men to fill a whole goddamn state would wanna kill you, they found you like this—and I might even be one of them, too, if I didn't already have bigger shit to worry about."

Initial rage expiated, he stood back up again, but his glare didn't lessen. "You spent one half your whole life thinkin' you were dirt, but the next thinkin' you were a man above all other comers, just 'cause you could draw faster and shoot better'n any of the rest of us. But ain't nobody gets to call himself a *man* who don't *clean up his own fucking messes.*"

The new door in Chess's brain swung open a moment. Immediately, Chess was submerged, still and breathless, under a bitter surge of anger, frustration . . . contempt, marrow-stunned with the hurt of it, the shock. Maybe because of its sheer inside-out impact, if nothing else, for to be loathed, looked down on, was certainly nothing new. But—Morrow's rush of disgust, temporary as it might prove, had nothing to do with the truths-turned-insults flung out. No. What riled Morrow ran far deeper—was the sheer perversity of Chess's own nature, that unbreakable wilfulness he'd always revered in himself, as sign and source of his innate freedom. His stark refusal ever to be bound, to obey aught but his own whim and want.

Because while he could walk free and hold a gun, Chess Pargeter answered to no man—no man, no law, no damn body, motherfucker. No ideal, no cause, no force but sheer chaos, bound and determined to move unimpeded and burn for the sake of burning. To never submit himself to ghost or hex or priest or even *God,* 'less he damn well *wanted* to.

No man except Ash Rook, that was—for a time. And after this last betrayal, from now on . . . not even him.

'Course not, Morrow's anger spoke back, unimpressed by Chess's well-tuned inner litany. *That's 'cause you're nothing but a brat who never grew up—a skillet-hopping little hot-pants who knows everything 'bout killing and nothing at all 'bout living. Who spits on friendship, duty and honour not 'cause he's above them, so much, as 'cause he don't know what they even mean—same way you don't really grasp how anything's real, 'cept if you want it, or it hurts you. And that's why you ended up givin' everything you had to a man who skinned you alive, then left you stranded down in Hell—'cause he was what you wanted, and Christ forbid Chess Pargeter ever admit what he* wanted *was a goddamn bad idea. You made it easy for him, Chess, you damn fool. 'Cause you couldn't believe you deserved anything better. And me? I'd never do that to you, or anyone. Never.*

The door between them slammed shut once more, leaving Chess alone in his own head, wrung out with surprise and confusion. And Morrow—he didn't seem to have even noticed their momentary communion. Just folded his arms, jaw set, and repeated: "So get dressed, I ain't gonna tell you twice. There's more goin' on than just *you*—and for once, you're gonna help fix it, instead've doin' every damn thing you can to make things worse."

And me wearing guns, Chess thought, amazed. Of course, Morrow *had* gone ahead and emptied the damn things first.

Chess knew he should be spitting mad, going on history alone— but it seemed more effort than it was worth. Still equal bone-tired from his long sleep and sharp awakening, he unfolded the shirt slowly, barely able to pry its buttons apart. Morrow evidently saw his fatigue as well; after a moment he huffed impatiently and stepped over the pictographs Chess could barely stand to skirt, bracing himself to help Chess dude up.

Damn, when'd you get so nice? a voice from the past said, in Chess's ear. But Chess brushed it away, like it was one of those dying dragonflies.

Boots now firmly wedged on, Morrow got his shoulder under Chess's arm and lifted him to stand. Freshly rendered decent, Chess felt the shirt and pants grate all scratchy-stiff against his skin, yet managed to force at least half a smile. Asking, "No pomade?"

Morrow snorted. "This ain't no Presidential Suite, Chess. Just have to wait 'til you're back on American soil for the little amenities, I—*what the shitfuck Sam Hill?!*"

Came so out-of-nowhere quick it almost made Chess bust out laughing, 'til he caught a snatch of his own shirt-sleeve going by. The plain denim was simply gone, replaced by *his* clothes—same rig he always bought, no matter where, or from whom: purple shirt, near-black trousers, burgundy-bottle vest, all clean and fragrant, as if fresh-laundered and pressed. Even his gunbelts were back around his waist, guns neatly holstered. And the boots were the exact ones he'd broke in months ago, no matter he *knew* they and all the rest were still lost somewhere outside this entire world.

"Oh, shit, Ed." He looked back up at Morrow, mouth open in dismay. "I'm a damn *hex*."

"All but indubitably, Mr. Pargeter."

As Chess's eyes went to the door, Morrow stepped smartly back over the circle, realigning himself with those who had just entered.

So they told ya don't come in here, Chess thought, and filed it away.

Songbird came first, her all-red rig pretty much the same as when he'd last seen it, except for wearing her too-white hair down rather than up. Still as elegant and finely dressed as a bleached-out baby whore could be.

She met his eyes full-on and threw him an evil little smile, murmuring: "*Ni hao,* English Oona's boy—so nice to see you once more, even after all the trouble you made for me, back at Selina Ah Toy's. But very much especially so, now that we both *know* each other . . ." *For what we actually are.*

That last part "said" extra-loud and direct, a spike punched straight through to his brain's own stem, the way most hexes probably joshed with each other—'cause they damn well *could,* and get away with it.

Allan Pinkerton, on the other hand, he knew from posters—a big, burly, check-suited man with a full bushy beard and a bowler hat. And then came a third figure, the man who'd spoken—some white-haired, bespectacled old fool, looked like the dimmer sort of medicus you sometimes found taking refuge from parts Eastern or Northern. Or would have, if his washed-out blue eyes hadn't held the most keen regard of all.

Chess tensed. He'd expected fear, smug triumph, stupid dismissal—all the old touchstones—and there was more than enough of all of them in Pinkerton's and Songbird's eyes to go 'round. But the old fool's gaze was different—clinical, passionate with fire Chess barely understood. As though Chess was the walking answer to some riddle gone unsolved all his life, a living quizbook ripe for reading. Or maybe a vivisection-bound (in)human curiosity, all fit to get strapped down and cut into.

It pissed Chess off—and spotting Hosteen hangdogging in back, like the bastard didn't have enough nerve to push past these strangers stink-eyeing Chess, only made him angrier. *Guess this here's the sorta situation where you're finally apt to be more careful 'bout your own skin than mine, for once, old man? You hypocrite—*

But then a strange thing happened. Hosteen squinched shut his eyes, fast as if Chess had actually pasted him one 'cross the chops with the above, rather than just *thought* it at him. Held his head, morning-after skull-ache style, and stared at Chess with wild, wounded eyes. At which point Songbird turned, silks flowing, to look first at Chess, then to Hosteen, then once more to Chess—like she'd just caught him at something, and it was making her happier than a shit-dipped hog.

With a tiny little smile, she raised one finger and wagged it back and forth, approving-reprovingly. Then whirled the finger and yanked, sharpish, as if first wrapping, then *snapping* some invisible thread.

For half an instant, Chess saw something—a flicker of light, a shimmer of heat—ripple up from the circle around him. A stinging chill came both down and up him at once, a giant pair of tailor's shears, *cutting* the air between Chess and Hosteen. Chess had no idea what, hadn't even known it was there, 'til it snapped back into him.

He staggered, grabbed the bedpost and glared at Songbird, who only shook her head with that same tiny smile: *Ah-ah-ah-ah,* gweilo!

Oh, that is fuckin' well it.

Chess felt it rush into him with a tingle, an ill-summoned current of power sent flooding outwards to prickle in both palms, which he clenched into fists. Almond eyes narrowing, Songbird's lip lifted in a snarl—and just as suddenly, a heat-haze crackled between the two.

"Doctor," said Pinkerton, low but urgent, to—the white-haired man, who'd been staring in open awe and delight, but now came to his senses with a shake of the head. Swiftly, he popped that odd timepiece of Morrow's from his own weskit-pocket. Morrow frowned to see it but said nothing.

Old Doc Whoever flipped it open, releasing its usual frantic clicking and clattering into the air. From another side-pouch, he drew a reel of dull, silvery-looking thread, spun off a length and snapped it free. He wound its middle once 'round the watch's fob and threw the end out the window, deftly swift, like he was laying a fuse. Chess followed it all only from the corner of his eye, barely truly clocking it, gunfighter-poised to meet whatever Songbird was conjuring with the hardest possible return strike he could muster. That he had no idea either *what* he would do or just *how* to do it didn't matter, not right then.

But that was when the doctor tossed the other end of the thread forward into the circle, to land squarely between Chess and Songbird. And that, that . . . was when shit commenced to *hurt*.

Compared to what-all he'd suffered down Mictlan-Xibalba way, 'course, this agony was second-rate at best. But for sheer surprise alone, it nonetheless took most of Chess's will to keep his teeth together as his body locked up, and all that freshly accessed hexacious firepower came sliding greasily out of him.

Songbird was far less sanguine. She threw back her head and screeched, indignant, as pinkish-white-green lightning arced from her and Chess both straight to the silver thread's end.

"*Ai-yaaah! Zhè shì shénme làn dongxi?*"

Which meant something like *what is this garbage?*—if Chess recalled his Chink insults aright. Though damn if he didn't almost feel he could "hear" it in its entirety, red-on-black-lettered inside his own skull, with the part she hadn't said at all—only *thought*—as an echoing aftertaste: *Kewù de lao bàojon* (*horrible old bastard*), *hao le ma* (*that's fucking well enough, okay?*)—or was that maybe *huàile* (*shit on my head*)?

Meantime, the symbols she'd inked upon the floor turned black, smoked, and melted into char as twisting, writhing arcs of power leapt from them too, lashing down the thread, through Morrow's device and out the window. Light flashed outside with deafeningly sharp cracks, the sound of a revolver emptying its chambers right shy of your ear. Followed by silence but for echoes, Chess all a-sway with his part-blinded eyes blinking, feeling light-headed and horribly empty.

Faint tendrils of steam curled up from the silver thread, snake-ghosts dissipating slow on the heavy air. Chess stared at them like the thread itself was a king rattler with its warning beads took off, bare inches from his naked heel.

"Private Pargeter, as was," said Pinkerton, his voice gone distant and buzzy in the racket's wake. "Seein' we all already know *your* reputation, I'd like to introduce Joachim Asbury, late of Columbia University's division of—what's the formal name, Doctor?"

"Experimental Arcanistry," supplied Asbury, with a smile both unsteady and forced. It came to Chess that Asbury maybe hadn't expected quite so violent a reaction himself. Then again, from the glare she was sporting, neither had Songbird.

So this ain't nearly as picture-perfect planned an operation as you-all want me to think, is it? Left hand and right not talkin' much?

"Though Mr. Pinkerton flatters me with the term 'division,'" Asbury continued, voice gaining strength. "With some experimental proof of my theories, however, I'm anticipating considerably more interest in the cross-application potential of individuals such as yourself, Mr. Pargeter—and you, of course, Miss Songbird—"

"Potential?" Songbird snarled something else in Chinese. "*Cong míng de, chùsheng xai-jiao de xiang huo!*" (*Very clever, animal fucking bastard.*)

Then whipped her hand backwards in Asbury's general direction, all five fingers tiger stance-clawed—and spasmed again, letting fly another yowl of pain admixed with sheer disbelief, as whatever hex she'd formed broke apart and crackle-sparked down into the silver thread on the floor, vanishing out the window once again. Rubbing her hand, Songbird glowered at Asbury with eyes full of furious venom.

"Unkind," she managed, eventually. "And . . . impolite, given our current alliance."

"As any wire of iron or steel grounds the galvanic energies of lightning, or similar phenomena," said Asbury smugly, "so a certain alloy of silver, iron, and sodium in its metallic form serves to ground magical energies where they manifest, conducting them away to discharge harmlessly elsewhere. Which is why any further active hex-working in this room—young lady, young sir—" he bowed to both Songbird and Chess, who shared an equally enraged glance at the inappropriate familiarity of being thus linked, "—will be neutralized in the moment of its launching."

Active hex-working? Chess had no idea what that meant. A hex was a damn hex, far as he was concerned. But he could still feel the smugness coming off Asbury as the man droned on—and only all the keener, now, with Songbird's far more sophisticated spellbinding self-evidently pulverized by the same device. With narrowed eyes, Chess forced himself to focus in on it, willing himself to relax and open up rather than lash out.

All at once, the smug buzzing transmuted, with shocking suddenness—same way Songbird's Chink-to-English inner babble had, into genuine *words*: *A lifetime's worth of unexpressed hexation, and more. Clearly this young man has no idea of just how powerful he could be . . . already is. And so we see why Reverend Rook chose to usher him through his transition with such overblown violence. Because doing so would allow him to keep control, stay the dominant partner in this invert ménage of theirs, thus avoiding the sort of overt conflict which might end in his own destruction. . . .*

Chess couldn't help but shy at the feel of it, so thumb-in-the-eye *pointed* as it rung, fair bruising his skull's bony confines. His gaze whipped over to Pinkerton, hoping for respite. But the crack only widened further, damage irreparably done—he plunged headlong into a burred Scots stream of words and images combined, oft times so close-knotted as to be barely coherent.

Sly little sodomite/catamite, properly, if Morrow's reported right/ wouldn't trust him so far's I could heave him, and that'd be some distance/ killer's eyes/take what readings you need and fast, doctor, then distract him/a bullet in the pan ought to do nicely/Madam Songbird's hex enough for our purposes, and you already have to keep her leashed/a mad dog/ for all your curiosity, can't think even you'd be foolish enough to let this monster live.

Mouth open, Chess turned to Songbird again and slapped up against an invisible barrier, hurting-hard—she'd locked down, no doubt feeling his intruding thoughts creeping loose through her brain. But after only a second's concentration, he began to make out shadow-show silhouette-cutter shapes moving *behind* those shields, coming abruptly into clarity with black-edged focus.

Big man in a flowing coat, shredding under a stream of flying shapes . . . Ash?

Same man, standing atop a mountain with a web of black strands tying him to a hundred, a thousand different figures everywhere, a great dark shadow rearing high behind him . . .

Ash, yeah . . . binding every hex in Arizona to him, maybe, like he'd said. And was that *her*, now, in the back? Or . . . Smoking Mirror?

A bearded man and a balding one, sinking down, with black blood flowing from their mouths. . . .

Pinkerton and Asbury, snared fast in whatever revenge Songbird had planned for their double trespass, their malfeasance toward her.

Oh, you stuck your damn hands in the hornets' nest for sure, boys, cuttin' a deal with that one . . . but then again, maybe that's why you ain't too inclined to want to do the same with somebody like me, *anytime soon.*

He slammed the door shut himself, cutting off the triple influx of soul-talk at its root. Jesus Christ, was this the sort of shit Rook'd had to deal with all the damn time? How'd he stood it? Panting, Chess made himself straighten. It all seemed to have gone by far faster than actually *hearing* the same "words," out loud. Indeed, Asbury himself was still talking, clearly having noticed nothing amiss at all.

". . . how the scientific study and deployment of your powers would offer vast benefit to our war-weary nation. Not to mention, of course, the spectacular opportunities for profit, for yourself. . . ." Asbury gave him what was clearly meant to be a sly, coaxing smile. Chess met it grimly. Nobody ever really got that it had never been about the money, did they?

I did what he wanted, and he returned the favour, in spades. 'Cause that's what a marriage of true minds is: loyalty. To hold fast and stay true.

Wasn't though, was 'e? that *other* voice murmured, far too deep down inside to ever be shut out. *Not really. Not when it bloody counted.*

But they'd settle that little point of difference later, when he'd caught up with Ash Rook once more. When he and that Mexican ghost-bitch'd had their fun, and the score'd been settled rightwise. When Chess finally had his boot laid right on that big bastard's rope-scarred throat, ready to stomp and *grind* the End-of-the-World Bible-foolery right out of him. That, or go down fighting, whichever way the chips might chance to fall.

One way or the other, he was never gonna throw his hat in the Pinkertons' slimy ring—a damn gang like any other, for all they had that staring sleepless eye-totem to watch over them, and drew their cheques at the same government trough as the Bluebellies. No matter how nice one particular agent might feel while all up in a man's business.

Here his bitter train of thought derailed. The true pain of his situation rushed back in, pouring him brimful with soreness and futility. Like getting your goddamn *heart cut out* by the same bastard you thought'd finally proved Ma wrong, who'd taught you love *did* exist, that you really were worth something more than a blow-job for a bullet, an extra gun at a knife-fight, or any other sorta flyin' fuckin' *fuck*. . . .

Think you can pull my *strings with greed, gentlemen and "lady"? Think there's any tune whatsoever you can play will make* me *dance? Think there's a thing on this whole damn earth you can tempt me with, now the one damn thing I ever* wanted *is gone forever?*

He snorted, loud and harsh, and saw Asbury frown, Pinkerton redden. Songbird's ghostly eyebrows lifted in an odd sort of respect . . . which frankly only made him want to punch her all the harder.

You got nothin' *I want, the none of you,* he thought, knowing at least *one* of them could hear him. *So fuck you kindly, very kindly—or rather, not. Fuck* all *y'all.*

To Asbury, with a smile so sunny it gave the lie to itself, curdling atop the acid ill-hid in every syllable: "Got something you maybe want to *ask* me, doctor, under all that syrup and sociability? Then I suggest you do it straight out, 'cause we're burning daylight."

Asbury coloured, thrown off his born pedant's stride. "Mister Pargeter," he began, stiff and direct—before slipping sidelong again into inquiry: "By the by, is 'Chess' your entire given name, or . . . a mere sobriquet, perhaps?"

"What exact part of 'get the fuck to it' was it you didn't understand most, mush-head?"

"Sir! I must protest, volubly—"

A brief flash from Morrow: *Jesus Christ, please don't*, with a side-order jolt of nasty amusement—from over Songbird's way.

"*Mister* Pargeter, if you please," Pinkerton amended, laying in thick with his battle-captain's knack of making his voice fill a room without seeming to shout. "For all you may find Dr. Asbury's methods a tad, eh . . . offputting, I think we've still one offer you might find of interest, nevertheless. Would you care to hear it? Given what seems to have occurred during your sojourn down in Hell's belly, for the good of America, if not the whole world—we aim to *destroy* the Reverend Asher Rook. And . . . we want your help."

"*Need* it, you mean," Chess snapped back, without thinking.

Pinkerton didn't much like his tone, that was clear—would've been no matter what, even without the accompanying in-rush of *damned puppy/queerbait bastard invert/how DARE* . . .

And—didn't it scare Chess, somewhat, how used to that he was getting?

Pinkerton, cold but calm: "*Need*, then. If you're willing to give it."

"Why would I be?"

"The way he's betrayed you, humiliated you, torn you stem to stern and then left you behind, for your worst enemies to pick up? Why *wouldn't* you, would be *my* question."

"Why indeed," Chess repeated. "But . . ."

Was that Morrow at the back of his head, now, slicing in all of a sudden from behind him, and probably not even thinking he was doing so? Showing Chess *himself*, slant-viewed, in ways he'd never previously dreamt on. How he maybe wasn't quite as black as he was painted, not even now, with Smoking Mirror's pitch-smeared face lookin' down over his mental shoulder.

Ask yourself why Chess does so much of any *damn thing, overall, and it's always pure contrariness—Oh, you think you KNOW me? Think you know what I'm capable of, which way I'll jump? Think the fuck again!—*

That's what Pinkerton don't care to understand, and Asbury just ain't even halfway equipped to reckon. Though Songbird probably knows it, or I'd be much surprised.

Jesus, Chess thought, head swimming, *and we only lay down together the once, too. Who knows what-all the Pinkerton son-of-a-bitch might've found out, Rook'd only stayed away a few nights more?*

He buckled without warning, eyes wide, and puked another splatter of hot and coppery blood that hissed as it struck the char-smeared wooden floor. Songbird's mouth tightened in distaste—then slackened, as Asbury gasped and Pinkerton's eyebrows rose, when the thickened mass inside the blood stirred, pushed upwards, swelled into a floral bud of the same carnal colour. In the silence of astonishment, the faint cracks of roots working their way into the floorboard's grain was clearly audible. Leaves unfurled along the stem. the bud grew further, spreading out red petals. With a dancer's grace the blood-flower revolved to face Chess, opening wider as it did, as if yearning for the sun.

Its central petals irised apart, revealing a bell lined with lamprey teeth that pulsed and tensed, a swallowing and hungry throat.

"My . . . good God," breathed Hosteen.

Chess made a sound too sharp and harsh to be a laugh. "Oh, you *think*, Kees?" He rounded on Asbury. "Fuck your money, Doc, and fuck your mission too, Pinkerton. I'll find Rook, all right—but not for you. He's *mine*. 'Cause . . . that's just the kinda bitch I am."

Songbird leaned slightly in Asbury's direction, and murmured: "I told you so."

Pinkerton drew himself up to his full height, mind hardening and darkening. Behind Chess, Morrow tensed. The two currents met queasily in Chess's midsection. "You'll not earn the dignity of a second chance from me, Pargeter, if that's your only answer." Then his scowl skewed to puzzlement. "What in God's name is *that*?"

His eyes went to the nightstand. Chess turned—to see the thing he'd always thought was Morrow's pocket-watch (Asbury's famous *Manifold*, he plucked forth—all unsummoned—from that same gentleman's over-hot brains), the device now eating all trace of magic from the air, come alive once more with its trademark chatter-whirring, ramping up ever louder and faster. More thought-stamps followed—from Morrow, a new surge of alarm and fear. Asbury's mindstink cloud had frozen up too. Chess could taste the old man's slimy terror in his own throat, bile mixed with blood.

"Agent Morrow." None of Asbury's fear was in his voice, unless that flat evenness was itself the fear. "What—*exactly*—did that . . . woman . . . say she wanted to do, with Mister Pargeter?"

"Sacrifice him, as I recall it." Equally flat, equally controlled. a voice Chess had never heard from Morrow. The Manifold clattered and buzzed, the pitch of its gears winding higher and higher. "Make him some kind of a—skinned god. A god . . . who dies? Like Christ Jesus, I s'pose. Only—bloodier."

Asbury turned away, paced frenetically back and forth, unable to keep still in his ferocity of thought. "Sacrificial re-enactment," he breathed, slapping his fingers against one palm. "The role of the avatar, rendered literal—yes, yes, with sufficient power directed upon it, bolstered by the faith of the worshippers . . . it could happen!" He stopped, excitement flash-flooding into dismay and horror, so vividly and powerfully Chess felt it strike everyone at once, for just that moment. "Oh, good Lord . . ."

"What *is* this, Doctor?" asked Pinkerton, low and the more dangerous for his own fear. "What the hell did we take into our fold on your say-so?" He spun to Morrow, abruptly shouting. "Morrow, what did you bring us?!"

Songbird, meanwhile, overtop—her mind's voice shattered glass and smoke: *KILL him, fools, while he's distracted, kill him NOW—!*

Hell, Chess thought, *and me with empty guns.*

The Manifold screamed on, a miniature steam-engine running at breakneck full-throttle, derailment-fast.

Asbury panicked. Chess felt it happen, more than saw it—the shattering of every ounce of vaunted rationality in one thoughtless burst. Knew, even as the old man scrabbled for Hosteen's gun, what he was going to do. Lifted his hand helplessly as Asbury wrenched Hosteen's pistol from the startled outlaw's holster, cocked it, spun to aim it at Chess's breast.

And then, right at that same instant: the crimson flower on the floor swivelled around and *struck*, lamprey-teeth closing fast on the silver thread-end beside it.

A double-flash of light blinded the room, one carmine, one actinic white, as the flower vapourized, the thread liquefied instantly, and the Manifold burst with a flat sharp crack that buried smoking shrapnel in every wall. Battle instinct saved Morrow and Pinkerton, both of them dropping to the ground when they saw the flower move. Songbird's shields had already snapped on, deflecting flying shards around her every which way, a jagged metal-and-glass halo. But Asbury yowled and fell to his knees, hands pressed to a long, bleeding gash traced all along his cheek.

Hosteen swayed slowly in the doorway, one hand wandering up to his neck, where a thick red flow drenched collar, shirt, and vest as it spattered onto the floor. He subsided against the doorframe and slid down it, without haste. Chess gaped at him, barely able to see for the flash-blindness blurring his vision.

The old Dutchman didn't have enough strength left for a smile, but Chess felt the last of his thoughts curl around Chess's own: *Made you a damn . . . god, huh? Well. Always knew . . . you'd matter. To him . . . to me . . . always . . .*

His eyes went flat and fixed. A terrifying emptiness yawned for a moment inside Hosteen's skull. Then—nothing. The thing in the door might as well have been a wax sculpture, for all the resemblance it bore to a man Chess'd fought beside and cared for.

He glanced over at Morrow, met the man's eyes, and was startled to find them equally stricken.

Footsteps thundered up nearby stairs, down the hall. Pinkerton lunged to his feet. "*Stay back!*" he roared. "For the love of Christ, stay clear!" He whirled and drew his own piece—which promptly lofted out of his grip and clattered against the wall. Songbird lowered her hand with a look of deep disdain.

"Silence from you, *gweilo*," she ordered. "This is a matter for your betters, now." Turning to face Chess, lightning crackling in her hair, as her own power—newly unshackled—puffed her like a windy sail. "Well, *boy*? Shall we finish at last that conversation we started, back in Selina Ah Toy's?"

Chess clambered to his feet, feeling power surge along nerves and muscles, electrifying and painful with his fury. Magic welled out from him, pushing back the inflood of thought and leaving him blissfully alone in his own head once more. "Sure you wanna do this? Seein' what I am, I mean."

On nothing but sheer impulse, he swept his hand, palm-out, 'cross the air in front of him. felt an invisible flame spill down into the floorboards, wrenching them up and apart as a decade's worth of vines and ivy grew in an instant, mounding up six inches high, curved before him in a tiny wall.

Heat-shimmer rippled up between them from the vegetation, distorting Songbird's face to a monstrous grimacing mask—but she just shook her head, and replied: "Oh, you *are* powerful, yes. But I—I *know* more."

She moved a mere finger in a minuscule yet complex pattern— and in an instant, the power flowing from Chess into the vine-fire wall simply went *snap*, a rotten log cracking in two. The barrier vanished, ivy withering. Energy backlashed into Chess, convulsing him with a startled yell of agony.

"Prince of flowers," Songbird scoffed. "Does your new skin chafe? Perhaps we will cure that itch by taking it off for you, once more."

"Get the hell offa me, you kinchin dollymop *bitch!*" Blindly, Chess spat more blood at her—only to watch it sizzle redly through mid-air, vitriolish. Songbird flipped her left hand up, a half-second too late. The hasty ward stopped all but one droplet, and she shrieked as it coursed down her face in a steaming red runnel, like she'd been hit with acid. By the time she mustered hexation enough to wipe it away, it had left a weeping, smoking scar near four inches long behind, running right down one perfect cheek.

Disbelievingly, she touched the wound with diffident fingers, tracing its path. Took them away to look at the blood. Then looked up at Chess—and all sense vanished from her face in a mindless demonic scream of fury as she threw herself upon him, the air between her fingers a-pop with ball-lightning, blue and vicious. "Ai-yaaah! Lotus-boy *ch'in ta*, uneducated *gweilo* whoreson *bastard*!"

With absolutely no idea how to shield himself from her vengeance, Chess switched right on back to his old tricks, and punched her full in the face—a round-house haul-off, nothing fancy but nothing pulled, worthy of any given ball-house tap-room brawl. Songbird's front teeth cracked across with a sound that filled the room as she went down, forehead-first, right at Pinkerton's boot-tips.

As it turned out, Pinkerton packed more than the one gun. Which wasn't much of a surprise, really—though hellish inconvenient, 'specially now he was brandishing the damn thing right in Chess's face.

"I knew this was a mistake, from the very get-go," Pinkerton told him, levelly. "Mad dogs should be put down, not catered to, no matter *what* other tricks they're capable of. So here's a proper end to it."

Chess held himself in some pride for not even flinching. Wasn't like he hadn't always thought this was the way he'd go out, after all.

"Better go on ahead, then," he said, "and drop your damn jawin'—'cause my only regret's I didn't kill a sight more of your men while I was at it, Mister King Shit Almighty Pinkerton. And if these guns of mine *were* loaded, I sure know where I'd start."

"A fine thing for me that they're not, then."

Yeah, too damn bad, Chess thought—then whipped his head 'round, as he heard almost the exact sentiment echoed from behind him.

"Too bad, yeah," said Morrow. "But still—"

Songbird looking up, at the same time, her mouth's pain a spike through the tongue: *What is that in your* mind, gweilo?

"Still *what*, agent?" Pinkerton demanded, as Chess and Morrow locked gazes.

To which Morrow answered, slow but distinct, "Still, occurs to me . . . since you *are* a hex, Chess, with at least as much juice as Rook, if not more . . . just what the hell's it matter, anyhow?"

Pinkerton opened up his jaws, drill-sergeant quick, like he was just about to bark at Morrow to *shut his mouth*—but it was too late. As though just giving the idea voice, however obliquely, had turned a key in Chess's gut, filling him back up top-to-toe with a virulent force that suddenly made all things possible.

Chess grinned, wolfish. "Always did like you, Ed," he said.

And cross-drew, fulfilling every outlaw's dream in one fell swoop with two impossible shots—that of shooting Allan Pinkerton in the face—or close as made no never-mind, clipping the Scotsman 'cross one ear-top as he swerved and went down ass-backwards, biting his own tongue so badly Chess could see the glinting muscle—with no ammunition but a *spell*.

He heard Asbury cry out. Heard Songbird laugh, even through her own pain, in sheer delight.

The bedchamber door heaved and sprang from its hinges, and a flood of agents spilled in, all blazing-ready to defend their sire. Chess turned to meet them head on, automatic, his guns already up. Only to have Morrow grab him up under the arms and sling him headlong through the white-curtained window, bursting out onto the first-floor roof in a spray of glass. He rolled and fell to the dusty street below, turning mid-air to find his feet like a cat.

Following hot on his heels, Morrow landed far heavier, with a yelp and a curse—jerked up and started limp-loping down the street, yelling back over his shoulder: "Jesus Christ, Chess, they'll be on us in a minute—you *comin'*, or what?"

Chess shook his head, but only to clear it. There'd be choice words 'tween him and Morrow later on, obviously regarding—various issues. For now, however . . . he turned, reholstering, to make better speed.

CHAPTER TWENTY-ONE

That they ended up in a graveyard, after—a cramped stripe of yellowing grass and tilted Spanish-carved stones, fenced off by black iron from the surrounding alleys, shaded by a dilapidated church to the west and new-raised houses on every other side—couldn't help but strike Morrow as entirely fitting. The new houses' whitewashed pinyon walls, he noticed, were superstitiously free of windows facing the tombs. What few did exist had been boarded up. Chess leaned against the back of a worn and grey sepulchre, bent over and panting hard.

Morrow stood with his arms crossed, shivering, thinking: *Everything I had . . . everything I am. I just sent it all up in fuckin' smoke, and for what? For who? The son-of-a-whore who's gonna kill me too, like as not, once he's got his damn breath. And that's a fact.*

It would make sense to run, he supposed. Run, keep running, see how far he got. But his legs hurt—and frankly, given what he already knew Chess could do, he didn't much see the point.

Chess straightened—made to spit, but then thought better of it and just wiped his mouth instead. "Tell you one thing," he said finally, without looking up, "that was some shindig, back there."

"Sure was."

"Guess you'll be in pretty bad odour with the big boss from now on, too, considering."

Morrow nodded, face lodged where between grim and blank. "Yup. Don't doubt it—"

At last Chess turned to glance up at him, but immediately shied away, hand over his face as if to shade his eyes from the sun. "Uh," he snarled. "Just . . . stop *lookin'* at me!"

Too tired to argue, Morrow complied, fixing his eyes on a smallish headstone. *Assumpta Francisca Xaviera Contesquio,* it read. *17 abril 1832 – 20 enero 1839.* His Spanish was rusty, but he thought the line beneath read something like, *Her beauty would only have grown greater.*

He thought of the Mexican woman whose body Ixchel wore. Wondered who *she'*d been, before the goddess-bitch took up residence—her life, her name. Did anyone still live who'd want to commemorate her with a stone recording their sorrow?

Christ knew, Morrow sure couldn't think offhand of anyone who'd bother doing the same for him.

"Ain't so bad, when you don't look," Chess said, unexpectedly. "I mean, I still feel it comin' off you, like standin' by an open window with a rainstorm outside." His voice dropped. "But when you look, it's like the wind changes, and it's blowin' right *through* me."

For half a heartbeat, the chill in Chess's voice touched Morrow to his bones, for all the Mexico sun continued to blaze down upon them.

"What's 'it,' Chess?" he asked, not really wanting to know, but feeling he should, somehow.

Chess thought hard on that one, an uncommon long span of time. "Might be . . . what you're thinking. What's inside you. The past, the future—I get it all the time now, from every-damn-body. Even Songbird, and I couldn't make out the *half* of what she had goin' on, let alone . . ." Chess trailed off, then struck the sepulchre's wall with one palm, flat and angry. "And it's always there, always, and I just can't get rid of it, can't block it out. Might be you, might be some other fucker a half-mile back, but it's *so loud,* and I *can't fuckin' make it stop.* Goddamn, if I ain't gettin' to wishing I'd let Pinkerton finish the job. And on a related note, just who the hell told you to help me back there, anyways?"

Morrow shrugged. "Who'd ya *think,* you ass? Rook."

Chess stiffened in shock. "Why?"

"'Cause . . ." Morrow took a deep breath. "He said you'd laid a spell on me—not to your knowing, just that you *had*, on instinct. Said if I wasn't an idiot, I'd have to keep you alive long enough you'd learn how to take it off yourself."

"Huh. Sounds the sorta thing he *would* say." Chess put one fist to his mouth, eyes narrowed. "Assumin' it ain't more'a his bullshit, though. What if I don't? Maybe I should just shoot your knees out and leave you here." A sidelong glance. "Let you find out how long it takes whatever it is I laid on you to eat *you* up, from the inside."

"Fuck if I know, you little piss-artist!" Amazing, really; no matter how far beyond anger Morrow thought fatigue had taken him, Chess still managed effortlessly to scrape up further irritation. "Think I really give a damn, this point?"

Anger sparked anger, and Chess rounded on him, green light flaring in his eyes. "Oh, but I think you *do, Agent* Morrow." He shot out a hand and slapped it upside Morrow's face, paralyzing him instantly, as swift and effective as Rook's charm-bag ever had. Chess leaned close in to Morrow, seeming to shimmer as his power roused.

It felt like the Howe-clasp on a rich Easterner's coat locking shut, mind hooking into mind at a hundred different points at once, rippling painfully through Morrow from scalp to anus. He flinched as Chess mercilessly tore away layers of pretence and wilful blindness, then smiled grimly at what he found. Then let go, as Morrow gasped, reeling.

"Yeah," Chess said, aloud. "You give part of a damn, at least." But the smile abruptly crumbled, leaving Chess to peer around the empty graveyard, disconsolate. "Much good as it does either of us."

He fell back against the sepulchre, boneless with annoyance, then slid down it, taking a seat on the ground. Morrow followed suit, as the truth of their plight sank in deep. Alone, penniless, hunted, and hundreds of miles from the American border, with no gang left on Chess's side. Hosteen dead—and whose fault was that? Near-equal on each part, Morrow reckoned—Rook rejected and gone, and no Agency on Morrow's side, not anymore.

"That Goddamn Asher Rook," said Chess eventually. "I'm gonna find him, and then I'm gonna kill him." There was no heat in it, no affect at all. "And it sure ain't to save the damn world, neither."

"Yeah, well." Morrow pulled off his hat and raked his hair back wearily. "I think he halfway wants you to."

Chess shrugged. "Then fuck him, maybe I won't." He caught Morrow's eye for a moment. An urge to smile pulled at them both. Both felt it, and felt the other feeling it, and it died. Carefully, Morrow turned away.

"I'm . . ." Morrow let out his breath. "I'm not sure it matters where you go, or what you do. Rook . . ." He sighed. "Rook beat me, Chess. Outthought me at every step, knew what I was gonna do 'fore I did it and planned on me doin' it. I don't know if it's hexation or just native wit, but if he could do that with me when he didn't know me from Adam, how the fuck you think *you're* gonna surprise him?"

Without looking, changing expression—hell, without even seeming to *move*—Chess's gun was in his left hand and raised to point at Morrow's temple. "By killing you? I mean, he seems to want you to stick by me. So why shouldn't I make sure you can't?"

Morrow's mouth hung open for a moment. Then he closed it. "Shit, I got no answer, Chess," he said at last. "Do what makes you happy."

He closed his eyes, wondering if he'd ever open them again.

There was no warning. That hundred-handed grip seized on Morrow's mind again, twined in and held, painfully hard. As little as six weeks ago the pain would have been bad enough to level him. And even stagger Chess—the mind-lock was hurting both of them, he only now realized.

Both saw in the other exactly what they recognized in themselves—the agonies and memories of their shared journey through Mictlan-Xibalba had changed both of them forever, even if only one of them had emerged as something more than human.

Might have been that resonance that opened up the link. Might have been part and parcel of the connection itself, or maybe only Chess's complete lack of hex-training. But as Chess's mind sieved through Morrow's with clumsy, savage power, his own memory unfolded to Morrow's sight as well, inverse mirror-images ricocheting off each other from touchstone concepts so fundamental, so absurdly different, it was like learning a new language with next to no terms in common.

Mother—

(a ragged, redheaded English girl curses and spits and beats a small boy with equally red hair, in a dark corner of an opium-stinking 'Frisco brothel / a tall, plain, rawboned woman calls three lanky boys and their father in from the farmyard, while a stew of beef, potatoes and carrots simmers on the stove and five clean tin plates wait on the table)

Fellowship—

(standing with eleven other men as Allan Pinkerton hands out badges, speaks words of congratulations, alive with pride, joy and satisfaction / watching over an absinthe glass as men you've bled beside drink and fight and fuck like animals, in absent disdain lessened only by the consolation that at least this vileness is honest)

Desire—

(one night born of boredom, anger, perversity / desperation, fear, loneliness / well-worn paths of flesh limned in shocked discovery / forgotten names of scores of men, release traded for release / a handful of women's bodies, echoes of clumsy tenderness and soft curves in the dark / the weight of one man, chosen for lust, kept for—)

Love—

(a father's hand on the shoulder / a young man not yet a Pink, laughing with fellows in a Chicago groggery / a greener, colder graveyard than this, standing silent for a brother fallen in war / a murdered lawman's wife-turned-widow, weeping with grief and terror, huddled over a wailing infant while awful salt-whiteness creeps up both their flesh at the behest of . . .)

Rook.

Chess tore free in a burst of agony, collapsing back onto his ass with a look of stunned incomprehension. Like any other man might have looked staring on Bewelcome, or Calvary Cross, or Mictlan-Xibalba itself. The shreds of their communion still raw, Morrow keeled over as well, nerves afire with the same pain—but he knew its meaning immediately, because it was no revelation for him. Hoist on the petard of the exact same truth-compulsion he'd turned on Morrow, Chess couldn't tell himself what he'd seen was a lie . . . and couldn't lie to himself about what it meant.

You really did *think we were all fools,* Morrow marvelled, half to himself and half expecting Chess would hear it anyway. *You really did think any man talked about love was talkin' out his ass—lyin' to himself, or everyone else, or both. And any woman talked about love was just lookin' to profit, some way or other. Whatever the words, you thought you had the truth of it. Thought you were safe.*

Until him. Until . . .

ROOK.

It was a surge of fury mixed with helplessness and hurt, curdled milk boiling over—and something sick and dark beneath, violent and deathly. Chess hauled himself to his feet with the support of a convenient headstone. Breathing harsh and ragged, he snapped open first one gun, then the other, and touched his finger to each empty barrel, watching with grim intention: *reloading,* by God. Each touch filled the chamber with—Morrow couldn't see what, exactly. A tiny, roiling mass of flame and shadow, nothing he could name. Fear crawled into his stomach and along his skin.

"Chess . . ." He didn't even mean to speak, but the words forced their way out. "Down there, the Rev—he told me that none of this would've worked, you couldn't've *survived,* if it hadn't been real—true in *your* heart, even if it wasn't in his." No change in Chess's look as he kept on loading, and Morrow's stomach knotted. He pushed himself up. "Christ knows, we've seen how many sins each of us's racked up—but you can't make this one of them. You can't. It'll kill you."

"Give me one good reason—" Chess snapped one gun shut, "—why I, you, anyone—" *click-clack:* the other gun closed, "—should give a tick's ass-fuck whether I live or die."

"*'Cause when somebody's as good in the sack as you are, they really do owe it to the rest of the world to keep themselves upright just as long as they can?"*

Chess whirled, but Morrow—stunned at the words that had come all unsummoned out of his own mouth—saw it like he was looking through the wrong end of a telescope, plummeting far and back away as if tumbled off a cliff-high gallows. A thick black weight engulfed him, swathed him, deadening the sound in his ears. All avuncular malice and power and . . . *concern?*

Chess straightened, all expression falling away from his face. The guns dangled, but he didn't holster them. As toneless as a sleep-talker, blurred and distant like he was underwater:

"Ash."

"*Darlin'.*" The feel of Rook's voice through Morrow's throat made him want to gag. A burning ache spread through mouth and jaw as alien intonations and stresses overrode his own. The very weight of his body shifted as he stood, suddenly inflicted with a far heavier man's sense of balance. "*You want to kill me, and none alive could fault you for that. But try shootin' me now, and . . .*" Rook spread Morrow's hands, shrugged his shoulders. "*Won't even inconvenience me. And for all his faults, I think you still might find Ed useful enough, in future, to not throw away so quickly.*"

It was hard for Morrow to make much out, but he thought Chess might have tilted his head. "Maybe I don't care any more 'bout what *you* call useful, Ash."

Rook shook Morrow's head, brought a laugh in his deepest register up from the gut, so low his throat felt sore. "*Well, maybe not, at that. But I seem to recall you do take pride in payin' your debts, Chess—bad and good. And can't none of us deny without Ed's help, you'd never have seen blue sky again.*" The tides of feeling around Morrow shifted, washed toward true pain, regret, and . . . something else. "*That'd've been an awful waste. Wouldn't it?*"

Rook stretched Morrow's hand out to Chess's face, stroked it as he had caressed it in the underworld, and Chess closed his eyes. Mortified, Morrow fought to retreat deeper—but the response sizzled along his nerves anyway as Rook leaned him in close, used his mouth to kiss Chess, gently as any husband with a blushing virgin bride. The blackness smothering him flushed dark as wine, sweltering with sudden heat, while Chess's mouth worked against his. Something wrenched at Morrow's groin and stomach like a cable, pulling him in and down, vertigo and arousal spinning up together.

Until—a hard push threw him off balance, and he actually felt Rook's presence *slide sideways*, halfway breaking free, before Morrow caught himself on a headstone.

Heaving in gasps, face red, Chess held out a hand palm-up before him, as if to brace a wall from falling. And snapped, "Not this time, you bastard—not now, and *not* like this. Not using someone else." The hand clenched into a fist, which he shook in Morrow's face—but at a careful distance, as if touching even Rook's shadow in another man was too great a temptation. "You want me, you meet me face to face, where I can rip my answers outta your lyin' fuckin' brain-pan myself."

Rook laughed. It racked Morrow's guts. "*Answers? Hell, sweetheart, those were yours for the askin', each step of the way. All you ever had to do . . .*" A sly, mocking note, "*. . . was ask.*"

Chess's face went blank again. Morrow tried to find some shred of will inside to brace himself, expecting the guns to thunder any second. But Chess surprised him—surprised Rook, too. Morrow couldn't mistake the startled mind-blink as Chess's hands fell open.

"What was it you did to me?" Calm, quiet, almost despairing. "*You* even know, for sure? Everything I touch . . ." As he swept a helpless hand over the graveyard, Morrow deliberately made himself recall the hotel battle, and relished as best he could the astonishment in Rook's mind as the images sank in. "I didn't mean to do nothin' that happened back there, any of it. And I don't do *nothin'* I don't mean!"

Morrow felt Rook marshal his thoughts. "*Had to, Chess,*" the hexslinger used his lips to say. "*Otherwise . . . you'd've gone to Hell. The real one, forever. unending agony, God's last Judgement. That Hell.*"

"Oh, do *not* turn preacher again on me *now*, you son-of-a—"

Rook shook Morrow's head. "*None of that. Just—you'd've never given me up, doomed yourself, and called it fair. This way . . . well, I still might burn. But you won't. That's good enough, for me.*"

Chess stared at him a long moment, uncomprehending. Morrow knew he could also feel Rook's total certainty, the irrefutable "truth" lurking behind that claim, however insane it might seem to anyone else.

Confusion whirled into frustrated rage. Chess surged forward and grabbed Morrow's shirt in both fists, twisted hard, so the cloth came up in bunches. "Just what the fuck are you even *talkin'* about? You incredible goddamned dumbass!" He shook Morrow savagely. Wrapped in Rook's presence, Morrow felt barely a twinge, but knew he'd be aching tomorrow. "Where the fuck you think I *was*, all that damn time? I've Christ-well *been* to Hell already, Ash. That's where *you* put me!"

Morrow felt Rook's grip slacken—confusion welled up, weakening the bond it bled through. And suddenly, for all his furious fear of the Rev's supernatural trickery, Morrow found it ten times more terrifying to consider how Rook maybe might not really *know* the exact parameters of what he'd set in motion.

"*You . . . remember that? But you weren't supposed to—*"

"*She* tell you that, you stupid donkey?" Chess roared. "And you believed her? Well, look *this* over a spell!"

He slapped his palm to Morrow's forehead, sent memories geysering into Rook's mind through Morrow's like superheated steam. Where far off, Rook's mouth opened wide, opening Morrow's with it.

(Mexico City, near a full fifth of it, levelled. Pinkerton's voice echoing, from Morrow's mind: *This sort of thing starts bloody wars. . . .*

(Oona Pargeter, gutted, metamorphosing into a black inhuman giant with obsidian ribs and a stone plaque for a foot: **I'm your Enemy, son—yours, an' every other's . . .**

(Lightless cracks in the earth, felt more than seen, seeping slow poison and dream-sickening corruption. One beneath the ruins of Mexico City, one in a Tampico hotel room, one under the salt-flat plains of a devastated town named Bewelcome. A half-dozen others, opening even now—as they "spoke"—in various strange and silent places.

(And that *voice* once more—Oona's, but not. Informing all three of them at once, with a scornful, half-crazed cheer: *Went on ahead and ended the whole world, him and you, with your Godlessness: that's what you did. Sure 'ope you're happy now. . . .*)

Did you really think you could go down so far and come back up alone, little kings? Little priest-consort, little sacrifice-turned-god, little husbands?

The mind-flood cut off at last, a sluice-gate slamming shut. Morrow collapsed to his knees, painful-sharp aware that Rook had just nearly done the exact same thing over a thousand miles away, only holding back for fear of *her* attention.

Shock and awe, not just at how bad things really were, but also from the sheer scope of what'd come along with it, from Chess: hatred, true as a blade. Not just the spite of a born pariah for the world ringed 'round against him, nor the casual cruelty that had always let him kill as surely and impersonally as a force of nature, but a near-Biblical fury, a desperate pain and loathing, which could come only when unlooked-for *love* found itself abruptly used up, betrayed, destroyed.

A low sound rippled up from Morrow's chest, and he felt sick to realize Rook was laughing.

Chess's green eyes widened. "You motherfucker," he whispered. "What makes all this so *funny*, to you, again?"

"*You, darlin',*" Rook wheezed, "*you. 'My only love, turned to my only hate.'*" He made Morrow get up, regaining control. "*Listen, Chess—I made a mistake. I know that now. I need for you to set it right, even if you gotta kill me to do it.*"

Chess smiled. "Oh, you don't have to fret yourself none on *that* account. I'm comin' for you."

Rook made Morrow's mouth smile in reply, oddly gentle. "*I know.*"

"I think . . . I might be stronger than you, now."

Morrow felt Rook's hold start to fade, releasing him one part at a time, yet saving his mouth for last. "*Sure hope so,*" Rook murmured.

Why? Morrow thought, numb. But the answer wasn't long in coming.

"Listen. You hear that?"

"What?"

"Shut up, darlin'. Listen."

Chess opened his mouth. Stopped, brows furrowing. Then turned, a hound tracking a cry on the wind. Helplessly, Morrow strained his own ears, more than half certain it was pointless—'til he heard it too, at last, a distant echoing howl sliding through Rook's hex-senses into his. Rook's grim consent pulsed within him, a wordless nod:

You need to know, Ed, just as much. If not more.

It came from nowhere in the graveyard. Only the faint noise trickling in from nearby streets, the mutter and rumble of human traffic, made any real sound here. But behind that there rose a noise that Morrow could name, immediately—a high, nasal wail, underscored with rattles, clacks, and irregular thumps, strange glassy crashes, guttural growls and roars. And not a single note in all this cacophony that sounded even halfway human.

Morrow's skin didn't just crawl. It lurched, as though his primordial fear was trying to rip it from his body. And a sickening second later, his stomach plunged as he realized the fear was as much *Rook's* as it was his own. Which meant—

Oh, shit, we're well and truly fucked.

No beginning, and no end—only an insistent grinding, a key turning in some locked door so large it kept two whole worlds separate.

But—no more. Distant dark places full of hateful, clamouring things. Fissures forming.

Chess scrubbed at his mouth, hard, and looked straight through Morrow's eyes, into Rook's. "All 'cause of us, ain't it?" he demanded. "'Cause you ripped me outta the dead lands, and left the door open behind you—some almighty sorcerer *you* are, for all your Goddamned airs. Your new wife know how bad you fucked up yet, Reverend?"

Rook set Morrow's lips. *"Suspect she's startin' to, yes. But then again, for all I know . . . she might not really care."*

Chess shrugged at that.

"'*Course*," Rook pointed out, "*it ain't just about me and her, Chess, or even me, her and you—you know that. There's that other fella, too.*"

The Smoking Mirror.

"He says he don't mean me any harm."

"*Maybe, maybe not. They're not like us, as you may've already figured—but some things* are *gonna change, no matter what. 'Cause he come up the same way we all did . . . and he sure didn't come up alone.*"

Chess made as though to snap a harsh line back, but something gave him pause. He looked down again, instead, sagging slightly, like the air in his lungs'd gone stale.

Quiet, he said, "He told me I . . . *was* him, now. One sort of him— or half, at least. 'Cause you fucked up in the makin' of me, just like I said."

"*That's right.*" Rook leaned closer, Morrow straining against him as he did—the resultant motion subtle at best, though Rook seemed to consider it significant enough to fight for. And heard his own voice drop even further, as Rook finished: "*But . . . you don't* have *to be.*

"*For here we have the key to write you a new gospel, Chess,*" came the words, out of Morrow's mouth. "*Every god needs a prophet. Every crusade, a messiah. John to Jesus, Stephen to the Apostles. She showed me how to make you something I didn't have to kill, or be killed by . . . and we're gonna show* her *that just 'cause she and her kin want back in, don't mean we'll leave the world to them without a fight.*

"*Make the common folk fear him, as much—or more—as they'll fear those who come in his wake, Ed.*" And as the world blurred out to black, Morrow thought he saw Rook's face swim up to hang before him, dark eyes deep and burning. Chess, the graveyard, the faraway wailing of the cracked world, all were gone. "*Spread the word of the Skinless Man, that the only way to save themselves is to let blood in his name. Draw it in a bowl, tip it out the front door, circle the house. Tell them what will happen to any as says no. Spill your worst nightmares on their heads—then tell them to pray that's all they endure. Or the Skinless Man will end them in ways no man can even think about and stay sane— let alone know yourself responsible for.*"

Rook did not smile, but the awful intention in his eyes was threat enough. "*Then by the time her kind have returned for good, every hex and every soul they might've claimed for their Machine will be already marked as ours, instead—and they'll have to either accept their place under our rule, or go back to the Hell they built themselves. Forever.*"

So caught up in his vision was Rook that, for a moment, Morrow's vocal cords slackened. He managed to draw in a rasping breath.

"And you think Chess'll do all this—let this all *be* done, in his name—just on our say-so? 'Cause you made him a god?" Astonishingly, he found a hacking laugh of his own. "Ain't the way any god *I* know's supposed to act."

Rook blinked. Then he returned the laughter, a dark, smoky chuckle. "*Well . . . knowing him the way we both do, Chess ain't too likely to be a god of* love, *is he?*"

And that last was so crazily, hysterically, absurdly true that Morrow found himself laughing right along, while the darkness washed away into the graveyard's dust-choked dimming sunlight— and Chess stared at him in furious horror, hearing two voices echo from one throat.

"I'm right Goddamn *here*, Goddamnit!" he shouted, at the both of them.

The final absurdity was enough at last to bust Morrow free of Rook's waning spell. He staggered, caught himself. Shook his head as Rook's influence boiled off faster than black tar cooking. "Two of you stuck together at the hip and such, for *how* long?" he gasped. "Plighting your troth for all the world, play-actin' the part of two souls in one body, or a heart torn in half reunited. And . . . in the end, *Reverend*, after all you've seen and done—you don't hardly know that little fucker at *all*, do you?"

Switching mid-word to thought, without meaning to, it all crashing out of him in one great wave hurled up against the thinning black cloud of Rook's shadow.

Chess Pargeter. Who's never done what anyone wants, for any reason, if he could help it—anyone but you, Rook. Chess, who's never been no man's tool and no man's toy—but yours. Chess, who's only ever played the fool for love, and only back when he didn't dream there even was such a thing. But now he knows better. Because . . . you taught him.

Chess tilted his head a bit at that, those poison eyes musing. "You maybe need to get on back to 'your' woman, Reverend," he said, without much heat. "That's what I think. 'Cause we all three of us know just how pissy she can get, when things don't exactly go her way."

He raised his hand in distinct imitation of Songbird, a backhand salute, to push every last trace of Asher Elijah Rook from Morrow's bruised soul.

Just past where Bewelcome glinted, Rook snapped back to himself, aching but whole. He touched a hand to his mouth, still feeling the trace of Chess's kiss on Morrow's lips.

"Is it done, husband?" Ixchel asked, from behind him—a dark figure on a darkening landscape, sky already shading down to dusk, hanging back with a strange courtesy. Willing to wait at least a few beats more for him to . . . commit himself, he supposed, given the gravity of what they were about to set in motion, and all.

"I believe so," he answered. "One way or t'other—he's coming."

She came up behind him, rested her forehead against one shoulder blade, inhumanly affectionate. "He shall come. He has no choice. All this was fated a thousand years before your births. Are you ready to prepare him the Way?"

"As I'll ever be," he replied, at last. And felt, rather than saw, her smile.

She took his hands in hers as he turned to face her, fisted them together in profane prayer, and began to chant. Within moments Rook heard himself echoing her as the spell enveloped them, aligned them, before unfurling itself, parasol-wide, across the land. Power fanned out from Bewelcome's salt-flat ruin in a hundred directions at once.

Down ley lines, the invisible currents of power running through air and soil. Along the rails of the Pacific Overland and its tributaries, near two thousand miles of steel. Through the continental copper mesh of Western Union's telegraph lines, chattering with Morse code. The spiderweb reached out all 'round them, lighting up, a silvery-glint net cast over half a continent to catch—their own kind, gathering and weaving together any who fell somewhere between those strands.

Sending out the impulse: *Come. Come seek out Ixchel, the Mother of Hanged Men. Come stand before Her priest-king, to offer up your service. Come to build the First City of the Sixth World—the world of wonder, the world of power. Come, and join New Aztectlan.*

Not every mark would prove receptive, obviously. Songbird and Chess, at the very least, would fight the call as hard as possible, and Rook didn't doubt that they'd succeed.

Many others either wouldn't try, or would try and fail—and then they'd end up here, lost and delirious, throwing themselves headlong into the famous Machine's endless suck-hole. As many as necessary, for Ixchel-Ixtab-Yxtabay-and-all-the-rest's purposes.

Yours as well, Reverend, supposedly. Yours as well.

For leagues on every side, the wires hummed and sang, lit and clicked. *We call this category of crime "lightning-theft,"* Rook told her, without moving his mouth. *Means commandeering telegraph wire-service without payin' for it—committing bank-fraud, or suborning fools to commit it for you, under duress. It's a Federal offence.*

And this, predictably, she found more amusing still—though he couldn't quite figure if her hilarity was sparked more by the ridiculousness of the charge, or the insanity of having one centralized government, supposedly, to reign over a hundred thousand separate territories that'd barely each support a law of their own.

Such ideas can never work efficiently, little king . . . at least, not when left to mere humans' administration. Then, cheerfully: **But we shall fix all that, you and I . . . while my brother watches, and your paramour is driven by hungers he cannot fathom to soften the land before us, whether or not he thinks he wishes to do so.**

Rook nodded, slightly, watching her close for any sign that the pressure of supporting such a massive, complex binding was distracting her—which it was, increasingly, the spell itself a choir of iron bells and stone gears all set drainingly a-clank, louder and louder and louder. Loud enough to drown him out when he finally allowed himself to think, soft yet clear, beneath the tumult of cemeteries blooming fresh from sea to shining sea—*oh, goody*.

Remembering that moment down in Mictlan-Xibalba, when Morrow's bullet hit Ixchel's brain—that unholy *snap*, throwing him clear for one cold instant from his warm bath of predestinate fate, that fine, slickly impenetrable shell of *need to get this* finished, *worry 'bout the cost later*. When he'd looked down and seen nothing but the horrid meaty undeniability of what he'd caused to be done—fuck that, what he'd *done*, himself, with his very own reeking hands.

Chess, and the awful damn mess he'd made of him, with all his bad intentions. Chess, dead and split open, staring vacant, when all he'd ever told himself was that he wanted him kept alive, kept running: a hundred times magnified, saved and salvaged, eternally rendered powerful, beautiful, unstoppable.

And now Rook knew the result—had seen it himself, albeit through Morrow's eyes. But that wrench persisted. It wasn't enough, and never would be.

Made a mistake, I know it now. Need for you to set it right, 'cause . . . I just can't.

For the first time since her death, he found himself ruminating a bit on Grandma. It occurred to him only now that maybe the reason she'd faced him alone hadn't been predatory at all. Or at least, not mainly so. For Injun hexes seemed to favour working in bunches with true shamans, the preachers of their kind. Them as were human, yet able to tap a-purpose into something far larger than themselves, perhaps that same force he'd felt boil from poor Sheriff Love's Word-struck pores.

From that angle, Grandma might actually have thought she was protecting her people by going hand-to-hand with Rook solo. Old and crafty as she was, she'd have known Rook's proximity would rouse her hungers and smother her honour—put her at the mercy of her power-thirst, like any "normal" magician. And then her people would've been caught in the overspill, her focus torn, forcing herself to care about making sure they came out okay.

Faith could produce miracles, no question. But hexes, perhaps because they bred miracles automatically, seemed to have no access to faith's power, unless they could somehow *become* gods, themselves.

Human sacrifice was the key, Rook thought—the worst taboo of all, worse than rape, patricide, or cannibalism. Gods fed and bred on the death of others, spiked higher-than-high with two parts suffering to three parts ecstasy, mirroring the blood-echo of their own. The God Who Dies . . . but not a milkwater Hebrew messiah, content to overspend his coin-flesh in others' service 'til He was good and broke. No, this was a shell-game god whose hungers ebbed and flowed in earthquake-driven tidal waves, meeting out glorious, cyclical destruction. Like Ixchel and Smoking Mirror.

Like Chess.

Chess, whom Rook had held, watched sleep. Chess, who fit in his arms as if he was made for it. Chess, who'd kill him, if he could . . . and very well might, when all was said and done.

But no such godhood for Rook, never; that boat had good and sailed. Only the vague sense that while he couldn't right now conceive of anything to do for Chess, for Morrow—he still knew himself at least willing, when the time for it came 'round, to at least *try*.

His palms still red and sore, even in her coldly imperative, power-soaked double-grip, where the Bible had burnt him.

My guilt talkin', that's exactly what that *was—stand-fixed, as ever, on how I don't deserve to use His Word. How I never did.*

But she'd the right of it too, he knew—the Good Book *had* been just a crutch for him all this time, and one without which he could get along perfectly fine, as their current spectacular working all-too-well proved.

Still, he couldn't say he didn't miss it. Almost as much as he missed—other things.

Ah, but which parts *of your Word do you miss most, Ash Rook?*

whispered a voice like Chess's, if only a little, in his inner ear. *The part says repentance brings forgiveness? Or the parts that tell how Vengeance Is Mine?*

The spell was winding down, resolving itself reel on reel, a wound-back thread from the world's force-ravelled cloak. Ixchel's gaze came back to him, re-possessing his Judas heart and argumentative Satan's mind, eating him alive. Yet Rook stood free a moment more, idly considering his hands in the sunset's glow, as though they were still gloved wrist-high in the cooling red of Chess's insides.

And for once, something came to him that wasn't from the Bible at all: something unbidden, new, slipping sidelong into his head. Shakespeare again, *The Tempest*, which he'd seen performed once back in Crickside, albeit heavily bowdlerized. Gonzago the shipwrecked Venetian courtier, of his boatswain: *I have great comfort from this fellow. Methinks he hath no drowning mark upon him; his complexion is perfect gallows.* Or the vengeful magician Prospero, or savage witch-boy Caliban—two points on the same compass, inalienable: *This thing of darkness I acknowledge mine.*

To which Caliban, his myriad sins found out, replies, ". . . *I shall be pinched to death.*"

Rook said it aloud—trying it on his tongue, weighing it like it came lozenge-sized, while little miss Snare-and-Trap Ixchel just stared at him, her flat black eyes particularly empty.

Replying, after a moment—"I do not understand."

Rook shook his head. "Wouldn't expect you to."

. . . *darlin'.*

In the cemetery, things were growing just as dark. From beyond the gates, scattered throughout shrouded Tampico, Morrow heard screams begin to rise. He laid a tentative hand on Chess's shoulder, only to find it shaking.

"Christ, oh Christ, what *is* this?" Chess choked out, liquid, scrabbling at his eyes. "I'm cryin' fuckin' *blood*, here. I'm . . . back to coughin' up Goddamn *flowers*. . . ."

Remembering what'd come along with those last time, Morrow

almost shied away, but half-hugged Chess instead, for all the smaller man's frame was so tense it hurt and sweaty enough to stick. "Should prob'ly get a move on, come full nightfall."

He broke off as Chess gave an inarticulate cry of frustration, punching both fists straight down into the dirt. There was a pulse, barely visible, and a sound of innumerable mice scrabbling. Bare seconds later, bones began pushing their way out around them, driven upside by a glut of vines and roots: whole, fragmentary, unidentifiable shards and crania with some skin attached, clacking jaw-harnesses, chittering unstrung teeth. They skittered around, circling Chess desperately, seeking a guiding will from a god too new to know what that might be.

"Shit!" Chess shouted, like he was near as surprised as Morrow—for all that seemed *highly* fuckin' unlikely.

"Got *that* right," Morrow yelled back, kicking ossuary junk away with both feet at once. "Make them lie down again, Goddamnit!"

They were both upright, back-to-back. Morrow swore he could feel Chess shake his head frantic-fast, where 'round mid-spine. "I'm *tryin'*—I think. But—"

—problem is . . . you just don't know all too much, really, about any of this crap. Why it happens. How to stop it.

Now the stones themselves were getting in on the act, rocking and shuffling like they'd been hit by an influx of mole-diggery, spraying dust and earth in plumes, up high. The bones leapt and tangled, trying their best to reassemble themselves, or maybe cobble something entirely new out of their own ruin—strange and teetery, spider-legged, all grabby-stroking pinchers mated from fingerbones and shoulder blades, tentacles of re-beaded vertebrae dragging 'round in spasmic switching tails. Weird growth of marrows and tubers putty-sticking skull to skull, ribcage to ribcage. Flower-eyes a-bloom and seeking blindly, soft scrabbly root-clumps gone hectic as millipede legs.

And all of it closing in at once, like it wanted to *kiss* Chess. Lick his boots with its vegetable tongues, leaving a pungent trail of rot and growth behind.

"Chess, for Christ Jesus' sake, *c'mon*—"

Above, a swarm of bats flapped by, their wings squeaking slightly. At closer vantage, they proved to be butterflies made from black volcano-glass, filigreed, rough-hewn. Dipping in formation as they flew, they made a strange back-and-forth mutual flutter, as though *saluting* Chess with the synchronized rise and fall of their shadows passing by: fluid and staining, same as gunpowder, or ink—or those hellish-cold rivers they'd waded through, near-endlessly, on the road to the Moon Room.

You're one of them, now, Morrow thought, looking anywhere but at Chess. *One of their kings. And they love you for it, all of them.*

"Chess—*please*—"

"Beggin' again, huh?" So deadpan-dry, it took Morrow a second to realize Chess Pargeter had made a *joke*. Like any man faced with craziness and death, and the choice of either laughing or going mad.

Morrow gulped. "Well," he said, balancing on the fulcrum of his own rising hysteria, "I . . . I did recollect hearing how you liked it that way. . . ."

Which was maybe flirting with intent, or even skirting too close to Chess's Ma's old stomping grounds. But at this point, Morrow wasn't minded to be finicky—just about anything that got them both out the gate would do.

Seein' how, whatever's comin', I'll definitely stand a far better chance of surviving if I got you by my side.

Chess flickered a grin at him, his old devil-take-everyone-but-me grin. "Ed, you got more guts than smarts. And you already had too many smarts." Without a second's pause he turned, held up his hands palm-together, then swept them apart with a cry: "*Begone, Goddamnit!*"

So thoughtless instinct succeeded, where lack of conscious skill had failed. The bone-creatures, black stone butterflies, bouncing stones and writhing vines, all parted Red Sea-wide, then fled away and out of the graveyard, vaulting the fence or sliding between its iron bars, into half a dozen alleys and out the main exit.

Within moments, the dull background of screams ramped up

sharper, harsher. Closer. Running shadows crossed the nearby streets, and a general smell of panic and blood filled the air.

Chess lowered his hands, gaping. After a moment: "Aw, shit."

"It's *you*," said Morrow, coming to stand by his side. "You bein' here, what you are, that's what's causin' it. We leave, this ends . . . I think, leastways."

A narrow sidelong look: "'We,' huh?"

Then, before Morrow could marshal further arguments: "Ah, hell. Might as well."

From Bewelcome township's dead heart, meanwhile, a tiny stream of ants—unseen, unchecked, under Rook and Ixchel's noses both— bore salt away into the desert, grain by tedious grain. To where a black-faced figure squatted by an empty campfire at the crux of a thousand dead roads, studying the future in his own mirrored foot: past and present converging, diverging, splintering.

A million possibilities. Pick one, plant it, water well with blood. See what grows.

Looking deep into the wavy greyness, to seize—at last—upon one particular face and *pull* . . . hard enough to draw a devotee down once more from his own promised Heaven, to twin him with vengeance unslaked. Rebuild him, particle by icy white particle, then turn him loose—*why not?*—for no better reason at all than simply to see what happened next.

A man of salt opening his eyes, coughing out the residue of his lungs to glitter on the night wind. And turned his head only slightly, just far enough to catch what light remained aglint off the sharp-filed points of his resurrector's awful smile.

***Your name, little earth-apple . . . give it to me, and quickly. What did they call you, when last you were alive,* mi conquistador?**

Stretched out full-length, the man coughed again—gathered his strength even in devilry's overt face, like any warrior of the one true God.

Then rose to meet his brave new life, unashamed in his tall, salt-glazed nakedness, and replied—

". . . Sheriff Mesach Love."

TO BE CONTINUED IN
A ROPE OF THORNS

ABOUT THE AUTHOR

GEMMA FILES

Gemma Files was born in London, England and raised in Toronto, Canada. Her story "The Emperor's Old Bones" won the 1999 International Horror Guild award for Best Short Fiction. She has published two collections of short work (*Kissing Carrion* and *The Worm in Every Heart*, both Prime Books) and two chapbooks of poetry (*Bent Under Night*, Sinnersphere Productions, and *Dust Radio*, from Kelp Queen Press). *A Book of Tongues* is her first novel, and will be followed by a sequel, *A Rope of Thorns*. Find out more about her at http://musicatmidnight-gfiles.blogspot.com/.